GOD LOVES
A MADMAN

GOD
LOVES
A MADMAN

MATT HADER

A NOVEL

Books by Matt Hader

God Loves a Madman
Two-Seven Remainder
Amika Press

Bad Reputation: The Complete Collection
The Core
West Bound
Breaking
Balmoral
Bad Reputation
Thinkbox Entertainment

Confessions of a Rock Star
Famous Monsters Music

God Loves a Madman © Copyright 2017, Matt Hader

First Edition   ISBN 13: 978-1-937484-59-0

AMIKA PRESS   466 Central Ave #23 Northfield IL 60093   847 920 8084
info@amikapress.com   Available for purchase on amikapress.com

Edited by John Manos and Ann Wambach. Cover design by Sarah Koz and John Rose. Designed and typeset by Sarah Koz. Body in Maiola, designed by Veronika Burian in 2005. Titles in Modesto Condensed & Balboa Condensed, designed by Jim Parkinson in 2000 and 2001. Thanks to Nathan Matteson.

FOR DAN & RICK

One of the deep secrets of life is that
all that is really worth the doing
is what we do for others.
—Lewis Carroll

1

J AKUB "PIES" Jakubowski had to see the mother of the woman he killed. He would locate Milena Chlebek, and face-to-face he would apologize to her.

As he stood alone and listened to the loud arguments and agonizing screams reverberating off the concrete walls outside the cell's steel door, it was all that mattered to Pies—to apologize.

The wrinkled white shirt and dark gray suit combo he squeezed himself into was stretched to its limit across his upper back and biceps due to the chiseled muscle he had developed over the past five years. The pants now fit a bit more snugly around his trim waist and made his upper physique appear like a wide V. He'd worn the exact same suit into the prison, virtually swimming in the cloth, but he'd walk to freedom with the material bulging to its tensile-strength breaking point.

His close-cropped, self-buzzed hair completed his overall intimidating appearance.

The penitentiary was the first place Pies had ever attempted to exercise. He'd grown prolific with his regimen, to the point where some of the others surreptitiously mocked his obsession—which was in itself remarkable given so many men on the inside worked out incessantly. The calisthenics Pies used were simple, but they lasted for hours on end. Push-ups, pull-ups, deep knee bends, as well as constant pacing within his cell and the yard, that's how he achieved his current build.

When he paced, especially while in the yard and common areas, no one got in his way. During those supercharged tense moments, Pies appeared more like a frantic zoo animal patrolling its tiny territory than a man doing his time, and the others would walk wide berths so as to not cross paths with him.

He'd done so many callisthenic repetitions over the course of his incarceration that his nickname among the other prisoners was "PP," shortened from "Push-Pull." The nicknames were rarely mentioned to his face, though.

Pies entered the penal system with an incredible amount of aggression, anger, and hostility over what his life had become. Tacit violence oftentimes seemed to ooze from him. No one wanted to be the first to challenge him for fear that the newcomer, Pies, would cause not only physical harm but also irreparable damage to their own precarious standing among the other prisoners.

Soon, Pies became somewhat of a junior statesman among the ceaseless arrivals of new prisoners, and his cycle of never being tested continued to go on and on.

Conversely, Pies did not receive psychiatric treatment for what were—obviously—severe manic episodes. Thankfully, the manic times inside the prison had diminished over the past eighteen months. It was almost as if he had paced and exercised himself to better mental health, if that were even remotely possible.

Pies twitchily paced back and forth within the holding cell and thought briefly about Milena's husband Blaze, who had died of a heart attack three years ago. He had read the obituary on the *Chicago Tribune*'s website on one of the prison computers a week after Blaze's passing. Blaze was such a good, solid man, a master baker who had absolutely trusted Pies with his daughter, Vicki. Pies could only assume that Blaze's early demise was due, in part, to Vicki's shocking death.

Vicki's mother Milena was now the lone survivor of the Chlebek family.

Ever since Pies squeezed the revolver's trigger in a desperate attempt to kill his crime boss Bast Zielinski, the source of lifelong torment, he was constantly working up to this apologetic moment.

Practicing.

Every day as he exercised, he would silently rehearse the act of contrition—thinking up various verbiage, inflections, and body language to make sure that Milena Chlebek understood how truly sincere he was.

Previous to the shocking developments earlier this particular day, though, when he was advised he'd be leaving prison, Pies's plan had revolved around inviting Milena to the penitentiary complex and making his case to her in the visitors' room. He would have to adjust his strategy—that was painfully obvious. The apology would now materialize sans the cynical, hooded-eyed gaze of the prison guards.

It would be only Pies and Milena.

Alone.

Time and time again, as he'd find himself training for what he would say to the woman, he'd stop himself. How could he rehearse something as crucial as a sincere apology? And he realized, even prior to his receiving the startling news of his early release, Milena would never consider coming to the prison to visit him in the first place.

What in the hell was he thinking?

Deep confusion and anger clung to Pies like painful, itchy burrs as he continued to pace within the cold concrete and steel structure of the Stateville Correctional Center north of Joliet, Illinois. He must have walked back and forth past the well-worn, overstuffed backpack that lay on the floor some two hundred times by now.

He paced and paced.

Utterly rattled that he was being set free barely past the halfway mark of an eight-year sentence for manslaughter, Pies was furious that he'd not seen the parole coming sooner. He kicked himself for missing something important in his last parole hearing. But he also knew some paroled prisoners were not given their exact early release dates as a safety concern, so that any enemies they may have created in prison wouldn't be operating under deadlines to hurt the exiting inmates—and vice versa.

The stark cell he currently occupied was the last stop for a paroled prisoner before being picked up by friends or loved ones—or given a bus or train ticket if friends and loved ones had forsaken the detainee. The departing inmate would also receive whatever cash he still retained in his facility bank account and then be sent on his way. If he were completely broke, the penal system officials would dispense a few twenties for the parolee's return-trip expenses.

Before they allowed Pies to depart, the prison authorities would run his name through various national criminal-justice data systems, checking to make sure he wasn't wanted in any other state. If an arrest warrant existed elsewhere, the jurisdiction in question would be contacted and awarded just enough time to head south of Chicago to pick up Pies before he was set free.

There would be no such legal obstruction this particular day because Pies was otherwise clean—in the judicial system's eyes, anyway.

Up to this point, it was a judicial system that had let him down at every turn. Pies was guilty of so much more than accidentally killing Vicki Chlebek. He would have been in prison for the rest of his life if all of his crimes had been properly tallied and the prosecutor and judge handling his case hadn't dropped the ball.

But life in prison was just not to be for Pies and that angered him. As this newly formed irritation began to creep into the deep recesses of his mind, he quickened his pacing speed, and he was able to successfully push back the rage where it would cause no further distress.

He rolled his head back and forth and attempted to loosen the tight dress-shirt fabric from of his neck, and he forced himself to conjure up what would happen to him in the future.

He reckoned he could throw a beating at the next corrections officer he made direct contact with. As soon as that thought fired in his mind, he knew it wasn't going to happen though, and for good reason.

Right after breakfast, a stout and humorless corrections officer named Chandler nosed right up on Pies, slapped an approved release form against his chest, and said, "Today's your day, killer. Time to go out and into the world. Parole board came through for you."

Pies snatched the paper away and quickly read.

Before he could even verbally respond, Chandler handed him a black smartphone with a paused video displayed. Pies was reeling from the CO's notification of parole, and he didn't understand the offering of the smartphone at first—until the humorless guard pressed the play button.

Exhibited on the smartphone was a shaky and muted surveillance video of an unsmiling Milena Chlebek. She was dressed in a windbreaker and blue jeans and was working in the front yard of her Edison Park home, sweeping the walkway. It was obvious by the way she mindlessly worked away, never once looking into the camera's direction, that Milena didn't know she was being surveilled. The video seemed so benign—a sturdy woman in her late sixties sweeping a sidewalk—and yet, Pies knew instantly what it meant.

Milena's life was being threatened.

Visually speaking, it was not a very exciting video to watch, but the point was clear.

The Chicago Outfit, who Pies had worked indirectly with before his incarceration and who certainly were responsible for the video, were correct in their assumption that Milena meant a great deal to him. He could never allow her to be harmed by the mobsters. She was an innocent. As loose as Pies's moral code had become over the years, it still always called for innocents to be protected whenever possible. He couldn't allow for another one of his mistakes to cost an undeserving someone his or her life.

The humorless CO Chandler said, "Your friend from Oak Park

will be in touch." He then slipped the phone into Pies's front pants pocket, and before he backed away, he tossed a phone charger on top of the cell's bunk.

Pies understood that he was leaving prison for certain. He couldn't cause trouble and delay his release. If he didn't cooperate, Milena would be killed. The Chicago Outfit would see to that.

So now, an hour after the CO gave him the phone, dressed in the too-tight gray suit, Pies continued to pace within the holding cell.

He paced—and anxiously awaited his future.

2

THERE WAS a bunk in the Stateville holding cell where he had spent his last eighteen hours in prison, but Pies couldn't make himself lie down. He didn't want to risk allowing the restorative benefits of sleep to permit him to reevaluate his duty. It was a must that his primary task be completed. It had to be done today. He'd find Milena Chlebek at her bakery on Northwest Highway, and he would apologize to her for killing her daughter and tearing her family apart.

His goal was set.

With quickly depleting adrenaline levels, the groggy Pies barely managed to appear unaffected by exhaustion as he stumbled and dodged other downtown Chicago pedestrians on Canal Street. He quick stepped, as best he could, away from the Amtrak station and in the direction of the Ogilvie Transportation Center, where he'd catch a Northwest Metra commuter train to Edison Park.

Soon, he'd be face-to-face with Milena.

Earlier, as he was riding the Amtrak train from Joliet to Chicago, he contemplated his other major concern outside of making his apology—how to keep Milena safe and free of the Outfit's sway.

First, he would have to carefully ferret out the new mob underboss and see what he wanted. A higher-up may have called for Pies to be sprung from prison, but in Pies's experiences with the Outfit, it would be an underboss running whatever show they wanted him for.

And as fatigued and as surly as Pies felt, he had enough of his wits left to consider taking a major risk once the Outfit made their plans known to him. Deep down he knew the mobsters would never truly be "done" with him. If he agreed to one job, he'd be obligated to do them all from here on out—until his usefulness was depleted. At that point he'd become expendable, and most likely he would end up dead.

The coming few days would be a precarious high-wire act for the newly paroled Pies. And, these would be nearly sleepless nights, for certain.

He wondered if he should work it so that the new Outfit under-boss would go the way of the last one. Pies could make it so the victim wouldn't even see his demise coming. He'd done it before with the use of some simple items—household repair parts and shotgun shells—all of which could easily be picked up at nearly any hardware and sporting good stores. It wouldn't be difficult to set up.

Some of the criminal cohorts who Pies had operated with in the past made the fatal error of repeatedly underestimating him. Nearly all of those men were moldering now.

Perhaps, after he apologized to Milena, he could quickly get her to a safe place. Maybe they'd go to Wisconsin? He recalled a trip the Chlebeks took him and Vicki on to lift his spirits after his mother died all those years ago. The excursion lasted for only two nights, but the outing allowed the young Pies to see some natural beauty for a change, after experiencing the brutal end days of his mother's life. The location was in Delavan, a place not too far from Chicago. Maybe an hour or so drive. Pies and Milena could stay out of sight long enough to work on a better plan to get farther away from the Outfit. Permanently.

Another thought immediately fired in Pies's mind. He could always circle back from dropping Milena off in Wisconsin, find where the Outfit underboss lived, and kill him before he did any work at all for the man. If Pies died in the commission of setting Milena free, so be it. She would be okay. His debt would be paid.

An hour later, seated on the Metra commuter train to Edison Park, Pies read through the release packet he was handed as he left the Stateville Correctional Center. He was assigned to a halfway house located on Bryn Mawr Avenue near Oleander Avenue, in the Norwood Park neighborhood on the Far Northwest Side. He would have to report to the halfway house by 6 P.M. that day, and he would also have to meet a parole officer on Belmont Avenue soon.

Naturally, he was placed under some strict parole guidelines. The documents that he scoured were riddled with boilerplate material: can't associate with known current parolees, can't possess a firearm or a dangerous weapon, can't drink alcohol or partake in any illegal stimulants, and can't be peripherally involved in such activities. He must adhere to the rules set forth by the halfway house where he'd be residing, and he was required to treat the supervisor and residents there with respect. He would have to immediately obtain a legal paying job and keep on a strict non-felonious trajectory. The document went on and on. If he didn't obey the rules for the next few years or if he was arrested for any reason, he'd find himself back in Stateville doing the remainder of his time.

Of course, that's exactly what Pies wanted, but since Milena's life was being threatened, he was on a new mission to stay free—for now, anyway.

As the outbound Metra train slowly rolled away from its fifth stop, Pies reclined in his seat and slipped the smartphone from the side pocket of his backpack and brought it to life. He located the contacts file on the phone's display and opened it. There was only one name and phone number on the programmed list. Pies figured that this singular contact name and number most likely connected to another burner phone like the one he held in his hand. Pies smirked sadly as he noticed the name the Outfit chose for the phone contact.

One word: Mother.

"We are now approaching Edison Park. Edison Park is the next stop," said the barely audible, automated voice over the train's scratchy-sounding PA system.

Pies slid the phone back into its hiding place, slung the backpack over his shoulder, got to his feet, and shuffled down the center aisle. He pulled the sliding interior double doors open and went into the train car's vestibule. This was an outbound train operating in the early afternoon off-hours, and he was the only one exiting that particular car. He peered out the grime-smattered door window as the train slowed and saw the familiar low-slung commercial and residential buildings of Edison Park slip past, right to left. It was years since he'd seen his old neighborhood, and he was pleasantly surprised that nothing had really changed.

The train came to a smooth stop, the doors hissed opened, and Pies stepped from the car. He kept his head down and awaited the train's departure. Once the train rolled on, he would cross the tracks and go directly to Chlebeks' Bakery on Northwest Highway. It was only a block and a half away.

But then a thought came to him. He spun on his heel, walked around the fence that surrounded the train station's platform area, and crossed through the tiny park that bordered the tracks.

The Chlebeks' family home was less than two hundred feet away, and Pies wanted to see it up close before he went to the bakeshop where he knew Milena would be. Throughout his lifetime, Pies never knew of a regular workday when Milena Chlebek would be anywhere but her bakery. She would have, most likely, hired a trained baking professional to keep the quality of their goods intact, but she'd be at the bakery running the place, Pies was sure of it. Back before he was sent away, he remembered that master baker Blaze Chlebek would always arrive at the shop at 3 A.M., and Milena would show up by 5 A.M. to get the front of the house ready for their customers to arrive at six.

Pies could see the Chlebeks' humble brick house the moment his shoes hit the patchy grass of the park. He slowed his pace and tried his best to enjoy the view of the pretty little neighborhood, the shade trees, and the well-maintained homes bordering the park.

He approached a park bench, where a couple who looked to be in their forties sat enjoying the day. Pies smiled and nodded. "Hi, how are you today?" he said to them.

Both the man and woman nearly smiled back, but then the man recognized Pies and nudged the woman. The woman gave the man an odd look, but then she, too, recognized Pies. Fearful, the couple stood and walked in the opposite direction.

Pies cleared his throat and kept walking.

He got to the sidewalk in front of the Chlebeks' home, and he silently observed the structure. He had no intention of getting any closer.

The house appeared slightly different from the last time he viewed it. It wasn't dramatic, but Pies noticed immediately that the paint on the soffit was peeling, and the gutter on the left side hung lower than the right due to a series of fastener failures. The shrubs in front were dead—brown and withered. Pies began to wonder why Milena hadn't maintained her home, especially since he had secretly given her and her husband Blaze a backpack containing $300,000 before he turned himself in to the police. What became of the money? Maybe she tossed it away once she figured out that the neat bundles of $100s were from him.

He backed away from the home and headed toward Northwest Highway, as he originally had intended.

Within minutes he'd be face-to-face with Milena. Perhaps he would ask her what she had done with the $300,000 he'd given her. As soon as that thought passed through his mind, he wiped it away. It was none of his business.

Pies walked across the Metra tracks, and he paused for a moment at the alley opening that led to the exterior, backside door for the apartment where Vicki used to reside above the bakery—and where Pies violently ended her life. Anxiety-induced perspiration sprouted along his hairline, but he forced himself to push forward.

He was seconds away from Milena.

It would be all done with soon.

Vicki's mother would either accept or reject his sincere apology.

A small portion of his life's burden would be lifted and he could then work toward getting Milena to safety and taking care of his Outfit enemies.

As he concentrated on each step he took, his breathing became ragged. He began to hyperventilate slightly as he rounded the corner onto busy Northwest Highway.

He was thirty feet from the bakery door.

Twenty feet.

Ten.

He could see the plate glass window with "Chlebeks' Bakery" painted in bold red and white lettering. Through the glass, he noticed a woman's shoulder as she stooped behind one of the display cases within, and he knew that it was Milena.

As Pies squared up fully in front of the store, Milena straightened and turned toward the back interior kitchen doorway.

She hadn't seen him.

All he had to do was reach out, grasp the bakery's door handle, pull, and step inside the shop.

Instead he slowly backed away and nearly fell as he pivoted and jogged across the street, dodging honking cars as he scurried along.

He reached the opposite sidewalk and moved to the right and directly inside of the diner located there between a travel agency and an Irish tavern on the corner.

He knew the diner well. One warm summer morning, when he was a teenager he perched on his bike at the corner across the street and observed two men sitting in one of the window booths of this very same eatery. He made sure his potential victims were securely in place before he pedaled off to put the finishing touches on his preparations for their imminent murders.

The glorious aromas of fresh coffee and cooked sweet peppers and onions met Pies at the diner's door and comforted him, until he tossed a look over his shoulder and saw Milena working away in the bakery across the street.

"Go ahead and sit anywhere, handsome," the scrawny waitress said with a wink, as she shuffled past with a delicious-looking plated sandwich.

Pies wedged into the small corner booth where the sidewall met the floor-to-ceiling front windows. His seat was right next to where his victims had been parked years before. From his current vantage point he'd be able to keep an eye on Milena. After a bit of food and coffee, his mind would be right. He would complete his task. He was sure of that.

The waitress approached with a menu, but Pies knew what he wanted.

"Coffee. Corned beef hash, poached eggs, rye toast—"

"Whoa, there, good-looking," said the waitress. "You been squirreled away in the woods without any food or something, sweetie? Hold on a sec."

She gently tossed the menu on the table and got her pencil and pad out of her front apron pocket. As she did this, a few crinkled dollar bills fell to the floor. She stooped to retrieve the bills and tucked them back where they came from.

Her words "squirreled away" and the sight of the money made Pies's mind flash to his old house's garage and what was hidden there many, many years ago. He'd forgotten about that until that very instant. "Oh, yeah...," he said, absently.

"What's that?" asked the waitress.

Pies shook his head as a response.

She said, "Okay, corned beef, poached, and you said rye toast, right?"

Pies barely nodded once, turned away, and watched the bakery.

"Anything else?"

Pies ignored her, so the waitress slowly painted on a pleasantly confused expression, picked up the menu, said, "Okeydokey," and made her way to the kitchen pass-through.

Pies continued to watch Milena for a long while as she dealt with a male customer. The customer must've ordered quite a selection, because Milena reached under the counter for a large, folded white cardboard box. She popped the box into shape and began filling it with assorted doughnuts and pastries.

"You skipped breakfast, didn't you?" asked a woman's warm voice from five feet away.

Pies was so wrapped up in observing Milena that the woman's interjection made him flinch and snap his head in her direction.

"Sorry, I didn't mean to pry," said the stranger with the easy smile, stylish gray hair, and an understated elegance. "I presumed you skipped breakfast because you're ordering eggs in the afternoon."

Pies quickly sized the woman up and concluded she meant no malice. He shrugged, "Yeah."

"I have two boys. Men now, like you. But I could always tell when they'd spent a night without sleep. Barhopping. All that. You know."

The waitress delivered Pies a cup of hot coffee, and he winced as he took an immediate, and painful, sip. His nervous hand nearly shook some of the coffee free of the cup until he was able to successfully set it on the tabletop.

"Food's on its way," said the waitress as she retreated. The waitress gave the gray-haired woman a little shrug and the woman smiled in response.

"They're responsible men now. Both have good jobs in the city. Wives and kids. The whole shebang," said the woman. "Dependable."

"That's good," said Pies, trying his best to remain polite. It'd been so long since he had a passing conversation with a fellow neighborhood resident. Inside prison, Pies kept mostly to himself, and that meant very little conversational interaction with his fellow detainees. "You must be proud," he added, hoping to cease the conversation.

The woman's facial expression froze for a moment and then transitioned from pleasant to weary. "I am." The woman stared for what seemed an eternity. Pies could barely keep his eyes on the bakery because of the woman's odd stare. He picked up his cup to steal another sip.

"I know you," she said with a quiet, clipped delivery.

Pies put the cup back on the table and blinked a few times.

"What are you doing? I mean...why are you...here? You should be in prison." She was still calm, but her facade was beginning to wither. Pies sensed violence rising up in the woman. She was so physically close she could effortlessly stand, lean forward, and strike him.

Pies wasn't going to shy away from uncomfortable situations involving old neighbors. He was free now, and he had to make the best of his situation. "I was paroled," he said, nearly inaudibly. He cleared his throat and continued, "The prison let me go, ma'am."

"She trusted you," she said, spewing a bit as she began to visibly shake.

Pies extended his view past the angry woman and made eye contact with the waitress. The waitress gave him a "thumbs up" that his food was on the way.

"You killed them all. Not only did you kill Vicki, you killed Blaze... and you killed her, too. Look again. Look. Turn around and look," said the gray-haired woman, rather forcefully.

Pies turned and observed Milena.

"I buy my bread there. She still breathes and walks and works every day, but she's dead. You...you...*dupek!*" she shouted, rather loudly, as the few other patrons and the waitress couldn't help but hear her outburst. Even the line cook poked his head out of the kitchen pass-through to take a peek.

Pies turned abruptly to the woman's red face, and then he spun back away, embarrassed, and directed his gaze across the street once more, through the front windows of the bakery—at the surprised Milena Chlebek. Milena stood with an empty metal sheet pan in her hand. She just remained in the same spot and stared back. Milena set the pan down on the front counter as her mouth slowly opened.

Pies was frozen in the moment—his eyes wide in surprise, as were Milena's.

"*Dupek.* P-yes Jakubowski," shouted the woman. "Leave. *Zostaw nas samych*, dog Jakubowski."

Pies dug into his pants pocket for some money, tossed a twenty on the tabletop, picked up his backpack, and ran. His backpack banged off an empty seatback and knocked the chair over as he pushed his way out of the place.

"Hey? Where are you...? Your food?" called out the waitress.

"*Dupek*," shouted the gray-haired woman as she finally launched herself to her feet, her face hardened with rage.

But Pies didn't hear either woman, and he didn't stop running until he found himself four blocks away and on the side street, south of Touhy Avenue, where his old house sat.

He couldn't bring himself to use the alleys behind the homes in the area. The alleys held too many bad memories for Pies. Deadly memories. Murderous recollections associated with the diner he'd just run from and the two men who had lost their lives to booby traps set up by the subjugated sixteen-year-old version of Pies.

Now he was five doors away and across the street from his former residence when he spotted a man about his age, seated on the front steps of the boxy Georgian-style house. The man was clean-cut and dressed in a sweatshirt and blue jeans, but he looked perturbed, anxious. Pies surveyed his old house as the man's foot tapped out a ragged pattern on the walkway cement. The exterior of the place hadn't changed that much. The new owners had painted the metal awning over the front door a dark-blue color instead of the army green it was when Pies owned the house. Nothing else appeared to be different.

Over the years of his incarceration, his imagination continuously spun imagery of his old neighborhood. Some of those images were pretty dramatic—drastic even—and involved the bulldozing of the area homes to make way for high-rises and massive retail projects. A sad smirk poked out from the corner of his mouth when he saw that the only change was the awning's new paint color.

Four houses up, on his side of the street, sat Stan Zielinski's and his son Bast's old place. There was a construction company's sign in the front yard now, but no workers were in sight. It appeared as if the structure was undergoing some sort of a rehab. The awning over the door was gone and all the shutters had been removed from around the front-facing windows. Upon closer inspection, Pies could see that the windows themselves were all newly installed replacements.

Pies's attention was pulled to across the street as a pretty young woman angrily shoved herself out of the screen door of his old house. Cradled in her arms was a cute little toddler girl. The man seated on the steps below got to his feet, gently took the little girl from the woman's arm, and walked quickly toward a dark-colored minivan that was parked at the curb. The woman's irritated state didn't allow for her to pay any attention to her surroundings, but Pies pulled a quick left turn anyway and hid behind the bushes next to the nearest home. He did not want to be noticed just now. He watched as the woman closed and locked his old home's front door and then walked to the minivan.

The man secured the little girl in a car seat in the back of the minivan and slid the side door closed, and he and the woman, apparently his wife, got into the vehicle's front seats. The engine leapt to life, and they drove off. The car got to Touhy Avenue, took a right, and was gone.

Pies slowly crossed over the side street and walked right up to his old house. He slipped down the gangway between the house and the next-door-neighbor's place to the left and entered the backyard without even looking around. At the time of his arrest five years prior, Pies had been working in a sort of reverse undercover job as a 9-1-1 communications officer for his crime bosses, the Zielinskis. The only reason he was ordered to take the position with the police department was because he was arrest free and, on paper, a great candidate for the job. What the police didn't know at the time of his hire was that Pies was a master burglar, working the job since the time he was a fourteen-year-old boy. One of the things he learned over his years as a professional burglar was that to successfully complete the job at hand, with fewest complications, you had to be confident—and look as if you belonged in whatever space or situation you were working in.

However, once Pies made it into his old backyard he tripped to a halting stop. He immediately realized that this was truly no longer his place. The obviousness of the situation hit him hard because the space seemed both comfortable and oddly alien all at once, and that made him feel slightly off-balance.

The back porch of the home was decorated with overflowing and colorfully hand-painted planting pots, as well as a smattering of kids' toys. There was a tiny pink tricycle in the middle of the back walkway that led to the garage's side access door and the alley beyond that. A four-foot-tall, pink-and-purple-colored plastic playhouse in the shape of a medieval castle, outfitted with a tiny door and side window, sat next to a sandbox in the grass.

Pies slowly shuffled down the walkway around the tricycle and tried to turn the garage's doorknob. It was locked. Without hesitation, he leaned forward, wedged a shoulder tight into the doorjamb, twisted the locked knob once again, and pushed hard on the door itself. The door popped inward without much fuss and without damaging the locking mechanisms. He'd done the same maneuver when he owned the home and had accidentally locked himself out of the garage.

Pies went inside the mostly empty garage and closed the door. The smell of gasoline and stale yard clippings crowded his nostrils and welcomed him to the cool, dark space. Once acclimated, he searched for something to stand on but couldn't locate anything of substance other than a tiny push lawnmower and a plastic one-gallon gas can. The garage was otherwise empty. Pies moved to where the closed overhead door and the sidewall met.

He slipped the backpack off, inspected the rafters overhead for a moment, and then leaped upward and grabbed an exposed joist. He hoisted himself up and wrapped his left arm over and around the joist next to the aluminum track system for the garage door. Once he was steadied, with his free hand he reached out and tapped a few times on the wooden top plate of the garage's exterior wall.

Each tap echoed its hollowness underneath. Pies knew that he was in the right spot.

He wriggled the secured wood top plate back and forth until a sixteen-inch section became quite loose and then totally free. He tossed the piece of wood onto the garage floor where it clattered to silence next to his backpack. He reached into the void he exposed and rooted around for a second or two, smiled, and then pulled, one by one, three plastic-sealed stacks of hundred-dollar bills from within, tossing each to the floor as he worked. Two of the bundles of cash that lay on the floor were thicker than the third. He started to lose his hold on the joist, so he readjusted his arm and then proceeded to reach down a bit deeper into the wall opening. After rooting around for a few more seconds, his eyes widened. His hand pulled back from the wall with a wire lock-bump device pinched tightly between his forefinger and thumb.

"I forgot about you...," he said softly.

Pies studied the device, which if used properly, acted as an alternative "key" on most key-locking systems. He tossed the lock-bump onto the backpack and reached down farther into the wall. "There we go," he muttered. He let go of the joist, and his feet touched down on the cement floor of the garage. He held a final banded stack of $100s in his hand. It was a bit thinner like the other bundle on the floor.

Now that he was back on terra firma, he placed the last cash bundle under his left arm, grabbed up the other money and the lock-bump, and leaned over to stuff them into the backpack. He hoisted the backpack from the floor and then kicked the piece of wood aside. He zipped the backpack closed, took the cash under his arm into his right hand, and exited the garage.

Back into the sunshine, Pies eyed the plastic playhouse for a moment, then leaned forward and tossed the thinner packet of cash, $5,000 worth, through the open side window. The money landed on a tiny table within and flipped over a delicate plastic teacup.

"What the hell are you doing?" said a man's voice.

Pies snapped his gaze to the side of the house where the new homeowner stood in the gangway entrance glaring at him. Pies could see now that the sweatshirt the man wore was emblazoned with the words "Notre Dame High School Alumni Association" across the front.

"This isn't your place any more, dude," said the man. "I...I know who you are."

"I'm not here for trouble," said Pies. He really did not want to hurt this anxious man standing in what used to be his own backyard.

But he would if he had to.

"Our friends said we shouldn't have taken this place because...because of who used to lived in it."

"You won't see me again," said Pies.

The man took a menacing step forward.

Pies uttered, "Don't."

The way he said it, the man froze in place. One word delivered with such authority and promised violence, that the simple command achieved the desired result. The man stayed where he was.

An angry car horn blared out in front.

Pies slowly shifted his gaze toward the plastic playhouse, and the man turned that way and saw through the tiny window the stack of cash on the table inside. The man's eyes snapped back to Pies.

"Keepers fee. For your troubles," said Pies.

The car horn honked again, and in the distance, Pies heard the man's wife loudly call out, "It should be on the porch. She left it on the porch. Come on, we're late."

The man blinked a few times, both agitated and confused by what was happening. He then relaxed and raised his chin to show that he agreed to let Pies go without any further delay.

Pies let out a slow breath, backed away, and hesitated at the partially opened chain-link gate that led to the alley out in back.

There was no other escape route for Pies to take but the alley, he thought. It was, of course, one of the places where he felt ill at ease in Edison Park. If he chose to turn around and go back the way he arrived, down the side gangway of his old house, he'd have to walk within a foot or so of the man in the sweatshirt. In that split second, standing at the alley gate, Pies wondered if he did walk past the man, would the new homeowner suffer a change of heart and become physical with him? Pies just couldn't stomach hurting an innocent.

He tentatively shoved through the gate and into the alley.

He tried to act casual as he walked south in the narrow backstreet —garages, garbage cans, and fetid air his only companions. But as his eyes swiveled about, he took in the familiar surroundings of his youth, and with each heel blow that his feet doled out to the worn pavement below, his stoicism crumbled.

As Pies reached the rear of the Banasik's old house—where he had murdered Mr. Banasik with a booby trap when Pies was a mere six-teen years old—he began to physically tremble. Pies never wanted to hurt anyone, let alone Mr. Banasik, whose daughter, Dana, was his friend, but he was very young and impressionable at the time. He'd been deceived into the act by his father figure, Stan Zielinski.

Pies searched the Internet for Dana Banasik's name while at State-ville and discovered, nearly four years after his incarceration began, that she'd somewhat successfully turned her life around. Shortly after her father's death, Dana had quit college and started drinking heavily. Pies's Internet search found her now married and working on the East Coast for a major financial firm.

Pies felt so tired as he stumbled down the alley—so tired and weak.

He couldn't do right by Milena and apologize. Not today, anyway. And the people from the neighborhood obviously had deep hatred for him that hadn't eased with time.

The realization washed over him—Edison Park was no longer his home.

A fusillade of downward-headed thoughts fired rapidly through his mind. Thoughts of his peculiar upbringing, his lost love Vicki, and the people he killed in his youth...and also later in life. All of the memories pinging around his mind made Pies begin to hyperventi-late and then visibly shake once again. He tripped to a sudden stop and leaned forward, hands on knees. "Stop. Please stop...."

He was so, so exhausted.

The tears flowed.

After a few moments, Pies composed himself, took a few deep breaths, and pushed on toward the Edison Park business district. Once there, he retraced his steps through the small park near the railroad tracks. He then made his way to North Shore Avenue. He proceeded toward the north-south thoroughfare of Ozanam Avenue and made sure to walk an extra block so he wouldn't have to see or be seen by Milena at the bakery.

His best-laid tactics for apologizing needed some work.

Clearly.

Pies silently fumed at his bungled attempt to offer Milena a bit of sincere regret. There would be no possibility for forgiveness this day, though. He would have to regroup and find a way to see Milena soon. Maybe he would go back to the bakery after he checked into the halfway house and got some badly needed sleep. And food. He had not eaten in the past twenty-four hours, and his stomach grumbled audibly.

He gently pushed Milena from his thoughts by planning his walking route to the halfway house. The mundane chore of hoofing it for the next mile or so would be the perfect tonic to help clear his head. He settled on taking Ozanam south to Talcott, then onto Oriole Avenue, and past the backside of the Resurrection Hospital grounds. He'd make it to his destination in the next twenty-five minutes. He'd check in, hopefully get some food and sleep, and, only then, take his next actions in getting acclimated back into the world.

As he walked along, Pies happened to look down the block as he reached two intersecting sleepy side streets.

He tripped to a halt.

A young girl rode slow circles on her bike in the middle of the block. Pies took in a sharp breath as he watched the girl carefully navigate her bike between and alongside some parked cars.

His gaze was directed down the block where his old boss, and one-time childhood friend, Bast Zielinski's house was located—the one Bast purchased after moving out of his father's first home across from Pies's old place.

Pies knew the girl in the frilly pink T-shirt and blue jeans.

Itty-Bitty, now ten years old, was oblivious that she was being observed from four houses away. Pies could hear her softly, happily, humming and singing as she pedaled along. She was twice as tall as she was when Pies stopped two 9mm rounds from ending her life years earlier. Seeing her now caused an involuntary guttural sound to croak in his throat and a sad smile to spike the corner of his mouth. The constantly painful twinge in Pies's upper left back, where he had been shot, brought him back into focus as the screen door of the Zielinskis' house swung open.

Bast's beautiful widow, Rebecca, pushed her way out of the home to check on her daughter. The woman stood with crossed arms and observed the little girl. Pies knelt and pretended to tie his shoelace, while keeping Rebecca in his peripheral vision. Rebecca's eyes flashed Pies's way, but then she fully turned and called out to her daughter, "Be careful now, okay, Bit?"

"Okay, Mom," replied the young girl.

Pies finished fiddling with his shoelaces. He stood and adjusted his backpack—and that's when a dark-haired man with prominent facial features and an imposing demeanor backed his way through the front door, holding a cup of coffee for Rebecca. She turned, carefully took the cup in her hands, and said, "Thanks, babe."

The man looked Pies's way, and Pies quickly walked toward Ozanam Avenue.

Rebecca was never a friend or a supporter of Pies, but Pies was happy to see Itty-Bitty as part of some sort of a family unit once again. Pies considered it imperative to have a positive father, or father figure, in a young person's life. He didn't really have that during his own crucial teen years, and, given how he turned out, he reckoned that it must be important.

Pies continued toward the halfway house. For some reason, maybe seeing Rebecca and Itty-Bitty, he could no longer keep his mind clear of negative thoughts.

The pessimism flooded back in, and he had little will left in his current state to stop it.

His thoughts at first began to drift and then rapidly fire—culminating with his recollection of a parole hearing he attended at Stateville Correctional Center. It was only three weeks back, and it was essentially his first and last hearing at the same time. The memory began to crowd his thoughts because he knew it was the reason he was now freely walking the streets of Edison Park.

He recalled how one of the parole board members displayed an envelope to the other four board members in the room, but nothing was said, and the woman made no eye contact with him. The session was quickly adjourned. Pies appeared at that parole hearing only because he was required to, but at the time he had an idea in the works that would automatically keep him locked up for good, so that he could do his proper penance for killing Vicki Chlebek.

Pies always seemed to have some sort of tactic in place to adjust to whatever life tossed his way. To be prepared with contingencies —plans A, B, and C, so that he could accomplish his intended criminal goals.

Pies's ideas for staying incarcerated called for violent actions to be taken with less than one year left on his eight-year prison sentence. He'd start trouble as much as possible. He'd fight, hurt deserving people, maybe get hurt in the process himself—which didn't matter to him—and have years and years tacked on to his sentence. He'd continue these vicious actions until his last breaths were consumed.

Little good his plan would do him now that he was out of prison and walking along Ozanam Avenue on Chicago's Far Northwest Side.

3

FIVE YEARS ago...

"Those first three counts are the ones that'll get you what you want," said State's Attorney Mary DiCicco. "About the other seventy-two counts? I'm sure you had a hand in them as you've admitted, but they're just window dressing, as far as I'm concerned. Overkill," she continued.

"Like we talked about, I plead guilty to everything, I go away for good," said Pies, thin, hollow-cheeked, and dressed in a loose, dark-gray suit. He sat at the long table of the Leighton Criminal Court-house's fourth-floor conference room and slowly read through the thick document that rested in his unsteady hands. He involuntarily rolled his left shoulder up and around to fight back at the lingering pain from being shot there months earlier.

"You admit to all of this in open court, especially counts one and two, the Banasik and Bartosz murders—"

"What about count three?"

"And...also count three. You plead to those in open court, and Judge Shapiro will sign off. And then you'll be on your way to the penitentiary as agreed upon, that's the way it'll work," said DiCicco.

DiCicco was a rather large, monochromatic-pants-suit-wearing woman who liked to pace as she met with defendants for interrogations or for hammering out plea deals. She exhibited all the grace of a hobbled water buffalo—but she usually knew her way around lawbreakers like Pies. DiCicco, whose own father was a retired Chicago cop, had absolutely no fear of hardened criminals.

Usually.

Pies's case was a different animal for the state's attorney, though.

In a loose grassroots assemblage, the public and then the media began to toss their overwhelming support behind Pies in spite of his major criminal—and murderous—flaws. That throng of taxpayers had their leniency for Pies cinched after learning he saved a little girl in the shootout. The nearly 10,000 e-mails, letters, and calls that SA DiCicco had received, so far, in favor of going easy on Jakubowski was a new twist and something she'd not seen in her fifteen-year career. DiCicco was good at her job, but she was also in the midst of a tight primary race to retain her position. She was compelled to do something she'd not done in her career up to this point, and that was to more closely study the public tea leaves. DiCicco had to make sure that she was on the winning side of the ones paying her salary and, more importantly, voting for her.

Count three of Pies's guilty plea agreement was the most important one in his estimation, though, and it was imperative that it be absolutely hiccup-free. There could be no mistakes as it pertained to his pleading guilty to manslaughter for the death of Wicktoria "Vicki" Chlebek. He must pay for accidentally killing his childhood friend, the only women he ever loved. After a few cursory passes, he reread the particular criminal count extra carefully to make sure there were no errors—spelling or otherwise.

Pies's attorney, a slovenly man named Mitchell, sat in a corner chair twenty feet away. The guy wore a food-stained necktie that was probably last dry cleaned in the mid-1980s. That tie crested over his vintage discount-department-store-shirt-wearing gut. Mitchell paid little attention to the others in the room and allowed his fingers to peck away at his cell phone. "Look good to you, Jakub?" he asked, with faux concern, without even looking up from his smartphone.

Pies did his best to ignore his attorney, DiCicco and her neurotic pacing, and also DiCicco's assistant, a fidgety pimple-faced young man who was tightly wedged into a cheap suit not designed for his plump physique.

Pies squeezed his eyes shut, reopened them, and then took a deep breath to reset his concentration and read, and reread, count three of the plea agreement once again.

"This will seal it all up. I know you were concerned that the grand jury I put together didn't indict you—"

"Because of the little girl?" Pies asked, his eyes locked onto DiCicco's.

DiCicco paused before she again paced and said, "I only went the extra step of seating that grand jury to bolster this agreement. Just because they didn't indict doesn't mean that the deal won't be accepted. I'm fairly confident that it's a slam dunk." But as soon as she finished her sentence, Pies noticed that DiCicco looked out the window and downward. It was something she'd done several times in the last few minutes of her pacing routine. This time, Pies sensed some unease wash over the woman.

Pies shifted his gaze back to the pile of paper before him, "How many years will he give me?"

"Oh, hell, you got the manslaughter of the lady and then the two men you took out when you were a sixteen-year-old kid...? At least twenty-five to, ah...um...you know," said Mitchell, as he fleetingly looked up from his cell phone. "You're not getting out. Just the way you wanted."

Pies acknowledged Mitchell and then allowed his eyes to scan the agreement once more.

Mitchell chimed back in. "Oh, and a couple of the networks have requested interviews from you. They'll wait until you land, you know, wherever..."

"Most likely Stateville," interjected DiCicco.

"Stateville? Really?" asked Mitchell. He then gave Pies a look of concern that was not lost on the doomed man. "Once you're settled in, you contact me, and I'll set it all up," Mitchell continued.

Pies's mind was drifting once again, like it'd done many, many times since he killed Vicki. As he fell into these funks, especially when he was around others, conversational flow would get away from him, and he'd sometimes become confused. Lost.

Mitchell picked up on Pies's confusion, and he sat up a little straighter. "The media interviews. There's going to be a few of them. We can do them all in one sitting, I'd bet. People love that 'true crime' stuff. They're interested in the...the, ah...what did that guy at channel seven call you?"

"The Blemished Hero," said the SA's chubby assistant.

Pies let out an angry breath and allowed his eyes to settle back on the document. He said, "The judge made me hire you, you know. You get a little something for setting up the interviews, too? I paid you with my house for all of this, that wasn't enough for you?"

"Jakub, buddy..."

"No interviews."

"Jakub, please think about—"

"No. No, interviews," said Pies.

His attorney fake coughed away the embarrassment of being slighted by his own client and went back to perusing his cell phone.

DiCicco actually smiled at Pies, although he didn't notice. She stopped pacing and looked through the conference room window and down to the street forty feet below once again. There were several television news crews set up alongside their parked vans and about one hundred people milling about on the sidewalk and the green space across the way, some carrying signs. One read: "Free Jakub. Hero not criminal."

The crowd seemed to be growing, too.

"Shit," said DiCicco, to herself.

Pies reread count three of the agreement—with the headline "The Manslaughter of Wicktoria Chlebek"—several times, and now he flipped through the other pages. The text at the top of each page shouted the headline of the crime that was meticulously detailed below it. The myriad burglaries he had set up and executed. The 9-1-1 communications officers job he illegally obtained so he could feed his burglary crew information on the residences and businesses whose alarms were malfunctioning. Nearly all of his crimes to date were mentioned in the document. All of the crimes that Pies could remember, at least.

However, none of the pages contained any mention of the murders of the two Outfit members that Pies carried out the same day he accidentally killed Vicki Chlebek. The victims were Zielinski burglary crew handler and Outfit made man Donny Noretti and his lethal bodyguard Luke. Both of the men sucked in their last bloody breaths while seated in a parked car in the Cook County forest preserve bordering Park Ridge. The two men had wanted Pies to continue working B&Es for the Outfit after they permanently took out the last of the Zielinski crewmembers. Pies saw it differently and made sure that the mobsters truly understood his unyielding stance in the matter.

The Outfit members had more than earned their demises, Pies thought, and he would go on allowing the police to believe that his immediate boss Bast Zielinski killed the men before he was dispatched in the shootout where Pies saved the girl. If Pies ever did admit to killing the Outfit guys, he would suffer a quick execution within the penitentiary walls. The Outfit would see to it. But Pies couldn't have that. He wanted to do his penance. He had to pay for what he'd done to Vicki.

"They deserved what they got," said Pies, in a near mumble.

"What's that?" asked Mitchell.

Pies waved his own comment away, not even realizing he'd spoken out loud.

"Look, Jakub, buddy, I can reschedule the interviews for after you—"

Pies shot Mitchell a look that stopped the man mid-sentence.

DiCicco motioned to her assistant in that instant, and the doughy young man slid a pen across the conference room table to Pies.

"Sign it," said DiCicco.

Pies snagged the pen in his right hand, flipped the agreement to the last page, and signed.

DiCicco made eye contact with her assistant, and he took the few steps to stand alongside Pies. He gently removed the pen from Pies's grasp and then went to the door, opened it, and said to one of the uniformed bailiffs outside, "We're ready."

*

"YOUR HONOR, this is unconscionable. You can't do that," said DiCicco, her face reddened and the veins angrily protruded from her thick neck. "He's pleading guilty. He's pleading to all counts, Your Honor. We had videotape rolling while we first put this all together."

The large, walnut-accented courtroom, with its raised judge's bench, empty jury box, and pew-like seating area, buzzed with guttural and joyous outcries from the standing-room-only audience.

Pies repeatedly blinked, and he couldn't truly understand what was happening. He reached sideways and grasped the sleeve of his attorney's suit jacket, but Mitchell didn't even notice. He, too, was flabbergasted by what the judge had just said.

Pies half turned and caught sight of his childhood friend Dana Banasik sitting shoulder to shoulder with the others on the right side of the jam-packed courtroom. Dana's face was screwed up in agonized surprise, and as she reached her hand up to cover her mouth, she slowly made tearful eye contact with Pies.

Pies immediately looked down and away. He was so ashamed of what he'd become and how he ruined Dana's family when he murdered her father those years before.

Judge Shapiro, who was soundly on the life cycle downslope, balding and looking more like an agitated tree sloth than an officer of the court, cleared his throat and motioned for DiCicco to take a seat. He said, "Please. Quiet down. Quiet. My decision's been made."

DiCicco slowly lowered herself back into her chair and turned briefly toward Pies and then back to the judge. Her assistant put his forehead into his hands and searched the tabletop in front of him for an answer that wasn't there.

Judge Shapiro peered at Pies for a good long moment and allowed the occupants of the room to grow even more still and quiet. He finally said, "You were coerced, sir. Nothing that you did, of a criminal nature, was of your own volition."

"Your Honor," called out DiCicco.

"Madam State's Attorney, I'd remain seated and silent if I were you," said the judge. He gave DiCicco an extended hardened glare before eyeing Pies once again and continuing. "I'm convinced that you had no say in the acts you carried out. You're a twenty-eight-year-old man sitting before us today, but you were a child at the time when you built and deployed the shotgun-shell devices that killed Mr. Banasik and Mr. Bartosz in Edison Park. You were bullied and criminally coerced into that and these other offenses by a ruthless and lawless element, Mr. Jakubowski. You were a child. You were the Edison Park version of a 'boy soldier,' in my estimation." The judge flipped quickly through a few pages of the plea agreement and continued, "These burglaries you've pled guilty to committing over the years, all of them, this extensive and exhaustive list, I cannot except that you were a willing participant. The criminal skills you acquired early on and used over the past years...I can't...I cannot accept that you knew what you were actually doing. And because of these very serious and significant circumstances, I am vacating the near entirety of this plea agreement. The state's attorney will have to come up with actual physical evidence of your participation in these past crimes, if she wants me to accept the majority of this deal."

The bulk of the utterly shocked occupants in the courtroom did not know that Judge Shapiro had also received e-mails, letters, and phone calls from concerned citizens wanting to ensure that Pies received leniency—closing in on six thousand such correspondences so far. Shapiro, too, was embroiled in a very tough primary, and his job was on the line.

"However, Mr. Jakubowski, I'm willing to accept your guilty plea on this, ah...," the judge quickly shuffled back through the agreement on his desk. "Yes. Count three of the agreement, the question of Wicktoria Chlebek's manslaughter. I believe that you did, indeed, take the young woman's life in the accidental shooting."

Pies's eyes welled up, and he lowered his head. He studied his wrists where they were still red from the handcuffs he wore but a few minutes ago when he was ushered into the courtroom. Something about his irritated red wrists disturbed Pies, but he couldn't fully understand why in that moment.

Judge Shapiro shuffled a few more papers, silently read and then reread a document, signed it, and said, "I sentence you to eight years of confinement at Stateville Correctional Center. We're done here." He slammed his gavel down, stood, and left through the rear courtroom door.

Two uniformed bailiffs approached Pies. He stood, head down, and placed his hands behind his back. His eyes darted about the room as the lawmen snapped handcuffs on his wrists.

No one else in the courtroom stirred or even made a sound for a long three-count. They were momentarily shocked into rigidity by the proceedings. But soon the news media reporters in the back of the room filed out, including a few who tucked sketch pads under their arms. Illinois still did not allow cameras in some of their courtrooms, and courtroom artists plied their trade for local television stations and in newspapers—especially during lurid cases like Pies Jakubowski's.

Finally, DiCicco and her assistant stood and gathered up their materials and briefcases off the prosecutor's desk. As they exited, Pies heard DiCicco mutter, "And a killer goes nearly free. This one's over for me. No more."

Pies turned her way to say something, but he couldn't get the words out in time and she was gone.

The audience started to shuffle out as well—all except for Dana Banasik. Dana sat and eyed Pies with what seemed to be a mixture of sadness and contempt.

"You take it easy, Jakub," said Mitchell, but Pies ignored him.

There were still two people Pies had not seen in the courtroom so far. They were Vicki's mother and father. In his previous public proceeding, his arraignment, and now the plea hearing, neither Milena nor her husband Blaze had shown up. Pies could hardly blame them for not wanting to see him. He'd taken so much from them.

"Come on," said the larger of the two bailiffs, and Pies was led through the left backside doorway of the courtroom.

"Your audience awaits, my man," said the smaller of the bailiffs as the three men walked down a long hallway toward an open elevator. "Your ride is downstairs."

"I'm not going back to county lockup?" asked Pies.

"Nope," said the larger bailiff. "The sheriff wants you gone. Too many man-hours keeping you segregated, and too much of a media circus."

"Media cir— What are you talking about?"

"You wait, my man, you wait," said the smaller bailiff.

*

PIES COULD hear the boisterous crowd before he saw the people. It sounded like hundreds of them, and they were chanting, but he couldn't make out what they were saying.

The bailiffs walked Pies to a nondescript, gray prison van, complete with a cage in the back, parked at the courthouse's covered loading dock. Two uniformed Illinois State Troopers stepped away from the van, one holding slack a set of chain waist and ankle shackles. Pies also noticed what seemed to be an unusual number of Cook County Sheriff's Police in what seemed like a perimeter around the van. They seemed to be a SWAT unit.

Since Pies was being housed in a segregated unit of the county lockup he had had no access to Internet, television, or newspapers. He had no idea that the public had begun to find his case so fascinating and thought-provoking. The only whiff of notoriety he witnessed for himself was the few days of television news he watched while he was in the hospital after the shootout in the Zielinski's Insurance offices. That was the first time he heard the Channel 7 investigative reporter call him the Blemished Hero. How he hated that nickname.

Pies remained docile as the bailiffs and state cops worked to get the cuffs off and the shackles on. Once secured, he was relocated into the back of the van and locked inside. The van reeked of stale urine and vomit, but Pies barely noticed as he took a seat. His mind was racing, and the chanting crowd was not making things any better.

The troopers got in, and the vehicle rounded out of its parking spot at the loading dock. Pies was finally able to catch sight of the massive crowd on the street in front of the courthouse.

On the other side of the locked gates several hundred people were shouting, some carrying signs with Pies's real name, Jakub, written or painted on them—all with various messages of support for the shackled man in the van.

"Hold tight, Jakubowski, this could be trouble," said the trooper in the driver's seat of the van.

"Damn," said the other. "Take it slow. Don't hit anyone."

"No shit," said the driver. "They'll roll us over like a big box turtle."

Cook County SO officers opened the locked gate, and the van inched forward and into the surging crowd of people. Several riot-gear-wearing officers, batons in hand, methodically shoved back the throng of protestors as the SWAT members slipped in on all sides of the van. The SWAT members created a walking human shield.

Pies was mesmerized at the sheer size of the crowd. He didn't even know where to look, there were so many eyes aimed his way.

"They want me dead, don't they?" asked Pies.

The trooper in the passenger seat removed his wide-brimmed hat and turned in his seat. "No, asshole. They want us to let you go. They hate us, not you."

As the van slowly made a right turn onto the main street and began to methodically emerge from the protestors crowding the avenue, one particular thing caught Pies's attention. Farther up the street, about three-quarters of a block away, where the protesters were not congregated, a woman dressed all in black climbed up onto the hood of a parked car, and then onto the roof of the vehicle—apparently to get a better view of the prison van.

"What the hell is she doing?" said the trooper behind the wheel. "Keep an eye on her."

The trooper in the passenger seat pinched his shoulder-mounted microphone and said, "Anyone have eyes on this lady? On the car?" The radio receiver on his belt crackled with overlapping responses, none of them making sense. The trooper un-holstered his sidearm and held it two-hand style between his bent knees, keeping his eye on the woman.

As the SWAT members on foot peeled away from the prison van, two Chicago police cars, both with activated light bars, tucked in front of and behind the vehicle as it cleared the last gaggle of protestors. The mini convoy began to gain speed, and Pies could not keep his eyes off of the woman, who was now standing quite boldly on top of the car as a breeze played at her long black skirt. As the van drew closer still, Pies noticed that she was wearing a black wig, a dowdy-looking black jacket, a plain white blouse, and a billowing black skirt.

Her garb was sort of old-fashioned, and Pies remembered seeing women dressed like that in the predominantly Jewish neighborhoods of Skokie and also on the North Side of Chicago. What set the woman apart, though, was that her face was so very, very beautiful—stunning and angelic, actually—and her pleading dark brown eyes seemed to call out to Pies. The wind kicked up, and her wig blew from her head. She caught it before it got away from her. The woman's natural hair was buzzed close to her scalp.

Pies stared for a brief moment, mesmerized by the woman, but instead of acknowledging her presence with a nod, he looked down and squeezed his eyes shut.

"What the hell was that?" asked the trooper in the passenger seat as the driver stomped down on the gas pedal and the convoy sped onward and toward Joliet.

4

"FROM WHAT we've learned, defendant Jakub Jakubowski will be pleading guilty to all charges here at 26th and California in about forty-five minutes. Once he's entered his guilty plea, and the judge accepts that plea, the sheriff's office is telling us Jakubowski will be immediately transferred to a state penitentiary. By the looks of this growing crowd of protestors, supporters really, nearly all in favor of some sort of leniency for Jakubowski, the authorities may have to postpone any transferring process at this time simply for safety reasons," said the humorless female street reporter for Channel 9 News on the television.

Faigy Tambor stood motionless in the kitchen of her Lunt Avenue two-flat. She sported a freshly buzzed head and kept her unblinking eyes locked on the small TV that sat on the granite countertop. She showed a keen interest in the crowd around the reporter. There were hundreds of people, and most seemed agitated while others carried protest signs in their hands.

Faigy blinked a few times and looked down at the two pieces of rye bread she held in her hands, which hovered over a paper plate. She took a half step away from the counter and dropped the bread onto the paper plate, and then she rubbed her hands together and knocked free any lingering crumbs. She smoothed her ankle-length black skirt, straightened her posture, and adjusted her simple black jacket, under which she wore a crisp white blouse.

She stopped all motion again and stared at the television, and in that instant a compulsion washed over her. She couldn't quite explain, but the urge had been growing ever stronger since she first heard about Jakub Jakubowski's legal troubles, redoubling in intensity the past few days, as the man's court appearance neared. Simply seeing Jakubowski on television wouldn't be enough to quench her cravings now. She couldn't explain the impulse if asked, and yet she still had to see Jakub Jakubowski in person.

Since the moment she heard on the local news about Jakubowski's criminal history and the heroic act he'd selflessly performed during a bloody shootout, Faigy had to know more about the man.

Jakub "Pies" Jakubowski had unknowingly worked his way into Faigy Tambor's life as she was having what some people would deem a "quarter-life crisis."

Faigy had been questioning her choices of late, chiefly, her marriage to Herschel Tambor six years ago, when she was an unworldly nineteen years of age. There was absolutely no chemistry between them. The only reason she agreed to marry Herschel was to please her parents, both of whom would leave her when they died within a few months of one another, three years after her wedding day.

Faigy Tambor was brought up in, and mostly adhered to, the teachings of the Hasidic sect of her Jewish faith. She dealt with a brief hiccup in her family's lifestyle when she went "emo" for a few short months and was also arrested on a misdemeanor vandalism charge during her fourteenth year. All through that tumultuous time, she wore garish makeup and baggy black clothing, which was absolutely nothing like the conservative black garb the people of her religion wore. That brief breakaway from her sect was later chalked up by her parents and their rabbi to hormonal growing pains more than anything else. Or so the elders thought. In actuality, the fourteen-year-old version of Faigy had been attempting to help a classmate fit in with the social hierarchies of their rather conservative school. The fellow student, a meek and lonely girl named Ann, was emotionally pulling away from the others in their private school and beginning to act out by causing minor disruptions—mostly ripping motivational posters off of hallway walls and talking back to the faculty.

Faigy placed it upon herself to reach out to Ann and to simply be a friend to the troubled girl. The turmoil Faigy caused her own family in dramatically changing her outward style caused a minor rift in her house, especially after she and Ann were arrested for removing thirty light bulbs from the exterior of their school and smashing them on the pavement late one Saturday evening. Faigy only acted out as a way to show solidarity with her new friend. She figured, at the time, that she could possibly coax Ann back from the emo brink once the troubled girl got to know her better. The ploy didn't quite work out that way. But at that time, Faigy knew that she at least needed to try and help the girl.

Everything returned to normal at Faigy's home after Ann and her parents moved to New York City two months after the light bulb incident. Faigy's father and her rabbi were able to get the misdemeanor vandalism charge dropped and to secure an agreement for her to remain in the school, if she paid restitution and apologized.

Five years after that moment in her life, Faigy's parents were the ones who pushed her toward the nuptials with Herschel, a Michigan Avenue jeweler. "He'll provide like no other, Faigy, I can promise you that," her father Bernard told her a few days before her wedding day. "There will be children, and Herschel Tambor will provide generously for them, too."

However, Herschel proved to be sterile, and cracks began to form in Faigy's existence, once again, after her parents' passing. Yes, Herschel Tambor provided for his young bride by way of his ownership of a lucrative jewelry store, but Faigy required more than what money could afford her.

She dutifully buzzed off her hair every week, as dictated by her faith, to show her loyalty to her husband. And in public she donned various conservatively styled wigs, depending on the day or the event she and her husband were attending. And, nothing too flashy was ever worn. It was all part of the Hasidic tradition for Orthodox women to dress typically in sensible white blouses and long black skirts, opaque stockings, and black shoes.

And to always do as her husband instructed.

Always.

At least those were Herschel Tambor's unyielding methods for following his faith. And he made sure that Faigy adhered to his rules.

As the television news rambled on, she grabbed up her car keys and a black wig from the kitchen table and scrambled from her house through the back kitchen door. There, she leapt down the wooden steps two at a time while trying to fit the wig on her head.

She got into her two-door Toyota that was parked next to the brick garage and started the engine.

Her frumpy husband, Herschel—a balding man with long side-curls called *payots,* who was exactly twenty-one years, two months, and seventeen days her senior—stumbled out and onto the landing at the first-floor rear door. He buttoned his white shirt as he called out, "Faigy? Where are you going? My lunch... Woman, get back here."

Faigy ignored her husband and soon found herself frantically driving southbound toward the courthouse at 26th and California. She had to get to the building in time to catch a glimpse of the man who she'd grown to admire, despite his many faults.

Forty minutes later, she illegally parked on California Avenue just in time to see the gray prison van carrying Jakubowski exit the courthouse grounds a block away and slowly weave its way through the group of supporters. As the vehicle neared her location, she had barely enough time to successfully clamber on top of her parked car, where she thought she'd get a better view. Once on top of the car, and in spite of nearly losing her wig to a stiff breeze, she was, indeed, able to make eye contact with the very man who risked his life to save the little girl.

*

"FAIGY, DEAR, he's concerned for your well-being, not trying to get you into...trouble. There's no trouble, my dear," said Rabbi Greenman, an elderly man who, paradoxically, looked both plump and skinny at the same time. His head was round and quite large, and it was highlighted by his long, gray *payots*. Curiously, his tall body was rail thin, which made him appear more like a hastily scratched-out caricature than a living and breathing man. He was dressed from head to toe in black, including a wide-brimmed, beaver-fur fedora.

Faigy sat nearly knee to knee with the rabbi in the well-appointed living room of her Lunt Avenue home. An hour after laying eyes on Jakubowski, Faigy returned home to find the friendly, albeit apprehensive, rabbi in her living room—and her husband Herschel anxiously pacing all about the house.

"I feel... I want to talk to you... But I can't do this," said Faigy, as her eyes darted to the pacing Herschel, who was now hovering in the hallway that led to the kitchen.

Rabbi Greenman motioned that he understood. He gently cleared his throat and said, "Herschel, could you give us a bit of privacy, if that wouldn't be too much trouble?"

Herschel, his back to the living room, angrily spun on his heels. "In my own house, I can't even—" And then he caught a glimpse of the rabbi's watery, all-knowing eyes. He softened and said, "I'll, ah... I'll be in the kitchen." He slinked from view.

"Now, please, go on, Faigy. It's going to be okay. Unburdening is good for the soul," said the pleasant old man, with another warm smile. "What's been upsetting you? Herschel said you've been infatuated with this Jakubowski man from the news broadcasts."

In that moment, Faigy didn't feel patronized by the rabbi. She had love and respect for the man. Rabbi Greenman had been instrumental in helping her through the grieving process after each of her parents passed on. She in no way wanted to upset the rabbi or for him to know that her faith was being rattled.

"Is this similar to the time when you were a teen?" the rabbi asked, apprehensively, and with the touch of a well-meaning smile. "With all the makeup and the breaking of things?"

Faigy blinked a few times and then shook her head. "I don't think so. No, I need...I have a need to..."

"It's okay, Faigy, I'm here," said the rabbi.

"I have no purpose, Rabbi," she said. "I'm devoted to Herschel, but ...I want more."

"No purpose?" he asked, thoughtfully. "Hmm. How do you mean, no purpose?"

"There must be more to our lives. Look at you. You have the shul to watch over and care for. I don't really have anything outside of... You see, I watched this man on the television, and he had absolutely no reason at all to aid a helpless person—the little girl," said Faigy. "But he did without thinking of his own safety."

"Yes, I read about that," said the rabbi.

"In fact, his life would've been easier if he had run from the situation. Just run away so he could live another day and go about his life doing...doing...whatever. But he risks everything. Everything, Rabbi," she said.

Faigy noticed the rather shocked look on the rabbi's face.

"Oh, no, it's not that I'm willing to die, it's just that... It's that I don't really do...anything. Nothing."

"Nothing? It's nothing that you do, is that it, woman?" shouted Herschel, who now angrily stood at the edge of the living room and the hallway. "So now I'm nothing to you? Is there not enough satisfaction in your life for you to take care of me in a proper fashion? To cook my meals, and to—"

The rabbi stood and put his hands out in a calming gesture. "Herschel? Please. Let your wife speak her mind to me, it'll be fine...."

"Get out of my house," said Herschel, who was now seething.

The rabbi didn't budge, so Herschel took one angry step forward.

"Get...out of my house, Rabbi. Leave me and my wife be. Please."

Faigy remained seated, and as she dejectedly dropped her chin to her chest—her black wig slipped from her head and plopped heavily onto the floor between her feet.

Rabbi Greenman didn't dare stoop down to retrieve it. He left the premises without another word.

Faigy, with tears streaming down her face, stared at the wig on the floor.

"Fantastic. Dinner will be late now," was all Herschel said as he backed out of the room.

*

THIRTEEN MONTHS later...

"No, no, just go about what you're doing. No posing. I want a natural shot," said the grinning and very relaxed Faigy. Her hair had grown out to about three inches in length and was styled in a pixie cut. It appeared as if a bruise on her left cheekbone was about halfway healed. She held a high-end Canon digital camera with neck strap to her eye and snapped off a succession of photos.

Two bright-eyed, rangy, and elegantly dark-skinned African— and newly American—women named Abua and Minika were her photographic subjects. The Nigerian immigrant sisters were carrying neatly stacked piles of heavy-looking cardboard boxes from the rear door of the Enduring Horizons complex in Evanston. Their friendly dogs, a yellow Labrador and a Border collie mix, hopped around excitedly at their feet but stayed close.

Abua and Minika were both taken in by the "women-helping-women" organization after landing in the States as refugees eighteen months prior. Enduring Horizons occupied a massive, three-story, hundred-year-old mansion on Ridge Road and typically housed twenty to thirty displaced women on a regular basis. If the women requiring services had children, those children were housed too. Most of the organization's clients were tangled in violent domestic situations, but occasionally women like Abua and Minika were assisted, as well.

"Are you going to help, or just take silly photos?" asked the smiling Abua in her accented English as she lugged another heavy box to a parked rental van positioned on the blacktop at the rear of the building.

Faigy snapped another quick photo, let the camera dangle from the strap, and helped the women finish their loading. "I'll frame some of these for you, for the new apartment," she said.

Minika placed the last box inside the rental van, and Abua motioned for the dogs to get into the vehicle and then shut the back doors. The sisters both moved closer to Faigy and hugged her tightly.

"Okay, okay," said Faigy. "Let a girl take a breath," she giggled.

"We would not be doing any of this without your help," said Minika. "You have done so much. We owe you everything."

Faigy completed the hugs, and the two sisters hopped into the front seats of the van and took off.

"Faigy? Faigy, do you have a minute?" asked a pleasant-looking, gray-haired woman, as she stepped closer.

"Of course. What's up, Melissa?"

Melissa briefly examined the bruise under Faigy's left eye. "That's healing pretty well," she said.

Faigy unconsciously grazed her fingertips across the bruise, and her mind briefly raced with an image of the squat-looking man with the pockmarked skin and the horrible temper who threw the punch at her. It happened two weeks ago when Faigy aided another woman in finding a permanent place to live—away from her abusive husband. Without their knowledge, the man had followed Faigy and his wife to the new apartment building. Faigy and the woman exited Faigy's car, and that's when the man assaulted her. Faigy ran away after being struck, and the wife, who had had enough of her abusive husband at that point, was able to hold onto the wildly flailing man long enough for the police to arrive and arrest him. From her hiding spot in the bushes three buildings down, Faigy watched as the police roughly detained the combative husband and took him away in their patrol car.

Faigy had wanted to do more in that violent moment, but her flight instinct had overruled, and ever since she'd been sort of kicking herself for not being braver.

Melissa continued, "I'm not sure how you saw this all progressing. What I mean is that you've done some exemplary volunteer work for the organization, but..."

"Oh, no. What is it?" asked Faigy, her eyes squinting with concern. "The fight...with the man?"

Melissa said, "Oh, no, dear lord, it's nothing bad, honey. I was wondering... I have to put my budget together for this coming year, and I was wondering if you've ever thought about coming aboard as a paid employee. Everyone who's come into contact with you gives the highest praise for your work. We'd hate to lose you."

Faigy's new direction in life all started quite innocently after she enrolled in a basic photography class at Enduring Horizons. She soon realized there was a definite need for volunteers to assist the female clients of the organization, some of who were in rather precarious domestic situations. Faigy quickly jumped in to help. It was the catalyst she thought she'd been searching for and hoping to find —to finally do more for those in need.

With her husband refusing to allow her to work outside the home, she felt trapped in the tedium of what her life had become. So Faigy went against Herschel's wishes and searched out activities that would keep her busy and fulfilled while her husband was away working fourteen-hour days at his jewelry store.

Faigy Tambor would not be denied the chance to help people in any way that she could. She was driven to be of service. It was her calling. And yet she still felt she needed to be doing even more.

At Enduring Horizons she met all kinds of people, women mostly, from many different backgrounds. Immediately, Faigy became a human cultural sponge. She loved learning how others grew up and lived, and where they came from. She developed into a human sounding board for the clients to unburden themselves.

She also became a one-woman relocation machine, helping displaced women find safe places for themselves and their children to live. Her clients could move forward from desperate situations and thrive.

It was while doing all of this that Faigy planted the seed in Herschel's ear about turning their unfinished basement into another apartment. When it was completed, Faigy would be able to offer other brave people who sought freedom from abuse a temporary place to stay. Herschel didn't know this was the reason for rehabbing the space. He believed it was to rent out for additional income. Once he found out the true purpose of the basement rehab, their marriage was over. Since it was Faigy's childhood home where they were residing, and she had clear ownership of the building, Herschel vacated the two-flat a few hours after their last argument.

Faigy was free.

While dealing with so many new people, some arriving at Enduring Horizons with heartbreaking tales of domestic violence, pain, and loss, there was no inquiry that became taboo for Faigy to ask of the others while she volunteered her time. She was so open and honest in her approach that she was rarely refused an answer. Nor did she fail to answer questions in return. The open dialogue she enjoyed with the women she served, she believed helped the demoralized women to heal—and for herself to heal from her own marital loss and cloistered ways.

Faigy never went beyond high school with her education, however, she was a voracious reader, of nonfiction, mostly. Her depth of knowledge was impressive even before she began her forays outside her home. She never likened herself to an anthropologist in the past, and yet that's exactly what she had become—a layman anthropologist.

She then began to utilize her camera to document everything she experienced. Her photos were good, too. Faigy was a natural master at balancing shadow and light. The photos she took told rich, layered stories without using any written words—like the series of photos she took of women and their young children. She had a knack for catching moments when her subjects' eyes were at their expressive best.

Now, as she stood with Melissa outside the Enduring Horizons building, it was Faigy's eyes that showed an overload of emotion. "I would...I would like that very much, Melissa. Thank you. Thank you," said Faigy, as she lurched forward to hug her boss.

"Here's the thing. The paying part of the job won't start until the beginning of the fiscal year," said Melissa. "I hope that's okay."

"I understand. This is wonderful news," Faigy replied. "Thank you, Melissa."

Melissa moved off and Faigy took in a deep and satisfying breath.

*

LATER THAT day, and still riding an emotional high, Faigy exited her local bakery with a white paper bag full of muffins in hand and a smile plastered on her face.

She cut across the narrow parking lot and was headed toward her home as Rabbi Greenman came walking into the lot from fifty feet away. He was dressed in his customary all-black garb and had on his wide-brimmed, beaver-fur hat.

Their eyes met, briefly, and Faigy cleared her throat as they neared one another.

"Good afternoon, Rabbi," she said with a friendly nod.

Rabbi Greenman's eyes flicked away, and he walked right past her without uttering a word.

The rudely calculated slight cut at Faigy. Instead of impolitely lashing out, though, she said, "It was nice to see you again. Please be well, Rabbi."

She heard the old man sort of snort and shuffle to a stop. He said, "I tried to help you, Faigy Tambor."

Faigy also skidded to a halt and turned.

Rabbi Greenman was carefully watching her. "I tried to help you through your...your...dilemma, and this is what happens?" He put a hand out as if displaying to the world what became of Faigy Tambor—who now stood in the parking lot wearing a casual blouse and blue jeans, rather than the traditional Hasidic garb.

"I was there to... I tried to help you, Faigy," said Rabbi Greenman as he turned and entered the bakery.

Faigy cleared her throat, looked at her shoes for a moment, and then raised her gaze as she moved out of the parking lot as quickly as she could. She tried her best to hold her head high as she stepped along, but she failed.

5

PRESENT DAY...

The halfway house was a nondescript, faded yellow brick, six-unit apartment building at the corner of Bryn Mawr and Oleander Avenues, overlooking the Kennedy Expressway. The place needed some basic maintenance performed, and soon—chiefly, new paint and tuck-pointing. Pies was familiar, and wholly unimpressed, with the arrangement sitting in front of him. Many other cheaply constructed replicas of the edifice dotted the area's landscape from the Far South Side up through to Zion at the Wisconsin border to the north. It was if the buildings were slapped together on some enormous assembly line and haphazardly flicked about like playing cards shuffled onto the unwitting Chicago landscape.

The three floors on the right side of the structure were each outfitted with a one-bedroom, one-bath apartment. On the other side, stacked one onto the next, were three two-bedroom, one-bath units. A small vestibule was situated inside the front doorway, and a singular interior hall and stairway bifurcated the building. The door at the other end of the first-floor hallway led to the alley out back. Before Pies even stepped a foot inside, he accurately guessed that it would reek of mothballs, pungent cooking smells, and dirty laundry. For him, every building he had visited like the one here had smelled the same, so why would this one be any different?

Pies thought that Stateville Correctional Center with its daily fights and 24-7 screaming matches was loud, but the corner of Bryn Mawr and Oleander was noisier. The cars and trucks zipping past below on the Kennedy Expressway could definitely beat Stateville in a head-to-head, decibel-level sound off.

"New meat," said a man's friendly voice above the din of a passing short-pipe Harley.

Pies pivoted to his left, and a dumpy, undersized man of about fifty years of age smiled in his direction. The guy had smooth facial skin for his age and sported a goofy Beiber-like haircut above his matching half-inch gauged earrings. He was also wearing what looked to be an old Members Only jacket. As the man got closer, Pies could see that he was wearing foundation makeup in an attempt to cover his deeply pitted skin. The man was a walking contradiction, bridging generations and fashion styles, all wrapped up in an abbreviated 170-pound package. The man carried heavy cans of soup in clear plastic grocery bags in each of his hands as he crossed over the thin strip of grass that acted as the halfway house's front lawn.

"Only messing with you, brother. Come on in. It'll beat any shit-hole you came from, believe it, man. You are checking in, right?"

"Yeah," said Pies.

"I'm Jenny."

Pies narrowed his eyes and followed along as the man gathered both plastic bags into his left hand so he could open the outer front door with the key in his right.

"Dave Jenner. They call me Jenny," he said. "Come on, you gotta see the Nazi first. Guy that runs the place. Gunther Reinschmidt. You know, the Nazi, because of his name and—"

"Right," Pies replied as he edged forward and followed Jenny into the building.

Jenny stopped to key open the interior vestibule door as Pies crowded in behind him, allowing the outer door to snick closed. Pies blinked as his eyes watered from the stench of stale cigarettes and bacon grease that emanated from the man. The odor would temporarily offset the smell of the mothball/cooking/dirty laundry combination that soon awaited him.

"It's apartment one on the right. The number fell off the buzzer thingy there, but it's the top button, so you know," said Jenny.

Pies wanted to get this over with as soon as possible. The sooner he could check in and settle in, the sooner he could take care of Milena.

"Where'd you come from?"

Pies didn't respond.

"Everyone knows everything here after a few days, so—"

"Stateville," said Pies.

"That right?" Jenny shot a worried look Pies's way and continued, "Um. Good to be out, huh?"

Pies didn't answer, so Jenny completed the unlocking process and pushed the door fully inward. They went inside, and he motioned with his chin to the apartment door.

"They call me Pies." Pies knocked on apartment one's door and ignored any further interaction with Jenny.

"It's open," said a terse, deep voice from within.

Jenny, mouth agape and ready to speak, hovered for a two-count, and then he ascended the creaky steps.

Pies opened the apartment door, and his nose was instantly swatted with yet another wall of aromas. These were many-layered cooking smells. And although he still hadn't eaten, none of the odors was very appealing. It smelled to Pies as if Gunther was pickling something in his apartment's kitchen, possibly long-dead rodents.

Gunther, nearing seven feet tall, was skeletal, with a shaved head and an intricate patchwork of tattoos that crisscrossed the rail-thin arms that protruded from his short-sleeved shirt. The man sported an easy smile, but his cynical eyes broadcasted to Pies that he thought he was not one to be trifled with.

The apartment was decorated with cheap furnishings and mass-produced paintings. It appeared as if Gunther had attempted to spruce the place up with his own personal decorative touches, but without much success. There were pieces of framed sports memorabilia here and there on the walls—mostly autographed photos of athletes from all the major American sports.

The crown jewel, Pies determined, by its placement right behind Gunther's desk chair, was a framed Chicago Bears #9 jersey with the name "McMahon" imprinted on it in block letters. The white #9 was autographed with a sweeping signature—McMahon.

Gunther pointed to a wooden chair opposite the white lacquered desk that was set up in the middle of the living room. Pies let the backpack slip from his shoulder, set it on the floor, and took another quick glance around. He lowered himself into the chair as Gunther wedged into his own seat opposite him.

Gunther stared, like he was trying to calculate what made Pies work.

Pies wondered if Gunther's expression was an attempt to look tough, because it was not working. Pies did his best to fight down any semblance of a smile.

Gunther held temporary dominion over Pies, he thought, but Pies estimated that the man would not withstand a well-placed punch to the bridge of his nose if it were ever called for. The condescension Gunther displayed to Pies at that moment would've earned him that very beating on any given day in Stateville.

"I know you, Jakubowski. I don't give a shit what you've done in the past," said Gunther. "What you do here at my house is the only thing that matters from now on."

Pies's non-reaction seemed to shave a hint of cockiness from Gunther's approach.

"I mean saving that kid, you know, so there's no confusion. I really do know who you are," he continued.

Pies nodded once and said, "Sure."

"You're just another asshole like you were at Stateville. The only difference is that the doors are locked from the inside here. That's pretty much it. You screw up, you go back. Simple. For the next six months, I'm your daddy. After those first uneventful six, you'll be allowed to live independently...or not. It all depends on you."

Pies cleared his throat and intuitively leaned forward, he wanted so badly to reach across the desk and grab this skinny asshole by the neck and squeeze, but he forced himself to relax and nod instead. "Got it," he said.

Gunther smirked as he opened the top desk drawer and pulled out a small folded pamphlet and a single key on a modest, clear-plastic ring. He pushed both items across the desk and continued, "These are the rules for a successful stay. And that's for the front and back doors. Don't lose it. There's a $100 reissue fee. The individual apartments and bedroom and bathroom doors don't have locks."

Pies grabbed the pamphlet and key and held them in his folded hands without even taking a glance.

"After you get a bunk, you'll still have enough daylight to go out and start looking for a gig. There are some friendly greasy spoons around that are always looking for bussers. Most are right up Higgins Road. Some are on Harlem. You need to find work fast. If I sense you're not looking hard enough, not putting in the extra effort, you're going back," said Gunther.

Pies again nodded once.

"Ever work in a restaurant?"

Pies stared and then blinked. Casual. "Not really," he said. He had ripped off a few eateries and restaurant-supply warehouses in his former days as an Outfit-sanctioned burglar, but that was it.

"There's a list of the friendlies on the wall outside in the hallway," Gunther said as he looked past Pies to the door.

"The bunk?" asked Pies as he stood.

"Top floor on the left. There are three others with you in the apartment. Two of them are at work, but I think the other one you met as you got here—that creepy little fucker Jenny."

"Right, Jenny," said Pies.

"You could probably figure out pretty quick why he got locked up, right?" Gunther said with a wink. "He was 'at-risk' in Stateville, if you get me?"

Pies knew exactly what Gunther meant, that Jenny was a convicted pedophile, but instead he said, "What was he in for?"

Gunther lost his smirk, hesitated, and said, "Like I said, there are no locks here other than the front and back doors for our protection. Take advantage of the gift the state has handed you. And know that I like to keep a special eye on the newcomers with nightly room inspections."

Pies picked up his backpack and knew in that moment that he had made a mistake by grabbing up his hidden cash from his old garage so soon after his release. Now he'd have to find another hiding place. He sidestepped over and opened the apartment door.

He'd been with Gunther for all of two minutes, and he knew the guy was not to be trusted by the way he placed Jenny's life in danger. Was he testing Pies? Seeing if he could goad him into hurting Jenny and in turn get tossed back into prison? Jenny would deserve his ad hoc beat down, but still, if Gunther so easily exposed the weird little man for the sick person he was, he'd have no trouble screwing Pies over if the time ever came.

"We have a total of sixteen assholes like you under this roof right now, so you'll have to make nice with them all, okay. We're supposed to have weekly group meetings here to discuss your collective transitions back into the world and your feelings and all that bullshit, but I don't do them. No one gives a fuck about your feelings. That's my call, okay. As long as you're cool, you get to stay. Listen to me. I run your life now. I make your major decisions for you. I'm daddy, like I said before, and if you screw up, even for the piss-anty-ist thing, you go back."

"Right. You said," offered Pies as he opened the apartment door wider.

Gunther said, "Hero, criminal, whatever, I don't give a shit, Jakubowski. Get a job in the next few days and we won't have any troubles."

With that, Pies left the apartment on the first floor, turned right, and headed up the stairs to the third floor where the door on the two-bedroom side of the building was already open. Pies could hear

'80s rock music playing softly from within and someone clinking around in the kitchen.

He walked into the apartment and took a quick glance around. It appeared as if the same corporate decorator who outfitted Gunther's pad did this one as well, sans the sports memorabilia. He stood in a good-sized living room/dining room combination that opened to a kitchen. Everything was painted a cream color—walls, woodwork, and cabinets alike. There wasn't a sofa; instead four upholstered chairs were set up in a semicircle around a coffee table, all facing the lone forty-inch, flat-screen television. A four-seat dining room table was positioned closer to the kitchen doorway, and there was a truncated hallway to the left of the kitchen opening that presumably led to the two bedrooms and the bathroom.

The aroma of mothballs and dirty laundry aside, the place was rather tidy. Pies was certain that Gunther made sure of that.

"Hey, man, welcome. Come on in. Check it out, and settle in," said Jenny as he stood near the fridge in the kitchen, putting his groceries into the upper cabinets. "We're bunkies. The door on the right down the hall."

Pies walked toward his new bedroom and pushed the door open. Inside were two single beds, both were neatly made, but the one on the left had a ruffled pillow. Pies figured that this was Jenny's bunk. He took a seat on the bed to the right and placed his backpack on the floor at his feet.

He sat there and stared at the floor as exhaustion washed over him in increasing waves, and his eyelids sank to half-mast. His stomach grumbled loudly and that woke him back up.

"I don't snore, if you're wondering," said Jenny with a faux chuckle as he entered the room, trying to keep things light.

Pies considered the grinning Jenny, noticing how much the man in front of him wanted to radiate an outwardly friendly persona, but what came across, instead, was strange, forced, and awkward. It was as if Jenny was a poorly trained actor working on a sincerity exercise. Pies could tell something wasn't right about the man the moment they met out in front of the building. There was a reason guys like Jenny were sometimes kept in protective custody in the penitentiary. Regardless of what he had done, the man wouldn't last an hour in the general population before someone would beat him... possibly to death.

Even if Pies's baser instinct was to toss Jenny out the third-floor window, he couldn't. Milena's life was being threatened, and he would have to control himself until he could figure out how to get her to a safe place.

"Can you give me a minute?" asked Pies as he stood.

"Sure, brother-man. No problem," said Jenny as he backed his way out of the room and pulled the door nearly closed.

Pies stood very still for a moment and could hear Jenny out in the living room turning on the television. He picked up his backpack and unzipped it. He extracted the three stacks of cash and slid two of them into his front right pocket, the other into his front left pocket. Pies tossed the backpack onto the bed and then reconsidered. He tilted back to the bed and slipped the smartphone from its hiding place in the backpack into his front left jacket pocket.

His pockets bulged to a ridiculous state, but he didn't want to leave the cash, $25,000 worth, or the phone behind with the creepy Jenny in attendance. He secured the bottom button of his suit jacket so that the fabric would partially conceal the swells of cash in his front pockets. He left the backpack on the bed as he exited the bedroom.

As Pies entered the living room, Jenny, seated in one of the four cushioned chairs, turned with an expectant gaze. "Going out, huh?"

"Yeah," said Pies as he grasped the doorknob. "Going out."

"Take care, brother."

As soon as the door closed, it opened again and Pies reentered. He headed back to the bedroom. There, he retrieved his backpack and then made his way from the place once again, all under the open-mouthed gaze of the still seated and mildly surprised Jenny.

6

THERE WERE four people inside the crusty neighborhood tavern, and only one was a customer—Pies. It was still too early for the after-work, daily drinking crowd so the place was fairly quiet. The interior was dark and dated, but by the look of the well-worn seats, floor, and other furnishings, business was probably brisk most nights.

Pies did his best to pretend as if the news broadcast on the tavern's television was keeping his attention, but he couldn't help but notice the way the man at the far end of the bar was eyeing him ever since he entered the establishment. The man, presumably the owner based on the dog-eared ledger book and papers spread out on the bar top in front of him, was middle-aged, thin, and sickly-looking, with loose-skinned, tattoo-covered arms. He sat sideways on his barstool and faced Pies from twenty feet away.

Pies was truly weary but was still able to retain the noncommittal expression on his face in light of the angry eyes on him. He slyly scrutinized the man via the long and narrow, horizontal back-bar mirror, as he awaited his food and drink order. The sickly man seemed to be growing more and more stressed by the moment.

When Pies initially entered the corner tavern on Higgins Road to order a cheeseburger and glass of water, the pretty bartender, an agile brunette woman in her early twenties, wearing a black Steely Dan T-shirt with the *Aja* album cover, stopped stocking beer bottles into a cooler to welcome him with a bright smile and a, "What'll you have?"

Now, a minute later, that same bartender leaned into the open kitchen doorway and gave the cook Pies's food order. The cook was a man in his late forties and, by the look of his pallid skin and the weary and distrustful expression in his narrowed eyes, most likely a fellow area halfway-house resident.

The bartender moved back toward her perch behind the bar, but the agitated man at the bar grasped her arm and then motioned for her to lean closer. She bent forward, and the man whispered into her ear. The bartender bobbed her head up and down, straightened, and came around to the front side of the bar and right up to Pies.

"Hi, there. Can I talk to you?" she asked, rather politely.

The worn-out Pies didn't respond straightaway. He sized up the woman for a moment. "Sure," he said as his eyes, again, slid back in the ailing man's direction. It was in that instant that Pies realized he actually did know the man.

The guy was an area tow-truck driver who the Zielinskis floated betting markers to on occasion, especially when the Bears and Packers were battling it out. Pies recalled one time, right before he went to prison, when he used his Zielinski-backed influence to get the angry man to unhook Pies's car from his tow truck. He recalled how the man acted like a tough guy at first, but quickly relented when he finally recognized Pies.

"Not here," said the pretty bartender. She walked to the front door of the tavern and then pushed her way outside. Pies scooted back, stood, kicked his backpack tight under the stool, and followed.

Once outside and onto the sidewalk, the bartender halted and spun around, which allowed Pies to move past her. She now stood between Pies and the door.

"Hey, look, it's not me doing this. He owns the place. Bought it the week before he found out he's got that cancer...of the colon," said the bartender.

"That's tough."

"He talks about you all the time, especially since you got put away.

I don't remember much of it because I was in high school then, but he's always going on and on. Says the Zielinskis were assholes, but he liked it better when they ran the neighborhood. The new guys are worse."

"You're his daughter?"

She grinned and continued, "Then there's the lady that you... That you killed? Don't make me say all of this stuff, okay. I've been hearing it all for like, ever. I'm kind of sick of it."

Pies tried not to react.

The bartender continued, "I don't know. You seem okay to me. Dad's at the point where he can barely stand up. He's not going to be around much longer. And it's his place, so... He wanted me to tell you something else. He wanted to..."

The bartender didn't want to talk anymore, and she didn't want to make eye contact, either.

"Go on. It's okay," said Pies.

"He said...he said that you're lucky he didn't pack today, because, well—he'd never see prison if he took your head off. He'll be dead soon, and...anyhow, look, it's not me..."

"I got it," said Pies through a woeful half smile. "It's okay."

She looked Pies up and down and then adopted a sad smirk of her own, spun on her heels, and walked back toward the front door.

Pies edged forward so he could retrieve his backpack from inside. The door violently flung open and nearly struck the bartender in the face. The angry man stood as proudly as his disease would allow. He held the backpack in his trembling hand. The bartender squeezed past the bar owner and entered the tavern, and the sickly man used all the strength he could muster to unceremoniously toss the backpack onto the sidewalk. The man stared and quaked with rage, and it seemed as if he wanted to say something, but he was so upset by Pies's presence that he couldn't even get the words out.

Pies picked up the backpack and left.

*

THE TWO grayish-hued rotisserie hot dogs Pies purchased from the convenience store a block from the tavern and slugged down on his walk back to the halfway house, were now trying to make an escape back up through their entry point. He lifted the bottle of water that he purchased with the nasty-tasting dogs, chugged, and foiled their flight.

As he crushed the empty water bottle and tucked it into his backpack, he burped.

"Oh, no…not this…," he said, as he stopped and nearly vomited. He righted himself, took a few breaths, and began to walk again. "Jesus…"

A local television station's van zipped past him on Bryn Mawr Avenue—and then another. They were colorfully decorated vans with microwave dishes on top used for live broadcasts. He could see from two blocks away that they were slowing and stopping in front of the halfway house. There was already a Channel 7 News van parked in front and a crew of three people busily setting up for a live shot.

Pies grasped immediately that either Jenny or Gunther had sold him out. The media knew that the Blemished Hero had been set free.

"Damn it," seethed Pies as he swallowed hard and quickened his pace. As he got to within 100 feet of the news crews, he could see that the Channel 7 investigative reporter, wearing heavy pancake makeup under bright production lights, was doing a loud microphone test count for the sound woman, who stood alongside a gum-chewing male camera operator.

So as to not tip off the gaggle of news people, Pies very casually cut between the next two apartment buildings on his side of the halfway house. Once out of sight, he jogged down the alley to the backdoor of the halfway house, dug the key from his suit coat pocket, and made his way inside.

"That dude's wearing makeup. What an asshole," said Jenny, ironically, to no one as he looked out the front vestibule window from the interior hallway. He turned as he heard Pies step into the hallway behind him. "Look at that. What the hell's this about? Crazy, huh?"

Pies knew that it was Gunther who called, because Jenny wasn't that good of an actor.

Pies saw that Gunther's door was partially open. He tapped Jenny on the shoulder, freed the backpack from his own, and said, "Do me a favor. Take this to the room, would you?"

Jenny grinned, instantly believing he'd earned some trust from Pies, and said, "Sure, thing, baby brother-man."

Pies heatedly shoved his way into Gunther's apartment. Gunther, surprised, looked over his shoulder, then turned. "Whoa, hold up."

Pies charged, stopping shy of actually touching the skinny man. The halfway house supervisor's eyes widened and he swallowed hard. "Now, hey, hold on a sec. You need to back off of me. Now."

Pies quickly gathered up his composure and leaned away from Gunther. He couldn't get tossed back into Stateville. Not now. Not with Milena's life in danger from the Outfit. Otherwise Pies would've gladly dished out a beating to Gunther, immediately gone back to prison, and lived out his days in confinement.

Pies settled and he looked through the open apartment door as Jenny bolted up the stairs with his backpack. Pies stood very still. He controlled his breathing and then turned back to Gunther and said, "Why?"

"Come on, man. The people need to know," said Gunther through a crooked grin.

"How much did you get?"

Gunther casually waved away his comment, "What? I wouldn't do that..."

"You asshole." Pies's anger instantly redoubled, and his shoulders bunched, which frightened the halfway house supervisor.

Gunther put his palms out, "A few hundred. So what?"

Pies's dead-eyed, incensed stare caused Gunther to cough up even more words.

"Five hundred. The jerkoff right there in the makeup paid me. It was too easy, you ask me." He craned his neck and scanned out the window. "The others must've caught word on the scanner or something." His cell phone, which lay on the desk, vibrated with an incoming call. As Gunther reached to answer the call, he and Pies stared one another down again. Gunther finally broke away first and answered the call.

"Go for Gunther," said the supervisor into the phone. "Yeah?"

Gunther cleared his throat and apprehensively squeezed his eyes shut as he slowly turned away so Pies couldn't see his face. He lowered his voice and said, "I told him... No, that's not what I said... What? No. That's not... I'm good for it. Did I not just say I'd get it back to you?" Without looking at Pies directly, he angrily motioned for him to leave.

Pies slipped from the apartment and bounded up the stairs to the top floor. He stepped into his own apartment and softly closed the door and stood there in stunned silence.

How could he get Milena to safety with the news crews hounding him? He tried to think through various scenarios of how he could even go in and out of the building now without being noticed by the media. An odd noise from the back bedroom caused him to head down the hallway.

Pies quietly pushed open his bedroom door and he saw Jenny, with his back to the door, hurriedly rifling through his backpack.

Pies reached his boiling point, and he rushed into the room and quickly struck Jenny in the back of the head with a hard forearm blow. Jenny toppled face first onto Pies's bunk and tried to cover up his head with his arms, "No. I was... I thought you and the Nazi were..."

Pies edged in very close, and Jenny hurriedly flipped over and onto his back. His eyes were wide with fear, and he placed his shaky hands palms-side out, emitted a nervous little fart, and said, "Please, don't hurt me."

"I bet you've heard that a time or two yourself, you son of a—"

"Jakubowski!"

Pies, with his fists clenched, spun completely around. Gunther filled the doorway, also with his palms out in a calming fashion. "Please. Just hold on a minute, okay? It's going to work out."

Pies was livid. He bristled with the real likelihood of murderous violence. He could beat both of the men to death with his bare hands if he really wanted to, and he knew that both of the other men understood this as well.

"I'll get you out of here," said Gunther. "Come on, my car's out back. Please? It's going to be okay, I promise."

Pies tried to breath himself to calmness and it was barely working. "Where?" he asked as he began to successfully settle his homicidal inclinations. "Where the hell am I going to go now?"

"It'll work out, I swear it will," said Gunther rather softly and reassuringly. His cockiness was now completely dissipated. "We'll find a place. It's all going to be fine."

Pies hastily reached toward the bed, and Jenny flinched and yelped, "Don't."

Pies completed his intended action of swiping his opened backpack off the bed, and he followed Gunther from the room. As Pies exited through the apartment's main doorway, he could hear Jenny softly weeping in the back bedroom.

7

THE ANXIOUS Gunther, who was barely able to fit in the cramped driver's seat, steered his off-brand, tiny two-door, car south on Harlem Avenue. He glanced to Pies in the passenger seat every few seconds and finally said, "Man, I'm so sorry for how I acted earlier. You have to believe me. I mean that, okay. I didn't want to—"

"That must've been an important phone call you took," said Pies, knowingly.

Gunther didn't respond to Pies for a few blocks of drive time. He didn't even want to look his way after his last comment, but finally he said, "I have to play the hard ass with some of the guys who come to my house. It's nothing personal. It's an act. I'm sure you understand with the type of men that I have to—"

"Sure," said Pies, unconvincingly.

"Here's the deal. I have a lot of discretion with my parolees. If they're cool, you know, if they stay clean, do what they're supposed to do, follow my rules and all of that, well, I can be cool, too. Do you understand where I'm going with this? If I can trust you to check in regularly with your parole officer—wait. Hold on a sec. You should've gotten a name and contact info before you left Stateville."

"I did."

Gunther continued, breathlessly, "Great. Well, then...if I can trust you to not screw up, you can live wherever you want. I'll cover for you if a parole officer comes around. I'll tell them you're at work or running errands for me or something."

"And you can make that happen?"

"I can do that. Hell, it's done," said the now uber-friendly Gunther. His smile was so fake and forced that his nervous cotton mouth caused his upper lip to stick to his top teeth as he spoke. It made Gunther look like a seven-foot-tall crazed marmot. "I only need to know where you'll be, you know. If I need to get in touch with you. An address. If you have one? Maybe a family member's address, or something."

They drove in silence for a few more minutes.

"Here," said Pies as he pointed to the curb near a corner gas station and a low-slung, one-story, downtrodden motel. Gunther pulled to the side of the street. He shifted the car into park, and they sat quietly for a few seconds.

"An address? For just in case, right?" said Pies as he pointed to the motel on Harlem near Foster Avenue where they were stopped.

"And a phone number, too. In case," said Gunther.

Gunther grabbed a pen with a gnawed end from his center console and waited to write the number on his open palm. Pies took the smartphone from his pocket, went to the settings, and quickly read the number aloud.

Pies finally reached for the door handle and said, "I'll need something to keep the room paid for. And for food."

"What's that? Oh, right. Sure, of course," said Gunther as he leaned back in his seat to dig into his front pants pocket for some cash.

"Six hundred should do it," said Pies.

Gunther ceased his motion, stared, blinked, and then recovered. "Okay, that'll work. Sure. O-okay." He pulled a wad of $100 bills from his pocket and handed it to Pies. Pies stuffed the money into his suit coat pocket and opened the passenger door.

"You, ah, take care. And good luck with your future...endeavors," said Gunther as he shakily extended his hand. Pies, standing now, ignored the man's outstretched hand and pushed the door closed without finishing the salutation.

Pies surveyed his surroundings as Gunther drove forward and turned into the parking lot of the motel. Pies could see that Gunther was craning his neck in an attempt to locate the address numbers on the building.

Pies's eyes settled on something else in the near distance—at the gas station next to the motel. It was a cream-colored, early 1990s Ford F-150 pickup truck with a "for sale" sign taped onto the cab's rear slider window.

Pies knew the Outfit had gotten to Gunther; it seemed obvious. Given the sports memorabilia scattered about the halfway house supervisor's apartment and the nervous phone call he'd taken, Pies figured that Gunther was probably on an Outfit-controlled bookie's payment plan. The Outfit operated nearly all the illegal gambling action in the city, so they could control Gunther, too, especially if he was having a losing streak.

Pies supposed that the Outfit was attempting to forge some goodwill by allowing him to stay outside the halfway house. Sure, they threatened Milena's life with the video clip, but they could also be faux-friendly if they chose to be. It was a ploy often used by the organization. They'd drop the hammer and then, sometimes, do a complete turnaround and treat their mark with respect to ensure the person did as instructed.

Pies also realized that to keep the mobsters off of his ass, he would need wheels that could get him around town and to and from the actual place he'd be living, which was not going to be the shitty motel on Harlem Avenue. He had a plan in mind to hide in plain sight. Pies, of course, always tried to have some sort of plan in the works. This one quickly gelled as Gunther drove away from the motel.

8

PIES PAID a passing high school boy $300 to purchase the Ford F-150 pickup from the gas station owner for him. He had also instructed the high school kid to pay an extra $750 to the original owner of the Ford to keep the insurance and license plates in the owner's name for the next few months. It was an arrangement that Pies knew the pickup seller would jump at. Pies didn't need the news media, or anyone else for that matter, tracking him through a vehicle's purchase and registration. Gunther had left fifty minutes prior, and Pies planned to never see the man ever again.

Pies adjusted the driver's seat and operational mirrors and then sat in a parking lot a few blocks away and searched craigslist on the smartphone. After a few minutes of phone surfing, Pies located a month-to-month apartment rental in the area where he wanted to live. It would be an ideal location for the time being because no one would ever look for him there.

An hour later, he headed east on Lunt Avenue. The old pickup truck bounced and rumbled through the tree-lined neighborhood that edged beautiful and lush Indian Boundary Park on the Far North Side of Chicago.

The Rogers Park neighborhood of Chicago was home to a large Hasidic community. The neighborhood was also close to an opportunity where Pies thought he could start work almost immediately. An old friend owed him that much, anyway. It wasn't money that was needed from the job—the set up would be a ruse to keep the parole officers satiated and off of his trail while he worked to get Milena to safety. It would be pretty much just a job in name only. Even though Pies had gotten out of living at the halfway house, he would probably still need to report to the parole officer on Belmont Avenue at some point. And that parole officer would want proof, a pay stub possibly, that he was actually employed. Legally employed.

Or not.

For a moment Pies considered how the Outfit had gotten to Gunther, and how they could've also, conceivably, worked it out so he wouldn't even be reporting to a parole officer. Time would tell. To hedge his bets, though, he'd still need to obtain a legal job, just in case, and he'd have to do it fast so as to not raise any undue suspicion with the parole authorities. Once he had the job, and then apologized to Milena, and ultimately transported her to safety somewhere, he'd figure out what to do next. Maybe he'd find a way back to the penitentiary, where he knew he belonged.

On his way to his current location, Pies purposefully drove past Chlebeks' Bakery a few more times. Through the front window he could see Milena working away as she was closing for the day, but he couldn't force himself to park, go inside, and talk to her. The apology would happen. It would. Pies simply needed time to get into the right mental space, set it up properly, and do it correctly.

What he really needed most, though, was sleep.

Pies drove along eyeing the natural beauty in Indian Boundary Park to his left, as well as the people all around. The residents of this area were predominantly Hasidic Jews, evident by the nearly all black and white clothing they wore—men, women, and children alike.

Pies found the address given by the man who was renting the apartment, parked, and approached the building. It was a solid looking and impeccably maintained, dark-brick two-story structure from the 1920s, and it had leaded-glass windows. The landscaping around the front of the place was trimmed to a precise tidiness.

He noticed to his right, two doors away, a pretty woman with short hair and a well-worn Cubs baseball hat working in her yard. She labored from a kneeling position and stopped her hand troweling to observe Pies with what seemed to be a suspicious eye. She then hastily popped up and onto her feet, and she stared and stared.

Pies thought her actions were quite odd, and he wasn't sure if there was also contempt in her expression, or if his presence simply caught her off guard. He acted as if he hadn't noticed her, nonchalantly leaning forward to open the front door of the two-flat and entering the building's tiny vestibule. Once completely inside, he pushed the top doorbell button labeled "Pila" and waited.

A few seconds later, Pies saw through the interior vestibule sidelight a balding, middle-aged man pop his head out from the first-floor doorway. The man sported *payots*, the long, curled sideburns characteristic of some Hasidic men, and he was dressed in a crisp white shirt with a small and tasteful company logo that read "Chi-Call Telephone." The moment the man saw Pies he narrowed his eyes and proceeded to shake his head.

"No. I won't rent to you," said the man, his voice muffled by the closed vestibule door. "You lied."

Pies thought he looked like an acceptable candidate to become a tenant, still dressed in his dark gray suit, albeit a bit wrinkled, so it couldn't be just his appearance that gave Mr. Pila pause. All Pies had done on the phone was to tell the man that he used to live in the neighborhood, hoping that the man would believe him to be Hasidic.

Pies knew exactly why Pila was balking. "Sir, I said that I used to live on California near Pratt when I was a kid," he lied. "I never said I was a member of your faith."

Mr. Pila stopped all motion. He seemed to be mulling over the proposition of having Pies live in the basement apartment. Then he shook his head once again, "No. I'm sorry, but you're not welcome. Goodbye, sir."

"Mr. Pila, please—"

Pila leaned quickly back into his apartment and firmly closed the door.

Pies backed his way out of the vestibule and walked toward his pickup truck.

Faigy Tambor, gently pushed up the brim on her Cubs hat and kept an eye on him, but Pies mostly ignored her this time. He got into his truck and drove off. Faigy immediately jogged toward a row of parked cars at the curb.

Pies needed to search online once again for an apartment. He had to find a place quickly, even a hotel room, because he was at his limits of exhaustion and he just needed to sleep. His patience was wearing thin, too, as he drove on.

He was so angry and perturbed that he didn't even notice that Faigy Tambor was following him in her dark blue Prius.

9

PIES JOLTED awake in the cheap, four-story hotel at the corner of Howard Street and Claremont Avenue on the Far North Side of Chicago. His eyes tried to adjust to the bright sunshine that cascaded through the broken blinds. He woke so abruptly that he was confused as to his whereabouts. Gone was the flat, locked, gray metal door he'd grown accustomed to seeing first thing for the past several years. He allowed his eyes to roam about, and he finally remembered where he was.

"Oh, man," he croaked, softly.

After he left Pila's two-flat on Lunt Avenue the evening before, he could barely keep his eyes open as he cruised the area in search of "for rent" signs in building windows. Pies had just enough wakefulness left to guide the pickup to his current location, rent the threadbare room for the night from the snaggletoothed desk man, plod up three flights of steps, unlock the room's rickety door, plug in his phone to charge, and plop down and fall fast asleep on the ratty bed.

"Yeah, I bet you wanted that, you fuckin' creep, but you didn't pay for that," said an angry woman's muffled voice in the hallway outside his room's door.

"Benny's gonna know about this," said a man's muffled, raspy voice in return. Pies winced as a door slammed shut.

"Fuck Benny," came the woman's reply as she retreated down the creaky hallway.

Pies sat up in the bed.

He was still wearing the suit and dress shoes he had on when he left prison. The clothing was now wrinkled beyond anything he could wear on the street. He shakily slid his feet off the bed and grunted as he reached to the floor for his backpack. He unzipped the bag and extracted a black T-shirt and blue jeans from within. There were also some dark-blue running shoes in the pack and a pair of dark-colored socks. He tossed the clothes on the bed beside him and began to rise so he could finally take off the suit and shoes, into which his feet had swollen tightly.

"Damn..."

As he stood, he wobbled but was able to quickly right himself. He'd not slept that solidly in five years, and he wasn't sure if it was a good thing or not. He was so unconscious to the world for the past several hours that he had unwittingly exposed himself to being completely vulnerable. As he allowed that notion to sink in, panic struck.

He held his breath as he hurriedly grabbed up the backpack and rifled through it. The stacks of cash he retrieved from his former garage were still in the bottom of the bag, as well as the lock bump.

Pies closed his eyes and took a series of cleansing breaths. He tossed the backpack on the bed, painfully peeled off the shoes one at a time, and then stripped naked. He gathered up the suit coat and searched all pockets to make sure they were empty. All he found was the halfway-house door key, which he left in the pocket. He dropped the coat on the bed and then went through the pants pockets. Once he was sure there were no valuables left in the wrinkled clothing, he crumpled up the entire ensemble, including the white dress shirt and the dress shoes, and crammed it all into the small plastic trashcan next to the bathroom door.

He slipped into the rudimentary bathroom and turned on the tub water. It gushed forth in a frothy and faintly rust-colored hue. A well-needed hot bath, rusty or not, was in order before his day began.

A faraway ringing sound confused Pies for a moment. He wasn't sure where it was originating from, until he realized that the noise was coming from under his backpack.

"Ah, damn it..."

He stumbled to his backpack and shoved it aside. Underneath, with the attached charger cord still plugged into the wall outlet, was the ringing smartphone. The lighted display on the phone showed: Mother.

Pies pressed to answer the call and hesitated for more than a second, long enough for the voice on the other end of the line to start the conversation.

"We figured you'd do something stupid, but we didn't think it would happen so fast," said the amused man's voice on the phone. "Pretty slick giving that asshole Gunther the fake address—that shit-hole of a motel on Harlem. We had a guy watching that place all night. That's some funny shit right there, Polack."

"What do you want?" asked Pies as he unhooked the charger and leaned back into the bathroom where he turned off the tub spigot. The filled tub looked more like a vat of diluted root beer than an invitation to relaxation and cleanliness.

"Don't fuck around, okay? Can you do that? Testing us won't work out well for you, or others. What we got for you is a big fucking deal, okay. Not some smash and grab shit, either," came the voice from the phone.

Pies didn't respond.

"You adjusting okay?" asked the man's voice.

"Let's get this over with," said Pies. "What do you want from me?"

"I could ask you where you are right now, but you'll just lie your ass off, I'm sure of that. Don't lose the phone, is that too much to ask? We'll give you some time to get your legs under you. You should go out and clear the pipes. It'd do you some good. Oh, and I'm texting you a little something after we hang up here to help keep you honest. That thing with Gunther and the motel on Harlem, you've got to pay for that. We'll be in touch," said the man's voice before the line went dead.

Pies tossed the cell phone onto the shabby bed, took another look at the rusty tub water, and said, "Nope."

The phone beeped once and a tiny red light flashed on the top left corner of the screen. Pies edged over and picked the device back up. He saw a number "1" in a red circle next to the text message icon. He depressed the icon and there was a message from "Mother" with a video attachment.

He tapped his index finger on the screen to play the video. The first thing depicted was a hospital hallway seen from a low angle, as if the person making the video was seated. Pies recognized the location as the place where he convalesced after being shot five years ago. Three seconds after the video started, Pies watched as two large men in cheap suits, Chicago PD Detectives who were there to question him, stepped up to the room's doorway and waited to enter. A moment later, Naomi Gott, the woman who had trained Pies at the Northcomm 9-1-1 Center, and who had become disturbingly enamored with him back then, exited the room in a hurry. Once in the hallway, she lowered her head and began to weep. The video stopped.

Pies tossed the phone back on the bed and rubbed hard at his forehead.

"Shit...shit...shit..."

The Outfit was threatening two people he knew—Milena and, now, Naomi Gott. Pies paced the room as his mind raced. He quickly came to a conclusion that one of those threatened persons deserved his protection before the other. He didn't possess the means to watch out for both of them at once. It was a heartrending choice because he knew that he couldn't get both Milena and Naomi Gott to safety at the same time.

Naomi had chosen to interject herself into Pies's life back before he was sent to prison, Milena had not. Milena Chlebek was truly an innocent in the shit storm Pies had created by killing her daughter.

Naomi Gott would have to fend for herself.

10

PIES STOOD inside the cozy house, just back from the window glass, and observed the beautiful lake that was 100 feet away and the manicured lawn to the rear of the structure. A twenty-six-foot-long white and maroon motorboat was tethered to the dock out back, gently bobbing in the water.

Beyond the boat dock, and a half mile across the gently undulating lake waters, he could just make out the outline of the rustic resort buildings where the Chlebeks took him all those years ago after his mother passed away.

"Boat rentals are two blocks up on South Shore Drive. You'll have full use of the dock, just not that boat. The owner's kind of picky about who operates his baby. They have Jet Skis, too, and canoes, you know, at the rental place," said the friendly, blonde woman with the blue eyes. "So, ah, are you interested, Mr. Edison? You look like you're ready to pull the trigger."

Pies gave her serious side-eye at the mention of pulling the trigger. His mind raced as he took in the lush green, sunlit, surroundings outside the window. He mentally kicked himself for not thinking of a better fake name than Bob Edison. Edison? Edison Park? Stupid. Someone could trace the name back to him if they were creative enough.

The lakefront house on South Shore Drive and Holig Street in Delavan, Wisconsin, would do a fine job of keeping Milena out of public view for a few weeks. And it was only an hour-and-a-half drive from where she lived. Pies could get to Milena and secret her off to this location rather quickly—if she'd go along with the idea.

The interior of the ranch-style home sported an open floor plan with back-facing, wall-to-wall, windows that directly overlooked beautiful Delavan Lake. The home's grounds were tree-filled and private. The landscape obscured any view of the home from three sides, leaving only the lake-facing side of the building wide open. Pies figured that that would be good enough—as long as no one driving past on the road out front could get eyes on Milena if she were lounging in the back of the house by the boat dock.

"I think this'll work," said Pies. "You mentioned a grocery-delivery service on the way over."

"Yes, of course. It's on our website. We send you an electronic list of items, and all you have to do is check off what you want and provide a credit card number. The service people will buy everything and stock your fridge before you arrive. All top quality products. Okay, then," said the blonde woman as she stepped over to her briefcase that lay on the soapstone countertop in the kitchen. "Let's get this application going. Once we accept the application we'll e-mail you a confirmation number. All your client will need to do is have that confirmation number at the time of check-in at our office. They'll be handed the key, and that's it. You were interested in how long of a stay?"

"A month," said Pies. He slipped one of the thicker banded stacks of cash from his pants pocket—$10,000 worth—and continued, "My client is extremely private. We were hoping that there wouldn't be a paper trail. I'll give you a list for the groceries and some cash to take care of that. And, um...I'd like the confirmation number now, if that's not too much trouble."

The woman said, "Oh, I am so sorry but—" Her eyes darted once to the cash, and then again. She closed her mouth.

"There's a $1,000 bonus in this for you, too," said Pies as he painted on his best faux smile. "For your discretion."

11

BECAUSE OF the beer-bottle-sized hole in the top loop of the letter *P* in the restaurant's partially shattered white-plastic sign, it looked as if the eatery was called "Bertena's llace."

The sign hung above the door of the arbitrarily constructed one-story building at the intersection of Simpson Street and Dodge Avenue on the sometimes-precarious west side of Evanston. Bertena's Place was one mile—and a world away—from the tidy Northwestern University campus.

The flat-roofed structure was comprised, front to back, of three different types of building materials: dark-red brick, light-gray cinder blocks, and tan-colored aluminum siding. It appeared as if the building owner's rehab funds were consecutively halved during each successive phase of construction. The vertical demarcation lines of the various construction materials gave the building the look of bland, unappealing Neapolitan ice cream.

The large pane of glass in front, with a hand-painted sign advertising Bertena's authentic Jamaican jerk chicken, was also cracked from stem to stern, and the screen on the door was ripped open in the middle from overuse. However, by the look of the smiling faces of exiting customers and the inviting, wonderful, and many-layered seasoning aromas emanating from the establishment, Bertena's was home to good food and neighborhood warmth.

Something caught Pies's attention as he walked away from his parked pickup truck with his backpack on his shoulder. There was a small black kid, who looked to be about eight years old, pestering a woman who stood near the street corner with a cell phone to her ear. The woman gently shoved the kid away and said, "Ain't no way. It's my phone. And quit crowding me." Pies took note of the kid because the boy seemed to be speaking with a British accent.

The boy, dressed in a baggy green golf shirt with a jet plane logo over the heart and cargo shorts and sans shoes, took a couple of steps from the woman and scanned the street for someone else to approach. As his eyes settled on Pies, he froze briefly, then quickly moved off.

Two dreadlock-wearing black men on high-performance motorcycles sped past from the left, and Pies watched as the boy ducked low behind a parked car and then took off running to the right. He was gone from sight within a few seconds. Seeing the troubled boy gave Pies a pang of memory, a sense of himself looking for something, anything, to help the world make sense again, especially now after every aspect of his life had torn apart. He shook away the thoughts.

Pies pulled open the creaky screen door and went inside Bertena's Place. As he did, a well-built, dark-skinned man with long dreadlocks, wearing a brightly colored yellow T-shirt, shoved into Pies and then past him. Pies gave a look, and the man stopped and squared up. Pies slowly faced the man and let both of his hands dangle by his sides. He was relaxed...ready for anything. At the sight of Pies centering himself, the well-built man puffed out a sigh and walked away.

All five of the mismatched tables inside the restaurant were filled with customers, and a man, two women, and three kids stood in line at a high counter along the back wall.

Bertena, a lanky, stoic-looking black woman in her seventies, wore a black T-shirt with her company's "strutting chicken" logo on it and stood behind the counter taking orders from the customers.

The second the screen door slapped closed behind Pies everyone inside the place stopped moving and stared his way for a brief moment before going about their business.

Pies gazed up at the wall and the hand-painted menu located there. After a few seconds, he casually got in line with the rest of the folks at the counter. There were only eight items on the menu, different preparations of chicken and goat, and Pies rightly assumed that Bertena crafted each and every item in the proper Jamaican way, by hand and fresh every day.

"Waddup, mon. Not going to find no chicken nuggets on that menu there," said a beefy man with the Jamaican accent at the crowded table closest to Pies. Pies detected that the man's delivery of his line was tinged with a bit more anger than the smart-assed bent he had hoped for. The man's tablemates, four other big men wearing oil-stained work coveralls, chuckled and stared unblinkingly at Pies.

Pies, without hesitation, and in no mood to play, turned and faced the man who spoke.

"Take her easy, why dontchya. I'm just joking, mon," said the beefy man. Two of his tablemates immediately lost their smiles, and the third gagged a little on some rice before righting himself.

Pies smiled slightly, which made the big man who spoke, lose his casual grin. The man shifted his eyes to the friend next to him, as if he was making sure his tablemates had his back if the situation turned violent.

Pies edged in even closer.

"Paul. No. Paul, don't. Paul, don't get up. Don't do it, mon. Keep your ass in the chair," came the booming Jamaican-accented voice from in back of the high counter. "Do not, mon."

Pies remained silent, but he knew the voice from behind the counter. It came from the man he was looking for when he arrived at Bertena's Place.

Rondy Clarke, who looked like an out-to-pasture NFL defensive end, carefully slipped past Bertena and around the counter. He wedged himself between Pies and the men seated at the table.

At the sight of Rondy, all of the other men at the table, except for the one, Paul, smartly went back to eating silently, ignoring their tablemate.

"This batty hole gets preferential treatment, is that it, Rondy?" asked the still-seated Paul as he gave Pies an angry once-over.

Rondy put a hand on Pies's shoulder and began to lead him to the kitchen area behind the counter. He shot a look over his shoulder and said, "I saved your teeth, mon."

"My teeth?" asked Paul.

"All ya's teeth, damn it," said Rondy. "Every pearly last one of 'em."

The men at the table traded confused stares for a second—then they went back to eating. Paul cleared his throat and made a show of picking up his fork in a quick, menacing fashion, and then he ate.

Rondy roughly pushed Pies along, into the ramshackle kitchen area, past two women who diligently cooked away, and through the screen door. Once outside in the alley in back of the building, Rondy finally stopped and spun Pies around.

"I don't owe you nothing, mon," he said. "You go on and go now, Push-Pull. You're not welcome here."

"I need a job," said Pies. "At least a paycheck or two."

"I don't have to do this. That was all inside, PP. We're out here, in the world. That fuckery don't count out here, you know."

Pies stared...waited.

"Hold on. How did you get out?" asked Rondy.

"You're really that interested?" asked Pies.

Rondy studied Pies for a beat or two, and then he said, "Don't owe you nothing no more."

Rondy and Pies enjoyed a rather strange relationship that mostly revolved around Pies saving Rondy's life—twice.

The first time Pies saved Rondy's ass was in the months before they were both incarcerated at Stateville. The second time occurred while they were inside the correctional center.

The very first time they laid eyes on one another, Pies was posing as a 9-1-1 communications officer for his B&E crew chief. As a requirement of his official communications officer training, Pies had to partake in a police ride-along to experience what officers on the street dealt with on a daily basis. During that ride-along, Pies landed in the middle of a violent street altercation as he and the officer he was with were dispatched to the scene where Rondy was demanding reimbursement for unpaid drug transactions from an associate of his.

Rondy held the bloodied man at machete-point, and he was soon surrounded by armed police officers, all of them only one misdirected twitch away from ending his life—and most likely his associate's life too.

However, the moment Rondy and Pies caught each other's eye that day, the big man with the blade saw something in Pies that scared him more deeply than the police and their guns. In that instant, Rondy knew that he and Pies shared experiences. He couldn't quite explain how or why he knew, he just knew. They both had killed before.

Shortly before the scene on the street, Rondy had been released from state prison after doing time for a manslaughter conviction. He was tying to murder someone else when he accidentally killed his childhood friend instead.

At the time Pies was still a few days from unintentionally killing Vicki Chlebek. But Pies had murdered people in the past. Inexplicably, Rondy could sense all of that in Pies's eyes, in his demeanor, and in the movements he observed that day. Pies's overall aura frightened Rondy so profoundly, he could see in Pies what he would become if he killed the man he held at machete-point. In that instant of trading hard stares with Pies on the street in Evanston, he knew that killing again would rob him of his very soul. He was sure of it. And he wasn't even a spiritual man.

That nonverbal exchange transformed the Jamaican-American man's life. Never again would he use violence to solve his troubles. Or so he promised himself.

Rondy was, of course, arrested for the felonious assault with the machete that day, and he wound up doing a little over four years in Stateville for the crime. In prison, he and Pies crossed paths again, and for baffling reasons that only the two of them knew, they ended up having one another's backs from time to time.

Now, as they stood nearly toe-to-toe in the fetid air of the alley behind Bertena's Place, the flies buzzed about their heads, and Pies edged in closer still. He poked Rondy hard in the chest with two rigid fingers and he said, "You would've been gutted if I hadn't stepped in."

Rondy looked away and absently rubbed his chest, he didn't, however, retaliate for the hard poke. His facial features actually softened.

A year ago, while they were both still in Stateville, Rondy took advantage of the staggered meal shifts, when one-third of the inmates were fed at a time, enabling him to execute a drug rip-off.

As one shift of inmates was ushered into the mess hall for their meals, Rondy, who was in the third group, made his way into the open cell of a lifer and prison gang member named Spud, so he could steal the man's stash of hydrocodone pills. Rondy knew Spud had received a package for his prison gang to sell because Spud's girlfriend had visited earlier that day. Rondy witnessed the exchange firsthand.

Spud's girlfriend, a shapely dark-haired woman with the face of an angry anteater, and an intricate neck tattoo of a spider, simply paid the guard who ushered her inside the visitors' room to look the other way as she placed a small packet of drugs, about ninety pills worth, into Spud's pants pocket. She made this all happen in a practiced, lightning-fast exchange—routinuely slipping a small bundle of pills from the waistband of her skintight jeans into Spud's front pocket the moment she arrived.

Touching was forbidden in the visitors' room, so Spud and his girl worked quickly once they approached one another. The guard who regularly took the payoff was always on duty the day Spud's girl visited, because she would call the guard on his personal cell phone the morning of the visit to make sure. If that guard were not going to be at work, her visit—and thus the exchange—would happen during his next scheduled shift. Unbeknownst to Spud, his girlfriend was also using the guard's cell number to set up well-compensated liaisons with the flabby lawman during his down time.

Once Spud's girl surreptitiously slipped the drugs into Spud's pocket under the guise of a hug, the crooked guard would wait a few seconds and then loudly call out, "No touching" to sell the ruse to any other official who might happen to be passing through the room at the time. Before anyone noticed what was really going on, the exchange was complete. After the visit was over, the guard would do a "search" of Spud as he passed through the door on his way back to his cell just to further sell the maneuver for anyone watching.

Rondy had seen the exchange happen five other times as he awaited one of his grandmother Bertena's weekly visits. He simply bided his time until he knew he could snag Spud's stash for himself. Rondy figured that he could hold the pills for a few days, and as Spud's gang's usual customers began jonesing for a fix, he'd charge them triple what Spud and his cohorts normally did.

Other inmates had seen the exchange between Spud's girl and the guard, too. They weren't stupid enough to mess with one of the prison's white supremacist gang members, though.

Rondy swiped a fly away from his nose as Pies leaned in closer still and shoved the big man so hard that his back bumped up against the restaurant's smelly dumpster. "I'm glad you let me know before you took it, because if I hadn't gone and stole it from you and then put it all back before they found out...things would have been very different."

Rondy wanted to rebut. Instead he remained silent because he knew Pies was right.

"I was your only friend...and I kept quiet," continued Pies.

If Pies hadn't intervened at Stateville, Spud's gang leader would've gladly killed Rondy for the theft—even a near theft—if he had ever actually known about the transgression.

Rondy's eyes finally locked onto Pies, and he seemed to acquiesce.

Pies said, "Okay. I don't need the money. Minimum wage, that's all you have to do. I'll sign my paycheck back over to your grandmother each week and pay her back the difference on the taxes they take out so she's not out a penny. I need the job to keep on parole's good side. Maybe a few weeks."

"A reverse 'no-show' gig," said Rondy.

Rondy stared for a long while, thinking it through. He then edged past Pies and opened the back screen door of the restaurant. As he headed inside he said, "No. Not going to do it, mon. Get away from here. No job."

Pies followed, and as both men moved into the bustling kitchen, one of the ladies cooking angrily twisted the temperature control knob back and forth on the deep fryer. "Damned thing. This? Again," she shouted in her Jamaican accent. "Bertena, baby, it's gone cold."

Rondy said, "Grandma, the switch," as he pushed out of the kitchen and into the front of the house.

Pies stopped in his pursuit of Rondy, put his backpack on the floor, and carefully eyed the deep fryer. The lady cooking there saw the way he was concentrating and got out of his way. Pies reached in back of the fryer and felt around behind the metal housing but didn't find what he was looking for.

Bertena Clarke, still at the counter attending to customers, turned away from the order she was currently taking and said, "Check the fuse, hon."

The female cook moved off toward the rear door and the bent-up metal circuit-breaker box that was located on the wall.

Bertena did a double take as Pies first crouched and then fully knelt on the greasy floor so he could peer up and under the fryer.

Pies craned his neck so that he could look toward the lady who stood at the circuit-breaker box, "Could you make sure that it's off, please?"

The cook looked Bertena's way, and Bertena motioned for her to do just that. The cook flipped the switch controlling the fryer into the off position, and Pies reached under the unit. He felt around for a second, and then everyone heard something snap firmly into place. Pies quickly got back to his feet. He waved to the cook at the circuit breaker. "It should be okay now."

The cook pushed the circuit breaker into the on position, and Bertena could hear the heating element under the fryer power up.

Rondy, with a defeated expression, peered at Pies from over the top of the front counter. "Ah, damn it," he said softly.

"You're Pies, is that right?" asked Bertena in her beautiful Jamaican accent. "Rondy's spoke of you."

"Yes, ma'am," said Pies as he extended his arm to complete the handshake Bertena offered.

"You need work, is that it?" she asked.

12

THE SKY was slowly evolving from blue into a wondrous glowing shade of purplish-gray as Pies, with the backpack securely on his shoulders, exited the rear door of Bertena's Place with a large, black-plastic garbage bag in each hand. He swung one bag up and into the dumpster, swatted a pesky fly away, and hurled the other bag to its doom. His first shift at the eatery ended soon after Bertena herself gently shooed an elderly couple from their table and shut the front door of her establishment at 8:17 P.M.

Pies was paying Bertena for the privilege to "work" at her establishment, but he still wanted to put in a few days to righteously sell his ruse to the parole people, if they ever investigated her restaurant.

"Pies, my friend," said Rondy with a crooked grin as he began to pull the rear door closed. Right before he disappeared from view, he added, "You played my grandmama today. You asshole." His loud laugh evaporated as the door snicked tightly closed.

Pies did his best to let Rondy's abuse harmlessly dissipate as he took a step toward exiting the restaurant's back alleyway. He looked skyward and hesitated. It was so silent and still as he remained there behind the building. It was a calm that he had not experienced in some time, an eerie serenity that felt right. He enjoyed the way the purplish night sky danced between the shadowy leaves of the gently shifting neighborhood trees. He turned up his face and allowed for the light breeze to wash over him. The draft shifted direction and picked up nasty bits and pieces of air from the dumpster, and Pies coughed once and quickly rubbed at his nose.

He glanced toward the street and thought he again saw the boy in the green golf shirt and the khaki cargo shorts. Curious, Pies walked to the street, then to the corner when he didn't see the boy. He casually walked along the block and turned into another alley. He saw movement near a dumpster and moved deeper into the darkness. Pies thought he saw the boy again. He pulled his cellphone from his pocket to use it as a flashlight—and that's precisely the moment something hard hit Pies on the back of the head. Immediately, the pavement rose up and slammed into his cheek. As Pies's nose involuntarily sniffed the warm, rank odor of the alley, everything slowly morphed into black nothingness.

*

"HELLO, THIS is 9-1-1. I can hear you breathing. Are you okay? Hello?" said the female voice. Pies, lying on his back in the alley, and uncomfortably across the still secured backpack, attempted to open his eyes. The cell phone lay on the ground next to his left ear. He blinked several times and rolled to his left. As he did this, his nose slid across the face of the cell phone, which made enough noise on the other end of the line for the 9-1-1 communications officer to say, "This is North-comm 9-1-1, are you okay? We have a general fix on your location and an officer is attempting to locate you now. Do you understand?"

"Damn it...," said Pies as he tried to get to his feet. He stumbled and fell onto his ass instead. He reached over and deactivated the call and picked up the phone. He gradually got to a standing position. As he slid the phone into his pocket, he looked up and down the alley. The kid was long gone. Pies had no idea how long he'd been unconscious, however there was still a hint of daylight left, so it must not have been too long.

Pies turned to look in the direction where his pickup was parked, and an Evanston police patrol car rolled past the mouth of the alley —the officer's eyes were aimed forward, though. Pies stumbled back and pressed up against the sidewall of a garage. After a few seconds, he had enough wits to walk out of the alley on his own accord.

He made it into his pickup truck, started the engine, and sat for a long moment. He allowed the sight of the frightened kid to flood his mind, and he wondered what kind of trouble the little guy might be in.

He immediately shook those thoughts away.

He had too much going on with his own life at present to interject himself into something he didn't understand and would be unable to follow-through on. He put the truck into gear and as he drove along, he passed the returning Evanston patrol car. Despite the throbbing pain on the back of his head, he forced a grin and exchanged a friendly wave with the officer.

13

THE BRIGHT headlights of a passing car momentarily pierced the front windows and slashed the darkness within the closed Chlebeks' Bakery. The only other illumination inside the place came from a streetlight across Northwest Highway sixty feet away and, to a lesser effect, from the digital displays on the coolers in back of the front counter.

In the bakery's back room, it was darker still, but there was just enough illumination from the front of the store to light the old-fashioned clock that hung on the wall next to the rear door. The hour hand of the clock was on the two, and as the minute hand clunked loudly into place over the twelve, the back door quietly opened.

Pies, dressed in the darkest clothing he owned, the black T-shirt and blue jeans combination, slid the lock-bump apparatus out of the deadbolt keyhole and slouched his way inside the business. He closed the door and stood still to acclimate his eyes to his surroundings. He wasn't worried about an alarm going off, because he knew the Chlebeks would never spring for the installation of an expensive system like that. He could hear Milena now saying in her clipped Polish accent, "A few thousand to put system in, and then I got to pay by month, too. No, no, no."

Pies slowly stepped to the cash register on the front counter. The register was open and the tray removed, and that was okay with him. He wasn't here for cash.

Pies slid a folded piece of paper from his back jeans pocket and placed it inside of the open register. On the front of the paper was written "Mrs. Chlebek." Inside the folded note was a heartfelt, hand-written apology to the mother of the woman he loved and had accidentally killed.

He wasn't proud of his cowardice, but one thing he had decided since leaving Bertena's Place earlier was that he didn't have it in him to see the face-to-face apology through. He never guessed that actually seeing Milena in person could be so heart-wrenchingly difficult.

He had to first let Milena know how sorry he was, and then he would invite her to the house in Delavan, Wisconsin, to hide out for the time being—and yet he wasn't able to say any of those things aloud. The note would have to suffice.

Out of the corner of his eye, Pies noticed stirring outside near the front window and he froze in place. A large dog on a leash sniffed at the window from the sidewalk as its owner, an unaware hefty man in too-tight plaid pajamas lit a cigarette. The dog reacted to Pies's scent and barked once, loudly, at the window. The man tugged at the dog's leash and said, "Shut up, would ya. Dumb dog." He and the dog slowly moved away and Pies breathed once again.

Pies's eye happened to catch sight of the child-sized chair the Chlebeks had stationed behind the front counter. It was a tiny chair that had been in its current location since their daughter Vicki was first able to take steps on her own. When things got hectic in the bakery, Blaze or Milena Chlebek would have Vicki take a seat so as to not get in the way and so they could keep an eye on her.

In the chair now sat a ratty teddy bear with mottled "fur" and a missing eye. The chair and teddy bear combination was nothing new to Pies. He'd seen the chair his entire life each and every time he visited the bakery. The worn backpack sitting in the chair next to the teddy bear was out of place though. It was the backpack that Pies secretly dropped off for the Chlebeks shortly before he went off to prison. At that time, the backpack was filled with $300,000 in cash.

Pies grabbed up the bag. It didn't have any weight in his grasp, but he felt the need to unzip it anyway to see if the money was still inside. He slowly opened the bag and tilted it toward the front window to aim some light at the bottom. He reached in and took out the only thing that was housed in the backpack.

It was a single photo—a photo of a cheerful and cute, seven-year-old Vicki Chlebek with her arm around the smiling seven-year-old version of Pies. In the photo, Pies's two front teeth were missing.

Pies swallowed back his quickly rising emotions, gently flicked the photo back inside the backpack, closed the bag, replaced it next to the teddy bear, and exited the bakery's back door. The sound of the deadbolt bumping back into the locked position cut through the darkened space.

As the time clock's second hand clunked into the 2:06 spot, the deadbolt snapped open once again, and Pies shoved his way back inside. He stumbled directly to the register, snatched the note from the open machine, and stuffed it into his back pocket.

He then made a hasty exit, locking the back door as he went.

14

FORTUNATELY PIES had reread the parole packet in his hotel room before he headed in for his second day, an earlier prep shift, at Bertena's Place. He'd not gotten much sleep overnight, and the precarious wave of exhaustion he was currently navigating almost cost him. He missed a notation that required him to call the parole offices within seventy-two hours of his release to set up his first meeting with his new parole officer. He made the call that morning while on a break at Bertena's. His appointment was scheduled for 4 P.M.

He still had a few hours until his meeting, so for now, his eyes were glued to the smartphone's screen, his elbows were braced against his pickup truck's steering wheel, as he sat parked at the outer edge of a retail lot on Western Avenue. He couldn't stand another night in the cheap hotel on Howard Street. A quiet apartment would suit him just fine, even for just a few weeks worth of stay time—if he could ever actually locate one that was available for rent. Checking into a nicer hotel would probably deplete his supply of cash in no time at all, and he'd probably need a credit card at check in. All he had now was the cash. So that option was out.

As he searched the Internet, his mind wandered. Soon, he lost all ability to concentrate on the simple task of surfing the web. He found himself wondering about the kid with the British accent. It was odd how that brief encounter—not really even an encounter, since they had not interacted—stayed with him. Something about the boy made Pies think the kid was in trouble. He absently rubbed the small, painful knot on the back of his head.

Pies nudged his drifting mind back on task. He reviewed the smartphone's screen as a warm breeze kicked up through the open truck window. His nose captured gentle notes of a pleasant floral scent mixed in with the city's usual robust exhaust fumes.

"Hey, there. I've seen you before," said a woman's lovely toned and friendly voice.

Pies, startled, half turned and shifted his eyes to the left. There was a pretty woman, maybe thirty years old, standing there, holding a heavy reusable shopping bag in her left hand. The bag had an illustrated imprint of the Chicago skyline on it. The woman had dark hair that was cut quite short in a stylish pixie. She also wore a weathered Cubs baseball hat on her head. Her forgiving brown eyes could not be ignored. They made her appear kind and approachable. She immediately reminded Pies of the actress who played a troubled ballerina in a movie he saw with Vicki Chlebek years back. And that was the moment Pies recollected where he'd seen the woman before.

"I remember you," he said.

Faigy Tambor's heart leaped, and she placed the bag down on the asphalt. "You do?" She thought, *How in the world would he remember me from that day he was transferred from the courthouse to state prison? Or did he see me following him last night?*

"You had that same hat on. Working in your front yard next to the Pilas' place. On Lunt?" said Pies. "The guy who has the apartment for rent?"

She recovered quickly and flicked the brim of her baseball hat with her forefinger and said, "Sure, of course. Are you going to be renting the apartment?" Faigy thought she knew the answer to her own question, though, because she couldn't help but notice Pies's disappointed expression when he left the Pilas' place only a minute after arriving. She had also followed Pies's pickup truck and saw it park, a mile away from her home, at the cheap hotel on Howard

Street. She figured, correctly, that Pies's apartment search had not been successful yet.

It was actually just dumb luck that she happened upon Pies in the parking lot where she occasionally shopped for groceries. But the fact of the matter was, the hotel on Howard, the parking lot where they currently stood, and Faigy's building were all less than a mile from one another.

Just then Pies's cell phone buzzed with an incoming text message. He opened the message, which read: "Olmsted Inn, 30 minutes."

It was from "Mother."

Pies stared at the text message for a moment and then cleared it from his phone. Earlier a thought had crossed his mind while he chopped some tomatoes in the prep area at Bertena's Place. The Outfit wouldn't go all in just yet and kill Milena, or even Naomi for that matter. They still needed a carrot to dangle in order to get Pies to do what they ultimately wanted from him. He didn't have a lot of extra time to play with, a few hours...a day or two maybe...but he had a little wiggle room. He figured he'd ignore the Outfit's requests for meetings for the moment and use that additional time to rest and to decisively come up with better escape plans for himself and Milena.

"The Pilas are constantly looking for tenants, and...they're kind of picky," she continued. "I've seen people come and go. Mostly go."

"Picky's a good word," said Pies.

"Mr. Pila is like...a part-time Hasid. I'm not exactly sure how devout he is. I should talk, though, right?" she said.

Pies wasn't sure what she was alluding to. "Yeah? Is that right?"

She continued, "It's a great neighborhood if you can find a place. A lot of demand for apartment rentals there."

"I'm Pies," he said as he extended his right hand.

"I probably shouldn't be speaking badly about my neighbors. That was rather insensitive of me," she said with a snort. "Sorry about that." She stepped forward to complete the greeting and said, "Faigy Tambor." Pies squinted his left eye in a dubious fashion, and she continued, "With a name like Pies? That's the reaction I get?"

Pies grinned and shrugged, "It's a nickname. Real name is Jakub."

"I like Pies better. Sounds like home. Warm pie. Faigy is no nickname, unfortunately. It's a family name, but I've grown to appreciate it."

"Well Pies is actually...," Pies stopped himself from going further and letting Faigy know that "Pies," when correctly pronounced as "p-yes," actually meant "dog" in Polish.

There was a brief and awkward silence.

"So, how *is* the search coming along?" she asked.

Pies shrugged again and said, "I found a job. So there's that."

"Where? I mean, if...you don't mind me asking," said Faigy. "Boy, I am really forward today."

"Am I that interesting?" asked Pies.

Faigy grinned. "You have potential." Pies was more handsome up close, she thought. Healthier appearing then she remembered. Of course, she last saw him skulking in the back of a prison van.

"Bertena's Place in Evanston," said Pies.

"I love Bertena's. Pretty spicy food over there, but very good. Okay, now I know why you're looking in Indian Boundary. It'd be very convenient," she said.

"Yeah. Convenient."

"So, did you find a place to live?"

Pies raised the phone and said, "On the hunt."

"Is that right?" shot back Faigy with a crooked grin.

*

PIES CAREFULLY edged past Faigy, so that he wouldn't make physical contact with her. As it was he was already uncomfortable around the pretty woman, and he didn't want to chance any accidental touching. He stepped into the darkened space of her building's basement and took a look around.

Since meeting her in the parking lot on Western Avenue and following her Prius to the building she owned, Pies couldn't shake the conflicting emotions of being in such close proximity to the beautiful woman and what it was doing to his psyche. He had been isolated in prison for years, and the only woman that ever came to mind was, of course, the only woman he ever loved—the raven-haired, blue-eyed, Vicki Chlebek.

Puzzlingly, now he was confused, nearly to the point of outright self-resentment, that this Faigy woman could elicit such strong feelings—and so soon after meeting her. He also had the sense that he knew Faigy from somewhere. There was something in her eyes that caused him to question whether they had already met somehow.

Faigy Tambor didn't look at all like Vicki or even remotely act like her, however. She was uniquely lovely in her own ways. She was confident and straightforward in her interactions, sure, but she was also feminine and charming. Her natural beauty was causing Pies some genuine anxiety. It was deep-seeded uneasiness over realizing that a woman, other than Vicki, could catch his eye in this manner—and so soon upon his release back into the world.

Would there be other Faigy Tambors heading his way, he wondered. Would those women elicit the same reaction he was feeling toward the woman standing no more than five feet from him now?

Faigy reached toward the light switch adjacent to the exterior door and Pies flinched a little. She smiled and completed her action, clicking the lights on, and the place lit up and unveiled an unusually bright dwelling for a basement apartment.

Faigy left the exterior door open as she tread fully into the space, which allowed Pies a differing view of the four concrete steps that led up and back into the small rear yard—and also to the brick garage beyond that, where her car was parked.

She said, "It still needs the trim work completed, the baseboards, and some touch-up paint, that's about it. Please, have a look. Take your time. I have to admit I didn't think I was even ready to show the place yet, let alone rent it. Here we are, though. You need a place, and…well…go ahead, look around."

Pies stood in the middle of the studio apartment and tried to let his eyes settle only on his surroundings and not the beautiful woman in the Cubs hat.

What he saw as he cautiously allowed his eyes to wander about the apartment, beyond the incomplete paint job and finishing details, impressed him. It was a big space for a studio apartment, about six hundred square feet in all, including a spa-like bathroom, complete with custom shower tiles, as well as a separate Japanese soaking tub. Everything in the apartment—from the tastefully appointed kitchen alcove with stainless-steel appliances to the lighting fixtures in place—was top quality. Pies was familiar with the upscale brands, because on more than a few occasions he worked B&Es in supply warehouses where he snatched up some of these kind of high-end items.

"Will you go month-to-month?" asked Pies, knowing it would be a difficult task to be near this woman for too long. He couldn't trust himself to not act on any romantic feelings, and a month-to-month lease would offer him the freedom of just picking up and moving on if need be. And as soon as he asked, he thought, *What difference does it make? I'll be gone soon anyway, once I get Milena to safety.*

If Pies reflected on it, he could acknowledge that there was also something so much deeper at play in his benign month-to-month request.

Pies believed that he no longer deserved love.

Not anymore.

He destroyed his chance with Vicki, and there would be no others because of that. He would make sure of it. So even if there were other Faigy-types to enter his life in the future, he would sidestep them, romantically speaking. If he felt he needed physical love, he'd hire someone for that. It was crass, of course, and he hadn't resorted to anything like that yet, but that's how he was feeling in that moment. And as soon as that thought passed through his mind, he tossed it in the mental trash pile.

He'd simply go without love altogether.

There would be no "Faigys" or hired lovers to act as Vicki surrogates. The lack of love and sex would be his self-imposed prison sentence. It would last a lifetime for Pies, he was sure of that. If the state didn't want to punish him, he would just do it himself.

Faigy's eyes narrowed, "Oh, I'm afraid...I'd have to have a year's lease: $650 a month with deposit."

The way Faigy scrunched up her mouth and placed a hand on her hip after she delivered her ultimatum, as simple as the gesture was, caused Pies to lose his breath for a moment. It seemed that nearly everything she did, every word she spoke, every small little gesture she made, caused Pies a pleasantly uncomfortable feeling deep inside.

What in the hell was he doing? It really didn't matter to Pies about the lease at all. "I'll do the $650," he blurted out.

Faigy grinned broadly. "Great. Oh, and the second floor is also available, too, in case that's better suited for you. I just had a woman and her two children leave last week. It's a bit larger. Two bedrooms. Fully furnished."

Pies dug into his pocket and extracted a roll of hundreds. "This place right here will work."

"My husband and I were...my ex-husband and I were having this place fixed up right until..."

Pies continued to count bills and pretended not to hear her last statement, and she seemed to appreciate that. The instant the words escaped her mouth, she was mentally kicking herself for allowing them to slip out in the first place.

The smartphone buzzed again, and Pies took it from his pocket and opened the message. It read: "Meeting now. Don't fuck with us."

Pies ignored the message and slipped the phone back into his pocket. He then extended his hand with the money, and before Faigy took it she said, "A couple of things."

"Oh, okay," said Pies.

"No loud parties, or anything."

"Sure, that's not a problem."

"If you're going to smoke, please do it in the backyard. Oh. And no guns. I just don't want them in the building. I work with clients who've had some bad experiences, and I don't like them around."

At the mention of guns, Pies absently and gradually pulled his hand with the cash back to his chest. Faigy squinted her eyes and said, "That a...deal breaker?"

Pies's mouth opened, and he wanted to explain to Faigy how he killed the only woman he ever loved with a .38 revolver. Instead, he waited a full three seconds before he bolted from the apartment.

The surprised Faigy took a step back as Pies jostled past and said, "Hey, where are you..."

Pies called over his shoulder, "I have to be—"

"What about...the apartment?" she called out.

Pies was gone, leaving Faigy to wonder why her "no guns" requirement was so upsetting. And then it dawned on her. "Oh, shit," she said as she ran after him. When she rounded her building to the front sidewalk, Pies's pickup truck was already gone. She spun and sprinted back to where her own car was parked. After starting the engine, Faigy drove in the direction of the crappy hotel on Howard Street—one of the other places she'd seen his truck parked.

But after two passes of the building, Pies was nowhere in sight. Faigy slowly drove back in the direction of her house, and as she passed the north end of Indian Boundary Park, she saw the parked pickup truck and then Pies sitting on a bench fifty feet away. She pulled into the first parking spot she could find and got out of her car. Faigy stood next to her car staring in Pies's direction, and she wondered why she was even chasing Pies Jakubowski down. But she felt a deep connection with Pies. She had a feeling that she owed everything, her new life outlook, her new career, and her freedom to him. The paroled criminal didn't know that, but she did. She walked directly toward Pies, who had his head down and didn't see her approaching. When she shuffled to a stop ten feet away, he finally lifted his gaze and nodded for her to take a seat, which she did.

"There's a lot on my mind," said Pies.

Faigy didn't respond. She knew his situation and that he had been in prison. His parole and release had been all over the news the past day or so. She also sensed that he wanted to get something off his chest, so she remained silent.

Pies continued, "Sorry about acting so weird back there."

Faigy gently waved his apology away.

Pies stood and said, "I have to go."

Faigy didn't try to stop him, but she said, "The place is yours if you want it."

When he was thirty feet away he opened his pickup truck's door, turned, and said, "I'll get back to you." He got into the vehicle, started the engine, and drove off.

Faigy so badly wanted to assert her connection with Pies, to help him as she believed he had helped her but she also didn't want to completely scare him off by pushing too much and too soon. She knew where he was staying, and if she had it in mind to go and see him again, she would. She leaned back and looked skyward.

15

BEFORE HIS upcoming meeting with his parole officer, Pies drove out of his way to see Chlebeks' Bakery once again. Maybe seeing the business would prompt him to buck up some well-needed bravery and apologize—get it over with. The slow-moving traffic allowed him to get a good look inside the shop. He placed a hand up to block the sun and glanced through the front windows to observe Milena working away behind the counter.

He was playing a dangerous game avoiding the Outfit and their requests for meetings in order to fulfill his desire to apologize and find Milena safety, even so he still, inexplicably, could not get himself to park his pickup truck and approach her. He couldn't dredge up the courage. He lied to himself that the right moment would happen soon.

When Pies's pickup passed the bakery one last time, a physically fit, and bushy-haired young man in a dark T-shirt and blue jeans kept his eyes trained on the vehicle. The man was standing across the street from Chlebeks' Bakery and leaning against the brick wall of a shoe store. He immediately pushed himself away from the wall and sprinted to the passenger door of a parked, nondescript-looking, windowless white van. Once in the vehicle, the van peeled out of its parking spot and followed Pies's pickup truck.

*

PIES SAT with four others, three men and a woman, in the waiting area of the bare-bones parole offices on Belmont Avenue, and he couldn't help but notice that the people with him all looked like middle-school kids who'd just been summoned to the principal's office for flinging spitballs in history class.

Pies recognized one of the men. He was the haggard cook from the neighborhood tavern that he'd been tossed out of.

Pies kept his eyes on the main interior door behind the unmanned reception desk, waiting for it to open again and for his name to be called. He had watched as that scenario occurred twelve times since he arrived. He knew that at any moment he'd be called. Once in the back office, he would, most likely, have to sit opposite a humorless parole officer and lie to the man or woman. Pies lied when he had to, of course, and yet he didn't like to do it. Telling a parole officer that he still resided at the halfway house on Bryn Mawr made his stomach churn. Lying always made Pies feel small, even when it was for the greater good. As he sat there he also wondered how long it would be before the media figured out that he no longer resided at the halfway house.

"Shit," he said to himself in response to his own thought.

"Jakubowski?" said the large, round man in the cheap sport coat after he shoved the door open. Pies looked the man's way for a beat too long.

"Let's go. Come on, come on. Got shit to do," said the man as he irritably motioned Pies into the main office area.

Pies got to his feet and followed. Once on the other side of the door, the parole officer turned and offered his hand, "Sorry to be so abrupt. It's been a long day. My apologies. I'm PO Ramirez, Mr. Jakubowski. Have a seat over here," he said as he motioned to the nearest desk.

Pies sat on the visitor's side of the desk and took a quick look around the office. There were twenty desks, each sloppily stacked with piles of case files. Ten desks were unoccupied. The other ten were filled with unsmiling parolees sitting opposite equally unsmiling parole officers.

Pies scanned and then locked briefly on an attractive, dark-haired, female parole officer whose desk sat in a position of prominence by itself and near the windows. Pies figured that she was the supervisor. She offered Pies a brief smile and nod, but instead of reciprocating, Pies turned his head fully toward Ramirez.

"How's things with the Nazi? You fitting in okay over there?" asked Ramirez as he scribbled something on a piece of paper in Pies's file.

"Fine. It's good," said Pies as his eyes once again glanced over to the woman—this time, though, she wasn't looking his way. She had her back to him, and she was talking on her cell phone.

"Pay attention to me," said Ramirez, his pleasant demeanor beginning to erode. "I don't like when my parolees don't pay attention."

"Sorry," said Pies. He nodded to assure Ramirez that he understood and that he had his full attention.

"You find a gig yet?"

"Yes. Yes, sir. In Evanston. A place called Bertena's."

"Bertena's, huh? With a *B*?"

"It's a restaurant. I do dishes, prep work, and some maintenance."

Ramirez wrote again in his folder. "What's the address?"

Pies had asked for Bertena to print up a pay stub with one day's pay displayed just for this occasion. The address and phone number were on the stub. He leaned back and extracted it and his cell phone from his front pocket and happened to notice that he had received another text message from "Mother."

"I have this," said Pies as he slid the pay stub across the desk and kept the phone in his hand—but didn't dare glance at the message.

"Good," said Ramirez, taking the stub, standing, and walking a few feet to a copier. He quickly made a copy and took a seat again.

"Not the talkative type, are you?" he said as he handed the original back to Pies.

"No," said Pies. "No, sir."

Ramirez grinned and said, "You're jerking me, aren't you?"

"No, I'm not, sir...," said Pies. He didn't want to garner any special attention from the parole officer. "Just trying to keep to myself."

"Okay, Jakubowski," said Ramirez as he bobbed his head absently and then wrote a bit more inside the file folder. "See you in two weeks. Same time."

Pies hesitated and then half stood. "That's it?"

"Yes. You can get the hell out now," said Ramirez raising his head and grinning. "Keep it one hundred, Jakubowski. It's a marathon. Slow and steady, and you'll do just fine."

Pies acknowledged the advice, straightened up, and went quickly back out to the reception area once again. He made his smartphone come back to life and opened the text message. There was another video attachment and a message that read: "Tomorrow: 8 A.M. Steak & egg place. Higgins just east of Cumberland. Don't fuck with us."

He walked past the other men and the woman who were all still waiting, and he paused closer to the outer door. He hunched over the phone to block the sun's glare that was coming in through the lobby windows, and he hit the play button on the video attachment.

At first he wasn't even sure what he was watching. It was a one-minute, sixteen-second-long video of a woman and a little boy in the open field of a lush, green park. Pies stopped and restarted the video. He watched and then abruptly sucked in a breath and said, "Oh, no."

All the others in the waiting room turned his way briefly, before checking their shoes once again.

The video was of Naomi Gott, his former coworker at the Northcomm 9-1-1 Center in Northbrook. Naomi had trained Pies as a new employee at the emergency communications center. She also became romantically attracted to him to the point where she began to stalk him, as well. In the video, her hair was styled differently, longer maybe, and it appeared as if she had lost weight, but it was Naomi all right. Her son Jason, now eight years old, was quite tall for his age. Pies remembered seeing photos of the kid on the wall of Naomi's communications pod when they worked together.

In the video, Naomi and Jason kicked at a soccer ball and happily chased one another around. After thirty seconds, the video zoomed in and held only on Jason.

"Goddamn them...," whispered Pies.

Pies re-watched the video and then paused it. Something in the background caught his attention. He played the video another time, and then again. He held the phone closer and played the video one last time.

The picture was blurry, but in the distant background, nearly two hundred feet to the rear of Jason, the corner of the camera caught the image of a chubby man getting into a red sports car. The car backed up, hesitated, and then drove off, its growling engine heard over the audio of the clip.

Pies knew the man who had gotten into the car. He knew simply by the way the man moved about, literally waddling as he walked— like an over-confident duck.

Threatening Naomi was one thing, but bringing her son Jason into this ever-growing dilemma was evil. Jason was an innocent. He had to be protected somehow.

"What the hell is wrong with you?" said Pies to no one in particular as he backed the video up and watched the man get into the car yet again.

"Hey, screw you, man," spit out the tavern cook from his seated position across the lobby.

Pies turned his ire in the cook's direction, and the pallid tavern employee quickly looked away. Pies's inaction with the Outfit, ignoring their text messages, had now placed not only Milena Chlebek in danger, but also Naomi Gott and, just as importantly, her son Jason.

"Shit," he said, as he shoved the phone back into his pocket and walked from the lobby.

The other parolees, wondering what in the hell was wrong with the cook, formed a wall of dubious glares.

The cook then swallowed some of the bile he dislodged during his outburst and said, "That dude right there is a stone-cold killer, man. Seriously."

16

"I AM ABSOLUTELY serious, baby. Why would I make that up? I'm on the short list right now. Hell, I *am* the short list. Probably get supervisor in the next few months because of the shit that's going down," said the tipsy Tim Ketmen to the curvaceous female barfly with the overly made-up eyes seated to his left. "I'll be running the place soon, you'll see. I'd do a better job than those crooks. Hell, my old supervisor, you remember Soup? She used to come in here all the time?"

"Sure," said the barfly. "She was kind of a bitch."

"Yeah, she was."

Ketmen and the woman were two of six people, including the bored elderly bartender, currently sitting within the low-ceilinged and equally low-rent Skokie tavern. The only other noise being generated, besides Ketmen's verbal barrage, was from the stereo system playing generic country music.

"Yeah, well...she just pleaded guilty for her part in the scam and got four years in the pen," said Ketmen.

"Wow, I didn't hear that."

"Fucking A, wow. It was on the news. The whole communications center was built on bullshit. They told all the North Shore towns they'd save money, and it looked like they were for the first couple of years. But that asshole who started the place, that worthless prick from Cincinnati?"

"He was cute," said the barfly.

"Whatever. He was a skimming son of a bitch, is what he was. He skimmed from the building's construction budget. He skimmed from the yearly operating budget. He cooked the books. Asshole's doing time in Ohio right now for pulling the same crap there. When he gets out, Illinois gets to pick his ass up for another long stay here. Now there's no other choice for these North Shore towns than to pour a ton of money into the place and keep it running."

"Last call, folks. Last call," said the bartender.

Ketmen caught the bartender's eye and circled his index finger over the top of his and the woman's half-full drink glasses.

The barfly leaned a bit closer, her hot and stale alcohol breath on Ketmen's shoulder. She traced a fingertip along his wrist. "Can you give me a private tour sometime? You know, after you become supervisor?" she asked seductively. "A lot of cops hang around there, right? Like the ones from Northbrook. Or Evanston, maybe? Those Evanston cops are hot."

Ketmen's face screwed up with annoyance. He shrugged her off his shoulder and said, "We'll see." And then something near the exit caught his attention. He immediately stopped talking although his mouth remained open.

Pies, dressed in his black T-shirt and jeans, stood staring back, unblinking. After a few seconds, he shoved his way out of the tavern's door. To Ketmen's eyes, Pies seemed even more menacing than he had remembered, and with good reason—Pies had packed on several pounds of muscle since they last met.

Both of the men knew one another from the time Pies worked as a communications officer at Northcom 9-1-1. Pies recalled Ketmen as a blowhard. The kind of person who had an opinion for nearly every occasion, even when one wasn't required. Ketmen would constantly crow that anyone who didn't look or act like he did was taking our country down the shitter.

*

THREE MINUTES later, Pies sat in his parked pickup truck and watched through the windshield as Ketmen emerged from the tavern alone.

The exterior building lights of the business barely illuminated the parking lot, and Pies could sense the chubby man's eyes were darting about. As Ketmen passed closer to one of the parking lot light poles, Pies could see that he was sweating profusely. Ketmen slipped his keys from his front pants pocket and nervously fumbled them to the asphalt.

Simply by the man's stilted movements and quick head jerks, Pies knew Ketmen was attempting to locate him. He seemed like a neurotic duck now, seeking breadcrumbs to peck at.

From Ketmen's vantage point, Pies could be in any of the parked cars in the lot, or none of them. As he continued to scan, he stooped to retrieve his keys off the ground. Once he straightened up, he staggered to his red Camaro. He got in, started the rumbling engine, peeled away, and nearly sideswiped a Honda.

Pies waited a full thirty seconds before he finally started his pickup and put it into drive. He'd follow Ketmen at a safe distance, and his mark would never even realize that he was being tailed from a quarter mile back. There was no reason for Pies to crowd the asshole because he already knew where the man lived. He knew pretty much all there was to know about Ketmen and had ever since they first met five years back.

Earlier in the evening, before heading to Ketmen's home, Pies called Northcomm's nonemergency phone line, twice. The first time was to ask for Naomi Gott. Pies didn't feel the same sort of mental anguish about Naomi as he did about seeing Milena Chlebek face-to-face. Pies hadn't killed one of Naomi's relatives. If he could get Naomi on the communications center's phone, then have her call his cell phone so they wouldn't be recorded, he'd immediately tell her that she was in trouble and she needed to lay low for a while.

Pies wouldn't mention that it was actually Jason who'd been threatened; Naomi would be terrified enough finding out that she was in the Outfit's crosshairs. However, when he called he was advised that Naomi no longer worked at Northcomm.

Not wanting to tip off the people at Northcomm that something strange was going on—a man calling to first ask for Naomi and then for Tim Ketmen during the same call—Pies hung up, waited ten minutes, and called back again, this time disguising his voice. The second communications officer who answered, a woman whose voice Pies didn't recognize, told him that Ketmen was off duty for the next three days.

Pies traveled the nearly empty streets five miles north and west to a neighborhood dotted with tiny run-of-the-mill brick ranch homes, near the intersection of Central and Shermer Roads in Glenview. He turned onto a side road and passed one cul-de-sac, looked right and caught sight of the parked red Camaro, and then he turned into and parked at the next cul-de-sac.

Pies killed his truck's engine and lights and got out. This particular area of Glenview was a quintessential bedroom community, and very few of the neighbors were awake at 2:34 in the morning. Pies stood motionless in the quiet darkness. He stared down the gap between the two houses closest to him and could see the front porch light go out at Ketmen's house. He walked between the two homes and approached Ketmen's place head-on.

*

KETMEN WAS completely drenched in sweat, petrified, and appeared as if he'd hurl at any moment. He hastily stumbled around his place and turned off all the lights. Once that was accomplished, he tripped into his darkened bedroom to retrieve his .357 revolver from the nightstand.

The sight of Jakubowski earlier at the tavern nearly shocked Tim Ketmen into an instant vomiting jag right there inside the dank drinking establishment.

"Why's he out, goddamn it?" he asked aloud, near tears. "They should've never let him out. My God..."

When Pies had been arrested for his myriad crimes, Ketmen finally understood why the man from Edison Park never cowed to his needling when they worked together at Northcomm. Every other newbie Ketmen ever worked with, be it at Northcomm or any other job, always bowed to his smartass remarks and abusive ways. Not Jakubowski, though. Jakubowski had Ketmen figured out from the moment they met, and that made Ketmen feel off balance, small, and truly insignificant whenever they interacted.

Ketmen clicked the safety off the chrome-plated pistol, cocked the hammer back, and staggered about his darkened home, patrolling his tiny interior perimeter. Everything seemed status quo, even in his drunken estimation.

*

KETMEN AWOKE with a violent snort.

He had fallen asleep in an uncomfortable wooden chair next to the picture window in his living room. He coughed hard, settled, and allowed his bleary eyes to scan the darkened home and then the area just outside through the front picture window.

Everything seemed okay, but how long had he been asleep? The eastern sky was beginning to brighten. He noticed the time on the cable TV box's digital display. It was 5:03 A.M.

"Oh, man...damn...," he croaked, as he painfully got to his feet—just then noticing that he still held the loaded handgun in his grasp. "Jeez..."

He lurched forward, involuntarily heaved and coughed once again, and bent fully forward. He wanted to vomit, even if it had to be on the carpet, just to cleanse his system of residual alcohol and become more aware of his surroundings because he was still a little drunk. Nothing happened. The gurgling in his abdomen subsided, and he took a couple of cleansing breaths, straightened, and glanced out the picture window once again. He heaved a deep and satisfying sigh.

"How much did you get?" asked Pies from the kitchen doorway.

Ketmen spun, nearly lost his balance, aimed, and pulled the trigger.

Click.

Click. Click.

Click...click...

Click...

"Fuck," yelled the chubby man, as he still shakily aimed the empty pistol at Pies.

Hours earlier, while Ketmen was hanging out at the Skokie tavern, Pies had broken into the house and emptied the chubby man's revolver of bullets. The rounds were now literally cooling off in the refrigerator's salad crisper drawer. Pies had also searched the house for other hidden weapons but found none. Next, he searched for any piece of paper with Naomi's name on it, without any luck. He had tried Ketmen's laptop computer, too, but it was password protected.

Pies snapped on the dining room light switch. The cheaply constructed chandelier illuminated the bargain-brand, two-chair table below it and most of the living room as well.

Ketmen squinted, and as soon as he adjusted his vision to the bright light, he dropped the gun and dove for the landline phone on the table next to his well-worn recliner chair. He very nearly knocked the faux-brass lamp located there to the floor.

Pies just stood and watched. Casual.

Ketmen snatched the cordless phone out of its cradle and said, "Fuck you, Jakubowski. Fucking murderer. You'll see. I'm going to get... And then you're..."

Ketmen pressed the button to activate the phone, and that's when he noticed that it had a blank screen. He mumbled, "The cops will..."

The power cord of the unit had been pulled from the wall socket.

Ketmen began to visibly shake, and with a defeated expression on his face, he dropped the dead phone to the floor and spun around. He tumbled backward into the recliner and began to rub his head with both hands and weep openly. "I know I fucked up," said the chubby man. "I know what I did, man. I'm sorry."

Pies edged forward menacingly and fronted Ketmen.

Ketmen never looked up as he blurted, "His name was Sam some-thing-or-other. He said he'd pay me five grand to locate her. I'd get five hundred now and the rest later. If I didn't help, he'd kill me. Me? What was I supposed to do?"

"Go to the police."

Ketmen waved Pies's comment away and said, "The asshole never even paid me the rest. And I got the new car to pay for…"

"Where is she now?"

Ketmen heaved out a sob and then quickly tried to control himself.

Pies leaned in. "Tough guy. Hey, where is she?"

"You know what? Fuck you," oozed Ketmen, who abruptly grew quiet and pursed his lips. It seemed like his last attempt at defiance.

Pies snatched the lamp off the table and smashed the base of it across the side of Ketmen's head. Ketmen bent sideways and raised his right hand to protect himself from another blow.

Pies feigned another strike with the lamp and Ketmen flinched.

"Shit…dude," begged Ketmen. "Christ. Stop. Stop hurting me," he cried, his head bleeding.

"Killing's always been easy. You do it once…"

"Okay, okay," said the terrified Ketmen as he put his hands up in surrender. "After the state and the FBI came to Northcomm and took all the supervisors away, Naomi quit and I guess went to Merrillville."

"Indiana?" asked Pies, as he tossed the lamp aside.

"Indiana. Yeah. Did you know that Cincinnati ass-hat who ran Northcomm and his brother-in-law were skimming?"

Pies nodded. He'd read about it online.

Ketmen sniffled, "Naomi was done with it all…."

"What's her address?"

"This Sam guy. He's scary, man. He comes across like he's a cool guy at first, and… He didn't even know her name right off. He had a video of her by your hospital room from back then. I had to look her up online, you know? And…"

"What's her address?" asked Pies again, beginning to lose even the tiny thread of patience he still possessed.

"Okay, all right. On the counter. In the kitchen. In my phone book, there's a printout," said Ketmen. "Am I'm bleeding?" he dabbed at his head with his fingers.

"Yeah, you're bleeding," said Pies as he went into the kitchen. He had searched the blue book earlier after he had broken in, but he hadn't realized that the printout with the Merrillville address was for Naomi Gott. There was no name next to the address. He slipped the printout from the book and tucked it into his back pants pocket.

"I tried the phone number there, but it's out of service. You have to believe me. I searched all the social media sites and that's the only address for her that I could find. It was the right one. I pointed out her and her kid at a park and then never heard from that Sam guy again," said the defeated Ketmen. "Just...get it over with," he continued as his emotions disintegrated even further, and he slowly rubbed at the sides of his head once again. "What are you waiting for? Goddamn it. Just kill...me."

Ketmen lurched forward in the chair and turned his head sideways to get a view of the kitchen opening. "Hey? Where'd...? Are you there? Hello...?"

Pies was gone.

Ketmen's house was quiet and empty.

The chubby man sank his head back into his shabby recliner and blubbered.

17

HIS SMARTPHONE chimed with an incoming text message just as he parked. Pies pressed to read the text and noticed, again, there was a video attached. The text message from "Mother" read: "Don't be late."

Pies pressed the video play button. Whoever made the video was sitting in a booth at the diner across from Milena Chlebek's bakery in Edison Park. The glass on the front door of her business was completely shattered and the sidewalk was covered in shards. An upset Milena stood, with arms crossed, as she spoke with a uniformed female Chicago police officer. The officer bobbed her head up and down as she wrote on a clipboard. At the end of the thirty-second piece, a man in coveralls carrying a door-sized piece of plywood entered the frame. The video stopped.

Pies let out a slow and angry breath. He opened the pickup truck's door and got out. The Indian Boundary neighborhood was beginning to start its day, and Pies needed to lock down a semipermanent place to stay. He had had enough of the crappy hotel on Howard Street. The little sleep he'd gotten over the past couple of days was interrupted with loud arguments and more slamming doors than he would like to count.

He got across the street, and he slowed to a stop and let his eyes scan the two-flat apartment building that sat in front of him. It was a nice enough place.

Tidy.

His most pressing questions for himself were: Would he be able to contentedly live in the same building as the beautiful woman with the stylishly short hair and Cubs hat? Could he keep his mind on task and find Milena safety and get out of Chicago without tripping up and doing something that would get himself and Milena killed?

He shook off his mushrooming apprehensions and continued toward the building.

He opened the front vestibule door of the building and pressed the button with the name Tambor written next to it. He could hear the muffled buzz from inside the first floor apartment and then thumping footfalls.

The electric lock on the interior door buzzed, and he pushed through that door just as the first floor apartment door opened.

"I saw you park—"

"I'll take the place," Pies interrupted Faigy, who was already dressed for the day in a plaid shirt and blue jeans. He bounded up the steps and handed her a wad of hundreds and continued, "I've had a lot on my mind, and when... When you showed me the apartment..."

"Pies, there's no need... I know...I know your story," said Faigy. "It must be really strange being out in public after so many years...away. To adjust."

Pies froze for a moment. He then nodded and looked down. "Okay. That was sort of inevitable, wasn't it?"

"The place is yours," she said. "I went ahead and moved a futon down there, you know, just in case you ever came back."

Pies looked questioningly at Faigy.

"The futon separates into three parts. No biggie," said Faigy.

Pies was pleasantly surprised, and he grinned in thanks.

Faigy continued, "You don't know this, Pies, but there are people who are willing to help you get adjusted. I'm one of them. You need anything, you let me know."

Pies, eyes down, nodded. "I'm not sure there's anything you... I have to go, I'm..."

"Go. Go. I'll be around all day. If it's late, I'll hide a key under the flowerpot next to the garage for you."

"I appreciate that," said Pies. He lingered for just a moment more and wondered why she seemed to trust him this much—so soon after they met. There was an appointment to make, though, so he waved and backed down the stairs and was gone from the building.

Faigy Tambor slipped back into her beautifully decorated apartment, walked to the front windows, and watched Pies with curiosity until he got into his truck and drove off.

As she stood there and observed the park across the street, her mind raced back to those days five years ago as she followed Jakub "Pies" Jakubowski's news stories—his human foibles and his selfless acts, as well. Pies, without realizing it, she thought, had changed her life for the better.

Her doorbell chimed again, which startled her. Faigy went to the door, opened it, and saw that her neighbor, Mr. Pila, stood in the glassed-in vestibule. She reached to the wall-mounted control system and buzzed the man inside.

"Mr. Pila? What can I do for you?"

Pila painted on his best smile and said, "May I?" as he motioned his desire to come inside.

Faigy backed into her home and allowed the man inside. He was wearing his customary wide-brimmed beaver hat and his black jacket and slacks, and Faigy also noted that he was dressed in one of his white work shirts with the ChiCall Telephone logo.

"How have you been, Mr. Pila?"

"Fine, fine. I just saw the man leave your building, and I wanted to warn you that he's not what he says he is. That same man inferred to me that he was of our...of the Hasidic faith, but he is not," said Pila. "He's not to be trusted."

"Okay," said Faigy, wondering what business it was of Pila's to worry about her—especially since she was no longer tethered to her former faith. "I know who he is. I know about him."

"He's a criminal, is what he is, Mrs. Tambor. A criminal. Not just a criminal, he's a killer," said Pila as his temper began to bloom. "He's been on the news, this man."

"Yes, I do know, Mr. Pila, but he's done his time and he's free to go about his life now."

"His life? What about our lives? What about my children's lives, Mrs. Tambor? Don't they mean anything to you? This is unacceptable for him to be residing in our neighborhood. You will not rent your property to that man, Mrs. Tambor. I forbid it," said Mr. Pila as he angrily took his hat off.

"Get out," said Faigy, quietly.

"What? Get...get out? I don't understand," said the confused Mr. Pila.

Faigy felt a rage building inside her as she faced this man who had been present when she was forced into a marriage with a man who never loved her, a man who was many years older than she was. Pila hadn't concerned himself with what might or might not have been acceptable to a nineteen-year-old girl at that time, and now.... She erupted with rage, thinking about his silence and apparent unconcern when she actually needed someone to be worried about her welfare. "You lived here for as long as I have. You witnessed what was happening here those years ago. Why didn't you step in at that time, Mr. Pila? Where were you then? Where was your concern? Who was watching out for me?" Faigy demanded.

Pila allowed her words to sink in, and he actually seemed to soften his temper. "Okay, okay, I see I've upset you, and I apologize." His eyes began to roam about her body, and a tiny smirk spiked the corner of his mouth.

Faigy recoiled slightly and said, "What? Are you—"

Pila continued, in a syrupy tone, "I didn't mean to barge in like this. I wanted this to go another way. I've wanted that for sometime... And seeing that man once again, it got me angry. I apologize. We should, you know, start over." He reached out and gently brushed his fingers along her elbow. "Everyone needs a friend, right? We live so close, but we don't really know—"

Faigy immediately knocked his hand away from her elbow and reared back her fist, but then she relaxed as a thought came to her. She smirked and said, "Everyone does need a friend, don't they. I may just have to tell my friend Jakub Jakubowski about you. How you treat your neighbors."

Pila cleared his throat as his eyes blinked with embarrassment. "I'll just be... I'll go...I should go."

Pila backpedaled out of the apartment. He walked down the stairs, pushed the door open into the vestibule, and Faigy said, "Say hello to Mrs. Pila for me, would you? And the kids."

Pila slinked from view.

"Asshole," exhaled Faigy. And then she thought about how she just brought Jakubowski, a man she didn't really know, into her troubles. She said, "Oh, you idiot."

18

PIES ROLLED past the greasy-spoon diner on Higgins Road two times before he could make himself park the pickup truck and go inside.

During his first pass, Pies saw only four people inside the diner through the grimy street-facing windows: three men, two dressed casually, one in a green short-sleeved golf shirt and the other in a well-worn gray sweatshirt, and a third man seated with them in a crisp, long-sleeved, blue button-up shirt. There was a single employee in attendance, as well—the cook, in filthy, grease-splattered "whites." The cook had his back to the other men as he rapidly worked the grill.

During his second pass, Pies swung into a parking lot opposite the greasy spoon, hoping the unending stream of traffic would give him cover.

Briefly idling the truck across the busy roadway, Pies watched as a man who looked to be in his sixties stumbled up to the diner's door and tried to enter the business. Immediately, as if operating as a single organism, all three men sitting at the side table turned in the stupefied man's direction and angrily shouted at him in unison. The man recoiled and then froze for just a moment, before he let go of the door handle, lowered his head, and advanced down the sidewalk. As the man disappeared from view, the diner occupant in the long sleeves looked at the cell phone in his palm, tapped at the phone to answer, and placed it to his ear.

With four minutes to go, Pies finally parked a block away. He was ahead of the scheduled meeting time and fighting some serious second thoughts about following through. So much so that he hid the remainder of his cash in the torn seat cushion of his pickup truck in case he needed to make a hasty run for it after hearing what the mobsters wanted with him. If he bolted and headed for the border, would the Outfit follow through on their threats to kill Milena Chlebek and Naomi Gott—or her son Jason?

Probably.

Not probably.

The answer would be *yes*. Yes, they would.

"Shit," said Pies softly to himself, as he opened the truck door.

He approached the diner on foot, with his adrenaline levels on the rise. His respirations escalated to a series of rapid breaths, but he was finally able to soothe himself to a more composed state just as he grabbed the door handle.

He entered the diner, but the three men didn't yell at him. They were the ones who froze this time. The largest of the three, the man in the sweatshirt, was slightly smaller than Pies. The moment the man in the sweatshirt solidly laid eyes on him Pies could sense the man's apprehension, even from twenty feet away. The man seemed confused by what he saw. Pies figured, rightly, the men had been watching old local news video of him from five years ago when he was emaciated and swimming in his courthouse suit of clothes. This broader, more muscular, more menacing version of Pies didn't match their expected image of the former inmate.

"Holy shit. Look at Mr. Muscles here," said the man in the long-sleeved shirt. Pies assumed he was the boss since he was the first to speak.

Pies had seen the man before, too. It was when he was walking to the halfway house after his first failed attempt to apologize. The man in the long-sleeves had handed Bast Zielinski's widow, Rebecca, a cup of coffee as they both stood on the porch of Rebecca's home, watching ten-year-old Itty-Bitty ride her bike in the street.

"Come on, sit," said the man. "Yo, Clyde?"

The cook, the haggard-looking Clyde, spun around, and the man in the long-sleeved shirt continued, "Another order of steak and eggs." The man running the meeting then gave Pies an extra, smirk-filled once-over and said, "Make that two more orders. Our friend here needs his calories."

Pies turned to look at the cook and saw a short stack of printed photos on the long, well-worn lunch counter. He couldn't make out the image in the top photo from this distance, though. He then sat next to the smallest man, the one in the green golf shirt. He noticed that the shirt had a little blue-colored jet airplane embroidered on the chest.

Pies let out a breath and leaned back in his chair and waited.

"Sam Panzera," said the man with the movie star looks who was running the show, as he extended a friendly hand to Pies. Pies shook, let go, and awaited Sam's next move.

"This here is Chuckie Silano," said Panzera as he aimed his eyes to his right and the man in the sweatshirt. "And that's Angelo Brosillino. Just call him Brosi," he continued with a jaw jut in the direction of the smaller man sitting to the left of Pies. Neither of the other men offered their hands, and that was fine with Pies.

Pies had heard these names before, save one—the man doing the introductions, Sam Panzera. Pies was not aware of him, or his face, at least not from his days in the Zielinskis' crew. That wasn't uncommon in the Outfit's universe. The organization had a way of hiding, in plain sight, the ones who were actually the shot-callers. They were referred to as "sleepers." It made for a much tougher prosecution by the authorities if things went sideways and they didn't even know who was making the actual decisions.

Silano's and Brosi's names came up now and then when deceased underboss Donny Noretti, the Outfit member Pies killed five years back—along with his bodyguard Luke—discussed with the Zielinskis the countless nefarious activities they were partaking in to earn for the organization.

Silano stared back at Pies with a hooded gaze, not dissimilar to the corrections officers he'd been around at Stateville. Silano's mouth had that permanent twist to it, as if he were about to tell you to go fuck yourself. Just from the looks of him, he'd be a hard man to get one over on.

Brosi, on the other hand, looked like a soft and round human puppy dog. He was a short man in his forties, but with a constant grin and doe-like eyes that masked the killer beneath. Brosi beamed and said, "Hiya. It's good being out, huh?"

Pies ignored him.

Pies understood what it took for these three men to get where they were in the Outfit, and he knew he was seated with three killers.

"Glad we were able to finally get you to come and meet. Fucking asshole. Sam's been sending fucking messages. Pay attention now, Polack," said Silano, as he angled his chin toward Panzera. "You got a lot riding on this."

"Can I call you Pies? I know that's what they called you before. The Zielinskis," said Panzera. "Before all that shit."

Pies gave confirmation with a single nod.

Clyde approached with plates of food and carefully set them down in front of the men.

"Looks good, Clyde. Thanks, friend," said Panzera.

Pies could see that Clyde wanted to roll his eyes at the "friend" comment, but he stopped himself short.

"More coffee, too. Pies, you want coffee?"

Pies shook his head and ignored the plates in front of him. Clyde returned to the counter to retrieve the coffeepot, and the three thugs hurriedly dug into their food like rabid strays. Clyde filled their cups and then retreated once again.

Through a mouthful of pulverized steak and egg bits, Panzera said, "You ever work in Barrington?"

Pies said, "That was out of our area. We mostly had the North Shore. You know that."

"Easy, prick," said Silano.

Brosi nudged Pies with a gentle elbow and gave him a friendly don't-worry-about-Silano gesture with his eyebrows.

"We got a thing we need done in Barrington. Barrington Hills, really. Where the money is," said Panzera. "There's a piece of sports memorabilia we'd like to get a hold of. We got a buyer."

"You have people. Why do you need me?" asked Pies as he eyed Brosi first and then Silano—both ignored his stares.

"We're more into airfreight these days, you know, importing stuff," blurted Brosi, as he took another heaping bite of food.

Both Panzera and Silano's wary eyes flashed toward their compatriot. Brosi caught their glances and lowered his gaze as he chewed.

Panzera recovered quickly from Brosi's statement and continued, "Our guys? I don't know. This one's tricky. Our guys aren't into finesse. Lately, when it comes to pinching shit, we've done more of the volume jobs. Empty out a warehouse full of laptops while the security guy's getting a blow job. Shit like that. I got to be honest here, we don't have a local who could pull this one off. It's that complicated. And we don't want to bring in anyone 'cause we want this all for our own."

"You don't want one of yours to get caught if it falls apart, is what you're saying," said Pies.

"Hey, hey, pal," said Silano as he aimed his fork overhand at Pies. "One more goddamned word—"

Panzera put a hand on Silano's forearm and said, "You and Brosi take your chow to the counter. Leave me and Pies here to talk."

Silano and Brosi did as instructed. As Brosi turned away to stand, Pies happened to adjust his position, and he and the short man bumped shoulders. Brosi said, "Sorry 'bout that."

Once Silano and Brosi were away from the table, Panzera leaned in close to Pies.

"That's not exactly why. Looking out for our own, sure. Nothing wrong with that, and there's no reason to bullshit you, right? It truly is a tricky job. I swear. I think you can come up with a solution that we're not seeing right now. And, well...you don't really have a choice."

Panzera's declaration caused Brosi, who was fifteen feet away, to chuckle. When the human puppy dog noticed Pies giving him side-eye, he said, "Yeah, sorry 'bout that. It's just...it's...never mind."

"Not hungry?" asked Panzera as he slipped another forkful of the greasy steak and egg mélange into his mouth.

"When do I start?" asked Pies. He wanted this over and done with as soon as possible.

"How about when do *we* start. Me and you. Silano and Brosi will be our backup outside the estate. It'll be like old times for you. That's how you guys did jobs, right? Some guys inside, and some outside running interference?"

"An estate?" asked Pies.

"Like I said, this is a tricky one. I'll follow your lead because I know that you know your shit, but we're both in on this. We clear?"

Pies was confused, though. Why would this Panzera, the guy obviously in charge of at least this meeting, if not an entire Outfit crew, why would he get his hands dirty working on the front lines of a high-end B&E? Guys like Panzera, Pies knew from experience, would have layers of soldiers between themselves and the illegal action that was taking place.

"I see this is causing you concern," said Panzera. "Pies, I run the entire area up here to the north, there are twenty more of us in all. Here's the thing. We're not up on the high-end, night jobs, if you get me. This thing in Barrington Hills is for a small item, but it is big ticket. If I see the way you do things, I can kind of train these other monkeys to do this shit, and then you go on about your life. You'll be free to go on your way."

Pies didn't believe him. Once his usefulness was over with, he would be, too.

Panzera was holding back, but Pies wasn't sure what he was keeping from him. And what choice did Pies have? He had not apologized to Milena Chlebek as of yet or even come up with a plausible plan to get the woman to permanent safety. He'd also not been able to see Naomi Gott to let her know that she and her son, too, were in danger.

"What are we after?" asked Pies.

Panzera grinned. He looked to Silano and Brosi and then aimed his chin toward Pies. "It's a crazy little sports item. A Honus Wagner baseball card."

Pies squinted his eyes and said, "A...baseball card?"

"Thing's worth millions. There's only a couple of them around. This one we're going after was sold a few years ago for over two mill. It's worth more now. Double that. I've already confirmed it. Got an Arab oil fuck on board to take it off my hands."

"What's so difficult?" asked Pies.

Panzera motioned to Brosi, who picked up the stack of color prints off the counter and brought them over to the table. He slid them in front of Pies and then returned to the counter.

"The house...house? This fucking mansion was for sale a few months back. It didn't sell right away, so the asshole owner took it off the market. He wanted thirty-five mill for the place. Believe that? We got those off the real estate website back when we first thought about doing this and the house was for sale."

Pies kept an even disposition as he shuffled through the stack, quickly glancing at the photos. In the exterior shots, he saw nothing but unbridled opulence. Photo after photo of an impeccable facade, built of mostly limestone. There were eight beautiful carriage-style doors on the attached garage. The only interior photos were of a grand master bedroom suite, outfitted with high-end furnishings and thick carpets. There were also photos of the extraordinary master bathroom, finished in the finest marble and imported tiles.

Pies shuffled to a photo of the master bedroom's walk-in closet, and Panzera put a stiff finger on the paper and held it tight to the tabletop.

"Right there. That glass case in the middle of the closet... Shit, closet? That's bigger than my whole living room. That glass case looks like it's got ties and shit in there, right. Colorful socks, maybe. I don't know. That's where the baseball card is. The owner's got a big mouth. He's a twenty-three-year-old zillionaire trust-fund moron who acts like he's Howard Hughes or some bullshit. You saw the flick? With Leonardo? Hughes was a maniac," said Panzera.

Pies ignored his cultural reference.

Panzera gave him a little shrug and continued, "One of our guys was at an event at Arlington Park a while back, caught the asshole talking up his baseball card and where he kept it."

Brosi chimed in from across the room. "The kid owner of that place is in rehab more than he's out, if you get me? A real stronzo."

"Just because they're rich doesn't mean they're super smart," added Panzera with a crooked grin. "The owner is smart enough to travel around with a couple of armed bodyguards, though. Real pros. So there's no snatching him up and making him give us this thing. I mean we could do it, I guess. It's kind of risky, though. We'd rather do this nice and quiet, like we usually do."

"This is cake. You don't need me," said Pies.

"No, no, we do need you. This place has systems we don't know how to get around," said Panzera.

"Infrared beams," said Brosi from the counter. "Pepper spray blasters here and there. Automatic doors that shut closed if they get a whiff of something going wrong. Some James Bond shit. Place will lock down tight is what we know."

Panzera jabbed a finger in Brosi's direction and said, "That right there," and then he turned to Pies and continued, "the moron owner bragged about all this. The security. The, the, what...the beams, and that shit. We usually know how to get what we want, but this stuff... This stuff at that mansion, we don't know dick about. We figured you would."

"I've been out of this for five years," said Pies. "How could I even... Things change all the time."

"You'll figure it out," said the confident Panzera.

"What choice do you got?" added Silano, humorlessly, from his seat at the counter.

Pies was backed into a corner, and he wasn't sure he could work his way out of it. If he didn't do as instructed, people he loved and respected would be killed, and then he, too, would die. He could also be quickly arrested while trying to pull off the job and that, too, would lead to certain loved ones being eliminated. His mind fired rapidly trying to come up with something, anything—a buffer— that would give him space to work out an escape plan for himself, Milena, and Naomi and Jason.

"You want results from me?" asked Pies.

The question stopped Panzera's momentum. He lost his grin and looked at Pies.

Silano's forbidding grin also disappeared.

Pies said, "It's a simple question."

"What do you— Of course we want results," said Panzera.

"If you want the best I can offer, you have to leave the women out of this," said Pies.

"You don't give the orders. And what the fuck are you even talking about?" began Silano, before Panzera shot him a look that froze him.

Panzera pivoted back to Pies, and by way of agreeing with him, he said, "Let's get this rolling, okay? No more fucking around, you get me? Here's the address." He reached into his shirt pocket and extracted a folded piece of paper. He tossed it onto the tabletop. He leaned forward and took a folded envelope from his back pants pocket and tossed that on the table as well. "For your expenses setting this up. Figured you'd be broke, just getting out, and all. If you don't run on us and you do this thing, we'll all make out great. So don't be stupid and run, okay?"

Pies, with one hand, grabbed the folded paper and collected the photos and the envelope into a neat pile that he wrapped around his other hand. He said, "That it?"

"You scout that place and then get back to me the day after tomorrow," said Panzera.

"I'll need more—"

"No, my friend. We'll go over what you got then. If more time's needed, we'll work it out. I've been waiting a long time for this to go down. Like to get it done."

Pies didn't wait to be excused. He stood and walked to the door. However, something had truly bothered him since he arrived. He stopped and looked over his shoulder, "Why didn't you pat me down? When I got here... No one checked me over."

Panzera began eating once again and said, "My guys had eyes on you from the first time you drove past, and then when you parked right next to them for a couple of seconds. If you tried anything stupid, they'd take care of you. They used to do shit like that in Iraq."

Pies finally noticed the nondescript white panel van parked across Higgins on the edge of a closed bank's parking lot. It was the same van that followed him from Chlebeks' Bakery, but Pies didn't know that.

"See you soon," said Panzera, as Pies shoved his way out of the diner and headed back to his pickup truck.

19

PIES YANKED open the plywood-covered front door of Chlebeks' Bakery, his eyes wide with anticipation and his adrenaline pumping. He had to get to Milena—and immediately whisk her off to Wisconsin. The apology would come later, after he knew she was safe.

He didn't believe anything that Panzera told him moments ago and just a mile away from the bakery. Why would they need him to do this job of stealing a baseball card? It all seemed ludicrous.

"You okay, pal?" asked the young man with the wispy blond hair who stood behind the main counter wearing his clean kitchen whites.

Pies didn't answer the man—he simply walked to the kitchen in back. When he got to there, Milena was nowhere in sight. He pushed out of the back screen door and looked side to side. The alley was empty. Milena was not anywhere to be seen.

"What the hell are you doing?" asked the young baker as he entered the kitchen. When Pies didn't respond he added, "I'm calling the cops."

"Don't do that," said Pies.

The baker stood with his hand hovering near the kitchen's flour-covered wall phone.

"Where is she?" asked Pies.

The baker's face screwed up with confusion. It was confusion over finally recognizing Pies and wondering why he was here. "Jakubowski?

Dude, it is you. I used to live down the block from you, man. I'm little Bobby Petrowski—"

Pies crowded the baker and grabbed a hunk of his whites in balled fists. "Where is she?"

"I don't know. She said she'd be back later."

Pies let go of the baker and ran out through the rear door.

He didn't stop running for a few blocks until he was bounding up the steps of the Chlebeks' home. He repeatedly rang the doorbell and furiously knocked on the front door.

"Mrs. Chlebek? Milena, please. Open the door," said the anxious Pies.

The elderly man next door, sitting on his own front porch, got to his feet and said, "Hey, you there. Is everything okay?"

Pies ignored the old man and jumped off the porch. He headed toward the backyard of the home and tried opening both the back kitchen door and then the basement door without any success. He could've used the lock-bump to gain entry, but what good would that do. Milena was obviously not home. He stood in the yard and rubbed at his forehead.

The elderly neighbor made it into his own backyard. He leaned on the chain-link fence and said, "Son, she's always gone during this time of the day. Pretty much every weekday."

Pies sprinted to where he parked his pickup truck. If he couldn't warn off Milena right now, he would head to Merrillville, Indiana, instead. He had to do something—anything.

20

FAIGY BACKED into the illuminated basement apartment with an armload of bed pillows, linens, and blankets. She turned and dumped the items onto the opened futon that sat in the middle of the basement apartment. She took a couple of deep breaths and leaned over to separate the sheets from the rest of the bed linens.

As she worked she surveyed what she'd accomplished so far. She wanted the place to be inviting, so she added some of her own decorative touches here and there, photos and such, as well as some more reasonable additions, mainly cleaning supplies and towels.

Earlier in the day, when Pies had left after paying her the initial rent money, Faigy had some second thoughts about the former inmate living in her building. If she had to be honest with herself, her neighbor Mr. Pila, as sleazy as he was, had planted the notion in her head that she was making a terrible mistake. She wasn't completely blind to the situation. She knew that Pies had murdered in the past, but he was just a young boy when that all happened, as far as she knew. He didn't seem like a violent type now. But he had taken someone's life before...on three separate occasions.

"What am I doing?" Faigy said to no one.

A slight bumping noise coming from above startled her. She cautiously moved toward the basement apartment's door and heard another shuffling sound from above.

"Oh, my God..."

Faigy had left her cell phone on her kitchen counter, so there was no way to call for help—and there was definitely someone in her apartment above. She remembered she had also left her rear apartment door wide open when she came to the basement space earlier. "Shit...shit..."

She latched onto an idea. She quietly stepped from the basement apartment and ascended the cement stairs. She thought that maybe she could find a passing neighbor on the street and ask that person to call the police.

When she cautiously got to the last cement step, the rear door of her apartment pushed open, and she could plainly see two physically fit young men—both with thick black hair and both wearing dark-colored hoodies and blue jeans. The first man to emerge from her apartment locked eyes with her. Then both men bolted down the steps, nearly knocking into Faigy. They turned and ran toward the street out in front.

Faigy hesitated for just a second and—inexplicably—chased after them.

"Hey," she called out. "What in the hell!"

By the time Faigy arrived street-side, the men had already gotten into a white panel van and were speeding away. It happened so fast that Faigy couldn't even get a license number. She stood for a moment watching as the van rocketed through a four-way stop sign down the block and was gone. She could call the police, but there had to be thousands of similar-looking vans driving the streets of Chicago.

She spun and jogged back to her own apartment. Once up the stairs and into the kitchen, Faigy slowed her breathing and began to survey her apartment, looking to see if anything was missing.

After five minutes she was satisfied that nothing had been taken —even though she had an expensive computer system in her home office, which she used for her photography hobby. Neither the computer nor her photo-quality printer had even been moved.

The sinking feeling that her new tenant could be trouble, once again caused a wave of queasiness to roll through her stomach. After settling down for a while longer and drinking a glass of water, she decided to let it go for now and not call the police, unless she later found something missing. She was the one stupid enough to leave her back door wide open. She also felt sure that whichever jaded police officer showed up to take a report would tell her the very same thing.

21

ALTHOUGH MERRILLVILLE, Indiana, was in another state, it was actually just a little over an hour's drive from Milena's home—on a good traffic day. Pies headed southbound, avoiding toll roads and the prevalent camera systems employed to stop scofflaws. Intuition began to slowly filter into his consciousness and quickly grew to a molten state as panic washed over him. He jerked the pickup truck over to the right, cutting across several lanes of traffic on the Kennedy and avoiding honking vehicles. Once in the right lane, he took the Armitage Avenue exit.

A block later, he swung the truck into a grocery store's pothole-pocked parking lot and skidded to a halt. Pies was immediately out of the door and on all fours, crawling around and peering up and under the vehicle—feeling around the underbelly as he went.

He was searching for a tracking device. He'd seen them before, even used one a few times when he was casing B&E jobs years back. They were four-by-four-inch boxes with magnets on the outside and the electronics situated within the weatherproof plastic-encased housing. If Panzera's men in the van had served in Iraq, they'd be familiar with tracking devices.

"You okay, buddy," said a man's voice.

Pies pivoted to a seated position and looked up at the old black man in the driver's seat of a silver four-door Buick that was idling alongside him.

"Yeah, I'm good," said Pies, trying to be cool. "Thanks."

"Watch out for them potholes, buddy," said the grinning man, as he slowly rolled away.

After one last sweep, and feeling all around the underside of the perimeter of the pickup truck, Pies got back into the driver's seat and slipped the smartphone from his pocket. He tapped it, searched through the settings, then gave up on what he was looking for. The Outfit wasn't tracking the phone, either. Otherwise they would've been all over him from day one.

*

"REAL EASY now, one hand and then the other. Lace those fingers and put them behind your head," said Naomi Gott's father-in-law, Mike, a capable bull of a man, his post-retirement age notwithstanding. The former Chicago police detective had a 9mm pistol in his right hand, held tightly parallel to his own chest, with the muzzle aimed directly at the base of Pies's skull. A set of handcuffs jangled loudly in the other hand.

The Merrillville area's population had grown tremendously in the past twenty years, and townhome developments like the one where Naomi lived seemed to be more common than cornfields nowadays. Her place was not easy to locate, either, because the new townhome subdivisions all looked very similar to one another, most of them with some sort of tan-on-tan-on-tan color scheme.

Just as he had stepped to her front door and was about to knock, the door flew open and there stood Mike, casually armed with the pistol. Mike had carefully guided Pies to his current location, against the living room wall inside the no-frills townhome, and kicked the front door closed, so nosy neighbors couldn't catch a glimpse of what was transpiring inside.

"Naomi's in danger, sir," said Pies.

Mike snapped the cuffs on Pies's left wrist, carefully brought the arm down behind Pies's back, and then said, "The other one." He repeated the process with his right wrist. Once Pies was secured, Mike tugged him a few feet inside the townhome and shoved him into a chair at the small dining room table. Mike then placed the gun on the far side of the table.

"We saw on the news that they let you go. Damned idiots. What were they thinking?" asked Mike, rhetorically. "Didn't think you'd be stupid enough to show up here," he continued. "Glad I came by today. I had a feeling."

"I never wanted to get out, either...."

"Grandpa, who's here?" asked eight-year old Jason from up the stairs and out of view.

"No one, buddy. You go back to your reading now," called out Mike. He then turned his ire back on Pies. "She nearly lost everything because she got tangled up in your shit. You're an asshole. She's got a kid to take care of."

"Please. Is Naomi here? I have to speak with her," said Pies quietly. "It's important. Please."

"Mike, it's okay. I got this," said Naomi Gott as she tentatively slipped into the room from the kitchen area. She looked so different to Pies. Naomi was fit and trim now, standing there in a yellow button-up blouse and blue jeans. Her hair was a darker color and much longer than it used to be too. She was beautiful and looked confident, Pies thought.

"Mike, please. Let him go. He won't...he won't cause trouble."

"Mom, who's down there with you?" called out Jason once again.

"Jason, honey, stay upstairs. I'll be there in a minute, okay?" said Naomi, trying to keep her voice emotionally level and not betray her unease around the newly paroled Pies.

"Okay...," said a dejected Jason. His bedroom door was heard closing a few seconds later.

To demonstrate his sincerity, Pies slowly stood and half turned to give his wrists to Mike.

"For Christ's sake," said Mike, nearly imperceptibly. He dug his right fingers into his front pants pocket and extracted the small cuff key. Once Pies was free, he motioned for Naomi to take a seat, which she did. Mike grumbled, picked up his gun, and began to leave the room.

"Sir? Please. Stay. You need to hear this, too," said Pies, as he sat once again. "I don't want to keep anything from anyone."

Mike let out an angry breath, tugged a chair free of the table, and plopped into the seat. He expertly popped the clip out of his gun and slid the chambered round out and onto the tabletop. He scooped the bullet off the table and tucked it into his shirt pocket.

Pies waited for Mike to settle before he turned to Naomi. "I hope you understand now why I was so rough on you in the hospital back then. I couldn't... You couldn't be linked to me in any way. I didn't want to hurt you. I wanted to make sure that you were away from me and safe...."

"I understand, I do. It took a few months to sink in. I finally...I finally figured it out," Naomi answered. "Pies, I was in a weird place then, too, and I have to apolog—"

Pies gently waved her comment away—all was good between them now. There were more important events to discuss. "Here's the thing. The Outfit got an idea of how you were linked to me. They had you on video coming and going from my hospital room and they... they know who you are now. They know that you live here."

"Son of a bitch," blurted Mike, as he stood. "You damned fool. What did you do? Were you followed?"

Pies shook his head.

Naomi heard Jason stir upstairs and half stood to intercept him if he chose to come downstairs. All grew quiet, and Naomi sat back in her chair.

"It wasn't me," Pies said, his eyes holding steady on Mike. "It was a guy named Ketmen. He works at the Northcomm 9-1-1 center."

Naomi leaned forward and said, "Ketmen? Why? Why would Ketmen—"

"They threatened him. They didn't even know your name. There was cellphone video of you at the hospital from five years ago," said

Pies. "They told Ketmen if he didn't track you down, find your address, they'd kill him. You have to go somewhere else for a while now. You have to hide."

The room was silent for a long moment after Pies's last remark.

Mike's eyes scanned Pies's—as if something more important dawned on him. He then he looked toward the stairs.

"Naomi, I think Jakubowski's right. He could've just bolted from town and left you to die, but he didn't. We have to get you and my grandson out of here. At least until things settle down," said Mike. "You remember Dave Bush from my old precinct?"

Naomi bowed her head, indicating that she remembered.

"He owes me the use of his Pensacola condo for a couple of weeks. What do you say? You can pack light. We'll head down to the Indianapolis airport, maybe that way no one will trail you and Jason, and you can be on your way. I'll hang back and keep an eye on things."

Pies opened his mouth to correct the record and tell Naomi and Mike that he thought it was actually Jason who was really being threatened by the Outfit. He wisely chose to close his mouth and stay mum instead.

Mike noticed Pies's newly hatched anxiousness and said, "What's the matter?"

Pies shook his head and motioned that all was okay. He then said, "Thanks, sir, that would be great. Thanks for helping."

Mike's expression morphed into a withering glare. He said, "I'm not doing this for you."

22

PIES WAS utterly exhausted and in need of some solid sleep. But as he drove toward Faigy's building to pick up the key to the basement apartment, he balked. In the back of his mind, he was still unsure of how to proceed with the idea of living in the beautiful woman's building. He knew that he didn't deserve even the slimmest of prospects for the potential love and warmth that someone of Faigy's character could provide.

Instead, Pies managed to eek out a couple of hours of sleep in his pickup truck while parked on a side street near Indian Boundary Park—just three blocks from Faigy's place.

He was awoken by a phone call from Bertena. One of her refrigerators had stopped working. Once he made the short trip to Evanston, it took only a few minutes to recognize the issue with the fridge, a loose refrigerant connection, and fix it.

He considered driving back to Edison Park to see Milena once again but thought better of it for now. Her young baker would have already warned her that Pies had shown up the day before. Knowing Milena like he did since he was a kid, Pies assumed that she'd be defensive, angry, and unable to listen to reason. Pies really did not want to physically kidnap Milena and whisk her off to Wisconsin, even if it were for her own good.

He had to preliminarily go forward with the plan to burgle the mansion in Barrington Hills...at least for now.

*

PIES DROVE by a postage-stamp-sized used car sales/rental lot on Highway 14 in Fox River Grove. He made two passes just to make sure the employee in the window was truly by himself. Pies could see the man standing inside the tiny building, which was once an old gas station structure. Certain that the middle-aged man in the tight-fitting, black golf shirt was unaided, Pies parked the Ford F-150 three blocks away in a grocery-store parking lot near the intersection of 14 and Route 22. He tucked the truck in on the far fringes of the lot next to some other older cars, all with "for sale" signs in the windows. He rifled under his truck's seat and came up holding the original "for sale" sign that was in the truck's window when he purchased it on Harlem Avenue. Pies used the ignition key and scratched out two of the sign's phone-number digits, and then he placed the sign in the front window. No one would be able to make out the entire phone number to call if they were interested in buying the truck.

He left the pickup truck and walked to the tiny car lot, and he slowly began perusing the merchandise—fifteen cars of varying degrees of quality, all parked at various angles. Within forty seconds, he heard, "Hey, how's it going, my friend. What a bee-autiful day."

Pies smiled, looked the approaching salesman's way, and said, "This is a nice car."

The salesman, a toothy middle-aged man, picked up his pace as he noticed that Pies's hand was gently resting on a newer, four-door, black Mercedes-Benz E-Class.

"Oh, yes, indeed. Yes, it is. How about a test drive?" asked the salesman.

"Yeah, maybe. Maybe," said Pies as he sauntered slowly around, put his hand in his pocket, and eyed the other vehicles. "This the only Mercedes?"

"At the moment, yes, but we get new luxury cars all the time. Goes with the territory. You know, being located so close to Barrington Hills."

"You rent cars, too? Your sign says that," said Pies.

"Sure do, sir. Sure do. But, oh, not the Mercedes. Sorry, we can't rent that one. It's only for sale. Too risky to rent."

Pies let his hand come free of his pocket, and the salesman immediately noticed the fat roll of bills in it. "You sure about that?" asked Pies.

The salesman tossed a friendly nod for Pies to come into the office. Once they were inside, the salesman buzzed around the tiny counter, placed a half-eaten sandwich out of view, and said, "We can always cater to our clients as we see fit."

"I just need it for a week. I want to impress the in-laws coming in from San Francisco," said Pies. "They're sort of, ah, upper-crusty." His eyes casually surveyed the office and landed on the surveillance camera attached to the wall up near the ceiling in back of the counter. "My Jeep won't do the trick," he continued, with a wink.

"Oh, of course. Sure thing. Sure thing. Ah...I can go on a one week rental at, ah...."

Pies fanned out some crisp hundreds on the counter. "Would twelve do it?"

"Cool, cool, cool. Yeah, I can do that. Yes. Just have to do some paperwork, and then we'll... Oh, I'll need a credit card, too. In case there's any problems. You understand. Unforeseen stuff, you know."

"Of course," said Pies, as he extracted a shiny American Express Black Card from his back pocket. He handed the card to the impressed salesman, and the man began to handwrite a rental agreement form.

As the salesman looked down, Pies scanned about the tiny space once again. Something on the wall caught his attention, and he leaned a little to his right to get a better view. The white cable exiting the surveillance camera dangled freely alongside the edge of a cheap shelving unit. The camera wasn't attached to anything—it was just for show.

"Okay, Mr., ah...?" The salesman checked the name on the American Express card, "Mr. Brosillino."

"Call me Brosi," said Pies with a grin.

"Brosi? I like that. Cool name," said the grinning salesman before he went back to completing the form.

Pies had surreptitiously snagged the wallet that sagged from Brosi's pocket back at the diner on Higgins when they bumped shoulders. He concealed the wallet among the printed photographs the Outfit guys had given him. After he had returned to his pickup truck, he rifled through the wallet, found the card, removed it, and tossed the wallet from his car window as he drove past the diner on his way from the meeting. He figured the Amex Black Card could come in handy as he went about his reconnaissance run. Pies was careful to leave the $900 in cash that was in the wallet so that if or when it was found by Brosi or one of his cohorts, the missing Amex card wouldn't be noticed. Not immediately, anyway.

"I'll need your driver's license, Brosi," said the salesman.

Pies counted out five more hundreds and said, "I lost mine last week. Waiting on the replacement."

*

PIES SAT casually in the driver's seat of the elegant Mercedes on the car lot. After he adjusted the seat and mirrors, he called Milena at home once again, without an answer. He tried the bakery, too, but she wasn't there either, and he didn't want to leave a message with the baker. He couldn't trust that the message would get through properly. He put his cell phone in the center console, cranked the engine to life, and placed the car into drive. As he rolled away, the salesman waved.

"Take care, Brosi. See you next week," called out the salesman.

Pies sped from the lot heading east on Highway 14. Once he was in the quaint village of Barrington, he found the commuter train station's main parking lot. Within minutes, he located two other black four-door Mercedes E-Class vehicles. Stealthily, and using only a quarter from the spare change he carried in his front pocket, Pies went about moving the plates from one vehicle to the next in a three-vehicle plate switch. If Brosi discovered the missing Amex card and called it in to the credit card company, the car lot would be notified of the crime, and Pies didn't want the original, hot license plates on the car as he worked in the Barrington Hills area.

*

Pies guided the luxury vehicle west onto Otis Road in Barrington Hills. Less than a mile up the road he took a right onto Wakelin Circle. Both sides of Wakelin Circle, like many roads in this area, were lined with ten-foot-high hedgerows that obscured the view of what lay behind the greenery. Soon, though, the hedgerows on both sides of the road gave way to open and gently rolling hills.

Pies pulled the car to the side of the roadway, glided to a stop, put the car in park, and took in what surrounded him.

Up ahead, less than a quarter of a mile away, were two massive mansions, one on each side of where the road came to an end at a wide cul-de-sac. The two homes were enormous and similar in color and design. Both were constructed of brick and limestone, and each was created in a wide, two-story-tall, V configuration. The front entrance of each house was located in the center of the concave side of the V.

The estate on the left had white, wooden paddock fencing that stretched in all directions as far as he could see, with the exception of wrought iron at the principal vehicle entrance gate. The white fencing enclosed the outbuildings, including a modern, metal horse barn. There was also a long gravel driveway that led to that same horse barn, this with its own wooden gate next to the road. The estate's paddock fencing wove onward, nearly to the line of trees at the rear of the property. Beyond those trees was the target mansion, the one that actually concerned Pies. At this hour, as the sun still shone, the targeted mansion couldn't even be seen through the thick foliage.

The estate on the right side of Wakelin Circle had dark-brown paddock fencing and similar outbuildings, and what looked like an equine training facility. Pies could make out the sight of two oval, fenced-in enclosures. He couldn't quite see all the details of the place on the right because the property was partially obscured by smaller trees that were planted neatly all about the perimeter.

It was quiet here in this corner of the Chicago area.

Pies felt the soft, low vibration first and then heard the gentle clip-clops of an approaching horse. He watched to the right as a dark-brown Arabian horse effortlessly sprinted toward the roadway. The horse was safely enclosed inside the brown-fenced paddock. As the muscular animal neared Pies, it slowed to a stop directly next to the narrow lane and poked its head over the fence. The beautiful beast cocked its head and looked directly at Pies for a moment and then took off, gleefully prancing about, running aimless circles in the sunshine.

Pies had completed burglary jobs in the well-heeled North Shore area of Chicago before, but he'd never once witnessed anything quite like what he was seeing in Barrington Hills. The North Shore was beautiful in its own right, but cramped by comparison. Pies imagined that the rolling landscape of the English countryside would probably look a lot like what he was seeing now. What amazed him most was that all that he saw was less than an hour's drive from the city of Chicago.

The extra space he was witnessing wasn't what Pies had imagined it would be, either. He figured the homeowners would let their surrounding lands grow to a wild state, allowing nature to run its course. But it was nothing of the sort. Everything within his sightline here on Wakelin Circle was manicured to near perfection.

Something in the near distance caught his attention.

The side of the well-maintained barn on the right side of the road, which was positioned on the edge of the horse training facility, had an enormous hand-painted rabbit on it. The painting was thirty feet high and forty feet across. Depicted was a rabbit with its head tucked down tight to its body, ears back, its eyes watery, squinting in the imaginary breeze that was bending back the long green grass blades the animal was nestled amongst. It was obvious that a professional had painted the piece. There was so much detail in the painting, in the animal's natural-appearing fur, which looked wind-blown, and the expressive eyes. The entire image radiated professionalism. In the fading sunlight the painting looked more like a photograph.

Pies's mind drifted as he sat there taking in the sight of the natural beauty, as well as the static artistic wonder of the oversized wall mural.

He couldn't help but think of Vicki Chlebek, the artist.

He imagined how she would look working on that rabbit painting. He could see her now. She'd be covered nearly head-to-toe in colorful paint splatters, her dark-colored hair tucked behind her ears and her stunningly beautiful blue eyes locked on her task with a laser focus.

He detected movement on the left and noticed a silver-colored vehicle nose out from the main gate of the estate located there. The car hesitated for just a moment and then drove onto the lane and headed toward him.

Pies tilted his face down, as if looking at his cell phone, and kept his peripheral vision on the silver Audi SUV as it rolled past. Behind the wheel was a gray-haired man who didn't even look Pies's way.

Once the SUV vanished from his side-view mirror, Pies placed the Mercedes into drive and edged forward. The end of the road, literally, approached up ahead. He needed to scope out the house on the left side of the cul-de-sac, here at the end of Wakelin Circle. It wasn't the house with the item that needed to be stolen for the Outfit, but it sat several hundred yards to the rear of the targeted mansion. He knew this because the Google map's satellite view had clued him into the fact.

Pies simply had to get a feel for his surroundings. He'd done the same type of thing when he was working for the Zielinski burglary crew in Edison Park. Scouting runs were the hallmark of Pies's criminal professionalism. That was *his* artistry. He'd never just walk into a job without first learning everything he could about what he'd be up against. Once he had the proper information, he could plan—properly.

At the wide cul-de-sac—the circumference was forty feet, the parkway manicured and tree-filled—he pushed the button that would raise his lightly tinted driver's side window and swung to the right side of the cul-de-sac circle first. He did this so that if anyone was observing or any possible camera was pointed in his direction, it would be more difficult to see him through the tinted windshield and all the closed vehicle windows, as he circled from right to left.

Pies passed the right-hand driveway, then noted the address number—221—on the left-side mansion's wrought-iron entry gate, from which the Audi SUV had emerged. He noticed something else, too.

A very tall Caucasian man dressed in a drab-green work uniform, complete with a brown jacket, stood just beyond the wrought iron gate of the estate at 221 Wakelin Circle. The worker rolled a fifty-gallon garbage can across the narrow asphalt driveway. He didn't seem to be paying any attention to Pies's car, but as the man stooped to pick up a couple of large sticks that'd fallen next to the driveway, his shoulder-holstered, chrome-plated, semiautomatic pistol dangled into view from under his jacket.

Pies remained calm, and, while retaining his slow speed, he kept driving and completed his loop of the cul-de-sac. He headed toward Otis Road once again, but he kept his eyes on his rearview mirror and the driveway at 221 Wakelin Circle. Once he was 150 feet down the road, he watched as a second man, this one in a dark suit, stood alongside the armed, supposed groundskeeper. Pies thought he could see the leathery edge of a holster under this man's arm, too. Both men looked in Pies's direction as he faded from their view.

"What in the hell was that?" Pies whispered to no one.

23

To MAKE the most of his recon run on the targeted property, Pies required the benefit of nighttime and the dark that the streetlight-free Barrington Hills afforded him. Darkness was an important component in the professional burglar's tool belt. To bide his time until darkness fully arrived, though, Pies would have to spend an hour sipping coffee while seated in the booth of a busy, twenty-four-hour pancake house on Barrington Road near I-90. Conveniently enough, the restaurant was located on the same ocean of asphalt as a sporting-goods superstore. He needed to pick up some supplies there before his real work began.

Ninety minutes later, seated in the luxury car and parked near the sporting-goods store, Pies activated the dome light. He carefully took a brief inventory of the items he had just purchased, which now lay piled on the front passenger seat. He wanted to make sure he hadn't forgotten anything.

The largest item was a white cardboard box that contained a spring-loaded, plastic BB gun. There was also a six-inch-tall bottle of white, plastic BBs; a black Magic Marker; and an eight-inch-long flashlight. Three black T-shirts and three pairs of new black-colored boxer-briefs, some batteries, and a small pair of cheap binoculars rounded out his purchases.

Earlier the man inside the sporting-goods superstore had shown Pies how to load the BB gun, so he got to work on filling the ammunition clip. He opened the box and drew out the black-colored toy gun with the bright orange-tipped barrel. He popped the clip from the pistol and laid both on the dashboard. He then unscrewed the pour-top cap off of the BB bottle and placed it and the bottle on the dashboard. He uncapped the Magic Marker and placed that on the dashboard, too, and then grabbed up the empty plastic bag and laid it flat in the palm of his hand. He reached over with his free hand and poured about twenty or so BBs from the bottle onto the plastic bag. He put the bottle down, picked up the marker, and began covering the white BBs with the Magic Marker. Once the BBs were all painted black, Pies gently blew on them so they'd dry more quickly.

He deliberately laid the plastic bag holding the now-black BBs on the passenger seat, so as to not spill them, and snatched the gun's clip off the dashboard. He proceeded to carefully fill the clip with the blackened BBs.

*

BACK ON Otis Road in Barrington Hills, Pies drove past a 1960s ranch-style house perched only one hundred feet off the road. There were still some more-modest-appearing homes in the area, like this ranch-style structure, but not many. Most of these older homes, he discovered on his fact-finding mission, were found closer to the roads for some reason, with the vast majority of their land to the rear of the building. This particular ranch home had an alarm company sign planted next to its driveway.

Pies set about running a quick test.

He noticed there were no lights on at the house, with the exception of the illuminated lamppost near where the front circular drive met the front door's walkway. There were also five plastic-bagged newspapers scattered about the driveway. The home's exterior layout seemed to be an optimal arrangement for what he had in mind, and it appeared that no one was home, either. On his second pass by the house, Pies stopped the Mercedes, rolled down his driver's side window, took aim, and fired off a plastic BB. The BB ricocheted off the brick next to the front-facing picture window with a "snap" and landed in the bushes. Because he had used the black marker on the BBs, they'd never be discovered wherever they wound up.

"Come on," he said to himself as he yanked the gun's slide back to reload the gun for another attempt.

As he fired the gun the second time, the black BB smacked loudly off the front picture window and bounced, once again, into the bushes. The window didn't break because Pies knew the gun wasn't packing enough power to do that from this distance, and that was fine with him.

The instant the window was struck by the BB, Pies began to silently count in his head. He got to forty-five, and the alarm finally activated with an ear-splitting, rhythmic, electric-sounding whine. Pies casually drove west on Otis Road for exactly one minute, gauged by the car's dashboard clock, turned around in the next driveway he could locate, and headed back. Once he had passed by the home and continued for exactly one minute in the opposite direction, he pulled a quick K-turn on the desolate Otis Road and headed back again. He encountered no other cars once his test began. He drove past the house with the alarm still sounding and continued for one minute more, turned, then headed back. As he got to within three hundred feet of the house this time, though, a blacked-out Barrington Hills police car pulled quickly into the circular driveway of the ranch-style home and stopped.

Pies didn't even look in the cop's direction as he drove the luxury car past the test house. He didn't need to, because he was now aware of how quickly the police responded to alarms in the area. It probably wouldn't leave him a lot of time to operate and do what had to be done at the targeted mansion.

His smartphone, resting in the center console, began to ring. Pies was startled. He didn't recognize the incoming number on the phone, and yet he answered anyway but did not speak. He just listened.

"Jakubowski?" asked the breathless man's voice on the other end of the line. "Hey, Jakubowski, you there?"

"Who is this?"

"Christ. I'm glad this is actually your number. I thought maybe you gave me a fake. It's Gunther."

"Gunther?" asked Pies, mildly confused.

"Gunther. From the halfway. The Nazi."

"Right," said Pies.

"We got a problem."

"Yeah?"

"That parole officer, his name…"

"Ramirez," said Pies.

"Yeah, yeah, Ramirez. He was here tonight, and I wasn't around. Jenny told him that you don't live here anymore."

"Damn it," said Pies.

"He just called me back. Like just now, he called. You got to be on Belmont Avenue at 7 A.M. tomorrow. First thing, he said. Man, I'm so sorr—"

Pies hung up and placed the phone back into the center console. He'd show up at the parole offices on Belmont Avenue as requested. However, he still had work to do.

24

THE MANSION on Chapin Way made the two homes beyond the trees out back on Wakelin Circle look quaint by comparison. Even in the darkness, Pies marveled at the sheer size of the place as he cautiously walked the perimeter, two hundred feet from the main building. He had parked the Mercedes on the gravel drive that led from Chapin Way to the property's horse barn. That was a full quarter-mile from the main house. He'd have to chance the police, a private security firm, or possibly a passing neighbor seeing the car. And even if that did happen, the police officer or passersby would most likely not pay much attention to the parked luxury car. He needed to get a closer eye on what he was up against. Something had been bothering him since he glanced at the real estate photos at the diner with Panzera. Why were there no photos of the rest of the interior of the house?

There were no distinct pathways here—no cement, crushed stone, or simple wear into the earth—linking the horse barn to the main house, If he could, he wanted to avoid tripping any motion detectors hidden on the expanse of the manicured grounds. Conversely, his confidence began to grow with each successive pass as he started to walk tighter and tighter circles around the enormous mansion. No automatic lighting systems tripped, and no one showed up to investigate.

The closer he got to the building, the more he felt sure that there were no hidden electronic exterior security measures in place. Not even security cameras, typically affixed to structures on the corners of an edifice in order to get the best visual coverage. There were no evident hallmarks of any surveillance systems whatsoever.

"This isn't right," said Pies aloud. "This is just weird."

The house was at least thirty thousand square feet under the one roof. It consisted of what appeared to be two full stories and an empty Olympic-sized pool in back, with four tennis courts adjacent to the pool. The pool house, a miniaturized, one-story-tall version of the main building, was larger than most single-family homes. The only difference was this— the windows on the pool house, and, for that matter, the guesthouse out front closer to the road, were covered in plastic-like blackout material. He couldn't get a look into either building.

The main house's exterior consisted of large limestone blocks, front and back, and eight soaring limestone columns four apiece on the front and rear facades. The place was not that old, no more than five or ten years at most, but it had the look of a stately one-hundred-year-old library.

It didn't appear as if anyone was inside the main building, either. Pies had been roaming around for the past few hours, and then he simply watched the home while seated on the edge of the deep end of the empty pool. He saw no movement inside the structure that entire time, but that could've been due to some of the windows being covered in blackout material. He wasn't completely sure, though, and he didn't want to chance getting too close to the main house just yet.

There were a few dim lights on inside the house that he could see —two lights to be exact. They were located in the front portion of the massive building and bracketed the front doors in the main hallway. They could be seen through the sidelights of the front doors and, just barely, from out in back of the mansion, where he sat at the pool. The lights didn't give off a whole lot of illumination.

Pies could've shined the flashlight inside the place, but that would only work to heighten his chances of being spotted. He wanted to do this right and take his time.

As Pies continued to observe the mansion, the dim interior lights turned off. No person hit the light switches, though. He figured the lights were on timers and clicked on and off to give pause to any un-professional burglars scoping the premises.

The grounds for the estate were well over one hundred acres in total. Pies counted four structures on the property—the mansion, the darkened pool house, a large horse barn (sans horses, and look-ing as if it had never been used), and a small, darkened guesthouse that was seventy feet off of Chapin Way near the main driveway's opening.

After hearing Sam Panzera and his cronies describe the possibly insurmountable security measures he'd be up against, Pies began to think they were given poor information.

Or they were lying.

Was this some sort of a set up?

Pies got up from the pool's edge, stretched his legs and back, and then casually jogged to his car. He opened the driver's side door and reached inside to retrieve his BB gun. He cocked the gun, loaded a black plastic BB into the firing chamber, and veered closer and closer to the main house. When he was one hundred feet away, he fired the BB gun at a second floor window, but missed and struck the limestone instead.

"Shit," he said softly.

Pies reloaded, and the second fired BB struck a window with some force, but the glass didn't yield. He reloaded the BB gun and fired at a first floor window, striking it on the first try this time, and with the same result.

Pies turned and trudged back to his car, counting silently in his head as he moved along. It was difficult to keep track of his count due to his ever-growing exhaustion. He did, however, succeeded in getting to three hundred before he ceased his tally. He heard no audible alarms cracking the silent night air. After he finally reached the Mercedes, he got in and started the engine. He rolled down his driver's window, listened carefully, and still could not detect any audible alarms whatsoever. That could just mean that there was a silent alarm in the main building, and the police would be on the way.

Or not.

There was something that just wasn't sitting right with Pies during this entire scouting run. Why weren't any alarms set off during the course of his recon?

Pies reversed the car off of the gravel drive and rolled slowly forward on Chapin Way toward the home's main driveway entrance and guesthouse. He stopped the car, opened the door with the BB gun in his free hand, stood, racked a BB into the chamber, and fired a shot over the roof of the car and at a front-facing window of the guesthouse. His aim was getting better. The BB hit its mark and loudly pinged off the glass on the first try.

Pies got back inside the car and drove away. After one minute he turned around and drove past the estate's entrance. He repeated his back and forth scrutiny of the estate, waiting for the Barrington Hills Police to arrive. If they did, they most likely wouldn't even look twice at the expensive luxury car driving past them. Pies never saw any activity at all, not even after ten minutes.

It was 3:36 A.M. and Pies needed sleep, but there was still something he had to do.

Naomi Gott and her son Jason were safely out of the picture, but he still hadn't met face-to-face with Milena.

He drove on Highway 14 toward the Northwest Side of Chicago.

Doing the Chapin Way recon was a required backup plan to keep the Outfit members appeased until his ultimate action could be put into place. Now he truly knew enough about the property to accurately report back to the Outfit on what he had come up against, if things came to that.

He had just enough time to drop in on Milena Chlebek, apologize, and give her the information she'd need to check into the lake house in Delavan, Wisconsin. Once she was safely there, and after his own 7 A.M. meeting at the parole offices, Pies could circle back to Delavan, and he and Milena could work on a more permanent plan to get away from the Chicago area.

It would all work out.

25

I T WAS 4:27 A.M., and the highly fatigued Pies stood on the front
porch of Milena Chlebek's home. The lack of sleep was causing
his muscles to physically quiver and tremble and his eyelids to droop.
He raised his hand to lightly tap, but stopped short of his knuckles
meeting the wooden door.

He initially considered ringing the doorbell, and then he had second thoughts, believing the chime would startle Milena. He didn't
want that. He didn't want Milena to be thrown off balance by his
early visit. She'd be surprised enough to see him at all, let alone at
this early hour.

He bounded down the steps and went around the house to the
back door. Even though she had the new professional baker working for her since Blaze passed on, the store's operations would still
require her to keep early hours. Pies knew she'd be awake by now.

The first place she would go once she was up and around, he reckoned, would be the kitchen. Milena loved her morning coffee. Pies recalled once when he was quite young, Milena serving him and Vicki
some of her morning Joe. Of course, he and Vicki were little kids
at the time, so the Joe was created mostly with milk and sugar and
just a splash of actual coffee to darken the beverage.

The home's windows and doors were closed tight, but Pies could
still hear dishes clinking inside and water running in the kitchen
sink. He carefully ascended the wooden steps that led to the back

kitchen door, and before he got to the fourth step, the water stopped running, and a second later the door partially creaked opened.

An angry-looking Milena, dressed for the day, stood with her left hand on the doorknob.

"Jakub, no. No. Not now. I'm not ready. I'm not ready for you, Jakub," she said with her Polish-accented English. "You go now."

Pies got to the top of the landing. "Mrs. Chlebek, I have to—"

"Jakub, please."

"Mrs. Chlebek, you're in danger," uttered Pies.

She squinted her eyes and pushed all the way out of the house and onto the small wooden landing. There was no more than three feet of space between them. To validate her anger, she allowed the screen door to slap closed loudly.

She eyed Pies carefully, indignantly.

"You don't think I know that, Jakub? Oh, yes, the man. The man follows me. I see him. Him with the...the...with the phone camera. He thinks he's very smart, but *glupi* he is. I see him."

"Those people want to hurt you," said Pies softly.

"Oh, he wants to hurt me? The...the man. The man I see with that Rebecca woman, the one who was married to that...that criminal Bast Zielinski? Let him try. I am not afraid."

Pies was taken aback by Milena's brazen attitude, and he wasn't sure what to do or say. "Please, Mrs. Chlebek, we have to find somewhere else for you to stay...I've got a place in Wis—"

"*Nie.* I will not. Now go. I'm not ready for you. I told you already. I'm not ready. I can't do this now."

And with that, Milena opened the screen door, went into the kitchen, and without looking back slammed the main door on Pies.

Before Pies took the steps down to the ground level, he could hear Milena weeping inside the house.

He exited her property as silently as he could and stumbled toward the parked Mercedes.

As he tripped along, his mind began to reel out a series of quick images.

Horrible images.

His mind's eye flipped from one ugly scenario to the next: Milena being strangled. Milena being stabbed. Milena getting into her car and being approached by masked gunmen who take aim and shoot.

"Stop," Pies called out, as he came to a halt on the sidewalk. "Stop...," he continued quietly, as he closed his eyes tight. "Please..."

*

WHEN HE opened his eyes, he was sitting in his old two-door car— from five years ago—and not the Mercedes.

The sun was out.

He jolted backward and away from the steering wheel as his confusion grew. His eyes scanned the interior of the car as if not believing what he was looking at.

"Vicki?" he said, as he pulled hard at the door handle and fell out of the car.

A passing van nearly struck him and honked its horn in displeasure as the frantic and now kneeling Pies tried to right himself.

Pies stood and sprinted in the direction of Chlebeks' Bakery. He hurriedly cut through the tiny park next to the train station. There were no pedestrians or moving vehicles in sight, and it was eerily still outside. Pies crossed over the railroad tracks, ran a half block to the alley opening, and turned left, angling toward the rear door for the apartment above the bakery.

He reached the exterior door and pulled hard on the handle. The door wouldn't budge, so he tried and tried, until finally the door gave. Once inside the building, he loped up the stairs that led to the apartment's kitchen door. He rammed his shoulder into the door at the top of the stairs repeatedly until it splintered inward.

Once he entered the kitchen, Pies noticed that Vicki's paintings were still stacked against nearly every wall in the small space, but there was no furniture. He moved through the living room and toward the apartment's front door.

He paused a few inches from the door and held his breath for a moment. As he breathed again, it was deep and shuddering. He reached out for the door handle with his right hand—and inexplicably there was a .38 caliber revolver grasped tightly in it.

He tried and tried but could not shake the gun free.

Pies stopped trying to dislodge the pistol and just stared at the weapon as tears welled in his eyes. "No," he said softly. "No."

And then, as if being controlled by an unseen force, his thumb cocked back the hammer on the gun. He tried to fight whatever had a hold on him, but it wasn't working. His body was then forced to first take a step forward and then a side step to the right. "Stop... No, don't do this." His body slammed tightly to the wall next to the front door.

The unseen force raised his gun hand and aimed the .38 revolver head-high for whoever might dare enter the apartment through the apartment's front door.

"No, please, Vicki. Use the other door. Use the other door," he cried out. "Don't make me. Please..."

He heard the front street-side door open below, and he repeated, "Please!"

Footsteps began creaking up the front stairs leading to the apartment. They were slow and methodical footfalls, almost mocking in their timing. A step, a long hesitation, and then another and another, until whoever was coming into the apartment's front entry was just on the other side of the quarter-sawn oak door.

Pies closed his eyes tight after he heard the soft growl of an approaching city bus down on busy Northwest Highway.

"No, please... Damn it...," said Pies in a whisper, as tears streamed down his face. "Don't..."

Pies tried to lower the handgun but his body still wouldn't allow him to. His arm was locked into place. He frantically tried and tried to lower it without any luck.

A thought came to him and his eyes brightened for just a flash. He couldn't lower the gun, but he could still control his left hand. He looked down at that hand and made a fist and then relaxed it. "Yes... Yes!"

Pies, with the gun still raised and ready to shoot, reached out and grasped the front door's knob with his left hand, twisted it, smiled widely, and yanked the door fully open.

"Vicki, run!"

There was no one on the other side of the door.

With his right arm still extended painfully in front of him, gun at the ready, Pies leaned forward and craned his neck around the open doorjamb and peered down the front steps leading to the glass-paneled door, vestibule, and sidewalk—there was no one there, either.

All was quiet.

Pies smiled through his tears, sighed deeply, and then chuckled, sadly. "Oh, my God, thank you… Oh, my God… Oh, my God…"

Then he peered at his right hand and saw a slight wafting of smoke coming from the barrel of the gun. Terror immediately overcame Pies as he shook the gun free from his grasp. The gun thumped to the floor.

"No."

He crumpled to his knees and wept. He leaned his head back, pressed his eyes closed as hard as he possibly could, and said, "I'm sorry. I'm so sorry."

*

WHEN HE leaned his head forward and opened his eyes once again, he was sitting in the driver's seat of the idling Mercedes Benz that was still parked in front of Milena's house.

The sun hadn't fully come up yet.

Confusion and terror washed over him, but soon he settled down and took many deep breaths. He peered all around, but no one was out at this hour.

That's when he remembered that he needed to head down to Belmont Avenue to see what awaited him with Parole Officer Ramirez.

After finally settling enough to safely drive, the exhausted Pies guided the Mercedes toward Ozanam Avenue, and as he stopped at the intersection where Rebecca Zielinski and her daughter Itty-Bitty lived, he looked in the direction of their home.

Sam Panzera, wearing a long-sleeved button-up shirt, which was opened to reveal a white T-shirt beneath, got into a dark-colored BMW—and Rebecca, hair tussled and dressed only in a robe, waved to him from her front porch.

Pies pulled over and out of view of Rebecca's home after clearing the intersection. He turned his car lights off and leaned away from his driver's side window. A few seconds later, Panzera drove by in his BMW. Once he passed, Pies straightened back up in his seat, turned his lights back on, and followed.

Panzera turned left on Ozanam Avenue and headed south. Pies got to within one hundred feet of Panzera's BMW, and he was able to make out the vanity plate number on the mobster's car and made a mental note of it—LB901.

The BMW took a right on Devon Avenue and headed west into Park Ridge. A few blocks later it turned right on Washington Street. Panzera was circling back, Pies was sure of it.

Pies pulled over again at Washington and Arthur Streets so he wouldn't be spotted so quickly and he waited a few seconds. He continued on and saw up ahead, a block and a half away, that Panzera turned right once again.

"Why's he doing this?" Pies wondered aloud. Maybe he knew he was being followed and was being coy?

Pies drove past the street where Panzera had turned so that he wouldn't spook the man in the BMW. He made a right at the next street. Pies got back to Ozanam Avenue in time to see the back end of Panzera's BMW glide across Ozanam and out of view. The car was basically going back toward Rebecca's street.

Pies turned right on Ozanam Avenue and glanced left as he passed the street where the BMW was now parked, twenty feet down, and at the right curb.

Pies drove for two more blocks and made a left and then another quick left. After rolling for a few seconds, he pulled to the curb and stopped. He was now on the same street as Rebecca Zielinski's home, but one block farther away, and one and a half blocks from Panzera in his BMW.

His eyes were hovering at half-mast, his exhaustion causing him to nearly shut down completely. He slapped his own face once, hard, and willed himself to stay awake.

Up ahead, on the right, Rebecca pushed out of her home's screen door. She was dressed in a sweatshirt and blue jeans now, and her hair was pulled back into a ponytail. She hurried toward her small, four-door, copper-colored Mercedes-Benz. She got in, started the car, and drove up to the next intersection, away from Pies, and turned right. A couple of seconds later, the BMW followed her, rolling right through the four-way stop sign at the intersection.

Pies pulled ahead as quickly as he could and turned right at the same intersection. He watched, as in the near distance, the BMW turned left over the Metra railroad tracks. He couldn't see Rebecca's car at this point, and he had to assume it was just ahead of Panzera's BMW.

Pies goosed the gas pedal of the powerful luxury car, sped past Milena Chlebek's home, and closed the distance between himself and the BMW.

It was still too early for the morning rush, so traffic was pretty light as Pies turned right onto Northwest Highway and followed Panzera's lead. Pies shadowed at a safe distance and kept an eye on the BMW. If the BMW stopped, Pies presumed that Rebecca was stopping, too. He couldn't even see her car from his current vantage point.

After traveling only five blocks, the BMW jerked to the right curb, parked, and extinguished its lights. Pies did the same, tucking his Mercedes behind a minivan three hundred feet from the BMW. He was parked next to a one-story commercial building.

Pies couldn't see either Panzera or Rebecca from where he was, and that was okay. His car would be out of their line of sight. Pies got out of his car and stepped toward the commercial storefront. He stood under the building's maroon-colored awning, pressed his back to the brick wall, and observed.

A block ahead, Rebecca walked away from her car and up to a three-story apartment building. The place looked a lot like the half-way house Pies was supposed to be residing in.

To Pies it appeared as if Rebecca took a set of keys from her purse and opened the outer door of the building. She then disappeared inside.

Pies could see Panzera slowly head bob from side to side, craning to see what Rebecca was doing.

"What the hell is this?" asked Pies of no one. He was confused but had to understand why Panzera would be following his own lover from her home to an apartment at this hour. Nothing was making sense right now.

A couple of minutes later, Rebecca emerged from the apartment building, stuffing something inside her purse and zipping it closed. She got back into her car and drove away—but the BMW didn't fol-low. Once she was out of sight, Panzera got out of his car and walked up to the apartment building. He tugged on the locked exterior door and then cupped his hands around his face and peered through the door's glass. He backed away, checked the names on the outer door buzzer system, and then walked around the side of the building and out of view for about thirty seconds. When he reemerged, he quick-ened his pace. He opened the trunk of his car but didn't locate what he was looking for. He slammed the trunk closed, got into his car, and angrily drove away.

Pies scrambled into his car, drove up the two blocks closer to the apartment building, and parked. He got out of the Mercedes, and as he walked to the apartment building, an older man in a gray work uniform pushed his way out the front door.

"Hey, man. Have to hate these early starts, huh?" asked Pies.

"Got that right, buddy. Have a good one," said the man as he walked away.

Pies slid into the secured interior vestibule of the building without the man even noticing. There were nine mailboxes on the wall in the vestibule, only one really interested him: the one with the name IB Gorniak in apartment #1.

Gorniak was Rebecca's maiden name before she married Bast Zielinski. Pies knew this because he and Rebecca had grown up together. The IB stood for her daughter Itty-Bitty, he was sure of that.

It wasn't quite 5:15 A.M., and Pies still had time to investigate. He pulled the lock-bump from his pocket and made his way through the interior vestibule door without much trouble. The many-layered cooking smells that Pies had grown accustomed to when visiting buildings like this greeted him directly. He could hear a few radios softly playing music as some of the other tenants prepared to welcome their days.

Apartment #1's door was right there on the first floor, at the rear and down the main carpeted hallway.

Pies gained access to the tiny apartment within seconds. He took a long look around the dimly lit one-bedroom apartment after he quietly closed the door.

The living room was outfitted with overstuffed furniture, like from the early 2000s. It was dark-green, large, padded furniture with rather wide armrests. It was nothing fancy. There was a sofa and a matching upholstered side chair. A coffee table and two end tables bracketed the other pieces. The furniture emitted a certain chemical smell that he couldn't quite indentify.

Pies leaned to his left and could see inside the tiny bedroom. There was a queen bed, a dresser, and side table. He poked his head into the bedroom and peered toward the empty closet. He then entered and opened the top dresser drawer and then all the drawers—they were empty, too. The bed had a thick comforter neatly spread over it. Pies pulled the heavy, and rather lumpy, comforter back, and he noticed there were no sheets on the bed.

The kitchen was next, and it was spotless, as if no food had been prepared there in quite some time. Pies walked in and opened the fridge and then the freezer compartment. Both were empty. He tried the cabinets, and all of them were vacant, the drawers, too.

He went back into the living room and stood there, wondering what in the hell was going on. The adrenaline that percolated to the surface while following Rebecca and Panzera had sharply elbowed him to a more wakeful state.

Something on the floor, near the end of the dark-green sofa, caught his attention. It looked as if the padding of the piece was out of place and dangling underneath. He edged in a bit closer and knelt to get a better look.

26

THE BLEARY-EYED Pies sat all alone in the lobby waiting area of the parole offices on Belmont Avenue. It was 7:01 A.M. His only companions were the twenty neatly arranged empty chairs that lined two of the rooms' walls.

The door that led to the offices in back popped open, and Parole Officer Ramirez leaned out.

"Jakubowski," he said and motioned with his fingers for Pies to follow.

The moment Pies cleared the interior doorway, Ramirez grabbed his shoulder and spun him around, "Hands behind your head. Lean against the wall."

"What's... What is this?" asked Pies as he placed his hands behind his head.

Ramirez shoved him against the wall. "You've been violated, Mr. Jakubowski. I told you what would happen if you broke my rules," said Ramirez, sort of matter-of-factly.

The parole officer quickly frisked Pies for weapons. He was clean. Pies had left the lock-bump and some extra cash in the parked Mercedes. Once Pies's hands were cuffed, Ramirez lumbered over to his desk and collected his keys, some paperwork, and his cheap sports jacket, and then he motioned for Pies to follow him.

Pies, with his eyes cast downward, walked through the near-empty offices. None of the five other officers working at that hour even gave him a glance.

Ramirez grabbed Pies by the elbow and they walked from the building and into the parking lot. Pies was led to Ramirez's official car, a silver four-door Crown Victoria.

All Pies could think about was Milena being murdered by the Outfit.

That would be a certainty now that he was headed back to Stateville. He had failed miserably.

Pies gently balked and refused to move. "Please. Can't we—"

"Was I not clear the other day? I stopped in the halfway house, and they're telling me you don't even stay there. The Nazi's got some questions coming his way, too," said Ramirez as he opened the rear car door. "Watch your head."

*

THE CHICAGO Police district house was only a few miles away. It was the notorious "Town Hall" station on Addison Street, mere blocks from the "The Friendly Confines" of Wrigley Field. Things had been cleaned up in recent decades at the 19th District, but in the past, Town Hall was well known as a place where recently arrested suspects would go to disappear for days, until they resurfaced with healing bruises and injuries—and solid guilty plea deals in place.

Ramirez delivered Pies to the smattering of bored police officers behind the main desk. For the next forty-five minutes, Pies sat cuffed to a table nearby while Ramirez completed some paperwork. Once the paperwork was finally finished, as Ramirez had explained earlier, a transport bus would take Pies to the county lockup. Stateville Correctional Center would be the next stop after that.

Ramirez stood and took his paperwork to a copier that sat thirty feet away down a narrow hallway. Once his copies were made, he left them on the machine, grimaced and lightly touched his stomach, and then disappeared into the men's room across the hall.

Pies was exhausted and defeated. There was no fight left in him.

He'd wind up going back inside prison, where he knew he belonged, and the very worst part would be knowing that he had gotten Milena, and possibly Naomi and Jason, killed. How could he be so stupid to trust Gunther or anyone at the halfway house?

"Damn it," he said softly.

"You okay, there, Pies?" said a pleasant female voice.

Pies raised his line of sight and stared back at the attractive, dark-haired, parole officer he saw the first time he met with Ramirez.

"I'm P.O. Supervisor Reedholm. I'm Ramirez's boss. You okay? Look tired," she continued with a weak smile. "Hungry?"

"You... You called me Pies."

She leaned in and gently took the cuffs off of Pies and then got him to his feet. Reedholm looked over and saw that Ramirez was still inside the bathroom, so she cleared her throat and motioned with her chin to the closest seated desk sergeant, a hefty man who looked to be nearing retirement.

"Let Ramirez know that I have this one, would you, Andy?" she said. She pointed to a clear plastic bag with his personal property inside that sat on a nearby desk. "This his?"

"Yup. That's his, Reedholm," said the sergeant. "Is Ramirez going to become upset because of this?"

"Yeah, he probably will," she said with a wink.

The sergeant shrugged "oh, well" and went back to doing his own paperwork.

Reedholm picked up the plastic bag and escorted Pies from the district building back into the sunshine. As they reached her dark-colored Crown Vic she said, "Get in front."

Once they were on the road, Reedholm extended her hand to Pies, "Joann Reedholm."

Pies stared at her beautiful hand with the finely manicured nails for what seemed to be an eternity before he finally completed the greeting.

"I'll drive through McDonald's and get you some chow. Maybe coffee?"

Pies wasn't sure what was going on, but he was beginning to like his chances of making this all work out.

"Is this even... Ramirez will just grab me up again, won't he?" asked Pies.

"No, I don't think he will. You're good. We're going to make this all official. I'm going to drive you to your place of employment. You do have a job, right?"

"I do."

"Fantastic. Once there, I'll ask the boss if you're actually employed, and if they say yes, cool, we're on our way. I'll want to see where you've been residing, too. We take care of those two action items, and I will make the determination that everything is okay. The report will say that a misunderstanding arose over where you were residing, but it has been cleared up, and that it was P.O. Ramirez who made the mistake," said Reedholm. "You'll probably never even see him again. You'll deal with me if something comes up."

Pies's eyes stealthily moved in her direction without his head turning. He was so confused and tired that he really wasn't sure which question to ask next. So he smartly remained silent.

*

"YA, LADY, he work for me," said Bertena. She suspiciously eyed Reedholm first and then gave Pies a once-over as well. "Sometimes he helps me open early and get ready for the day, sometimes he works late," she made it sound as if Pies had been employed there for some amount of time now, even though he'd only been out of prison for a couple of days. Bertena knew how to play the game. "What's this about? You don't believe him? He's a good man. He works hard."

They were all standing in the dining area of the small restaurant. Pies looked at the floor, embarrassed by Bertena's words. Pies never thought of himself as being a good man—ever. As he raised his gaze, Rondy was watching from behind the tall counter. Rondy slowly shook his head, waved a hand in disgust, and walked from view.

"I won't bother you any further, ma'am. Thank you for your time," said Reedholm as she motioned for Pies to follow her out.

When they reached her Crown Vic, she said, "Now you're taking me to where you've been really living. And no bullshit from you." She smiled and got into the car. Pies got in, too.

*

THE RAMSHACKLE lobby of the shitty hotel on Howard Street had a few unwashed and fetid occupants milling about as Reedholm and Pies arrived. There was no way that Pies would take Reedholm to Faigy's basement apartment. In reality, he'd not lived there yet. Not even one night.

The hotel desk clerk, an ancient-looking bearded man with the physique of a garden snake, took one look at P.O. Reedholm and hooted loudly.

"There's my little JoJo," he said.

"Long time, no see, Ralph. Things good with you?" asked Reedholm. "I thought you worked at the place you own on Irving Park Road."

"Nah. I got to stay close to home after that last DUI. I can walk to this property from my house," said Ralph.

Pies began to panic. He'd not actually stayed at the hotel for a night or so. Would this cause Reedholm to take him back to the police district?

"You know this guy?" she asked Ralph.

Ralph glanced at Pies and said, "Sure. He just got out, too, I bet. They all have that same look, you know. Like they're lost. Skin's sort of translucent. That the right word?"

"Pies, I think we're good," said Reedholm. "I'll get you back to your car."

"He still owes for last night, though," lied Ralph, with a half wink in Pies's direction.

Pies didn't actually owe anything to the asshole desk clerk, but to stay a free man, he played along. Pies took the only money he had on him, two twenties, and laid them on the counter.

"Much appreciated. Much appreciated," said Ralph as he scooped up the cash.

Reedholm said, "Take care, buddy," and headed for the door.

Before Pies turned to leave he watched Ralph cram the money into his own pocket and grin through a patchwork of rotted teeth.

Reedholm and Pies drove the entire twenty minutes to the Belmont Avenue parole offices in silence. After they arrived and Reedholm parked in her assigned spot, she turned the ignition off and faced Pies. Gone was any semblance of pleasantry.

"Quit your pissing around. You've got a job to do for my friend from Oak Park, so do the fucking job," she said, as she opened the glove box and extracted a business card. She slapped the card onto Pies's chest and said, "Panzera's giving you some extra time because of this shit today. Take advantage. Get some rest and then get back to work. Now out."

27

PIES AWOKE in a mildly confused state.

His brief respite was racked with memories of his father, a Chicago police sergeant, who died by his own hand when Pies was a four-teen-year-old boy. The thoughts and dreams—nightmares really —that he had just experienced were odd and difficult to decipher now that he was awake. The main image he recalled from these sleep-induced visions was of his father's wrists, which were injured and rubbed raw for some reason.

His initial confusion upon waking was replaced with new bewilderment. He painfully raised his head and tried to figure out where in the hell he was. Everything in the room looked foreign. It took more than a few seconds to correctly register his whereabouts—on the futon...in the basement apartment...at Faigy Tambor's building.

The fuzzy memory of arriving here around 10:30 A.M., after dealing with the entire parole offices fiasco, slowly seeped back into his consciousness.

He recalled finding the key under the pot next to Faigy's garage, opening the door, and plopping down on the futon. He also started to remember that he had done some Google searches with the smart-phone, and then his recollections stopped. He must've passed out in the middle of his investigative work, because he was still wearing all of his clothes.

He propped himself up on his elbows and surveyed the studio

apartment. He noticed that Faigy had sort of decorated the place while he was out exploring in Barrington Hills. There were several framed photographs on the walls. They were of the candid variety and portrayed many different people, of all different ethnic backgrounds, doing everyday activities. Some were people simply eating a picnic lunch, other subjects were standing and posing, and still others were young mothers with their babies.

As his eyes scanned, he counted twenty framed photos in all, hanging on the walls of the apartment. Pies concluded that the majority of the photos were most likely taken right there in the neighborhood, because he could see the distinctive and beautiful Indian Boundary Park in the background of many shots.

Looking through the open bathroom door, Pies noticed that Faigy had stacked some towels on the edge of the tub. On the kitchen counter there was a bottle of dish soap, a box of dishwasher powder, sponges, and dishtowels—all neatly laid out and ready for use.

He reached for his smartphone and instead felt the plastic bag with the new T-shirts and underwear from the sporting-goods superstore. As his fingers finally located the smartphone buried in the folds of the bed sheets, he saw that the time was 2:37 P.M.

"Shit."

He needed to go and let Bertena know he would be unavailable for the next day or so. Bertena had been so helpful to him, and he thought she deserved the respect of a face-to-face meeting, not simply a phone call.

There was more required surveillance to be done in Barrington Hills. Now that Milena had shunned him, Pies had to completely immerse himself in the Chapin Way B&E until, maybe, she changed her mind and would hear him out. He still had to protect her, though, and that now entailed following through on the job to steal the Honus Wagner baseball card.

PO Reedholm advised Pies that Panzera gave him some extra time, but the sleep he just enjoyed, as brief as it was, had still put him behind schedule.

He saw a scribbled note scratched on the BB gun box in marker ink, which was also tucked among the bed linens, and it quickly came back to him why the writing was there in the first place. Before he had fallen asleep, he had searched the Internet on his smartphone for the address of 221 Wakelin Circle and discovered something rather interesting about the occupant of the house located to the rear of his targeted mansion in Barrington Hills.

Pies hopped from the futon, stumbled until he could get some proper footing, peeled off his clothing, and headed for the shower.

*

PIES ASCENDED the wooden steps that lead to Faigy's back apartment door, and he lightly tapped on the screen door. The inner door was closed, and through the door glass he could see Faigy's anxious-appearing face quickly dip in and out of view down the hall that led from the kitchen to the rest of her apartment. Once she got a look and saw that it was Pies, she moved out into the hallway and to the door to let him in.

"Hey, how's it going?" asked Faigy. She backed up and motioned for Pies to come into her kitchen. As Pies got inside, Faigy nodded for him to take a seat at the small square table and said, "You want some coffee? It's already made."

"Everything okay? You seem nervous, or something," said Pies as he sat.

Faigy playfully waved his comment away and said, "What about some coffee?"

"That would be great," said Pies, grateful for the invitation.

"I have some coffee cake, too...."

"Kind of hungry," said Pies. "Thanks."

As Faigy opened her refrigerator to get some cream for her coffee, she caught the look on Pies's face. He was staring at a big bag of plump, seedless green grapes. "I can clean some up for you."

"I hope that's not asking too much? I haven't had a chance to shop for food," said Pies.

"Cream?"

Pies shook his head and Faigy took the grapes out of the fridge and placed them next to the cream on the counter. She poured two cups of coffee and handed one to Pies. As he sipped, she went about cleaning a handful of grapes at the sink and placing them in a bowl.

"Help yourself to the coffee cake. It's in the box," said Faigy. "Just use a paper napkin as a plate."

Pies opened the box and saw that the coffee cake was raspberry flavored and the pieces were pre-sliced. He grabbed a paper napkin from the holder next to the salt and pepper shakers and placed a piece of the cake on the napkin. As he did this, he caught a glimpse of Faigy popping a cleaned grape in her mouth followed by a sip of hot coffee.

She chewed, swallowed, and grinned when she saw the look on his face. "Cold, sweet grape. Hot, bitter coffee. A little yin and yang, you ask me."

"It's just—"

"Don't knock it—"

"No, that's not... It's nothing," said Pies, not wanting to explain that his father used to do the very same thing. For Pies the grape and hot coffee act Faigy just performed elicited happy summertime memories of when his father was still around. It was a strange coincidence, though. First he had the injured wrist memory of his dad, and now the grape and coffee combination. Pies took another sip of coffee and then a big bite of the cake.

"You missed all the excitement," said Faigy.

"How's that?"

"Pretty stupid on my part. I get too comfortable living around here. I really should be more careful," she said.

"What happened?"

"I was burglarized. Well, sort of."

Pies stopped mid coffee sip and placed his cup and the coffee cake down on the table.

"It was nothing. They didn't even take anything. I think I scared them off. A couple of kids, looked like to me," said Faigy.

Pies turned away and studied his coffee cup and nodded absently.

"What?" asked Faigy. "You don't look—"

"Did you see what kind of car they were in, maybe get a plate number, anything like that," asked Pies.

"A white van is all I noticed."

Pies gulped hard, and he scratched at his chin. His reaction was not lost on Faigy.

Panzera's men had found where Pies was staying. But how? Pies had been particularly careful not to pick up any tails, or so he thought. It had to be the same men in the white van he saw parked across the street during his meeting with the Outfit members. Those had to be the men who had entered Faigy's place. This was no coincidence, Pies was sure of that. He swallowed hard again as his eyes locked with Faigy's.

"They were near Milena's bakery," he said, in a near whisper. "That has to be it. They saw me...and you when I came to see the apartment."

"Who? Who are they?" she asked.

*

PIES HURRIEDLY moved about the basement apartment, picking up his belongings and stuffing them into his backpack.

"Pies, wait. I don't understand what's... Stop. Please, stop and talk to me. You're scaring me," said Faigy.

Pies caught sight of her terrified expression and dropped the backpack onto the futon.

"You weren't supposed to be part of any of this."

"What?"

"My... Everything... Everyone I come in contact with... I don't mean for it to be that way, but it happens. I can't have that happen here. I can't."

When he reached for the backpack once again, Faigy's firm hand grasped his forearm and stopped him.

"You obviously need some sort of help here," she said.

Pies shook his head and said, "That's not going— No. I can't do that."

"Those men who were in my apartment are part of something you're caught up in. I don't know what that is, but whether you like it or not, now I'm caught up in it, too."

Pies was taken aback at Faigy's convictions. But he said, "You don't know—"

"You need help. I want to help in any way I can. I've never been more sure of something," said Faigy, and she meant it. The man who had unintentionally helped her to find her own true path in life was standing right here in her building, and in need of some sort of assistance himself. This was no time to run and hide in the bushes, like she did when the man with the pockmarked face punched her all those months ago. "But...I won't do anything unless you truly want me to help. You have to ask."

Pies relaxed and plopped heavily down on the futon. Faigy remained standing.

"I can't be in both places at once... In Barrington Hills and... I have to keep her safe," said Pies.

"Who? Who needs to be safe?"

Pies stared at Faigy for a few seconds and then said, "Do you know where the Edison Park neighborhood is?"

28

THE SHOULDER-LENGTH black wig she wore was a bit itchy. She never recalled the wigs making her skin crawl this much in the past. It could've been because her head was buzzed short at that time and the wigs simply fit more snugly. Deep down, though, Faigy knew that her discomfort was probably due more to the fact that she was in over her head after taking on this chore for Pies.

The only thing that kept her on task so far was the friendly dog she was walking at the end of a ten-foot leash. If she focused on the dog, and trying to keep him from taking off after another dog, a squirrel, or a passing jogger, she'd be okay. The dog was courtesy of her Nigerian friends Abua and Minika, and a prop that Pies suggested she borrow for her mission. She thought Pies's idea was pretty strange, but the way he explained it, no neighbor would be suspicious of a woman walking a dog. And if Faigy were being honest with herself, if it weren't for the dog's warm presence, her apprehension would have caused her to bolt from the area a few minutes after first arriving.

As she scratched her head under the front edge of the wig with her left forefinger, the yellow Labrador jerked her sideways when it saw a squirrel dart up a tree.

"Ah, come on, dog," said Faigy as she held the leash taut. The dog took a step backward, and that allowed the leash to go slack once again. "Good boy. Or...um, I mean girl..."

Faigy fought back the thoughts of scrambling to the safety of her

own home, and on her fourth leisurely pass on the sidewalk opposite Milena's dark-brick home, the white panel van drove past her.

It was the same vehicle that sped away from her own home, she
was certain. She tripped to a stop when she saw the van park five
houses away from Milena's place. Faigy stood on the sidewalk for a
few long beats wondering what she should do.

Seeing the van again terrified her. She had to calm herself when
she noticed that she was actually quite close to hyperventilating.
The dog sensed that she was struggling and sidled up and leaned
against Faigy's leg. The dog's cozy reassurance had a calming effect
on her, and soon Faigy was breathing normally again. She instinc-
tively reached down to gently pet the dog's back.

If she kept going straight ahead, she'd be able to turn the corner,
walk completely around the block again, and wind up where her own
car was parked. She could make a clean escape without the van's occupants ever seeing her.

But Faigy had been preparing to take more and more chances these
past years, especially when it involved helping people who couldn't
help themselves.

Faigy did a casual U-turn, and she and the dog headed in the
van's direction.

With her heart pounding, and pretending as if she were about to
make a phone call, Faigy slipped a smartphone from her small purse,
raised the phone to her left ear, and with the inside edge of her left
thumb depressed the button that would start the video camera. She
crossed over the sleepy side street about thirty feet in front of the van
and made sure that the phone was angled to catch images of both
men in the front and the vehicle's license plate.

As she passed the front driver's compartment of the van, she kept
the video camera in the phone rolling but also surreptitiously caught
a side-glance of the men seated inside. From her line of sight, she
reckoned that the men were most likely brothers—they looked so
much alike. Both had dark mops of thick hair, and both seemed
rather physically fit. Neither of the men even looked at her as she

moved past. Both had their eyes focused directly on Milena's house.

Pies had instructed Faigy that Milena Chlebek would be home at this hour, just after shutting her business for the evening. And because they were parked here now, Faigy figured that the men in the van had the same intelligence. Pies also let Faigy know that if anyone approached Milena's home while she was there, to call the police on the burner smartphone he had procured for her earlier that afternoon at a dubious-looking cell phone store on Western Avenue. He didn't want Faigy's legitimate cell phone to be used in any of this activity. Even though she did volunteer to help, he tried as best he could to keep Faigy safe and free of any future police investigations if things went south.

Faigy put the phone away and took a stroll around the block once again, more to calm her nerves than anything else, and wound up in the park adjacent to Milena's home. She took a seat on a bench and the yellow Labrador lay at her feet. After forty minutes, she got up and walked a half block to where her Prius was parked on the opposite side of the small park. She got into the car, which was facing Milena's house, but a full block away, and observed the van for several more minutes. From her vantage point Faigy could just see the front right side of the van's grill and the driver's side of the windshield. It was enough of a view, though, to tell whether the men inside got out at any point and crossed the street to Milena's house, which they never did. The dog fell asleep on the back seat within ten minutes of getting into the vehicle.

As the sun was setting, Faigy could see the back kitchen light at Milena's house go out, followed by the only light illuminating the living room. Pies had advised Faigy, among other things, that Milena went off to bed at an early hour due to her morning routine at the bakery.

The occupants of the van saw the same, and within a couple of minutes of the house going dark, they took off.

When they left so soon after Milena's house darkened, Faigy figured that they probably had been there to see if Pies would show up.

Pies hadn't given Faigy all the specific details on why Milena was in danger, but he did say it was because some of the people he used to work with wanted him to do something for them, and that Milena was unwittingly being used as an insurance policy.

Faigy felt comfortable enough to leave as well. When she started the electric car, the dog sat up in the back seat, as if knowing she was going home, too.

"Hey, girl. I know I'm not all that exciting. We'll get you back now," said Faigy as she drove off. The dog poked her wet snout into Faigy's ear as she reached back to tussle her neck fur. "Okay. Okay."

29

THERE WAS no one at the targeted mansion on Chapin Way, Pies was sure of it.

In the fading sunlight, and as he moved to the edge of where the driveway met the attached garage's cobblestone-constructed apron, he could not get a line of sight on any other nearby neighbor's dwellings, either. Pies knew there were other residences in the area, because he'd seen the distant glow of their interior lights through the foliage the last time he was here in the darkness. In the dwindling sunlight, he couldn't even make out any other rooflines.

He peered through the cheap binoculars but could not see the main roadway, Chapin Way, only the top fringes of the roofline of the targeted property's guesthouse. He was free to roam about unencumbered by the peering eyes of any suspicious neighbors or onlookers, he was sure of it.

With the use of the natural light, he was able to finally establish that there were absolutely no visible security cameras anywhere on the exterior of the property. This seemed so odd to him.

Pies next turned his attention to the interior of the massive mansion.

He walked to the front door and then to the right side of the structure, all the while attempting to get a view inside the front-facing windows. They were all covered in blackout material, the same type he had first seen on the guesthouse and pool house on his earlier scouting run. He backtracked to the only windows not covered in the blackout material—the two sidelights at the wide front double doors. He looked through the glass there, but the light was so poor on the inside that he really couldn't make out any details.

Walking to the back of the huge home, he did establish that two of the ten side-by-side sets of French doors were not covered with blackout.

Pies leaned in close and cupped his hands around his face to get a better view of the interior, and then he immediately pulled away.

"This is crazy...."

He was confused about what he was seeing, but at the same time also experienced a bit of clarity. The photos that the Outfit members gave to him were missing key elements of the house's interior. He thought that was strange at first, but now Pies was beginning to understand why.

He placed the binoculars against the glass of the nearest French door and looked inside once again. What Pies saw was an interior that appeared more like an unfinished construction zone than a posh dwelling space. The ceilings were soaring, and yet completely unfinished. The exposed sturdy steel framework of the building's interior gave way to views of exposed wiring and plumbing lines. The interior walls had not been dry-walled to completion, save one. In the front corner, just to his right of the front hallway, Pies could see an open door and what appeared to be an upward-angled, enclosed stairway.

Oddly, there were also four professional-appearing skateboard ramps situated at various points on the first floor. They were enormous, like the ones found in a municipal skate park, but weirdly, these were *inside* the house.

"What the hell is this?"

He placed his eyes back onto the binoculars, and he could see near where the wide front hallway began, a folding table with unfurled blueprints on top. The two interior lights that bracketed the large front double doors were only cheap work lights that hung from bent nails hammered into the doors' unfinished, wooden frame. The lights were plugged into orange extension cords which snaked to a cheap timer system that was inserted into a nearby, unfinished, dangling wall socket.

Two eight-foot aluminum ladders lay on the floor near the table, but no other construction equipment could be seen. No table saws, no tools, or anything like that. The home was basically an abandoned work site cum-skate park.

Pies pushed away from the French doors, and he peered about the exterior grounds. He noticed that there were several large landscape stones bordering the vast paver patio next to the wall of French doors. The sight of the stones jolted him a bit, because he had forgotten to check them earlier to see if they were real or not. Sometimes, homeowners utilized realistic-looking fiberglass stones or boulders to house security cameras and sensors, or even extra house keys. He moved over to gently kick at some of the larger landscape stones, and a few of the smaller ones, too. The stones were all authentic and that allowed a cleansing breath to escape Pies's mouth.

He was confident that his scouting run for the outside of the house was complete. However, he still did not want to chance entering the main house and trip any security measures that he hadn't noticed yet—or wasn't expecting.

As he peered about, he could see that a narrow dirt footpath had been worn into the earth heading away from the mansion out in back—about 150 feet away from where he stood presently. Pies still had to know the lay of the land all about the targeted mansion. He tilted toward the path, and as he entered the thick foliage located there, the air seemed to cool a degree or two, and it smelled sweeter, too. The trees formed the natural barrier between the Chapin Way's estate grounds and the rear of the property at 221 Wakelin Circle, where Pies had seen the two armed men during his earlier reconnaissance run.

He carefully wound his way through the gently arcing pathway and noticed, through the foliage, that the fading sunlight glinted off of a body of water farther up ahead.

The smaller trail soon intersected with a wider, crushed limestone pathway. The trees and the vegetation still crowded in on this area as the wider path bisected neatly through the dense growth. Upon closer inspection, Pies could see many crisscrossing horse hoofprints in the crushed limestone. Horse trails, of course. Barrington Hills was famous for their horse culture and impressive trail system.

The horse trail bisected to his right and left, and he intuitively followed the right for fifty feet until another worn footpath branched away and angled leftward. After walking a hundred or so feet on this newly discovered narrow trail, Pies could smell the water before he was fully upon it. A few more steps farther on, and he came to the edge of a very large pond that was several acres in size. As he stood on the footpath, he paused to take in the beautiful sight and the fresh aromas.

It was so peaceful.

He sensed movement and flinched.

Pies smiled a little after he finally got a sense of what had moved.

On the right edge of the pond, nearly two hundred feet away, a spindle-legged blue heron stood in the shallows. The delicate bird was nearly stock-still as it peered down and into the clear water below. Pies just watched. In a flash the bird struck downward into the water, and as it came back up to a standing position, it leaned its head way back and completed the task of swallowing its small fishy catch. The telltale fish-sized lump in the bird's throat slid satisfyingly downward toward its digestive doom.

A warm breeze washed over Pies and he raised his nose up and closed his eyes to take it in. As he slowly opened them again, he jerked backward and began to puff out quick and anxious breaths. He was terrified.

30

PIES WAS fourteen-years-old again—in his mind.

Inexplicably, he was both a thirty-three-year-old man, and recent parolee, currently situated on the dirt path next to the pond in back of the Chapin Way mansion—and yet, he was also fourteen. He tried but he could not pry himself back to reality, because a strong and deep-seeded repressed memory had a hold of him.

Don't...do this, Pies thought. *Why am I doing this?*

As he looked around he saw trees and greenery in abundance, that was true, but what he was observing now was more manicured and stately.

There was no pond, either.

His confusion was gaining steam. Right before he scrambled away from and escape what was a strange mirage of some sort, a fourteen-year-old version of Vicki Chlebek swooped in to block his path. She wore a pair of white overalls, a red T-shirt, and open-toed sandals, and there was a rather concerned expression on her beautiful face. She edged in closer and closer to Pies.

Pies scooted backward, and that's the instant he saw his own father over to his left.

Jacob Jakubowski Sr., a robust and thickset man, sported a midlife paunch that stretched the material of his button-up shirt. He held a cheap camera in his hands and looked through the viewfinder. He was taking quick snapshots of the stunning and colorful flora that encompassed and sort of floated all around him. Pies finally realized that the images he was seeing were of a well-maintained garden—or something similar. He couldn't quite grasp it all just yet.

It slowly dawned on Pies, what he was looking at.

I remember, he thought, dreamily. *I remember, Vicki. It's so beautiful. My dad drove us here. The botanical gardens. We were here. I do remember.* He settled down some and even smiled and nodded his approval to Vicki, although she didn't seem to acknowledge him.

His grin gave way to terror again as he peered to his left once more. His father leaned forward to get a photo of a bed of vibrant purple flowers—just as Stan Zielinski materialized with a drawn pistol in his outstretched hand. The gun was aimed directly at the back of Pies's father's head. Stan Zielinski turned to peer in Pies's direction, and a menacing grimace formed on his old criminal boss's face. The sneer was one that Pies had seen before. It was the exact same expression that Zielinski offered Pies the day before he killed two men back when he was a sixteen-year-old kid. That was the very day that Stan Zielinski laid out some specific plans for who Pies had to kill, and exactly why. The entire time Zielinski spoke with Pies that dark day, he sported the same sinister look. Pies remembered it all so well and with so much detail. Stan Zielinski's eyes squinted in the same way, and he sported the same murderous expression. Devoid of spirit. Dark.

Pies thought, *No! Don't make me see this again.*

Abruptly, Pies was transported to the front seat of a Chicago police car as it slowly rolled and meandered through the narrow streets of his Edison Park neighborhood. Pies's father, in his sergeant's uniform, was at the wheel.

Pies could see his father's mouth moving, as he grinned and conversed, but he heard no words, actually no sound at all. Pies took a quick look at his own arms and hands—they were the hands and arms of a fourteen-year-old.

No, no. I can't see this. Please don't, Pies thought.

As the car came to a gentle stop at the red light where Ozanam met

Northwest Highway, a loud thump took fourteen-year-old Pies's eyes off of his father and directed them to the hood of the police car.

There, he saw a shapely and sexy-looking—yet angry—woman in her twenties, wearing a halter top and blue jeans. She furiously and repeatedly pounded on the hood of the car as she screamed—but, again, Pies could not hear anything.

Why is this happening? thought Pies. *I don't want to see this. I shouldn't have seen this.*

Jakubowski Sr. yelled something through his open car window and the woman stormed off to the sidewalk on Pies's side of the vehicle. His father then yanked the steering wheel, and the patrol car edged to the curb on Northwest Highway. His father launched himself out of the patrol car and toward the woman. He took her by the elbow so that he could walk her farther down the sidewalk.

Please...stop, thought Pies. *Not this.*

He could see his father turn toward him, toss a reassuring nod his way, and then pivot back to face the woman. Jakubowski Sr. spoke softly, but the woman's reply was the first sound Pies heard.

"This isn't Stan's fault, Jake," said the enraged woman. "Stan's not the one who made promises and then didn't keep them. You think I give a shit that you decided to walk away from his action," screamed the woman. "I need to be taken care of, like you promised. You said once your wife was gone, it'd just be me and you."

Pies saw that his father was doing his best to calm the woman, but she was inconsolable. She yelled, "You can't just cut me off like this. I need rent money."

The image of his father with the woman faded, and Pies could now see that he and his father, out of uniform now and in a white T-shirt and plaid shorts, were standing across from their own small house—at Stan Zielinski's first home in Edison Park. There were a couple of coils of thick rope laid out on the front lawn next to a twenty-foot-tall evergreen tree, and also a small chain saw sitting on the walkway that led to the front door. An eight-foot stepladder was opened and standing next to the tree.

Pies's sometime friend, fifteen-year-old Sebastian "Bast" Zielinski, Stan's smart ass of a son, was there, as well. Mr. Banasik—another neighbor whose daughter, Dana, was also a friend of his—was on the lawn too. Banasik was one of the men that Pies would eventually murder at Stan Zielinski's behest.

"How long before you're crawling back, huh, Jake?" said Stan Zielinski to Pies's father. "You get used to the life, it's hard to let go. But, eh, you made your decision...I'll respect that."

Pies finally understood what his father and Stan Zielinski was discussing and how it meshed with the memory of the angry woman in the halter top. All these years he had pushed down the fact that his father was a dirty cop and had been working on the side for Stan Zielinski doing...whatever, for as long as Pies had been alive.

Rapid-fire memories invaded Pies's mind; they were images of Pies, when he would hide and peek around a wall that connected their dining room to their kitchen, when Stan Zielinski paid late night visits to their kitchen. There was an envelope, with cash visible, being handed to his father, and then another envelope and another —and then many more. Flashing images, memories, of Pies peering out his bedroom window and seeing his father leave in his personal car with Stan Zielinski and Mr. Banasik late at night. Leaving again and again. Pies growing younger and younger as he witnessed the scenario play out over and over again. Glimpses of his father at his basement workbench surrounded by new camera equipment and various and expensive electronics equipment like video cameras, recorders, and the like.

Jesus, Dad. What did you do? thought Pies.

Seeing the evergreen tree again, Pies caught a furtive glance that young Bast, holding a chain saw, and Mr. Banasik shared. It was an odd, quick, and chilling exchange that Pies could only describe to himself now as murderous. He didn't know why the two would even share a look like that as they stood on the Zielinskis' front lawn next to the twenty-foot evergreen tree. Pies was so utterly confused by the exchange.

Everything sort of fast-forwarded, and now Pies saw two lengths of rope that were looped around the tree trunk twelve feet up. One of the lengths of the rope was being held by Mr. Banasik, and the other by his father. Stan Zielinski stepped down from the ladder after securing the ropes to the trunk. Bast fired up the whining chain saw and edged in close to the base of the tree trunk.

Over the din of the chain saw motor, Pies's father said, "Shouldn't you have a tree service do this?"

"I'm paying you one last time to help me," said Stan Zielinski. "Be a friend, huh?"

"Jake. Hey, Jake," called out Mr. Banasik.

When Pies's father turned in Banasik's direction, Banasik wrapped the two ends of his portion of rope tightly around his wrists and then grasped the side that was encompassing the tree trunk into his palms. "Like this. You'll have more control as it comes down. We have to keep it tight and pull it away from the house."

"Just paid it off," said Stan Zielinski with a wink toward Pies.

Pies's father wrapped the rope around his wrists and grasped it tightly just as Banasik had demonstrated. Bast began to cut into the thick trunk of the rather bushy tree, and as it started tilting toward the Zielinskis' home, Pies could see that Banasik allowed the rope to come completely free of his wrists, so that the heavy load was entirely in his father's grasp. Pies's father struggled, but he was a strong man, and he was able to pull with all of his might, lean back, and nearly sit, to keep control of the falling tree. As the tree plummeted, it briefly angled toward the house and then dropped harmlessly to the front lawn with a crunch and a thud.

Pies's father let go of the slackened rope and rubbed at his wrists. They were raw, and Pies could see smatterings of blood seeping up through his skin. "Seemed like I had the whole thing," said Pies's father.

Stan Zielinski reached into his shirt pocket and took out a couple of hundred dollar bills. He slapped them into Pies's father's opened palm and said, "Thanks, Jake. Couldn't a done this without you."

And then...everything was different.

Pies was outside on his neighborhood block. It was still daylight —and he was again only fourteen years old—but now he was standing on his own front yard and he could see his father seated in his patrol car, in uniform, waving goodbye to him as he pulled away from the curb.

Out of thin air, Stan Zielinski appeared...right in the middle of the street. His father had no choice but to jerk the patrol car to a stop. Zielinski moved to the opened driver's side window of the patrol car, and he spoke, but Pies could not hear anything. His father smiled, nodded, and motioned for Zielinski to get into the passenger seat, which he did.

As the car slowly drove off, Pies caught a glimpse of Stan Zielinski's face—especially his eyes. There was a malevolent darkness in Stan Zielinski's eyes. The same squinted eyes and the same murderous gaze Pies would see two years on. It was an expression that was devoid of human spirit.

What did you do? thought Pies, as he met Stan Zielinski's cruel gaze.

A few seconds after his father's patrol car gradually rolled away, Mr. Banasik and Mr. Bartosz, another neighbor, followed in Banasik's car. Both of Pies's neighbors had sullen expressions, as well.

Pies ran after both cars on foot, and right before he was able to touch the trunk of Banasik's car, it and his father's patrol car evaporated and were gone, leaving Pies standing in the middle of the street.

Fourteen-year-old Pies bent forward, hands on knees, huffing in great breaths of air and thinking, *What did you do to my dad?*

Pies was then immediately transported to a hushed, funeral home visitation room. There were no other living souls in the room except for Pies. He could see his father's casket, lid open, placed at the far end of the room. He edged slowly forward until he was standing directly next to the open casket, and his father's body. The body didn't even look real to his fourteen-year-old eyes, more like a sculpture you'd find in a cheesy wax museum somewhere. It had been three days since his father had left in his patrol car with Stan Zielinski.

In the hushed and empty visitation room, Pies stood and studied his father's face one last time before the casket lid would be closed. There were no other family members that he could lean on for emotional support, because Pies had no family whatsoever. His mother had died months before, and he was now alone in the world.

Images of his father's jam-packed wake, earlier in that day, began to flash in his mind's eye. Pies tried to shake the painful memories away, but little good it did him. One uniformed officer, then another, and finally rapid fire, eight officers in a row—all saying the very same words as they whispered to unseen others that were just out of Pies's line of sight. "He ate his gun."

"He ate his gun."

"He ate his gun."

Stop, Pies thought.

"He ate his gun."

"He ate his gun."

Stop it. Pies thought. *Please, don't...*

He ate his gun.

He ate his gun.

He ate his gun.

Everything finally, thankfully, quieted down. And standing there, peering at his father's motionless body, Pies could see no telltale signs of the injury that caused his death. Pies assumed that the lethal injury was probably in the roof of his mouth and the top of his head. His closed mouth and the hair on his head would hide that damage.

The funeral home's makeup artist had done a pretty good job of making his father appear peaceful, albeit waxy-looking. But the makeup person had missed something. Peeking out just below the starched and pressed cuff of his father's dark-blue Chicago police uniform jacket, a small bit of his injured right wrist was visible. The fresh rope burns were makeup-free, black and blue, raw and dreadful looking.

His father's eyes opened—and Pies jolted backward three steps, taking great gulps of air.

His father slowly got up and onto his right elbow, all the while casually keeping his eyes on Pies.

"Jakub, buddy, it's okay. Don't be afraid," his father said through a sheepish grin.

Pies could see that his father's upper two front teeth were cracked nearly to the gum line, and when he spoke, his tongue appeared to be burned and blistered. There was also a soft glow of light that filled up his mouth. Pies knew that the light had to be coming through the massive wound in the roof of his father's mouth and top of his head.

His dead father saw the way Pies was looking at him with terror in his eyes and said, "Oh, shit. Sorry." The dead man in the casket reached up with his left hand and adjusted his head hair a little. "Better?" said Pies's father—the illumination no longer present. His father then sat up and showed both wrists to Pies. "It wasn't my idea, buddy, this whole checking out thing. I know that you weren't ready. And holy shit, man, I wasn't ready. You believe this?"

Zielinski's eyes that day. Those goddamned eyes, thought Pies. *They tied him up, and... Goddamn them...*

His father's corpse tossed a little ta-ta wave, and he lay back down. In a few seconds the body became still again. Dead still.

Pies took some deep cleansing breaths, and as he settled himself, he heard a croaking-like sound coming from an interior darkened doorway to the right of his father's casket.

He tilted his head this way and that as he tried to get a better look at what was hiding in the darkness and making the strange noise.

A blue heron with a tiny, wriggling, fish firmly in its beak cautiously emerged from the funeral home's interior doorway. Fourteen-year-old Pies took an immediate step backward, not completely sure what the bird had in mind. It was a skinny bird, but it was about four feet tall, and it looked to be rather menacing with its beady, twitchy eyes.

The heron made the croaking sound once again and took a few more steps forward, until it was no more than ten feet away from the casket. It flicked the fish in Pies's direction. The fish hit the thickly carpeted floor with a tiny thud and flopped around, gasping for breath. Pies first took in the sight of the fish and then looked back to the tall bird.

I don't understand, thought Pies. *Please. I don't understand...What is this?*

31

"PLEASE. I don't understand," said the confused Pies, as he blinked himself back to the pond in Barrington Hills.

A freight train in the distance blew its loud warning horn, and he flinched.

Pies was sitting on the dirt of the small footpath and facing the water. He knew that the exhaustion he was experiencing and the stress he was under to protect Milena were inflicting some rather hard-hitting blows to his psyche. But he had been powerless to fight the deep dive into obviously repressed childhood memories.

Strangely, though, he felt a bit of relief too. Some painful recollections from his childhood were now making sense. The culmination of his lost childhood memories were a shit storm, yes, but at least he acquired some clarity. He also felt a slight lessening of the guilt he'd been carrying for years over killing Banasik and Bartosz. Without him even realizing it at the time, Stan Zielinski had provided Pies with an opportunity for a bit of vengeance when he ordered him to kill the two mob turncoats two years after his own father's death.

Pies needed sleep, clearly, and yet he stood and pushed on, stumbling forward, deeper into the woods in back of the house on Chapin Way.

He had no other choice.

Milena was counting on him.

Since the sun was still a little ways from fully setting, Pies needed to be careful not to get spotted by any nosy neighbors up ahead on the backside of the Wakelin Circle property.

The narrow footpath ended on the far right corner of the pond. Pies required silence and stealth to work his way through the tangle of trees and shrubbery that he encountered next. He finally had to crouch on all fours and crawl under the dense growth until he found himself on the back edge of the Wakelin Circle grounds.

He used the binoculars to eye the residence and surroundings from his shaded hiding spot. He was looking for sites to possibly hide a vehicle that could be used in case he and Panzera were compromised and were required to flee out the back of the Chapin Way mansion. It would be pitch-black during any escape, but with Pies's keen sense of direction, he was confident he'd be able to find his way.

Through the binoculars, he spotted an older red pickup truck with a snowplow blade attached on front and a green golf cart parked on the side of the Wakelin Circle estate's horse barn. There was also another green golf cart parked next to the pool area in back of the main house. A black Cadillac SUV was in front of the attached four-car garage of the main home.

Pies lowered the binoculars after he heard the start of a thumping bass beat from a powerful sound system within the residence. There were obviously excellent speakers mounted outside as well because some driving dance music punched into Pies's hiding spot in the next few seconds. The clear and precise sound quality of the high-end system was incredible, like one used in an upscale nightclub.

The setting sun pierced the glassed-in, rear first floor of the home at 221 Wakelin Circle and worked to highlight the beautiful, finely furnished and open living area within.

A very tall and athletic-looking man, dressed only in boxer shorts, danced into the room pushing along a smaller female. The female, wearing a white terry-cloth robe, did not look as if she wanted to join in the reverie. Her shoulders were slumped, and she shuffled as she walked. The man reached out and physically forced the female to dance with him. Pies could see the man yell something over his shoulder, addressing someone else. A few seconds later, the two men Pies had seen before, both then and now exhibiting shoulder-holstered handguns, emerged. All three men crowded in on the female as they laughed, danced, and pawed at her.

The tall man in the boxer shorts, while gyrating to the dance music, reached out and ripped the robe from the female's body, and she stood there naked and embarrassed and attempted to cover herself the best she could.

"Oh, no. Not this...," Pies said softly. He pulled the binoculars away from his eyes, blinked a few times, and said, "No...no."

As he placed the binoculars back to his eyes, he could see that the three large men had shoved the naked girl down onto an expansive pit-group seating area.

Through Pies's eyes, the girl looked to be only twelve years old.

After a few seconds, Pies dropped the binoculars to the ground and anxiously rubbed at his mouth. He started to hyperventilate and calmed himself as soon as he recognized his breathing had become too ragged.

He wanted very badly to charge across the three hundred feet of manicured lawn and into the mansion on Wakelin Circle to save the girl. But he knew he'd be killed the moment he went into the house. Two of those men now having their way with the female, revoltingly enough, still had their handguns holstered as they performed their sordid deeds. They didn't even have the decency to disarm themselves. *Why would they?* Pies thought.

"Animals..."

If Pies barged in, they'd not only promptly kill him, they'd have to get rid of the girl, too.

Pies had to do something.

Anything.

He turned and ran as fast as he could, dodging branches, back toward the targeted mansion on Chapin Way. He made it one hundred feet before he came, literally, crashing to his knees on the dirt footpath next to the pond.

The situation he just witnessed was so shocking that he had been caught completely off guard.

He didn't know how to help the girl.

He didn't know what to do.

An innocent girl needed help, and Pies was powerless to do... anything.

He began to wonder if he was cursed.

Truly cursed.

Pies, the man with a set plan of A, B, and C always at the ready, was clueless as to what he could do. He was helpless to act—to save, what to him, looked like a little girl from being raped by three grown men.

Why did he find himself in these strange situations where he felt compelled to risk his life in order to help people he didn't even know?

He was beyond confused.

He had the same sort of sensation when, five years ago, he was ordered to take a job as a 9-1-1 communications officer by his old crime boss, Bast Zielinski. He wound up actually *helping* desperate people who were calling the emergency line. He didn't want to help the people—he just couldn't stop himself from doing so.

There was some sort of instinctual glitch in his operating system, he thought. He wasn't trained as a young boy to care for others— he was just trying to earn for his Outfit-sanctioned bosses. So why had he continuously gone out of his way and placed his life in danger to help others?

He should have never put someone else's interests above his own —especially someone he didn't even know. But here he was, again, scrambling to where he left the binoculars, trying to think of an idea, something, anything, so he could help the girl.

Pies couldn't go off half-cocked, though. There was just, literally, too much ground to cover between the tree line and the Wakelin Circle building to even get close to doing any good.

He slid the smartphone from his pocket and began dialing 9-1-1 and then instantly disconnected the call. If he got caught up with the authorities over the sordid goings-on at Wakelin Circle it could possibly jeopardize Milena's life. He couldn't have that. If the police were crawling all around the property where he clearly witnessed a rape, it would be nearly impossible to pull off the Honus-Wagner-card rip-off next door. There'd be too much heat in the area.

Pies pounded his hand on the ground once, and then he stood and slipped the phone back into his pocket.

He needed to come up with a foolproof, solid plan. It would have to be as sure-fire as he could conjure up.

He needed time.

The sun was nearly set, and as he glanced once again through the binoculars, he saw that the three male occupants inside the illuminated interior of 221 Wakelin Circle were putting their clothes back on. Two of the men, laughing, backed away from the naked girl, and she scrambled from the room. The third man followed her, dangling a set of keys on his finger.

The other men began to gather up wallets, keys, and jackets. It looked as if they were readying to leave the premises. And then the man with the keys stepped back into the main room—with yet another girl. This girl looked all dressed up and ready for a night out, however, she was not smiling. She looked terrified. She was about the same age as the last girl, Pies presumed, but had much darker hair.

Then the music was cut off.

Silence.

Pies had very little time to react. He lowered the binoculars and quickly ran back toward his parked Mercedes. He stumbled and landed on his chest next to the pond. A panic washed over him as he lay there, and he spun to a seated position. His eyes quickly scanned the tall reeds, but there were no tall birds in sight. Pies hurriedly got to his feet and continued on.

Out of breath, he was still able to run across the Chapin Way grounds and get into the Mercedes. He started the engine, put it into drive, and goosed the gas pedal. He quickly found his way rounding onto Otis Road. Up ahead, just as his breath began to settle, he caught sight of the black Cadillac SUV turning off of Wakelin Circle and onto Otis.

Pies sped up, but he didn't get too close, for fear of spooking the people in the SUV.

The lurid activities on Wakelin Circle were gut-wrenching and complicated enough, until yet another thought crashed into Pies's mind as he drove. It was a vile sensation and he wasn't sure why it deposited itself there in the first place.

What if there were more girls in the house, beyond the two he'd seen?

"Oh, shit...," Pies said softly.

He had to figure out the best way to not only accomplish his task at the targeted Chapin Way mansion but to also get the authorities to the Wakelin Circle estate so they could correct a grievous wrong.

If he followed the SUV, maybe the endeavor would bear fruit, and he'd find a way to help the girl in the car up ahead—and any others back at the house. He knew that the girls were being kept under lock and key. Why else would one of the large men have keys displayed as he brought the girls in and out of wherever they were being kept?

The keys.

That's how the thought of multiple girls had entered Pies's mind.

"What the hell are they doing...?" he said as the SUV entered the quaint little village of Barrington. The light traffic began to build and tighten, though, and he didn't want to be right on the SUV's bumper within the small town's limits. He'd be readily seen, and that was not going to work for Pies, because the driver of the SUV, the man Pies had noticed before, wearing a suit jacket and standing in the driveway of 221 Wakelin, could certainly identify the Mercedes. He had seen the luxury car before when Pies drove a slow loop around the cul-de-sac in front of the residence.

Up ahead, the SUV passed by an old-fashioned movie theater marquee and turned left on Barrington Road. Pies made the traffic light in time and turned left too. The SUV continued for a few blocks until Pies could see its taillights bob up and down as it crossed over some freight train tracks. One block later, the vehicle took a left on the side street just before busy Highway 14.

Pies turned left and followed the same roadway to its terminus—which was a magnificent-looking public park, complete with man-icured baseball diamonds and a swimming pool area that would rival most upscale-commercial water parks. Next to the swimming pool area was an enormous, modern recreational center building, constructed of soaring glass walls and brick.

Pies slowed as he entered the parking lot of the complex, and he slipped the car into a front-facing spot a hundred feet from the main recreational building. He killed his lights and kept a steady eye on the SUV as it parked in front of the door in what appeared, from Pies's vantage point, to be a handicapped spot.

It was completely dark now, and with an assist from the overhead lights in the parking lot, Pies could observe the three male occupants quite clearly as they lumbered out of the SUV.

He was a bit closer to the occupants than he was back in the woods, too, so he could see more detail with his naked eye. One of the men, the one wearing the suit jacket the day before, was now in a blue windbreaker, and he closed the driver's door after getting out. The passenger, the man seen in a work uniform in the driveway at 221 Wakelin Circle, was now in a black sport coat over a white button-up shirt. He reached out and opened the rear passenger-side door.

Only then did the last man exit the SUV. He was the guy wearing the boxer shorts back at the house. Now he was decked out in an expensive and brightly colored tracksuit. The man in the track-suit walked toward the building, and the guy in the black sport coat reached back into the vehicle to help guide the petite, dark-hired girl from the SUV.

"Jesus," Pies said, as he watched. "She's a kid...."

The girl had long hair and wore an inappropriate-for-her-age tight tank top and a short skirt. The girl and the guy in the sport coat followed the man in the windbreaker and the man in the track-suit into the building.

Once inside, a gaggle of rambunctious teenagers began to flock to the man in the red tracksuit. Some of the teens wanted to shake his hand, and others were offering up their T-shirts for him to sign. Still others used their cell phones to take selfies with him. As he was being mobbed, the man in the red tracksuit nodded, and the man in the windbreaker took the petite girl by the hand and led her farther into the lobby.

Pies knew exactly why the man in the tracksuit garnered so much attention and adulation. Pies's earlier Google searches, and also the Magic Marker note on the BB gun box back in Faigy's basement apartment, guided him to the discovery.

The home at 221 Wakelin Circle in Barrington Hills belonged to twenty-eight-year-old Tin Tomic, a Croatian national and star professional basketball player for the Chicago team. Tin Tomic had been burning up the league as a small shooting forward since he was nineteen years old. His game, as well as his spoken English, had improved greatly since he moved to the States. His contracts grew, as well, allowing him to comfortably afford his Barrington Hills estate.

As Pies watched, though, he noticed that the man in the sport coat was no longer paying attention to Tin Tomic, as he dealt with his adoring fans. He was staring directly in Pies's direction.

Pies knew he'd been spotted, and he slowly lowered himself behind the steering wheel.

"Damn it..."

Pies wondered if the people in the SUV knew they were being followed the entire time—or just since they arrived at the recreational center building.

Pies put the car into drive just as the large man in the sport coat turned away when one of Tin Tomic's fans asked him a question.

With his lights off, Pies sped from his current parking spot to another one to the side of the lot and a bit farther away.

Pies could still see clearly inside the well-lit lobby, and as the man in the sport coat looked out again, he lost interest.

By that time Tin Tomic, the girl, and the man in the windbreaker were all well inside the lobby.

Pies caught a glimpse of an interior door opening, and he could see a couple of men in T-shirts and shorts in the heat of a pick-up basketball game, running back and forth inside the gym.

One of the teens, who earlier had taken a selfie with Tin Tomic, walked from the building, admiring his phone and, most likely, the photo he had just taken. He was about seventeen years old and wearing a T-shirt with a big, illegible autograph on the front chest area. He walked directly toward where Pies was parked.

Pies got out of his car when the teen was about thirty feet away.

"Hey, man, was that Tin Tomic?" asked Pies with faux-exuberance.

"Dude, that was so cool. I got a pic with him. The dude is tall, man. Check this out," said the smiling teen displaying his T-shirt to Pies.

"No kidding." Pies edged closer and continued, "Hey, man, ah... this is going to sound weird—"

"What?" Weird, how?"

"It's not that weird, dude," said Pies.

The teenager laughed and said, "Okay, what's up?"

A plan had formed for Pies in the last fifteen minutes. It was simple, but it could work. It had to work.

"I'll give you one hundred dollars to take my phone into the gym and video Tomic playing some hoops. That's all. Just like maybe five minutes, and that's it," said Pies.

"Two hundred and you got a deal, bro," said the teenager.

Pies agreed by handing the kid his phone. He said, "I'll be right here."

"What about the money?"

"You have to finish the job first," said Pies with a grin.

The teenager shrugged and then jogged back to the recreational center. After several minutes he emerged and handed the phone back to Pies.

"I checked it. The video quality's kind of shitty, but you can totally tell it's him," said the teen.

Pies watched and listened to a few seconds of what the kid had recorded and then paid him.

"That *was* weird man," said the grinning teen as he waved the two hundred-dollar bills at Pies as he backed away from the Mercedes. "But the cool kind of weird, bro."

"Thanks...bro," said Pies as he got back into the car and sped away. "Bro?"

Pies remembered seeing a large pharmacy on his way to the recreational center. It was a few blocks back and right off of Barrington Road. He pulled into the lot, parked, and ran inside.

He hurriedly walked the aisles but couldn't find what he was looking for. It wasn't where he first thought it would be—in the antacid aisle—so he continued to search.

"May I help you," said a friendly female voice.

Pies spun around and was greeted by a pleasant woman, who was as round as she was tall. Her purple punked-out hair made Pies grin just slightly. "You look like you need some help," she continued.

"Me? I do. I do. Thanks. Do you have that stuff that makes you puke...makes you throw up when you need to? I'd like to have it on hand in case my kid swallows something he shouldn't. The kid's been putting everything in his mouth," said Pies, forcing a grin. "I mean, what's that about?"

"Oh, my God, mine too. And he's getting into the terribles," she said.

"The terribles. Oh, right. Sure. Terrible twos. Yeah...mine, too."

"Ipecac."

"What's that?" asked Pies.

"It's called ipecac syrup. We don't stock it on the shelf, the pharmacist has it back over there," said the woman.

*

Pies sped back to the mansion on Chapin Way and was so certain that no one would even notice, that he parked in front of the main house this time.

He carried a plastic bag from the pharmacy as he sprinted around back and through the tree line. This time as he passed the pond, he forced himself not to look for fear that the heron would be peering back with its twitchy eyes.

He could've parked on Wakelin Circle, but he hadn't done any recon there and couldn't chance having the car spotted by a security camera.

He hurried across the back lawn's expanse on Wakelin Circle, and as he got to within one hundred feet of the house, a wall of bright lights hit him—and he froze for a second, blinking, and wondered if he'd been discovered. Nothing else occurred, though—no sounds, nothing. He realized that automatic security lights had been triggered. He didn't have time to mark the grass for the invisible line where the lights activated. It would be a task he'd complete later on, if he had time. He pulled the front of his shirt up and over his nose as he reached the side of the house where the back brick patio and pool area were located. He did this in case any security cameras were angled his way. That's the moment when the security lights automatically switched off and the yard darkened once again.

There was enough light coming from the interior of the house for him to finally notice there were actually no visible surveillance cameras in sight.

Pies went to the rear kitchen door, stood still for a few seconds, and listened. The place was quiet. He put the bag down, extracted the lock-bump from his pocket, and was inside the house in seconds. He picked up the bag, entered, and closed the door once again.

He stood in the kitchen and waited. There were no sounds here, either. No barking dogs. No alarms beeping. Nothing. It shocked him that these two expensive houses in Barrington Hills had such insufficient security in place. He allowed his shirt to drop down back into place.

The interior of the Wakelin Circle house was immaculate and obviously decorated by a professional designer—not a professional athlete. The place was enveloped in soothing earth tones and chunky masculine furnishings, lots of leather and wood.

The open area here at the rear of the house was where Pies saw the men raping the girl with the lighter-colored hair. Earlier, when the man with the keys left the area, he went straight ahead from where Pies stood at that moment—at the massive, marble kitchen island.

Pies quietly as he could went forward and strode down a very long, thick-carpeted hallway that was outfitted with four doors on each side. Again, all was very quiet. The equally spaced doors were bedrooms, he presumed. At the end of the hall on the right, the door was locked with a heavy-duty, padlock setup. It was a rudimentary system, but it would get the job done of keeping someone locked away, Pies thought.

He gently knocked on the door, and he heard panicked murmurs inside. "Oh, hey, it's okay. It's okay. I'm coming in," he said, as calmly as he could.

Pies began bumping the padlock and could hear muffled young female voices inside the room. They were speaking in an Eastern European language that he didn't quite understand. He knew Polish, but this was not a language he was familiar with.

He got the lock popped open, and he carefully pushed the door inward. "It's okay. I'm not here to hurt you. Hello?"

As the door was pushed fully opened, there was no one in sight. He saw immediately that the room was windowless and equipped with two sets of simple bunk beds and matching dressers. The bunks were each neatly made-up. The room was otherwise spotless and orderly. There was an attached, windowless, bathroom to the right.

Pies saw a white-socked foot tuck back under the bottom bunk of the beds to the left. He got down on all fours and peered under one bunk and then the other bunk.

In all, he saw three sets of eyes looking back—two on the left and one set on the right. "Please, it's okay," he continued in a soft tone.

"*Molim te, ostavi nas na miru,*" said a frightened, soft, female voice from under the bunk on the right.

"I'm here to help," he said.

To Pies, it sounded like she said, "*Moleem ta ostavee nas na mehoo.*"

He mouthed the words a few times, trying to think back if he could recognize the language.

"Oh, yeah. Yes, yes, yes," he said, as he grinned and dug his cell phone from his pocket. He tapped his phone, searched on the device, and pressed a few buttons.

While he took a few minutes to work on his phone, the girls began quietly weeping. Their muffled cries made Pies's heart sink. Conversely though, he was onto a plan he thought would get them safely to freedom—and all without Pies bringing them directly out of the house by himself. Pies just could not get "officially" involved in assisting the girls.

"Here we go," said Pies, as he punched a button on the phone and spoke directly into it, *"Moleem ta ostavee nas na mehoo."* The phone beeped and then an English-accented, electronic female voice said in a pleasant tone, "'Please, leave us alone.' That was identified as Croatian."

Pies leaned down and asked the set of eyes under the bed to the right, "Croatian?"

There was no answer, only soft weeping.

"Please, it's okay. Croatian?"

After a few seconds, a feeble *"Da,"* came the reply.

Pies was in business. He pressed a button on the phone and brought it back up to his mouth, and said, "I'm here to help."

He turned the phone toward the girl on the right, and the pleasant electronic female voice said, *"Jas am tu da pomogne."*

"O moj Boze," came the hushed reply from under the right bunk. Pies understood that because it sounded nearly identical to the Polish his own mother spoke. The girl had said, "Oh, my God."

All three girls, who looked to be about twelve years old to Pies's eyes, began to nervously emerge and scoot out from under the beds. As they shakily got to their feet, wondering what would happen next, Pies could see that they were very pretty young girls. He needed to keep his emotions in check, knowing what they were going through. He had to play this safe. He couldn't just extract these three girls without the other girl who was currently with the men. The girl at the rec center would, most likely, be killed so that Tomic and his men could cover up their obvious criminal activity. And Pies still couldn't do anything stupid like lay in wait and take care of the three men when they got back with the girl's compatriot. It would be too risky. All of the girls would be hurt, he was sure of that.

The girl who slid from under the right bunk, the one who Pies witnessed being raped, edged in a bit closer and he could see that she had crystal-clear, stunning, blue eyes and a small kidney-shaped mole on her lower left cheek. She hugged Pies tightly. He hugged her back and said, "It'll be okay. We have some work to do."

The blue-eyed girl broke the embrace and motioned to the smartphone. She wanted to know what Pies was saying.

*

PIES STUFFED the pharmacy bag in his back pocket as he exited, alone, and locked the back kitchen door to the house on Wakelin Circle. And then he remembered something else.

"Damn it..."

Pies bumped the door's lock once again and went back inside. He headed to the expensive-looking entertainment center on the inside wall of the enormous back room. He inspected the high-end audio equipment for the manufacturer's name and the model number. Once he located both on the front of the machine, he took his phone from his pocket and began searching for the manufacturers website. Once on the proper site, Pies clicked through a few pages, until he found what he was hoping to locate. It was a tab labeled "remote access."

As he moved to exit through the rear door, something caught his attention. It was a colorful, ceramic dog-shaped cookie jar that sat on the marble counter closest to the door. Pies took the dog's head off the piece and looked inside. There were two sets of keys there. He reached in and took them both out. One was a set of car keys, and the other set was shaped a bit differently—more stubby-appearing.

Pies put the dog's head back into place and exited the house the same way he came in.

He needed to test the exterior automatic security lighting system for where the trip point was located. The information could come in handy later, he hoped, when he planned to get the girls to freedom.

His plan was taking shape.

It was a simple yet time-consuming task, trying to locate the invisible line in the grass. First he would have to walk directly out and away from the house, farther than one hundred feet, where he knew he tripped the system earlier. Once that invisible border was located, Pies would still need to find the exact arching line of the system's perimeter. He knew automatic security lighting systems work on an infrared beam that spreads out in a wide semicircle away from the structure that's being secured. Pies hoped to have time to pick up a few of the rocks that edged the pool area and then drop them where the invisible line was located out on the lawn.

He took one step toward the invisible line, inhaled a sharp breath, and stopped. Something in the distance had stirred. It was way out in the back, near the trees that bordered the pond. Pies stayed as still as possible and watched.

Silently, one, then two, and finally three large deer, all females, slowly walked onto the lawn. They had emerged from the same spot Pies had earlier. The deer lazily poked their snouts at the ground and chewed at the grass. In Pies's mind their grayish-brown fur looked ghostly, nearly luminous, in the limited moonlight.

Pies didn't move a muscle.

One of the deer—the one closest to him, but still two hundred feet away—lifted her head, as if she caught his scent. The other two deer walked right alongside the first in a strangely choreographed move, as if they were forming a unified front. Then all three began to cautiously step forward—again, in unison. As they got to within 150 feet from where Pies stood, the animals separated and began to bound and leap all about the lawn. It was quite a display of raw and natural joy. The deer seemed to be gliding through the air with each leap, and when their hooves landed on the ground they pranced about like show horses.

Pies's breath caught in his throat at the sight of the frolicking deer. He couldn't believe his eyes, especially as all three deer stopped their dancing and carefully toed their way forward about fifty more feet, once again, in unison. The animals slowly, vigilantly, spread out and formed a sort of wide semicircle. They then all began to walk forward and that's when the security lights tripped.

Pies blinked away the lights and tried to adjust his vision to the surprising luminescence, and when he finally did, the deer were gone. He could now see exactly where their hooves had stopped their forward progress and precisely where the invisible security light line was located in the trampled grass.

"What is happening?" asked Pies, softly. He took a quick look around, spotted a pool towel on a chair nearby, grabbed it up, and bent down to pick up three of the rocks. He immediately brought them out and onto the lawn to mark the invisible line. Once that was done, he jogged to Tomic's barn where the golf cart and red pickup truck with the snowplow attachment were parked.

Pies took the keys he snagged from the cookie jar out of his pocket and opened the driver's door of the truck using the larger key. Once in the vehicle, he reached up and turned the dome light off. He made sure the door lock was open and then he put the ignition key in place and closed the truck's door. He stepped over to the golf cart and placed the other key in its ignition. The key fit perfectly. He left that ignition key in place and backed away from the golf cart.

As he made his way back across the expanse of lawn toward the massive Chapin Way mansion, headlights bounced up Tin Tomic's long driveway. Pies dove chest first to the grass, out of the security light's range, and remained still. The headlights angled away, and the SUV parked in front of the garage doors. Pies got to his feet and sprinted to the back tree line.

Even though there was limited moonlight, Pies was still able to successfully navigate himself back to the rear of the mansion on Chapin Way.

He got to the rear French doors of the house, pulled the lock-bump from his pocket, and made his way inside the mansion. As he had predicted, no alarm panels beeped, no lights activated, and, after standing still for a few minutes, no actual alarm was triggered.

Pies carefully stepped through the darkened interior of the massive space, past the folding table with blueprints, and directly to the enclosed, up-angled stairway in the front corner. He peered up the stairway and saw mostly dark nothingness, with just the hint of a red glow.

He backtracked to the folding table and found a nearly spent roll of paper towels there. He ripped off several paper towels and wrapped them around each of his hands, using them as improvised gloves. He went to the French doors and wiped the handles clean. Once that was accomplished, Pies stepped over to the table once again and lifted the paper blueprints, but he didn't see what he was looking for. The only other item on the table was a cordless transistor radio. He then went to what he presumed was the interior access door for the attached garage. He opened the door, and the darkness within told Pies that this was probably a closet of some sort.

As he tried the next door, he knew he was in the right spot. The empty and airy, eight-car garage was partially lit by the moonlight coming through a massive skylight in the middle of the tall ceiling.

Pies rooted about the garage, opening the doors of the wall-mounted cabinets as he searched. In one cabinet he found a flashlight, but it didn't work. He took it with him anyway because his small flashlight was still in his car. Four cabinets down, he found some painter's and drywall equipment that had been stashed. There were brushes and painters' masks, as well as a couple of paint-splattered pairs of coveralls—and rubber gloves. He extracted a pair of gloves with his towel-covered fingers, ditched the paper towels, and put the gloves on. He next discovered several sets of clear plastic goggles, no doubt for use in sanding or spray painting, inside a small cardboard box within the same cabinet.

Pies grabbed up the coveralls, painters' masks, and a set of plastic goggles. He also took along the nonworking flashlight, and he headed out of the garage.

Back on the main floor, he went over to the folding table, put everything down, and then pushed the radio onto its side. He felt around in the dark and was finally able to pop open the battery compartment on the back. He dug two batteries out of the radio, unscrewed the head of the flashlight, and slid the batteries inside. He clicked on the flashlight, and the space lit up. It was too bright though, so Pies immediately clicked the flashlight off.

He walked to the stairway once again, cupped a hand partially over the top edge of the flashlight, aimed it up the stairway, and clicked the light on.

After scanning the light back and forth a couple of times, he said, "That's kind of what I thought."

He turned the flashlight off and then shoved it into his back pants pocket. He went back toward the table and located one of the eight-foot aluminum ladders that lay there, and then he picked it up in his right hand.

He carried the ladder closer to the folding table and put it down momentarily. It was just long enough for Pies to quickly don the larger pair of coveralls and then place a painters mask over his mouth and a pair of the goggles over his eyes.

Milena had pushed him away for now, but other people, innocents, were still counting on Pies. He had to follow through with his budding plan to burgle the upstairs of the Chapin Way estate and to finally rid himself of the Outfit's oversight—and to free the girls on Wakelin Circle.

Pies hefted the ladder once again and headed toward the enclosed stairway.

32

"Hey, shit for brains, you don't call the shots," said a red-faced Chuckie Silano, as the spittle flew from his angry mouth. "What the fuck?"

Pies sat across from Silano and a calmer Sam Panzera at a table in the otherwise empty greasy spoon diner on Higgins. It was just after 7:43 A.M. and Pies still hadn't enjoyed any meaningful sleep since he was released from prison. His red and puffy eyes betrayed his mounting exhaustion.

Brosi leaned against the lunch counter and silently observed. Gone now was his previously friendly demeanor. He looked today like the killer he was, with a flat expression, tight mouth, and crossed arms—but still coiled and ready to strike if need be.

Clyde, the cook, was nowhere in sight.

"You went through a lot of trouble to get my help. This is how it happens, whether you like that or not. It has to be tonight," Pies said, rather forcefully.

"Listen to this shit," said Silano.

"I've done my homework. Just like I did for the Zielinskis' crew all of those times. I did just like you asked. I'm telling you, the window on this closes in about twenty-four hours. You want to wait? That's on you."

"Fuck your window," said Silano. He wanted to banter on, but he caught sight of Panzera's expression. "Shit...," he continued, "You're buying this?"

"Why tonight?" asked Panzera.

"Can't fucking believe this asswipe," mumbled Silano.

"Chuckie? Enough, already," said Panzera.

Silano got to his feet and stormed from the diner.

"Did I give you too much leash?" asked Panzera. "Huh, dog? P-yes. The Polish dog. That's how they pronounce 'dog' in your neighbor-hood, isn't that right?"

Pies didn't respond. He allowed Panzera to have his moment.

Panzera reached out and grabbed Pies's forearm tightly with his left hand. Brosi edged a step closer.

Panzera said, "How do I know you're not setting me up? Maybe you already got inside and took the thing I want, and when I get there tonight, the cops are waiting on me and you're far away? And then it's so long, Sammy P."

"Why would I be here now? I'd be gone already," said Pies. He took a deep breath and measured his next words carefully. "I didn't take the thing and run. I couldn't do any of that because Brosi was right. The last time we met, he said that there were some complicated se-curity measures in place inside the mansion. He got that right. Who-ever told you about that was not playing you. This isn't a one-man job, and it's not a six-man operation, either. You'll have to leave those two guys across the way in the van home on this one."

Panzera's eyes flashed toward the street for a beat and then back to Pies. "How is your kike friend, by the way? The one always with the Cubs hat? I've seen pics. Kind of a looker...eh?"

Pies smartly let the comment go by the wayside. He didn't want Panzera to know that he had hit a painful spot when he found out about Faigy and where he'd been staying. Instead, he kept the pre-vious thread going. "You've been around that Barrington Hills area, Panzera. The roads are narrow and tight. If we have too many cars driving around at that hour, we'll get the attention we don't want, even if we're all in Maseratis. The four of us here—me, you, Brosi, and Silano—is all we need to be in on this."

Panzera seemed to be taken off guard by Pies's statement. He let go of his arm, leaned back, and blinked a few times.

"We're going to have to cause an overload on the system so that when the alarm does activate, and it will, the cops will think there's a glitch," said Pies.

"Glitch? What glitch?" asked Panzera as he leaned forward again.

"If one alarm zone goes off, the alarm company thinks there's a break-in. They'll send the cops. Even if it's a bird flying into a window or whatever activates that one singular zone on the system, the cops are probably going to check it out. One zone, to them, means that there's a good chance someone is trying to get inside. The alarm company has to make sure to cover its butt, so here come the cops. You have to remember that these alarms are going off all the time all across towns like Barrington Hills. At night, that's mostly what the cops there are doing, checking activated alarms and, maybe, looking for DUIs."

"Okay, I get that," said Panzera, as Brosi came closer and took a seat.

Pies grinned and went on, "Now, if the alarm activates in the house, the guesthouse, and the horse barn, all at the same time, they'll think it's a power surge, or maybe a power outage or some other minor problem. Chances are, even if the cops are dispatched at that point, they won't actually go all the way up to the house. They'll just drive past the property and then check the neighborhood, you know, to see if there are any lights on elsewhere. When they see that other homes have lights, they'll think that the power's out at our mansion. Chances are, they'll call the power company, not be up our ass as we take the thing. You understand?"

"So then why don't you just cut the power for the mansion? Cut the power and then we just walk right in. Right?" asked Panzera.

Brosi was already shaking his head, and as Panzera turned to him, the man said, "You cut the power and those vault doors we heard about all close up tight. Automatically. It's a...the...um...the default."

Pies looked Panzera in the eye and added, "You remember what I was doing before I graduated from Stateville, right?"

"Right. Working for 9-1-1," said Brosi. "Dispatching cops and all. You know your shit."

"Chuckie and Brosi here can handle breaking in and activating the alarms at the outbuildings, you know, the guesthouse and the horse barn. You and me will do the main house where the item is located," said Pies. "Once the alarm is tripped we'll have more than enough time to get the thing and be gone."

"What about security inside the mansion? It's got to be tricky," said Panzera. "That place is worth millions."

"I have workarounds. I'll need a thousand more for some extra equipment. I've already gone through what you gave me," said Pies.

"No way. That comes out of your pocket," said Brosi.

Panzera said, "No, that's fine. I got it."

"It's for gas masks for me and you, and walkie-talkies, good ones, for all of us so we can communicate and get this done right," said Pies, as he exhibited a bit of exuberance for the job they were about to pull off.

"Gas masks?" asked Panzera. "Really?"

"See, I told you they had pepper spray blasters in the place. You trip the alarm near where that card is sitting in the display case, that shit gets sprayed from the ceiling, covers every damned thing," said the excited Brosi.

"Won't it hurt the card?" asked Panzera.

Pies shook his head and said, "Thing is sealed tight in that display case. The cards themselves, these million-dollar pieces, they're kept in plastic containers of their own. I've seen photos. It'll be fine."

"Okay, I think I get this," said Panzera through a cautious smile.

"It's going to be like old times for me," Pies said with a nod and a grin. "I didn't say we weren't going to get dirty, but you'll get what we came for."

"Why tonight?" asked Panzera.

"The guy who owns the place comes home tomorrow morning,"

said Pies. "He only stays in Barrington Hills for certain times of the year. He travels heavy. Bodyguards, the whole thing. We won't need to take care of guys with guns if we do it tonight."

"How do you know that?" asked Panzera, as he looked up and waved for Silano to come back inside.

Silano shoved his way back into the diner and stood a few feet from the table. He seemed to have calmed down a bit.

"The guy's desktop computer is in his home office," said Pies.

"Hold up. So you were already in...? You were in the house?" asked a concerned Panzera.

"I was," said Pies.

"Goddamn it, Sammy, he's fucking this up," said Silano. "What if he tripped something and the cops are waiting when—"

Panzera placed a calming hand on Silano's arm with immediate effect. "You didn't set off the alarm, did you?" Panzera asked Pies.

Pies raised an eyebrow, shrugged a little. Coy.

"How'd you did skate around that?" asked Panzera as he showed a bit more respect for Pies and his abilities.

"The only alarm on the first floor is connected to the front doors and the front door glass. That's it," he said. "I got a way around that."

"Fuck you, no other alarm on the first floor? How can that be?" asked Silano. "That's bullshit."

"I checked it out. The only guess I have is that the owner gets tired of setting off alarms, so he deactivated the majority of the first floor. And the thing is, I'd bet he believes—no, he knows—that everything of value is upstairs," said Pies.

"The Honus Wagner card," said Brosi.

Pies said, "So why bother with the first floor, right?"

"He only lives there part time, like I told you before, Sam. Remember?" said Brosi. "That's what our guy told me, too. Said he grew up around here but lives mostly in California now. Santa Barbara, or some fucking place. And that he's got some crazy security in place all around the card. The card is his baby. This all checks on what I've been hearing, Sam."

"When I got onto his home computer, I opened his calendar up, and it has his daily schedule. He's in...Santa Barbara, just like you said, right now, but arrives home by 8 A.M. tomorrow. He's taking a red-eye, some private jet that lands at the airport in Wheeling," said Pies.

"We know that airport well," said a smirking Brosi.

Pies said, "I wrote the plane's tail number down in case we need to track it."

"You can do that?" asked the impressed Brosi.

Pies took a breath and said, "We have to do this thing tonight if we want to do it clean."

"Under the radar," said Panzera. "In and out, no one knows what hit 'em."

Everyone seemed to acknowledge. Everyone except Silano, he was still looking a bit dubious about the entire affair.

"Get some fucking rest, why don't you? You look like shit," said Panzera as he took in the sight of the exhausted Pies. "But nice work."

33

PIES REELED out an impressive yawn as he pushed the shopping cart from the automatic doors of the big-box hardware store on Touhy Avenue. His cart was brimming with rolls of clear, two-foot-wide, industrial-strength, plastic wrap and also neat bundles of yellow, two-inch, nylon strapping—the type used in construction for lifting heavy materials.

The strapping would come in handy later when he met with Panzera in Barrington Hills. The plastic wrap was for the job that was now at hand, though.

He was so very tired and he nearly tripped over his own feet as he moved along.

He got to the Mercedes, and placed the majority of his purchases in the trunk and the remainder in the back seat, all the while looking every so often toward the far corner of the parking lot.

There were five men, day laborers, aimlessly milling about a stationary black-colored pickup truck, waiting for any gigs that could possibly come their way.

*

PIES STOOD in the center of the living room at Rebecca Zielinski's Edison Park home, and he stared out the picture window. He could see that Rebecca, herself, was still in front of the home, planting some flowers next to her front cement walkway.

Five minutes earlier, as he drove through the intersection four houses down the street from her home, Pies could see that Rebecca, wearing a wide-brimmed sun hat, was kneeling down to get some flower planting underway. He parked in the alley out back, left the car engine running, and made his way inside through the unlocked rear kitchen door.

His hope now was that the hat she wore would prevent her from getting a glimpse of him through the front windows as he quickly moved about inside the house.

In Pies's hand was a written note with a door key taped to it. It read: "It's been moved to 6601 N. Oketo Avenue, Apartment #1. Sam is not your friend. He wants what's yours."

Pies spun toward the kitchen, and standing just a few feet away, at the base of the stairway, was ten-year old Itty-Bitty. She eyed him curiously, exhibiting absolutely no fear at all. She smiled and tossed a little wave.

"Hello," she said.

Pies hesitated and then said, "Hey."

"Itty, come and show me that shortcut," said the small child's voice from upstairs. Pies immediately guessed that the voice would be that of Sebastian Jr., now five.

"In a minute, Sebby," called out Itty-Bitty. "He loves Mario now," she continued with a slight giggle. "I know who you are."

Pies looked at the front windows once again, and he saw that Rebecca was still at work. When he looked back in Itty-Bitty's direction he tried to smile but came up short. "You do?"

She nodded. "Sure. I remember you."

Pies tried not to react to her statement, but it hit a deep emotional corner of his heart. He always wondered if Itty-Bitty would be okay, emotionally, as she got older, especially after the murderous violence she had witnessed when her father was killed in a close-quartered shootout.

Itty-Bitty wasn't an adult yet, and Pies was obviously no psychiatrist, but, the little girl seemed well adjusted. She stood there in a confident manner and addressed him directly. She exhibited no fear of him whatsoever.

"I'm leaving this for your mom, okay," he said as he took one step toward the kitchen.

"Okay."

"I have to go," said Pies as he began to take another step.

"Thank you," she said.

And that made him hesitate. He wasn't sure if she was saying thank you for the note in his hand, or thank you for taking the two bullets that would have ended her life those five years ago.

He didn't want to find out. He had stayed too long already.

Pies placed the note on the kitchen countertop and left the same way he entered.

As Pies exited, Rebecca opened the front screen door and slipped inside the foyer. She grimaced as she took a look at her dirty shoes.

"Darn it," she said at the sight of the mud she tracked inside. She noticed Itty-Bitty quietly staring at her from the base of the stairway. "Hey, Bit, can you run and get me the watering can in the basement? It's on the front workbench. The yellow one."

"Okay, Mom," she said as she happily bopped through the kitchen. "That nice man left you something on the countertop."

Rebecca grinned in a questioning fashion and said, "What? What nice man?"

"That nice man who saved my life," said Itty-Bitty's fading voice as she descended the basement steps. "The man from the news."

Rebecca's face went to stone, and she launched herself toward the kitchen, leaving slanting mud prints as she scrambled forward. She found the note, picked it up, and read.

*

THE HYSTERICAL, and shoeless, Rebecca left Itty-Bitty and Sebastian Jr., a towheaded little guy, in her parked car as she bolted to the front door of the apartment building on Northwest Highway, the one that Sam had followed her to.

She unlocked the common doors, ran down the short hallway, and then shakily unlocked her apartment door.

"No...no!" her voice loudly echoed, as she entered the empty apartment.

Everything was gone.

The sofa, chair, and tables were nowhere in sight—even the bed and comforter were gone from the bedroom. She stumbled to the kitchen and flung open all the cabinets and drawers. The place was completely cleaned out.

She clawed into her back jeans pocket and took out the now-crumpled note with the key attached. She sprinted from the apartment and folded to her knees on the sidewalk out in front. There, she bawled loudly, inconsolably.

Itty-Bitty opened the passenger door and called out, "Mom? Mommy?" Just as Itty-Bitty climbed out of the car, Rebecca scrambled to her feet, wiped the tears from her eyes with the back of her hands, and reread the note Pies had left for her.

Her composure completely disintegrated, she looked up the street, first one way, and then the next. Her eyes locked on something across the street and a few buildings to the north.

She ripped the key free, separating it from the note, and ran right past Itty-Bitty as the girl reached out to touch her. She dodged two honking cars and made it safely to the other side of the busy Northwest Highway. She cried loudly, kept running, and headed to her left, as her tear-filled eyes searched for something.

Rebecca skid to a halt at the next corner, reread the note one more time just to make sure, and bolted across the sleepy side street that intersected with Northwest Highway. She ran to the nearly identical-looking apartment building—at 6601 N. Oketo Avenue. The building was only two hundred feet from the last one.

She fumbled to unlock the inner door with the key and then ran down the first floor hallway to apartment #1, using the same key to unlock that door, as well.

As she shoved her way inside, she took one look, inhaled a sharp breath, and then crumpled to her knees and began to sob, once again.

"Oh, God. Oh, my God...," she cried.

All of her furniture from the apartment across the street was piled into the living room of the tiny apartment here. All of it was mummified with industrial plastic, stretch wrap, even the comforter, which was rolled into a tight burrito shape and sat in the middle of the floor.

Rebecca crawled to the wrapped sofa and began clawing and tearing the plastic film away. After she created a hole that was large enough, she reached up and under the sofa.

It took a bit of effort, but her hand finally came back holding a banded stack of hundred-dollar bills. Emboldened, and yet still sniffling back tears, Rebecca pulled the plastic wrap off all the upholstered pieces. When she was done there, she unwrapped the comforter and mattress and the box springs, too.

When the chair was free of wrap, she shoved it onto its back and checked the underside. She gently pulled at just the corner of the loose, black material that hid the springs and saw that the chair was packed full of neat stacks of cash. The stacks were held in place by a crisscrossing web of nylon twine. She unzipped the chair's cushion, and there was no padding inside, only cash—stacks and stacks of cash.

She reached under the sofa and ran her hand lightly along the length and sighed in relief. Next, she stood next to the upright mattress and partially unzipped the side of the padded cover. Inside she could see that the money was in place there, too.

Nothing was missing.

Her improvised "bank" had held—at least her savior Pies had seen to that for her.

When Bast was killed, Rebecca needed to quickly hide all of the money her husband had accumulated and hoarded over the years. And the cash her deceased father-in-law Stan Zielinski had socked away before Bast inherited it. If she hadn't hidden the cash the way she did, she and her children would be leading entirely different lives. The money was initially housed in a couple of storage units by Bast when he was alive. Rebecca knew, though, that the police investigators would've eventually discovered the cash if she hadn't moved it when her husband died.

She couldn't open bank safety-deposit accounts, because the police would know about that, she was sure of it. And if the authorities ever found any of this money, Itty-Bitty and Sebastian Jr. would've, most likely, been turned over to Children and Family Services while Rebecca did her time in prison for tax evasion, and whatever other charges they could pin on her.

Her simple, yet ingenious, plan, which had worked for years now, was to rent an apartment in her maiden name; buy some oversized, cheap, used furniture; remove the majority of the upholstery padding; and neatly and meticulously stuff the furniture full of the money. If anyone ever broke into her secondary apartment, which they wouldn't, because the place was located within the very safe confines of Edison Park, they'd immediately see nothing of interest and leave.

"Mommy, are you okay?" asked Itty-Bitty, who now stood in the apartment's opened doorway along with an elderly woman who held a shopping bag in her hand.

The elderly woman said, "She said her mother came into the building, so I was just—"

Rebecca lunged forward and took her daughter in a firm embrace. "I'm okay, honey," said Rebecca. She gave a thankful nod to the elderly woman, who instantly walked away. Rebecca continued, "We're okay now, honey. Everything's going to be fine. Let's go get Sebby out of the car, huh?"

Rebecca knew right then she would have to relocate the money once again, just to be doubly safe. It would be a small price to pay for hers and her children's financial security.

As Rebecca tightly held her daughter, she noticed another handwritten note taped to the wall next to the apartment's door.

The note read: "For I-B and S Jr."

34

PIES PARKED the Mercedes four doors down from his old house in Edison Park and got out. This was not a stop he planned on making, but since he was close by, at Rebecca's place, he thought he could make the most of his proximity. The majority of the folks in the neighborhood were at work, so he didn't worry about being seen. And who would remember a clean-cut man exiting a Mercedes and strolling up to the house—the Zielinskis' old place that was directly across from his old house—anyway? Lots of guys in Mercedes-Benzes were in the area these days, buying up properties, fixing them up, and selling them for a nice profit. Pies could just be another one of these people.

He hesitated at the front sidewalk and saw that the place was mid-rehab, and basically a construction zone. But all was quiet presently, not a worker in sight. Maybe the laborers were at lunch? Pies made his way to the small cement walkway on the left side of the house, passing the weathered stump of the tree his father helped to fell those many years ago. The former homeowners, the ones who purchased the place from Stan Zielinski, and who then recently sold to the developer listed on the sign out in front, had used the foot-and-a-half-tall stump as a sort of table to hold a clay flowerpot. With each new spring, the pot was filled with different colorful annual flowers to brighten up the otherwise drab exterior of the home.

As Pies stepped into the backyard, he had to edge around pallets of construction materials, wood, cement patio blocks, and the like. He bound up the three steps that led to the back door and surveyed the piece of plywood that was screwed in place as a temporary door.

Pies kicked the wood inward and wedged his way into the house. There were no lights on, but enough sunshine made its way inside through the new replacement windows to illuminate the place. It was a small space, but the rehab crew had done a beautiful job. The appliances had been installed, and it appeared as if they were making some last minute repairs to walls, spackling, and such, before the painting would start.

Pies started to become quite anxious...being in the Zielinski place, where his father's murderer had lived. He began to puff out great breaths of air, and his face reddened. And all at once, Pies began to tear the place apart. He picked up a five-gallon bucket of premade Sheetrock mud and tossed it right through a recently repaired wall. He grabbed another heavy bucket full of hand tools and repeatedly slammed it into the polished wood of the new kitchen floor. Tools scattered all about the place. When he finally let the handle of the bucket go, he noticed that there was a small can of paint thinner on the new granite kitchen countertop.

Pies angrily snatched up the paint thinner and shuffled from the kitchen into the living room. The floors there had just been sanded and resurfaced to their old glory. Pies hurriedly popped open the top of the paint thinner can and splashed the flammable liquid all around the room, onto the floor, the walls, even the ceiling. He scrambled back to the kitchen and found some paper, what looked like a short stack of receipts from a hardware store, and rolled them into a tight tube. He stepped over to the new gas stove and lit the end of the paper on fire.

As he moved back into the living room to drop the lit paper onto the paint-thinner-soaked floor, he heard the faint and muffled sound of a baby crying.

Pies gulped hard and tried to both swallow his hate and settle his breathing. He backtracked into the kitchen and tossed the lit paper in the new sink and doused it with water from the tap.

As he left the house through the kicked-in temporary door, he turned to his right, and through the kitchen window of the home next door, he saw a young woman gently bouncing a tiny infant girl in her arms and attempting to feed her from a bottle. The woman didn't even notice Pies.

He exited the same way he came, and he would never happen upon his old neighborhood block again. He was sure of it this time.

35

"I WORE THE wig again. At the store," said Faigy. "Everything's in the bag. Next to the toaster. I got like ten or twelve, plus the one you asked for."

Pies's tired, half-mast eyes scanned to Faigy's kitchen countertop and the small black plastic bag that lay there. He then went back to re-watching the short video Faigy took of the men in the van on her burner smartphone. From what he could see of them, neither of the young men in the van looked familiar.

"I don't think they get too many girls in that place," said Faigy.

"What's that?" asked Pies.

"That place. I don't know. It was like they were seeing a unicorn for the first time. They were very friendly, though. Overly friendly," said Faigy with a sad grin. "I got an assortment, like you asked."

"That'll keep people off your trail. No one will ever put it together," said Pies, reassuringly. "That wig, it makes you look so different. No one's going to talk to you when this is done."

"I look older, right?" said Faigy. "With the wig?" She asked the question, but she didn't really want or need an answer. She was just making small talk until she could get to the meat of the conversation that she actually wanted to broach with Pies.

Pies popped a noncommittal shrug in response to her "older" comment.

Faigy was attempting to keep things light, but then she let out a nervous breath and opened her mouth to add that she didn't want to be a part of Pies's quest any longer. Doing the surveillance of the house in Edison Park, where the two men in the van were parked—if she were being honest with herself—scared the shit out of her.

Faigy was not cut out for covert work, especially where some possibly dangerous people could be involved. She had overstepped her comfort zone's red line, and she thought that backing out now was the only prudent action to take. She was good at reading people and situations, she had thought, and helping when folks were in need, but she was wrong this time. Pies could get her into some real trouble if she were to remain involved and perform any further tasks for him, like going to the sports memorabilia store she just returned from and being recorded by the surveillance cameras there.

Faigy had been agonizing over her decision to tell Pies she couldn't help any longer—and that she wanted him to leave her basement apartment. For several hours now, and through a sleepless night spent self-deliberating, she told herself that she just could not get involved in any criminal activity. The hazy details that Pies had provided for her so far about what he was planning, allowed her to realize that the vast majority of his future actions were not super legal.

Pies shook his head and said, "Older? Nah, that's not it. Like I was saying, I don't know how this is all going to work out. But you'll be fine." He took a slow sip from a glass of water. "You wouldn't happen to have an old computer here? Something you'd be comfortable throwing away."

"A computer?" Faigy retreated from giving Pies her ultimatum for just a few minutes longer. Maybe if he took the old computer and left that would square things. And as soon as she considered that option, she shook the notion away.

"Are you okay?" asked Pies.

Faigy painted on the best fake smile she could muster. "Yeah... I think I do. An old one." She snapped her fingers, pointed, and continued, "Yes, in the office closet. I got it from a garage sale a few years back." She stood and led the way out of the kitchen and down a long hallway to what had previously been a bedroom—now transformed into a formal office. After Pies grabbed the old computer from the closet and was heading out the back door of her apartment, she'd tell him that he needed to move on. At least then she'd have the exterior kitchen door to slam on him in case he became irritated with her.

His eyes roamed the neatly hung rows of framed photos displayed on the walls of the office—all of them taken by Faigy. There was an empty space and a nail in the wall where another framed photo used to hang. "These are...cool," he said.

"Thanks."

Pies said, "You...took these?"

"Do you like them?" asked Faigy, trying her best to act casual.

"Like them? They're excellent." He then caught site of the expensive, top-of-the-line computer that sat on the wooden desk. "I can't use that computer, it's too nice."

"Oh, God no," said Faigy, with a grin. She pointed and said, "In the closet." And the second she said the words she remembered that there was something inside the closet that she never wanted Pies to see. She tried to reach out to stop him, "Wait. No."

It was too late. Pies opened the closet door anyway and moved inside. The space was quite large and orderly in its design. He reached up and pulled the string that operated the single light bulb in the ceiling.

"Here, let me. I know where it is," said Faigy, in one last attempt to get Pies out of the closet.

Pies ignored her and didn't budge. Straight ahead he saw shelves with office supplies and stacks of empty photo frames. On the right were more shelves, these with neat stacks of black-colored clothing —men's clothing. Pies allowed his eyes to roam rightward, where on the floor, he saw a small flat-screen computer monitor, keyboard, and an old processor. He wouldn't need the processor for his purposes. As he gathered up the parts he required, he stopped.

His eyes settled on a waist-high shelf straight ahead and a framed newspaper article with a photo insert. The frame would fit perfectly in the empty space on the office wall. It was a photo of Faigy Tambor, dressed nearly all in black, standing on top of her car as Pies's prison van drove past. The headline read: Blemished Hero Gets Eight Years.

Pies stared at the newspaper photo and blinked a few times.

"I should've told you that...we've already sort of met," said Faigy. "I really should've said something."

Pies put the computer parts back on the floor, spun, and started walking from the room. Faigy inexplicably reached out and gently grasped the material on the back of his shirt, which brought him to a standstill. She should've just let him go. It was what she wanted, but the hurt and confusion in his expression touched her and she thought that she needed to explain herself.

"I didn't want you to think I was some...stalker. I'm not. It's just that you've... Your story. It's touched me very deeply. It's difficult for me to explain I was inspired by—"

Pies quickly turned and drew her in tightly to his chest. He stared down for a few seconds into her incredibly stunning eyes, and then he kissed her—tenderly. Both of their eyes closed. After their lips parted, he gently slid his cheek across hers and whispered in her ear, "You're so beautiful."

Pies lightly cleared his throat, let go of Faigy, leaned back to the closet, and grabbed up the computer parts once again. He balanced the monitor and keyboard under his left arm as he reached up and took down a pair of large, black slacks from the other closet shelf. The pants would be quite baggy on him, but that would work just fine for his purposes. He leaned out of the closet, took a look around the room at all the framed photographs, and said, "You should put some of your paintings in here, too."

"My...paintings?" Faigy stood there wondering what the hell had just happened. She was rightly confused. "Pies, I think you... Are you okay?"

Pies carried the stuff back toward the kitchen table. He put it all down on the floor and took a seat once again. He leaned back in his chair, as if nothing had been going on at all, and yawned.

Faigy carefully took her seat and studied him for a long beat. She knew he wasn't acting right. And it was most likely due to fatigue, she assumed. She needed to end this though, and right now.

"Pies, there's something else..."

"Getting those girls out of there is going to be dangerous. But...I think I have a way that'll work...," said Pies, absently.

"Wait. Wait. Girls...? What girls?" asked Faigy.

36

PIES HAD a significant amount of prep work he still needed to accomplish before he met Sam Panzera in Barrington Hills. He was worn-out, but he had to push forward.

He was also hoping that Rebecca didn't do anything stupid—like contact Panzera in regard to Pies relocating her "bank." He was hopeful she would keep it to herself because if she did not, she and her children would be headed for certain ruin. Pies could also only hope that Rebecca never saw or spoke to Panzera ever again. Pies would do his best to see to that, as well.

Moving her money-stuffed furniture was not something he ever wanted to get involved with, or even remotely planned to take on. However, some details that hovered around Sam Panzera and Rebecca Zielinski began to unfold for him over the past couple of days.

They were painful memories from five years ago. They began to resurface after he first caught site of Panzera's car's vanity license plate number of LB901 while following him to Rebecca's apartment.

He had a strong idea as to why Panzera was so hot on having Pies do the B&E, but he never set aside enough time to do some of the extra research to cement his hypothesis.

He sat in the driver's seat of the parked Mercedes with the door open and perused the smartphone's screen. Pies knew that the 901 in Panzera's license plate most likely denoted September 1. That date was never far from Pies's consciousness. It was the date Vicki Chle-bek died by his hand.

Pies next searched "Sam Panzera" and "LB."

As the results began to populate on his smartphone's display screen, he knew exactly why Panzera had plotted to get him out of the penitentiary and then to Barrington Hills by himself. It was ex-actly what Pies had begun to suspect.

He got out of the car, locked the door, and made his way inside the dingy military surplus store on Elston Avenue. Weirdly, and as always, the place stunk of recently repaired sewer lines and boiled cabbage, but the prices were right.

Pies was a regular shopper here when he was doing B&E jobs for the Zielinski crew. He knew his way around the aisles and also the idiosyncratic personalities of the undesirable people who owned the shop. They were friends of the Outfit and came highly recom-mended back in the day. They were so closely linked to the Outfit that the owners never installed security cameras in the place. They didn't want to help the cops track down their own if it ever came to light that mobbed-up criminals were purchasing items here.

As he grabbed a rickety shopping cart and moved through the place, Pies received serious stink eye from the balding and tattoo-covered, father-and-son owners who stood behind the long front counter.

Pies remembered that the owners, who were probable neo-Nazis based on the type of WWII German uniforms they proudly dis-played and wore around the store at times, were not talkative types but were helpful enough when he shopped here in the past.

Pies walked directly to aisle seven and examined the various mili-tary issue respirator packs and gas masks, hanging from the display rack in front of him. It took him a few minutes, due to his exhausted state, but he finally grabbed two of the most expensive respirators and tossed them into his cart.

He would also have to pick up some black backpacks, a box of black rubber gloves, a couple of small sledgehammers, some pry bars, and some duct tape, as well.

Once Pies had picked up everything he needed from the aisles, he'd take his chances with awkward conversation and ask the owners to open the locked glass case next to the front counter, where the bulletproof vests and high-end walkie-talkies were securely displayed.

"Hey, asshole," bellowed a familiar voice. "Leave the cart."

Pies turned and saw Chuckie Silano standing at the end of aisle seven. He impatiently motioned for Pies to follow him.

"What is this?" Pies muttered to himself, as he pushed the cart along. He ignored Silano's directive to leave his merchandise and rolled the cart to the front counter.

"I'm coming back for this and more stuff," said Pies as he left the cart and reached over to grab a short stack of the military surplus store's business cards from the display tray on the counter.

"You don't need all of those cards, man. Come on," said the older owner, angrily holding his hands to the heavens. Pies opened the front door, grinned at the owners, and exited. The older owner turned to his son and said, "Nicky, put his shit back on the shelf. He ain't coming back."

Once Pies cleared the doors of the business, he followed Silano as he casually sauntered to the driver's door of a black Range Rover parked in the corner of the strip-mall parking lot. Pies stuffed the business cards into his back right pocket, opened the passenger door of the SUV, and got in.

Silano said, "This thing with Panzera ain't happening," as he got in on the other side of the car.

"What?"

Silano plopped heavily into the driver's seat and shut his door. "Come on. Up," he said, motioning for Pies to raise his hands. Pies shut the passenger door and did as instructed. Silano quickly frisked him. He felt Pies's phone and a small stack of cash in his front pockets, and nothing else.

"Good thing my cousins called me when they saw you park, and

I live close by," said Silano. "Lean forward," he continued. Silano pawed at Pies's back left pocket and said, "No wallet?"

Pies, hands now on the dashboard, sort of shrugged. "Hadn't gotten around to it."

"What's this? Paper?" Silano asked as he jabbed his fingers into Pies's back right pocket but couldn't extract the contents. "Take that out."

Pies reached back to retrieve the pocket's contents and said, "Business cards." He extracted the small stack of cards, and Silano could see the military surplus logo on the top card of the stack. Pies continued, "I've been looking for a new job, and I try to get a business card whenever I—"

"Don't bother with this place," said Silano as he turned away, started his SUV, and guided the car southbound onto Elston Avenue. "They ain't hiring."

Pies palmed the cards, rubbed them surreptitiously and slowly on the thigh of his pant leg, and darted his eyes toward the rear interior of the Range Rover. It was just he and Silano in the car. Silano looked left before he turned left, and Pies slyly tucked the stack of business cards as deep under the passenger's seat as he could.

Silano drove in silence for about a half mile. Then he looked at Pies and said, "Shut it down."

"What does that mean?" asked Pies.

"I don't have to explain dick to you. You just need to know that the Barrington Hills job is not happening," said Silano.

"Does Panzera know?"

Silano let out an angry breath and said, "I don't want a beef with you, okay? Don't test me, dog. You're lucky my cousins called me. They remembered you."

"Good guys," said Pies.

Silano took a quick glance at Pies, and actually grinned. "They're a couple of assholes."

Pies shrugged in agreement.

"I'm not bullshitting. If the Barrington Hills thing goes forward, it would end badly for you. The people I report to don't even know you're in on this. I do. I'll make personally sure that things end badly for you."

"Okay," was all Pies said.

"Sammy's got this bug up his ass so deep... Word from the top says the job, as explained to them, is too damned risky. Me and Brosi confirmed all of this with the higher ups. So stop this shit. We good?"

"What do I do when Panzera orders me to Barrington Hills? I was sprung for this."

"I'm not requesting this from you, I'm telling you. Do not go and do this job. After we get Panzera to calm the fuck down about this goddamned baseball card bullshit, we'll be back in touch. I'm sure there's something else you can help us with in the future. Keep the phone charged, because we'll be calling. And what in the fuck are you talking about? We didn't spring you. Panzera heard you were getting out."

Pies was confused by that last remark. After a moment he said, "Isn't Brosi going to beef on this? Seemed to me that he was the one who started this whole—"

"Stop talking. I got it worked out. Brosi's with me, and he's staying with me on this. Don't worry about shit that doesn't concern you," said Silano as he pulled an illegal U-turn and began heading back to the military surplus store. "No more shopping, either."

The owners at the military surplus store would be refusing any of Pies's purchases today, anyway, so he made sure to note the time on the Range Rover's dashboard clock. It was 3:12 P.M. If he called in a favor as soon as Silano dropped him back at his car, he could maybe, just maybe, find an alternative source to get the equipment he still needed.

He had to be in Barrington Hills in time to meet Sam Panzera at a strategic rendezvous point.

Everything would go forward as planned.

37

Pies, in a black knit hat, black T-shirt, and baggy black pants, along with Naomi's father-in-law Mike, also in dark clothing and gloves, stood next to their vehicles. The cream-colored Ford F-150 pickup truck and Mike's gray Toyota SUV were parked in the rear of the neighborhood cemetery off of Dundee Avenue in the village of Barrington. The Chapin Way mansion, where the Honus Wagner card was located, by way of the crow, was a little more than a mile from their location.

The desolate backside of the cemetery was not yet "occupied," although there were narrow paved car paths that crisscrossed through the area. The majority of the gravesites were in the first one-third of the cemetery's property, up closer to Dundee Avenue. There was less threat of a visitor, or passing car, seeing them way back in their current location.

"You're a fuckup, Jakubowski," said Mike as he grabbed heavy-looking dark-colored backpacks with his rubber-gloved hands from the opened rear door of his vehicle. He placed the backpacks into the bed of Pies's pickup truck. "But I think you have your heart in the right place."

"We only have a couple of minutes," said Pies.

Mike was troubled as he got into the driver's seat of his Toyota. "None of the gear is traceable," he said, nodding toward Pies's pickup truck's bed. "So just leave it where you leave it. I don't need to know anymore than I do already."

"I'll be back here within an hour," said Pies. "If it goes right."

"Goes wrong?" asked Mike, not waiting for an answer as he placed his vehicle into gear and rolled forward ten feet—and then the SUV lurched to a stop. He craned his neck so he could get a good and solid look at Pies.

Pies said, "What is it?"

Mike's anxiousness was evident in his tightly closed mouth and his hard working jaw muscles. The older man looked Pies directly in the eyes and said, "Jason was the one, wasn't he? They threatened my grandson, not Naomi."

Pies's inability to verbalize an answer was all that Mike required. He softened his gaze a degree or two, let his foot off the brake, and slowly drove away.

*

PIES, NOW wearing black rubber gloves, watched in the darkness, as the white panel van, with lights off, drove rather leisurely over the cemetery's ridgeline.

The van rolled right up next to him and stopped. Panzera was in the passenger seat, and a baby-faced young man was at the wheel. As the side door slid open, there was yet another man inside, also young and baby-faced. Both of the men sported thick mops of black hair— they were the same men Faigy had videotaped earlier and who had entered her apartment. All three men in the van were dressed in dark clothing, as Pies and Panzera had discussed earlier on the telephone.

Pies disregarded Chuckie Silano's demand to stop the Honus Wagner baseball card job, and called Panzera to give him the meet-up location and time.

During the course of that earlier conversation, Panzera tried to improvise plausible excuses for Silano's and Brosi's absences...something about "things they had to do." Pies didn't really pay attention. He just needed Panzera to show up. That was all that mattered to him. Panzera also advised Pies that his two nephews, Tommy and Johnny, would be taking care of Silano's and Brosi's tasks during the B&E.

"Turn around," said Tommy, the man who had hopped from the back of the van. Pies did as instructed, with raised hands. Tommy edged in closer and expertly patted him down.

"They both did shit like this in Iraq. A couple tours each," said a proud Panzera. "Didn't take them long to pick you up and follow you to that Yid's house near the park."

Pies wanted to deliver a proper response to the anti-Semitism, but this was not the moment. He took a deep breath and said, "Yeah, you mentioned that about Iraq."

Tommy was satisfied that Pies was clean of weapons, and he patted Pies's shoulder indicating that he was okay. Pies immediately went to his pickup truck and reached into the bed area.

"Whoa, whoa," said Johnny as he sprinted a few steps forward and grabbed Pies by the wrist. Johnny could see inside the bed area that there were three backpacks and a black sweatshirt on the open tailgate. There were also two large bundles of yellow, two-inch nylon strapping.

Pies relaxed and said, "The dark blue pack is for you and..."

"Tommy," said Johnny. "He's my brother. I'm Johnny."

"Sure," said Pies. "The two black ones are for me and your uncle. You'll have two walkies in yours that are preset. Just turn them on and we'll all be on the same channel. You have small pry bars inside, too, to break some glass on your targets. One of you has to take the guesthouse, the other the horse barn. There are flashlights in case you need them. Don't use them unless it's an emergency. We want to stay as dark as possible."

Panzera edged to the pickup truck and as he reached to grab one of the black backpacks, Pies said, "You should put the gloves on first." He pointed to a box of black rubber gloves Naomi's father-in-law had delivered.

Once everyone put rubber gloves on, Pies slid one of the backpacks closer to Panzera. Panzera smirked at Pies, as if telling him he wasn't stupid enough to take the first pack Pies offered him. He shoved that first backpack aside and picked up the second one instead, this one identical to the last. He hefted the heavy pack and then unzipped the main compartment. With the help of the illumination from the van's dome light, Panzera saw a small sledgehammer, a walkie-talkie, and two bulletproof vests that were folded neatly inside. A roll of duct tape was at the bottom of the bag, and there was also an expensive respirator with attached sealed eye protection.

Panzera stared at Pies.

"We both have the same equipment," said Pies. "Either pack. It doesn't matter."

"What's with the vests?" asked Panzera.

"It's not about dodging bullets. They'll come in handy when we get to the main access door upstairs. I'll explain when you and I have eyes on it. You'll understand," said Pies. "You come with me. Your nephews can follow. It's not far, but stay close. And no weapons. If we have guns, and we get pinched, we're all doing life."

Even in the darkness, Pies picked up on the twitch that instantly manifested in the corner of Tommy's eye, so he continued.

"Guns at a B&E constitute a home invasion. You get caught with a piece, you're probably looking at life."

Panzera said, "Like you're going to scare these two studs. They've got confirmed kills." His confident grin grew askew as Tommy stepped to the van and came out holding a rather large assault rifle. Johnny lifted his shirt and unhooked the holstered .40 caliber semi-automatic pistol that was on his right hip.

"Uncle Sammy, I didn't know that part of it," said Tommy. "I can't chance that. I got a kid now."

Panzera's stricken expression relaxed. He shrugged and said, "Put 'em on the back side of that tree. We'll pick 'em up on our way out."

Tommy took Johnny's handgun from him and walked them over to a nearby, thick, old oak tree. He carefully placed the guns out of sight.

"Go ahead and take the walkies out and fire them up," Pies said.

Everyone did as instructed.

"We'll need them switched on for the drive over. Just in case. When you see me turn up the main driveway, you follow and then turn immediately right and park on the backside of the guesthouse. There's a blacktop apron there. Your van won't be seen from the main street. One of you stay at the guesthouse, the other will need to walk down the hill to the right to the horse barn. When I give you the go ahead on the walkie, break some glass and then lay down flat in the high grass. If someone is on patrol, they won't see you." Pies quickly read the nonchalant expressions on Panzera's nephews' faces, and he continued, "You guys know what you're doing. Your uncle and I will be in the main house. Once we're done, we'll get you on the walkie. We'll be in and out in about four minutes if this works right. You ready?"

Panzera and his nephews agreed with nearly imperceptible nods, and Pies said, "Okay then."

The two younger men hopped into the van and Panzera got into the passenger's seat of the pickup truck. Pies turned to the lowered tailgate and to the black sweatshirt that lay across the panel. He quickly slipped it over his head and adjusted it for comfort, and then he slammed the tailgate closed. He put his backpack on, too.

Pies picked up the box of rubber gloves and got into the truck. As he led the way from the cemetery, south on Dundee Avenue, he lowered his window and tossed the box into some bushes along the street.

Pies then turned the pickup truck west onto Otis Road—and finally, he took a right onto Chapin Way. He and Panzera never spoke the entire ride. However, Pies could sense Panzera's anger growing, and he knew exactly why the man hated him so much.

Pies swiftly guided the pickup truck through the mansion's open gate on Chapin Way and turned off the headlights. He could see in his rearview mirror as the van turned off its lights and parked next to the guesthouse.

Pies maneuvered the truck to the doors of the massive mansion, and then he pulled an abrupt half turn, so that the rear of the truck was aimed directly at the front double doors.

"Get your pack on," he said to Panzera.

Panzera did as instructed.

Pies lifted his walkie-talkie to his mouth and pressed the transmit button. "Ready?"

Pies and Panzera heard one voice on the walkie-talkie say, "Ready."

A moment later, the second voice, "Almost there. Stand by." Five seconds later, "I'm ready."

Pies put the pickup truck in reverse, pressed the transmit button again, and said, "In three, two, one. Do it."

He hit the gas pedal on the pickup, and the vehicle jolted backward.

"The fuck!" yelped Panzera as he tried to hold onto any part of the truck he could find.

The pickup smashed through the mansion's front double doors, splintering the doorframe and knocking out the two dim lights located on the interior side. After the truck finally came to a stop, it was well down the wide front hallway. Pies put the pickup into park, left the engine running, and hopped out. "Let's go. Come on."

Panzera was a bit shell-shocked but was still able to extract himself from the vehicle. He was not expecting this level of violence just to gain entry to the mansion.

There was enough moonlight coming through the rear French doors, which allowed Panzera, once he got out of the pickup, to see the inside of the huge building. He was shocked by what was there. "What the hell is this?"

What he saw resembled an unfinished construction zone that had been turned into a crudely assembled indoor skate park.

"We don't have time," said Pies as he padded to where the two aluminum ladders were positioned earlier when he did his reconnaissance run. This time one of the ladders was pinched and bent into a near-flattened state. Pies grabbed the undamaged ladder and carried it toward the corner of the first floor where the enclosed stairway was located.

Panzera followed and saw the table with the blueprints on top. Only this time there was also a flat-screen computer monitor and a keyboard. "This is his home office? I don't understand this place at all," Panzera said, in confusion.

Pies said, "The owner's a weird guy. This is more like a vault masquerading as a mansion. The entire building is a shell mostly. What's upstairs is where the real construction money was spent."

They both reached the enclosed stairway entrance and Pies took a flashlight from the side pocket of his backpack and shone it up the cave-like stairway. At the very top of the twenty steps, there was a thick metal door opened inward. It looked a lot more like a small bank vault door than a bedroom door.

"It's a panic room. Those real estate photos showed a master bedroom, sure, but it's really the owner's panic room. Now you don't have to wonder why the place never sold. There's nothing else here."

"What the hell...? What's that dim red light up there?"

Pies said, "The blaster plates have red lights in them. They're all up there to the left, if the real estate photos were correct. I checked out some of the blaster manufacturers online. They pretty much all work the same. Once we get near the case and we break the beams of those blasters in the walk-in, they activate. There'll be regular lights up there, too. The switch is just inside the door if the pics were right. See the two silver outlet plates on opposite sides of the fourth step from the top?"

Panzera acknowledged with a short nod. He seemed to be in awe of what was going on.

"Motion detectors. We trip those and that vault door closes on its own and bolts itself closed until the owner comes back with the combination to open it. See the keypad at the top left? There's another one inside the room. We don't have the code, though."

"This is crazy," said Panzera.

"I need you to take the vests out of your backpack once we get inside the room. We'll need them right away," said Pies.

Without another word, Pies put the flashlight away and hefted the ladder. Panzera shone his light upward, and Pies began ascending the stairs. As he got to the sixth step from the top, he steadied the feet of the ladder firmly in place and then angled the ladder up and over the motion detector plates so as to not activate them. He placed the top of the ladder onto the wall above the open door. He then kicked the feet of the ladder once again, securing them into the step he was on. "Follow me," Pies said. "Do what I do, otherwise this is over."

Pies effortlessly climbed over the infrared beam of the motion detector and swung off the side of the ladder and onto the master bedroom floor. Once there, Pies turned the room lights on.

Panzera put his flashlight away and followed. He was a bit shaky, but he was able to follow Pies's lead, and he made it into the room without tripping the security system.

Pies took off his backpack and extracted the two bulletproof vests he was carrying. Panzera mimicked Pies's actions and then glanced around the room.

The master bedroom's furniture was pretty beat up. The entire space was absolutely nothing like the real estate photos depicted. There were no linens on the stained king-sized mattress, and there was a hotplate and a microwave on a folding table that sat next to the bed. Also on the table were a well-used, foot-tall bong and a fat zipper-bag of loose-leaf marijuana. A mini fridge sat on the floor, as well. There were posters of naked women on every bedroom wall.

And there were no windows.

"The windows in the real estate photos were just posters, like these," said Pies. "I told you, it's weird, huh?"

"Holy shit," Panzera said softly.

"Brosi called it. Said the owner was a goof. He was right," said Pies.

Pies tossed two of the vests over the top of the main door. He then reached into his backpack and took out a fresh roll of duct tape. He taped the vests into place on the front and backsides of the door, so that they wouldn't budge. Panzera got the two vests from his backpack, and he handed them to Pies. Pies taped those in the same fashion to the door's open side edge, above and below the handle.

"If we trip something, bolts will come down from the ceiling and on that side of the door and lock this all down tight. The bolts won't make it through that Kevlar, though. I hope," said Pies.

"We fuck up, we're stuck here," said Panzera.

"That's right."

Panzera could see the polished ends of the one-inch-diameter steel bolts recessed into the upper and side metal frames of the door. The Outfit underboss then turned his head in the direction of the display case that was inside the opened walk-in closet. "And there she is," he said.

Prominently exhibited in the walk-in closet was the display case holding the Honus Wagner baseball card. Panzera was so excited to be this close to his goal that he took a step in the closet's direction.

"No! Don't," said Pies.

Panzera froze in place and watched as Pies extracted his respirator from his backpack and slid it over his face. Panzera followed suit. After they both had their respirators snugly in place, Pies grabbed the walkie-talkie and a small sledgehammer from his backpack and motioned for Panzera to do the same. They both left their backpacks on the bedroom floor and edged closer to the walk-in closet's doorway.

His voice muffled from the respirator mask, Pies said, "It's going to be hard to see in here once those pepper spray blasters activate. They'll probably fog the entire room." He then pointed to where three of the five blasters were located.

"The fourth one is above the doorway on the inside up there," said Pies motioning for Panzera. "Fifth one is the largest. It's part of that light fixture in the ceiling."

"I already smell it. Even through this thing," said Panzera, his voice muffled, as well. "The pepper spray. It burns a little."

"I bet the owner had the system tested not too long ago. That's probably why there's no clothes in here," said Pies.

"Right," said Panzera.

The blasters didn't look like much at all—basic four-inch-square, white wall plates with small, downward-aimed, red lights emanating from the lower left corner. There was also an eighth-inch-round hole in the middle of each plate. All of the plates were recessed into the upper wall on all four sides of the room. The fifth one in the ceiling was completely hidden as part of a decorative, hanging light fixture.

The three-foot-wide by three-and-a-half-foot-tall, glass over wood-grained-material display case was located in the very center of the massive walk-in closet. There were small, locked, double doors on the front side of the case.

"We're going to smash the glass in. The front doors on that case are steel that's made to look like wood. I can see it from here. We don't have the time to get inside through them. You ready?" asked Pies.

Panzera gave a thumbs up.

"Wait," said Pies as he stepped back over to Panzera's backpack, which lay on the floor near the door. He unzipped the outer part of the pack and took out a small bag of cotton balls. Pies ripped the bag open and took out a handful. He edged up to Panzera while stuffing a cotton ball first into his right ear and then his left. He handed the remainder of the cotton balls to Panzera and he mimicked Pies's actions.

"Because of the pepper spray?" asked Panzera.

"You got that right," said Pies.

They both stepped through the doorway and up to the display case. Two seconds later, a series of soft beeps emanated from the blaster wall plates.

"Five seconds," said Pies.

Inside the case, they saw the Honus Wagner baseball card sitting dead center and propped up on an angled, red felt pad, like something from an elegant museum display. There was absolutely nothing else in the case except the card.

"Do it," said Pies.

Panzera lifted the small sledgehammer over his head—and the pepper spray blasters activated with a loud hissing sound.

"Hit it," Pies cried out. Both men began hammering down on the glass with the sledgehammers.

The room filled with a stinging, pungent, thick fog of pepper spray. It was difficult for either of them to see through the masks.

Panzera coughed in his mask and said, "Shit's getting through, goddamn it. My ears still burn."

"That's okay. As long as it's not in the eyes. Hit it again," said Pies. "Let's go."

Panzera and Pies repeatedly whacked the glass with their sledge-hammers, but nothing happened. The hammer blows just bounced off the glass. Pies put a hand out and motioned for Panzera to stop swinging, which he did. And that's when the blasters stopped spraying and the room grew quiet once again. The fog started to dissipate, but it didn't completely clear.

"It's bulletproof glass," said the concerned Pies through his respirator mask. "Shit. Stay here," he continued, as he wiped his gloved hand across the faceguard of the mask to clear the spray residue and ran from the room. He grabbed a hold of the ladder and swung himself up and over the stairway motion detectors. Pies bound down the ladder rungs and then the remainder of the steps. As he reached the wide front hallway, he got to the bed of his pickup truck and grabbed the two bundles of nylon strapping. He brought the strapping up the stairs and tossed it over the motion detectors and onto the master bedroom's floor. He then climbed the ladder and entered the room once again.

He unfurled one of the bundles and gently shoved Panzera aside as he wrapped the strapping securely around the middle of the display case.

He could see Panzera pensively eyeing the hundred-year-old Honus Wagner card. The card didn't look like much at all. It was about three inches by two inches and was enclosed in a thick plastic holder specifically designed to encase the multimillion-dollar item. The card was an old-time photo of a man in a drab gray jersey. The word "Pittsburgh" was written in large letters across his chest. The ballplayer's hair was parted down the middle, and the background of the piece had a yellowish-orange hue.

"The panic room door is going to close when I use the truck to yank this from the room. The strapping is going set off those stairway motion detectors for sure. We can't avoid it. I'll need you to shove the ladder between the wall and the closing door when the strap goes taut. We can't have the door close all the way. You understand?" said Pies.

"What about the vests? They'll stop—"

"I'm hoping they work as a backup, but I don't want to count on them. The ladder should work. It should jam it all up. Just to make sure," said Pies through his respirator mask.

"We're still good out here. Everything okay inside?" asked one nephew's voice over the walkie-talkies.

Pies motioned and Panzera got his walkie-talkie off the floor next to the display case, he wiped spray residue from his mask, and pressed the transmit button. "Almost done," he said.

"You're at five minutes already," said the voice on the walkie-talkie.

Pies, walkie-talkie in hand, looped the strapping together to form a much longer piece. He dropped the strapping on the floor for Panzera. He snatched up his backpack and lifted it onto his shoulders. And then he went toward the main doorway and hopped up onto the ladder. Pies pointed toward the remainder of the strapping, and Panzera picked it up and tossed it over the motion detector's invisible beam and kept his hand up high so that the slacked strapping wouldn't break the infrared beam in the stairway just yet.

Pies loped down the stairs and quickly made his way to the trailer hitch on the truck. He securely tied off the other end of the strapping, stopped for a moment to adjust his sweatshirt, got into the truck, pressed the transmit button on his walkie-talkie, and said, "You ready?"

Panzera, walkie-talkie in one hand, strapping in the other, pressed his transmit button and said, "Ready, yeah, yeah."

Panzera let the strapping slack drop from his hand and then he reached out and pushed the top of the ladder from the wall above, which allowed the ladder's feet to kick slightly outward and the top portion to slide down the wall and drop into the bedroom. The ladder blocked the doorway—just as the panic room door began to automatically and swiftly close. When the heavy steel door pushed hard on the ladder, the aluminum bent, but did not fully give. The door remained partially opened. Panzera could also see the bolts slide from their recessed positions in the doorframe, but they had nowhere to seed themselves. If the ladder did fail and snap into two pieces, or slip down the stairway, the vests would probably still keep the door open...probably.

Panzera's eyes widened as the strapping snapped taut with a loud cracking sound, and the display case in the closet was violently yanked from its floor mount. Panzera jumped out of the way as the case ricocheted off the closet's doorjamb, swiped past him—way too close to his shins—and smashed into the partially opened panic room door.

The case split into two pieces—the bottom steel portion tore open, and the top glass portion flipped and tumbled down the steps.

Panzera saw that the ladder would not hold much longer, so he flung himself out of the room, squeezing past the partially closed door, and barely made it before the door fully crushed the ladder. He was able to remain upright and not tumble down the steps. He pulled his respirator over his head and kept it in his hand as he ran down the remainder of the steps after the broken glass portion of display case. When he reached the case, he smiled and extracted the cotton balls from his ears.

Pies had the pickup truck stopped now in the center of the driveway out in front of the mansion. His respirator was off his face and dangled from a strap around his neck. He, too, had extracted the cotton balls from his ears and shoved them into his pants pocket.

Pies slid off the driver's seat as Panzera confidently ambled from the mansion's shattered, front double doorway opening. The Outfit member was tenderly holding the plastic-encased Honus Wagner baseball card. He proudly displayed it in Pies's direction. He grinned and then brought his walkie-talkie to his mouth and said, "Bring the van."

Pies immediately ran directly at Panzera, whose eyes grew wide with surprise. Pies lowered his shoulder and collided hard into Panzera. The mobster tumbled backward and onto the driveway, while Pies stumbled, retained his footing, and dashed inside the mansion once again.

Panzera got to his feet, tossed the walkie-talkie aside, and shoved the baseball card into his front pants pocket. He pulled a compact .380 caliber, semiautomatic pistol from his back waistband and gave chase. He entered the construction zone that was the first floor of the mansion, but Pies was nowhere to be seen.

"I moved Rebecca's bank," said Pies's muffled voice from somewhere on the first floor. "You won't find it."

Panzera turned this way and that, but he couldn't get a fix on Pies's location. The space was cavernous and every sound seemed to echo. All Panzera could tell by the way the sound carried was that Pies was probably hiding in the back portion of the first floor.

Panzera grew more and more angry at Pies's statement, though, as he quietly and carefully tiptoed around the space. Every few steps he stopped and tried to listen for Pies's movements. He slipped past the table with the unfurled blueprints and the computer monitor and keyboard. He recalled Pies had told him that he checked the mansion owner's computer for his calendar and whereabouts, and that the job needed to be done tonight. As he leaned forward to inspect the computer a bit more closely, Panzera noticed that the monitor and the keyboard weren't even attached to a processor.

Panzera's eyes carefully scanned the darkened space. If he hadn't left the flashlight in the room upstairs, he'd be using it now. Panzera said, "Rebecca's easily led, dog. The cops thought that her asshole of a husband killed Donny Noretti and my cousin Luke in the forest preserve. Know why? Because I told them that's what happened. The cops are easily led, too. You and I know better, isn't that right?

Rebecca's got to still pay for what you did. You worked for her husband. It all connects in my book."

Panzera's license plate of LB901 had truly bothered Pies for the past few days. The Google search Pies did earlier while parked at the military surplus store came back with an article about Luke Bercovici and his criminal dealings. Luke Bercovici was Donny Noretti's bodyguard and driver. Pies had killed both Donny and Luke five years ago when they had backed him into a corner.

There was a photo attached to the article that Pies uncovered— a photo from Luke Bercovici's funeral. In the photo, front and center, acting as the lead pallbearer for Luke's casket was Sam Panzera.

"I could've reached out and had you taken care of in Stateville. After I got wind of your release, I had to do this myself. I knew my patience would be rewarded. After you did this one last job that paid me some major cheddar," said Panzera. "Luke told me where he was going the morning you killed him. No one else knew. I never said a damned thing about what really happened this entire time, because I knew I'd eventually get to you, you fuck! You stabbed my cousin in the goddamned eye. In the eye with a fucking pen. And then you shot him. The same is coming your way, scumbag."

Pies took off running from his hiding place in the back right corner of the space and crashed through a set of the rear-facing French doors.

Panzera aimed, fired, and missed.

Pies stumbled but still managed to scamper from view just as Panzera took off running in his direction.

Pies sprinted to the far side of the empty Olympic-sized pool and hid among the landscape boulders. He could hear the van's engine as it approached the front of the house. Pies hesitated for another beat and then raced toward the tangle of trees that formed the natural boundary between the Chapin Way property and the Wakelin Circle estate out back.

Pies had gotten a hundred feet from the pool, still in the open, when Panzera fired his handgun again. The bullet caught Pies in his lower right back, right under the backpack. He staggered from the shock and pain, but he continued to stumble forward.

Pies, gasping for breath, made it to the footpath carved into the tree line and slid his smartphone from his pants pocket. Through the thick trees, and on the other side of the pond, Pies could clearly hear loud music playing from the high-end sound system at Tin Tomic's estate. It was muffled, but it was there. He also heard the frantic and angry voices of Panzera and his nephews Tommy and Johnny. They were in pursuit.

Pies, with his breaths ragged, cell phone in hand, and his back in excruciating pain, zigzagged through the trees, making sure his backpack didn't snag on any limbs. He turned right as he reached the horse trail and then angled left down the footpath that led past the pond and onto Tin Tomic's estate. As he circumnavigated the pond, he flinched when another shot was fired. The round missed him again.

Pies bent forward and made his way through the trees that edged the back of Tomic's estate. He fully laid his eyes on the exterior of the Wakelin Circle residence and righted himself as he stepped upon the manicured grass there. He ran directly toward the house.

The interior of Tin Tomic's place was lit up, and Pies could see two girls dancing with Tomic's two bodyguards outside near the dimly lit pool area. Even from this distance, Pies noticed as the low light glinted off of their shoulder-holstered handguns.

The professional basketball player, Tomic, was nowhere in sight. The bodyguards and the girls hadn't spotted Pies yet, because he was still in the darkness outside the reach of the home's security lighting system. They wouldn't be able to hear him because the music they were gyrating to was extremely loud. The people at Wakelin Circle must not have even heard the shots Panzera had already fired—the music was that loud.

As Pies neared the back of the mansion, while still outside the line of marker rocks he laid earlier, it was very plain to see that the two girls were dressed in tight tank tops, miniskirts, and high heels. The girls danced in sad little herky-jerky motions, as if they were high. Then one of the girls bent over and vomited. The bodyguard dancing with her leaned away to avoid getting splashed. The ipecac the young women had laced into their own drinks was working.

Pies slowed his pace, and as he turned back, he saw the shadows of Panzera and his nephews breaking into the open field. The three men hesitated for a moment, spotted Pies's darkened form, and then charged forward. They were now running at full tilt.

Pies remained just outside the rock markers and took a parallel route to the right side of the house. Once he arrived at the driveway's cement pad and the attached garage, he knelt down and began to tap in commands on his smartphone.

The app Pies had downloaded earlier from the website of the manufacturer of Tomic's high-end sound system worked perfectly. The music stopped.

A second later, so did the dancing.

The second girl also vomited, and the bodyguards raised their hands in frustration and disgust.

"What the hell is that?" asked one of Tomic's bodyguards in his broken Croatian-English as he happened to look out and onto the wide lawn to the rear of the pool.

The other bodyguard, the one who was wearing a sport coat the last time Pies saw him said, "*Tko su ti supci?*"

The girls huddled together and ducked backed into the house.

Pies, still on a knee, pressed a command on his smartphone. The sound of gunfire, six fired rounds, cut through the darkness from the sound system's speakers. Both bodyguards intuitively ducked down a little. Then Tin Tomic's voice came shouting loudly over the sound system. It said, "Shoot. Shoot, damn it. Shoot!"

The audio was gathered when Tomic played in a pickup basketball game at the recreation center. The bodyguards didn't know that. They thought that their boss was giving a direct order. They slipped their chrome-plated, .45 caliber, semiautomatic handguns from their underarm holsters and aimed...as Panzera and his nephews crossed over the border of strategically placed granite rocks.

The very instant the surprised Panzera, Tommy, and Johnny were illuminated by the ever-so-bright, motion-detector-activated security lights, the bodyguards opened fire. Their expert shooting was not hurried, but staid and slowly rhythmic, very professional.

The confused Johnny took an immediate headshot above his right eye and died instantly. His brother, the other combat veteran, was unarmed and attempted to take up a defensive position among the inches-high grass. There was just nowhere to hide.

Panzera, still standing tall, aimed his handgun and returned fire, squeezing off three poorly aimed shots in the bodyguards' direction.

The bodyguard on the right took aim, fired, and the round struck Panzera in the right elbow—the Outfit member's arm was nearly ripped into two and dangled now, utterly useless. Panzera yelped and fell to the ground. He scanned the grass for his dropped handgun, but instead, his frantic eyes caught sight of Pies, kneeling over by the driveway.

Tommy tried as best as he could to stay low and to follow Panzera as he struggled back to his feet, but the bodyguard on the left took out the nephew with two tightly grouped shots to the side of his chest. The young man was no more.

Panzera, even under fire, was able to get to his feet, pick up one of the eight-inch granite rocks that demarcated the invisible security light field, hoist it over his head with his good arm, and aim it directly at Pies. "Goddamn you," cried Panzera. He only made it four steps before he was taken down in a six-shot volley from the bodyguards.

Pies, still out of view of the bodyguards, used the smartphone to turn the music back on and crank the volume even louder than it was before the shooting started. As he did this, he saw that there were two luxury cars parked side by side in the driveway. One was a dark-colored Bentley, the other a red Lexus.

The roomy and baggy black pants that Pies wore allowed him to comfortably stay low and duckwalk to safety. He then stood and ran at a full sprint toward Tomic's horse barn.

The bodyguards never even knew he was there.

Parked at the horse barn was the red pickup truck with the snow-plow on front and the electric golf cart. Pies scrambled to the red pickup and looked back to the Wakelin Circle mansion's driveway —where he saw two shadowy male figures scurrying along, naked and in bare feet toward the Bentley and the Lexus. Both of the men, balding and with some gray hair, carried scrunched-up bundles of clothing in their arms as they slinked along and reached an illumi-nated portion of the property near the garage apron.

Pies got into the passenger seat of the red pickup, and the engine sprang to life. He said, "Go! Get out of here."

Faigy, at the wheel and dressed head to toe in black clothing, in-cluding a pair of black rubber gloves, had an apprehensive look on her face.

"Go! Go!" said Pies.

"Take the golf cart to the gate. I'll meet you there," said Faigy, as her eyes canted forward and toward the luxury cars and the two naked men, who looked to be digging into their bundled pants for car keys.

Pies didn't argue. He got out and Faigy put the truck into gear and stomped down on the accelerator.

Pies watched as the red pickup, with lights out, angled toward the driveway and the parked luxury cars.

Earlier, when Pies had finally told her about what he thought was some sort of human trafficking/forced prostitution ring going on at the professional basketball player's home, Faigy realized she had to help somehow. Her previous trepidations immediately melted away when she knew young women were in danger and that there was something, even if it was minor, that she could do to help. Her persistence to lend support eventually wore down the exhausted Pies, and he agreed to let her come along.

In the plan they hatched, before meeting Mike at the cemetery, when Pies dropped her near the corner of Otis Road and Wakelin Cir-cle, Faigy was supposed to hide in the red pickup truck and start the engine after Pies remotely turned the music back on. Pies advised her at that time there was a chance he could be injured by Panzera and his nephews, and that he would need her to be at her best to get him back to the cemetery and Mike's SUV. Once to safety, and if Pies were bleeding, they'd burn the red pickup truck to rid it of Pies's DNA.

Pies hopped into the golf cart and made sure the lights were in the off position. He sat for a second and watched as Faigy drove the powerful four-wheel-drive truck at a steady twenty miles per hours across the dirt, smashing through the wooden fence separating the horse barn area from Tomic's more manicured front lawn.

Pies glanced toward the rear yard. The bodyguards hadn't heard the pickup taking out the wooden fence because the music was still blaring. They were more interested in keeping their eyes directed to the back tree line, as if waiting on other gunmen to approach.

Pies turned back and saw that Faigy and the red pickup were on a trajectory to collide with the luxury cars. The pickup slowed to about ten miles per hour and solidly rammed the Bentley broadside. The force of the collision was enough to shatter the luxury car's driver's side front and back windows and gently lift the car up on to its two right wheels and then push it tightly against the driver's door of the Lexus. The red pickup truck's engine revved louder, and the vehicle moved forward, pushing and skidding both of the luxury cars sideways for another ten feet before Faigy brought the truck to a stop. In the darkness, all three vehicles appeared to be meshed into one expensive hunk of steel—no light seeping between them at all. Neither of the luxury cars would be going anywhere tonight.

The naked men, frantic upon seeing their cars rendered basically inoperable, headed toward the dense foliage of the mansion's front-facing bushes to hide.

Faigy scrambled from the red pickup and sprinted across the open front lawn of Tomic's property to where the gravel drive met Wakelin Circle.

As Pies wheeled the golf cart around to head in the proper direction, he noticed a naked, and frantic, Tin Tomic scramble from inside of his house and out to the pool area in back. The tall man was flailing his arms and obviously screaming, but his voice could not be heard over the din of the music.

Pies pressed down on the accelerator of the golf cart and careened down the gravel pathway toward Wakelin Circle.

In the darkness Pies could see Faigy moving his way, so he skidded the golf cart to a stop, got out, opened the gate himself, and waited for her to arrive. When she got into the cart, in the partial moonlight, both Pies and Faigy took one last look at the rabbit mural on the side of the neighbor's barn across the way. Then they observed a couple of front-facing lights switching on at the main house of that same neighbor's estate. Pies goosed the pedal as he steered the golf cart toward Otis Road.

Eastbound on Otis Road, Pies turned to Faigy and said, "Back there...why did you—" He stopped himself from going any further.

Faigy saw the confused look on his face and said, "My ex, Herschel, didn't look the part, but he was strong. Strong enough to— He would sometimes hold me down..." She lowered her head and remained silent for another few seconds. "I had to do something."

Pies smartly didn't force any more of a response from her, and as they drove along, he caught the first glimpses of fast-moving police lights cresting a hill in the distance. He said, "Hold on," and veered into a ditch on the left side of the road. The golf cart became embedded into a hedgerow, which was just fine with Pies. The police wouldn't locate the cart until the next sunrise.

Pies and Faigy hopped off the cart and carefully crawled through the tangle of bushes, so they wouldn't scrape themselves and leave usable DNA samples in the bushes. Once safely on the other side of the hedgerow, the police lights flashed past them without stopping, and Pies and Faigy slanted through the estate grounds located there. They were both running on pure adrenaline now.

Pies used the GPS on his smartphone to guide them toward their intended destination. Halfway to the endpoint, Pies stopped to slip off the backpack. He removed the rubber gloves and shoved them into the backpack. He then slid the respirator over his head, and he pulled off the black sweatshirt. Underneath he was wearing a bullet-proof vest. Earlier he had tucked the vest into the sweatshirt making both garments appear to be one and laid that in his truck's bed before he met Panzera and his nephews at the cemetery. Panzera had no idea that Pies was wearing ballistic protection. Pies had surreptitiously fastened the Velcro side tabs as he went to tie the nylon straps to the trailer hitch on his pickup truck before yanking the display case from its footings in the master closet.

Faigy handed Pies the burner phone he'd gotten for her earlier, and then she just watched. No words were necessary.

Under his black knit hat was a clear-plastic shower cap. He'd done his best to keep the pungent pepper-spray scent off himself as much as possible. And Pies didn't want to leave anything behind with DNA that could be tested. His DNA was already in the criminal justice computer system. He would be too easy for the police to locate, and Pies needed to remain free for just a while longer

Pies stuffed the hat, plastic cap, burner phone, and every other extraneous bit of equipment on his person into the backpack, and then they both ran.

As they jogged around the perimeter of the last Barrington Hills estate before crossing into the village of Barrington proper, Pies saw ahead that the ground rose up. He knew that at the top of the berm would be the freight train tracks that bordered the rear side of the cemetery.

The ground rumbled with a repetitive and deep vibration. Three seconds later, they both heard the telltale metallic-clacking sound of an approaching freight train.

They ran as fast as they could toward the rise in the earth.

Pies and Faigy successfully crossed over the tracks fifteen seconds before the train rolled past at forty miles per hour. The conductor, had he been paying attention to the tracks ahead and not eyeing the porn site on his iPad, would never have sounded the train's horn anyway. Pies's and Faigy's black clothing did an excellent job of allowing them to blend into their surroundings.

From their raised vantage point, Pies could just make out the silhouette of Mike's Toyota SUV. They sprinted toward the parked vehicle. When they got to within thirty feet, the engine started up, but Pies ducked toward a white cemetery maintenance building instead, which sat one hundred feet away.

Faigy got into the back seat of Mike's SUV. She could see that Mike had duct-taped down thick, plastic sheeting to protect the seats and floor from any caustic pepper spray lingering on Pies and his clothing. She and Mike silently watched as Pies turned on the building's garden hose and took a painfully cold shower, clothes and all.

After he finished, the soaking-wet Pies rushed back and opened the front passenger door of the SUV and rested his head back.

Mike turned and nodded to Faigy and then said to Pies, "You stirred up some shit. I heard at least five cruisers so far."

"No toll roads," said Pies.

"Damned cameras are everywhere," said Mike.

Mike headed the SUV southbound from the village of Barrington and then took Algonquin Road east. They'd arrive at their intended destination in approximately forty-five minutes.

"Here," said Mike, as he handed Pies a cell phone. "This one will only get 911. Untraceable. Toss it when you're done."

Pies took the phone and said, "Thanks for everything, Mike. Naomi and Jason will be okay. No one's going to bother them."

Mike finally pulled over and parked on Ottawa Avenue just off of Higgins Road on the Northwest Side of Chicago. Without any conversation, because most every detail of this operation had already been predetermined, Faigy got out of the SUV, peeled off her rubber gloves and stuffed them into her front pants pockets, walked across the street, got into her Prius, and took off.

Mike aimed his chin to the back seat and said, "Clean clothes and the plastic bags are in the back."

Pies got out of the car, then opened the rear door and jumped back inside. He stripped off all of the tainted clothes he wore and shoved them into a fresh plastic bag. The backpack went into the bag next. He then slipped into the clean sweatshirt and pants that Mike had brought along. He was all set, and he reached out to shake Mike's hand. "Thanks..."

Mike didn't reciprocate.

"Listen, Mike...after I do this one last thing, I'm thinking of turning myself in, okay? I want to do my time," said Pies, softly. "I should be locked up. I'm with you on that."

Mike kept his eyes on the dashboard.

"You're a good man, Mike, and I appreciate what you've done. I do. No one's going to know about any of this," added Pies.

Mike still hadn't budged...or blinked.

Pies opened the door to make his exit. "Thanks...for everything."

Mike half turned his head and extended his hand. They shook, and Pies got out. As he stood next to the car he remembered something. He leaned back inside and opened the plastic bag. His hand rooted around and came back holding a wad of cash, the lock-bump, and the smartphone Panzera had provided for him. He closed the door, and Mike slowly drove off.

Pies walked back onto Higgins Road and turned to the east. His connection with Outfit member Sam Panzera, and by association the link to Parole Supervisor Reedholm, was over and done with. Pies no longer had a buffer that allowed him to live outside of the halfway house.

He desperately needed sleep. A comfortable bed was just three hundred feet away.

He used the lock-bump, and once he cleared the interior security door of the halfway house, Gunther's apartment door flung open, and there stood the lanky supervisor dressed only in wrinkled boxer shorts, holding a cup of coffee.

"What the hell, man? What are you doing?" asked Gunther with a croaking "morning voice."

Pies stared back for a second before moving toward the stairway. "I'm going to sleep for a couple of hours," said Pies.

"How am I going to explain this to... What are they going to think, you know, the guy who let you... Is everything okay?"

"Everything's fine," said Pies as he ascended the steps.

When he entered his assigned apartment, Jenny, who was sitting at the apartment's dining room table and eating a sloppy-looking bowl of oatmeal, stopped mid-bite. "Oh, no," he said softly.

"Relax," said Pies. "Keep it down out here for a couple of hours, would you?" he continued as he walked back toward the bedroom.

Jenny stood and wiped his mouth with his bare hand. "Sure thing, brother man. The other guys are already gone for the day. I'll keep the volume low, bro."

Pies didn't even acknowledge Jenny. He pushed open the door to the back bedroom, headed to the right bunk, and lay face-first on the bed.

Things were settling down, finally.

He allowed his eyes to slowly close—and within seconds, he was asleep.

38

"**W**HAT? No. The heron, man. Not the heroin. What the hell is wrong with you? I haven't touched that stuff in months. No, bro. At the pond," said Lucas Grayson, the twenty-three-year-old, trust-fund baby who owned the massive mansion/indoor skate park on Chapin Way.

Grayson was dressed in an expensive shirt and leather pants combo, and his spindly feet were adorned with five-dollar, gas-station-purchased flip-flops. The young man tried mightily to exude a bad boy vibe that just wasn't working.

Grayson sat alongside his lawyer, a stoic and baggy-eyed elderly man, in a conference room at the attorney's Deerpath Road offices in Lake Forest.

Two linebacker-sized bodyguards occupied the space that bracketed Grayson and the attorney.

Four FBI agents, two men and two women, all wearing customary dark suits, sat opposite Grayson and his entourage.

"You've been there for, what, like hours searching the place, and you're telling me that you haven't... The heron, man. The one that catches the teeny-tiny fish and tosses 'em at ya. It's really freaky, bro. You didn't see it? Oh, dude, you're missing out. You are in for a treat. If you sit on the path next to the pond, and you're real, like, still, he'll just keep doing it, too. Catching 'em and tossing 'em," said Grayson, mimicking the tall bird's movements with his own skinny face and neck. "Catching 'em and tossing 'em. It's freaky. Catching 'em and tossing 'em."

FBI Agent Alexander, the one in charge, a man with all the personal warmth of a snow-covered roof, cleared his throat and leaned in. He wanted so badly to reach over the conference room table and yank the actual owner of the authentic Honus Wagner baseball card by the neck and squeeze. Instead, he said, "No, sir, I have not seen the...heron. We're more interested in the people who lived in the estate in back of yours. You know, past the pond, at the home of the basketball player on Wakelin Circle. Can you tell us more about him and his activities?"

"Oh, the lanky dude with all the foreign chicks?" asked Grayson. "He's not only a player, broham, he's a playah, my man. Feel me?"

Grayson's attorney leaned sideways and whispered into his young client's ear. Grayson grinned and swatted away the man. "That kind of tickles, bro."

The attorney righted himself and motioned for Grayson to speak to the agent in charge.

"I think I'm all done talking for now, broham," said Grayson. "I bet that you sneaky assholes think I had something to do with this shit you're investigating, don't you? Nope, I am talking no more. I'm going to sit here and not say another word, man. Not a one. Because if I do—"

The lawyer cleared his throat and Grayson looked at him.

"Right. Oh, right, right. Cool, cool. I'll stop talking now," continued Lucas Grayson.

Agent Alexander caught the stoic attorney rolling his eyes.

39

SILANO AND Brosi had their anxious eyes craned to the wall-mounted television as the 4:00 P.M. news broadcast crackled with a breaking story. They sat, hunched, in the back corner of a dark and dingy tavern on Chicago's West Side at Harrison and Racine. The bartender, a middle-aged man with all the muscle mass of a wilted turnip, escorted an angry and flailing drunken old man from the bar. The drunk lost his poorly designed auburn-colored toupee when it slipped from his head and landed at his feet. The bartender stooped and snatched the toupee off the sticky floor and slapped it to the old man's chest, before he shoved him from the place and locked the door.

"Turn it up. Come on. Turn that shit up," ordered Silano. The bartender hurriedly grabbed the television remote, aimed it, and continuously pressed the volume button until the sound was blaring.

On the television screen, the buxom, overly made-up female anchor breathlessly got things started, "We're continuing our coverage of the shootout in Barrington Hills. Authorities have now confirmed that one of the three men shot and killed overnight was reputed Chicago crime figure Sam Panzera of Oak Park."

There was a mug shot of Sam Panzera displayed on the television. He was unshaven, grinning, and surly-looking in the photo. The mug shot segued to a map showing where Chapin Way is on the map.

The female anchor continued, "The other two men have not

yet been identified as of this time. The men were reportedly killed during a shootout while in the commission of a residential burglary. This all happened on Chapin Way in the exclusive enclave of Barrington Hills. Rob..."

Brosi took a shaky sip of his gin and tonic and said, "Chuckie, what happened? This is...this don't even make sense...."

Silano angrily waved for Brosi to shut up.

On the TV, the chisel-jawed male anchor jumped in, "Thanks, Holly. Police are saying that nothing of value was found on the deceased men other than a knockoff of a rare Honus Wagner baseball card. The genuine version is reportedly worth several million dollars. Other media outlets are reporting that the homeowner on Chapin Way is also the owner of record for the actual Honus Wagner card; authorities have also confirmed that for us. Police are not disclosing whether or not the mansion owner is involved in any criminal activity at this time. That mansion owner, who has not yet been identified by authorities, is currently being questioned by the FBI. Jon Rivi's at the scene in Barrington Hills, and he has more information about some new details. Jon?"

Chuckie and Brosi traded quick, quizzical glances and then turned their attention to the television once again.

Jon Rivi, the handsome reporter on the television said, "That's right. The killings here in Barrington Hills have led to another investigation, Rob and Holly." The television displayed footage of four women, all wearing robes, and for the most part, their faces purposely pixelated. They were being led to a police van parked in the driveway of the Wakelin Circle mansion, next to a crashed red pickup truck and an expensive, yet damaged, black Bentley. "The alleged shooters in this case are bodyguards of professional basketball player Tin Tomic. Tomic owns the estate here bordering the mansion that was burgled. As officers responded to the initial calls of shots fired in this area, they discovered the women being shown on the screen now, their faces obscured for privacy reasons, all of who have been identified as Croatian citizens. The women were discovered locked inside a room at Tomic's estate. Amazingly, the women have told authorities that they were being held against their will and that, quote, an angel helped them to freedom. Police speculate that the term 'angel' may just be phrasing that's somehow lost in translation."

Even though the robed females' faces were partially obscured, the kidney-shaped mole could be plainly seen on the face of the woman with the lighter hair—the girl Pies spoke with through the translator app...only she wasn't a child. She was well into her twenties.

The street reporter continued, "All four women, ranging in ages from twenty-four to twenty-nine, have been taken for medical treatment and then will be questioned by Immigration officers later today. And we're also being told that the armed bodyguards for Tomic and Tomic himself have all been taken into custody on a host of charges, some rather serious and possibly involving human trafficking. Two local men whose cars were discovered wrecked on Tomic's property have also been taken in for questioning. There's a lot to sort through here. More on this as the details are released. Reporting from Barrington Hills, this is Jon Rivi. Holly, Rob, back to you in the studio."

Chuckie Silano stood and poked Brosi in the shoulder with a forefinger, "Come on. We need to find that asshole Pies and pay him a little visit."

The men scrambled to the front door and unlocked it themselves. The bartender grabbed the remote and lowered the volume and then changed the channel to a game show. A few seconds later, the drunk old man reentered the place, his toupee askew, and took a seat at the bar.

Silano and Brosi reached the sunshine and, with heads down, they both walked right up to Silano's black Range Rover, which was parked at the curb immediately outside the tavern's door.

Brosi got into the SUV first, and as Silano got around to the other side and opened up the driver's door, five unmarked police cars roared up and skidded to a stop in a semicircle all around the parked vehicle.

"The fuck?" was all Silano could get out of his mouth, before ten armed, plainclothes officers descended with force.

"On the ground."

"Get down. Get down, goddamn it."

"Hands on the back of your head."

Silano, indignant, got to his knees and said, "Blow me."

A tall plainclothes policewoman with short black hair grabbed him by the neck and forced him, face first, to the oily asphalt.

"Easy, lady," said Silano, who then heard Brosi screaming and struggling from the other side of the SUV. "You fucks, you better not hurt him. Brosi? Brosi, are you okay? Brosi? Don't fight it, man."

The policewoman placed a firm knee into Silano's back as she cuffed him. "Relax. Your little fuck buddy's just fine, Chuckie."

"You can't talk to me like— Who the fuck," Silano strained to get a look at the officer's face, "are you talk to me like that? Goddamn... You can't... What's this about, goddamn it?"

Two male officers reached down, grabbed Silano by the arms, and roughly hoisted him to his feet. He spit in the policewoman's direction, and she just smiled and motioned toward one of the parked, unmarked police cars. Silano was led away.

On the other side of the SUV, Brosi was handcuffed and now sort of calmer and grinning and leaning, face first, against the back door of the vehicle. A rubber-gloved, male officer was already in the process of searching the car. He was bent forward and scanning the carpeted floor of the vehicle. He reached under the passenger seat and came out holding a smattering of the military surplus store's business cards and the Honus Wagner baseball card—the authentic Honus Wagner baseball card. The officer displayed the card to the grinning Brosi.

"You get a piece of bubble gum with that, officer?" said Brosi. "Probably a little stale now, huh. All these years, ya know."

The officer holding the Honus Wagner card asked, "Hey, Angelo, why would a Mercedes that you rented be found in the garage of the house where this card was stolen from? And also in the same vicinity of where your boss was killed? There a reason you bleached the entire interior of that Benz, Brosi?"

Brosi's eyes showed a bit of panic. As he began to speak, the same officer said, "Don't answer just yet, dumb ass. I'll read you your rights first. We'll make it all official."

Two male officers arrived and took the cuffed Brosi to another unmarked police car.

*

SEVEN HOURS later, Silano and Brosi, still dressed in the same clothes, quite wrinkled now, walked from the jailhouse at 26th and California.

An idling, dark-blue, older model SUV awaited them. Silano got in front and Brosi in the back passenger seat, and the vehicle drove away.

The driver, a man wearing a black suit and with a pockmarked face, whistled and said, "For how much cash it cost us to spring you guys? Christ. People are not happy."

"This is bullshit. They planted that shit," said Silano. "And why the...why did Panzera go forward with that baseball card bullshit? I don't get it. They told him to leave it be."

The driver gave a side-glance to Silano and said, "Where can I drop you two? I'm the lawyer, not a fucking ride share. I'll get you close to where you need to be. How's that?"

"Thanks man, for getting us bounced," said Brosi from the back seat. "Maybe the Kennedy at Lawrence, if you can swing that."

Silano was silently brooding now. After three minutes of drive time, it finally dawned on him that the lawyer was taking them west and south, instead of north—the direction where they both lived. He looked quizzically at the man behind the wheel.

That's precisely when a pudgy-faced, beefy man with a mop of black hair, wearing a brown leather jacket, slowly rose up from the back cargo area of the SUV. He gently poked the .40 caliber semiautomatic that was in his right hand to the back of Brosi's head.

"Chuckie?" said Brosi, quietly, in a near whisper.

Chuckie Silano turned around, saw the man with the gun—and then slowly cast his eyes downward.

The lawyer said, "We're going to need a cash reimbursement for that bail we just handed over. Tonight."

The pudgy-faced man said, "Couldn't leave Barrington Hills alone...."

*

THE DUPAGE County sheriff's officer parked his cruiser forty feet in back of the smoldering and haphazardly parked dark-blue SUV at 2:07 A.M.

He shined his side-door spotlight on the vehicle and pinched the transmitter on his shoulder-mounted microphone, "I've got a smoking vehicle off the roadway at...Powis Road north of Smith. Fire looks to be out, but it's still smoldering. Roll an engine, no lights and sirens, just to be safe. Send a tow truck, too."

The officer put his car into park and opened the cruiser door. The sickeningly sweet smell of charred death, an aroma he was familiar with from his time serving in the Marine Corps in Afghanistan, instantly swept over him.

"Ah, shit..."

He scrambled up to the red-hot SUV and shone his flashlight into the front seat, and there sat, side by side, the charred remains of Chuckie Silano and Angelo Brosillino. The men's clothing had fused to their bodies, and their blackened heads were cranked oddly backward. Their empty eye sockets looked heavenward, and their mouths were agape in a horrid, almost choreographed, death pose.

The officer put his sleeve to his nose, backed away, and bent over. He coughed, gagged, and reached to pinch his shoulder-mounted microphone and missed. As he straightened, he took a few stagger-

270 *   MATT HADER

ing steps away from the smoldering vehicle and a couple of cleansing breaths, as well. He successfully keyed his microphone and said,
"Send me a supervisor, now. Powis and Smith."

He released the microphone button and gasped, "Fuck me."

*

THE CHICAGO 16th district police patrol car bounced into the parking lot on Elston Avenue and came to an abrupt stop. Both side door
spotlights illuminated the front glass of the military supply store
—the front door was ajar.

As the two patrolmen cautiously exited their car, the driver, gun
drawn, peeled toward the front door.

His partner angled to the side of the building and edged closely
along the store's exterior brick wall, gun aimed forward. As the patrolman got to the back of the building, he quickly poked his head
around the corner, saw that it was clear, and turned, advancing to
the closed rear door of the business. He was just feet from the metal
door when it popped open, and his partner stood there grim-faced,
shaking his head.

He said, "Get the Sarge on the radio, we got a rubber-glove job."

As both of the patrolmen shuffled inside the tiny, rear interior
hallway, the driver darted his eyes toward an open doorway. The
other patrolman peered into the office—there, the empty floor safe
door was opened wide, and they observed the tattoo-covered, father
and son store owners, lying askew on the floor, each with a couple of
bullet holes to the side of the head.

40

TWENTY-SIX HOURS after Mike dropped him near the halfway house, Pies awoke with a start, his mind racing.

All he could think about was the Ford F-150 pickup truck that he had left at the burgled mansion in Barrington Hills. He had wiped the vehicle clean of fingerprints before he met Panzera at the cemetery and began their criminal project. But the previous owner of the truck would be asked some rather pointed questions once the VIN number was run by the police. While in his sleepy state, he was hoping that the former owner would skate on any trouble, and if he didn't, Pies would find a way to exonerate him.

He propped himself up on an elbow and was confused by his whereabouts, and then his eyes caught movement near the room's door.

"Hey, there, buddy. Man, you must've been really tired," said the smiling Jenny. "There's coffee in the kitchen, if you want some."

Pies sat upright, slipped his smartphone from his pants pocket, and saw the time. He barely recalled waking a few times over the past several hours, and each time when he thought that he would actually get up, he drifted back to sleep.

"Shit," he said as he launched himself from the bed, stumbled, righted himself, and then stood still for a moment.

"Take it easy, my main man," said Jenny. "You okay?"

"I need a shower," said Pies. "Coffee," he croaked.

*

PIES, LOOKING a bit more refreshed and wearing one of Jenny's tight, dark-blue T-shirts, turned the corner from Oshkosh Avenue onto Northwest Highway. He walked directly toward Chlebeks' Bakery.

Now that Panzera was taken care of, Pies had to do his level best to steer clear of Faigy Tambor for the time being. He did not want her involved in what he knew was coming, namely a police investigation into what transpired in Barrington Hills. Pies knew the police would be looking at him, since he was an Outfit-sanctioned burglary expert just recently released from prison. Maybe a month or so down the line, he'd reconnect with Faigy to see how she was getting along. At least that's how they left things with one another that night when they set off to take down Sam Panzera, Tin Tomic, et al.

Pies knew he could trust Faigy to remain silent—and she could trust him.

From the moment he left on foot from the halfway house, though, he had the sensation that he was being followed. He actually expected it. He tried not to make any quick head moves to locate the tail, but he knew one was there.

Five minutes earlier, when he walked past the Chlebeks' house, he went down the side walkway and around to the home's back door, out of view from the street. As he strolled along, he pulled the majority of the remaining cash he had, the lock-bump, and the smartphone from his pants pockets and tossed it all into a battered plastic milk crate located under the porch landing—all without stopping. If it was a police tail he had picked up, which he reckoned it was, he didn't want to have the lock-bump and burner smartphone on his person when they caught up with him. Either one of those items would get him tossed quickly back into Stateville Correctional Center, especially the burner cellphone with its rather damaging Internet search history.

After dumping the items from his pockets, he shoved some bushes aside, hopped the back fence at the Chlebeks' house, and cut through the park next door.

He would have nothing in his possession other than the seven dollars in his pants pocket when he opened the bakery's front door, went inside, and apologized to Milena.

Pies got right in front of the bakery and could see inside the store through the main front window, where Milena was wrapping it up with a female customer, as well as the reflection of outside the store where a black-colored Crown Victoria was moving along the curb behind him. The Crown Vic slowly pulled in front of a fire hydrant and stopped.

Pies tugged open the bakery's door, which was still covered in plywood, and went inside. The female customer slipped around him on her way out, and Pies edged in closer to the front counter—and Milena.

They stood and stared at one another for what seemed like an eternity. And just as Pies opened his mouth to issue his long overdue apology, the shop's door violently burst open, and four armed men, and two armed women, all in plainclothes, quickly piled into the space. They formed a semicircle five feet from Pies—guns aimed at his back.

Milena's eyes widened, but she remained silent for the moment.

"On the floor," said the tall, dark-haired policewoman in charge, rather quietly. She was the same officer who had taken Silano down. "Do it, now."

Pies complied, and when he was on his stomach and secured with handcuffs, the plainclothes police officers put their weapons away.

"What is this?" said Milena. "This is not good. This is not good in my shop," she continued angrily, in her broken English. "You must leave."

The cops ignored Milena's request.

Two of the male officers got Pies to a seated position and gave him a preliminary frisk. All he could do at that point was to peer up at

Milena with pleading eyes. Should he go ahead and issue the apology to Vicki's mother now because it could be his last chance to offer it face-to-face?

As he was about to say something, the policewoman in charge said, "We're going to find out where you were early yesterday morning Jakubowski. Then we're going to put you away," she said.

"Yesterday morning?" asked Milena. "He was here with me," she continued without hesitation.

The policewoman in charge lost the shitty little grin that had formed after her statement. She turned to Milena and said, "What? What do you mean?"

"The main oven. It doesn't work right. Dear Jakub made it work again," said Milena. Her acting chops were impeccable. "He's so good with the machines."

"What time was that?" asked the policewoman.

Milena didn't falter, and she grabbed a hold of a time she believed would offer the best false alibi for Pies. "My Jakub was here until five that morning fixing it. He's so good with the mechanical things, he is. He was here for over twelve hours. He's such a nice man," continued Milena. "And he refused to be paid."

One of the male officers chimed in, "That squares with what the Nazi and that little asshole at the halfway house told us. Said he got in yesterday morning and crashed."

The policewoman in charge nodded to the other female officer, and she bent down to take the cuffs off of Pies. After he was unhooked, she said, "Get up."

Pies grimaced as he painfully stood.

"Everything okay," asked the other female officer.

"Tweaked my back working on the oven," said Pies as he placed a hand close to where Panzera's .380 caliber round struck his bulletproof vest. While he was showering earlier at the halfway house, Pies had caught a glimpse in the mirror of where he was hit. An angry-looking and large, dark-colored bruise had blossomed at the site.

As he tried to rub the injured spot, Pies eyed Milena and wondered why she had lied for him.

"Let's do this the nice way then, okay? Mr. Jakubowski, would you please come with us. We have some questions for you. It'll help in a major crimes investigation," she said.

Pies said, "I don't understa—"

"We need to clear some things up. Chicago PD's taking the lead because there's a connection to organized crime. Now *that* you should understand. Barrington Hills asked for the assist."

"Barrington Hills?" asked Pies. "What's going on?"

The policewoman in charge smirked and said, "Right... Okay, Ace. Would you please come along with us?"

Pies was not under arrest, but he knew that he would have to go along. If he cooperated, then maybe the police wouldn't look so hard at him. He still needed to come back to the bakery and apologize properly. "Yeah, I can do that," said Pies. "Be glad to help," he added without a whiff of sarcasm.

41

PIES HAD been sitting in the conference room of Chicago's 16th police district for several hours—alone. This was the exact same building he walked into five years prior when he turned himself into the police.

This time, the police gave him a can of warm cola and told him to wait. At one point, as he silently wasted the time away, a humorless uniformed female police officer came in, dropped a bag with three cold fast-food hamburgers onto the table, and left. Pies never touched the food.

Pies was not locked within a windowless interrogation room, and that was a truly positive development. The police were treating him like a witness and not a suspect. But the hours and hours of waiting still had him a little off balance and growing more and more tense by the moment. He considered at one point that the cops had possibly found some damning evidence against him. Maybe he had left something behind in Barrington Hills and that's why the police allowed him to slowly stew in the conference room.

It was dark outside when the door of the conference room finally opened again. In lumbered a large man with a file folder in his hand. The man appeared more like a cheap-sports-coat-wearing brick wall than anything human. He smelled faintly of Italian beef sandwiches and French fries, and as soon as they made eye contact, Pies knew exactly who he was. The man had essentially gotten larger—wider—since he and Pies last laid eyes on one another.

Chicago Police Detective Stu Von Bargen, physically appearing as if retirement was just around the corner, gave Pies a sarcastic half grin. Pies and Von Bargen were first introduced five years ago after the shootout in Edison Park.

"You packed on the pounds," said Von Bargen, ironically, as he pulled a chair from under the conference room's table and sat directly across from Pies. "I heard you were an exercising maniac at State-ville. So it seems that I did not hear wrong," he continued, with an added whistle. "Look at you...."

"What do you want?" asked Pies, his patience totally gone. He did not like Von Bargen—especially after the detective had tried to jam him up by playing "good cop" the last time they interacted. Pies never bought Von Bargen's good cop routine because Von Bargen's true shitty disposition always shone through whatever role he was play-ing as part of his official police duties. Pies had also sensed, at the time, that Von Bargen was the type of officer who would callously sidestep pesky constitutional hurdles to make his cases stick if he was backed into a legal corner. Yes, Pies was a criminal, but crimi-nal cops still disgusted him.

Von Bargen leaned back and stared hard at Pies. He glowered for a good long minute, but Pies never looked away. Finally, the detective opened the file that he brought along and studied it for a moment.

"There's going to be a mountain of evidence to go through on this," said Von Bargen as he looked up once again. "It'll take a few months, I'm sure. Maybe even longer to lock everything down," he added.

"What happened?" asked Pies. "No one's told me. I keep asking. No one's telling me anything. What's this all about?"

Von Bargen smirked and said, "This has your paw prints all over it, Jakub. Looks like the work of the old Zielinski crew, you ask any-one here. We both know there's none of those Zielinski pricks left... save one. And I'm looking at him."

As Von Bargen conversed, Pies could sense that the big detective was troubled by something, but he was doing his best to act like he didn't have a care in the world.

Von Bargen smiled and continued, "We'll get something to stick, and when we do, you'll be back in Stateville before too long."

"I look forward to it," said Pies.

That elicited a confused facial response from the detective. "What's that supposed to mean?" he asked.

Pies didn't respond.

Von Bargen recovered by saying "We have a parole officer's report in here from an—"

"Officer Ramirez?" asked Pies.

Von Bargen gave him a cold glance, and then continued, "Ramirez was in possession of a substantiated report that you were not residing in the halfway house that you were assigned to. That's a violation, Jakub. That sends you back," he said with the hint of a grin.

"I was just doing what Parole Supervisor Reedholm ordered me to do. Isn't that what a parolee's supposed to do, Detective, follow orders?" said Pies. "She signed off on me living anywhere I wanted, just as long as I reported to Ramirez when I was ordered to. Ramirez knew that. There's a desk sergeant at Town Hall. A big puffy guy, looks a lot like you, as if he's about to give up on life—"

"There's no need—".

"He saw and heard the whole thing. He can back me up," added Pies.

Von Bargen took in Pies's last statement, and he seemed to acquiesce. He looked down, and swallowed hard. Whatever was bothering him could not be held in check any longer.

"Shit. Sorry to ruin your night," said Pies.

Von Bargen, while never raising his gaze, chose his words rather carefully. "They um...Supervisor Reedholm's body was discovered this afternoon at her Glenview apartment."

The news actually shocked Pies, but he fought to not let it show.

Von Bargen raised his eyes and continued, "She used her service weapon to, ah... She even killed her dog, for fuck's sake. That's why it took me so long to get here. I had to make a report because we're taking the lead on this Barrington Hills..." He stopped himself from talking and slapped the table hard. He blurted, "Goddamn it. Goddamn it..."

The detective took in a sharp and angry breath, slowly closed the file, cleared his throat, and stood. "Just, um... You can, ah... You can go...." Von Bargen spun around and headed for the conference room's door without saying another word.

"Detective?"

Von Bargen looked over his shoulder.

"Do you have a business card? Never know, I might hear something that could help with your investigation," continued Pies. "If I hear anything..."

Von Bargen squinted and looked a bit puzzled. "The fuck?"

"Serious," said Pies.

Von Bargen reached into his suit jacket pocket and extracted a card. He angrily flicked it onto the conference room's table and left.

Pies picked up his warm soda can and chugged the remainder of its contents. He set the can carefully back on the table. There was no need to worry about leaving behind prints or DNA here. The police already had a book on Pies's entire existence.

He rose to his feet painfully and stretched his stiff and sore back muscles.

A few brand new and different thoughts burst into Pies's mind.

If he was being honest with himself, he knew that he would probably never see or speak with Faigy Tambor ever again—not even a month from now—and that was okay. Jakub "Pies" Jakubowski had an uncanny knack of bringing injurious chaos into innocent people's lives, and he didn't want that for Faigy. A clean break was for the best. The woman was so very strong, and Pies appreciated that to no end. She did things in her own way, it seemed, and that was a certainty that anyone she encountered could rely on.

Once he apologized to Milena, maybe he'd give Von Bargen a call to clear up a few details about the Barrington Hills job. And then he'd gladly go back to Stateville Correctional Center to live out his days—however many that would be once the Outfit figured out what he'd done to their organization.

And as promised, Naomi's father-in-law Mike would never come up during any of his future police interrogations.

Maybe Pies would make Von Bargen's tough week worth the trouble.

Pies moved over to the end of the conference room table and lingered. He stared down at the card with the detective's name and snatched it off the table. He left the 16th police district without looking back.

42

VIHAAN VIRK, or VV as he was known to his close friends and regular customers, returned to the Harlem Avenue gas station he owned after spending several hours in the federal building in downtown Chicago. He was mentally drained from the badgering he received, first at the hands of some Barrington Hills police officers and then from Chicago police detectives, the FBI, and finally Homeland Security personnel.

The authorities even attempted a bit of theater when they initially transported him from his Northwest Side gas station to the federal building in an unmarked car. In an attempt to rattle the second-generation American, the cops led him, uncuffed, into the building past a throng of television news cameras and badgering reporters. But the faux perp walk hadn't rattled VV one little bit.

During his interrogation, VV was asked at one point by the FBI investigators if he wanted an attorney present during his questioning, but he declined. He had nothing to hide. The events VV outlined for the authorities were not imagined, they actually occurred in the way he methodically—over and over again—laid them out.

Mostly.

About a week before his questioning, an unknown teenage boy entered VV's gas station saying that he was interested in purchasing the Ford F-150 pickup truck that was sitting on his parking lot.

VV made the deal, took cash from the kid, signed over the title, and that was that.

VV broke no laws, and he never saw the kid or the truck again—until he spotted the Ford on television from the view of a circling news helicopter's camera. VV recognized his old pickup truck by the distinctive rust pattern—sort of like an elongated map of Rhode Island—in the bed of the vehicle.

VV had done nothing wrong...that he'd admit to. He did take extra cash to retain the vehicle's registration and insurance in his name for a couple months...but, so what? The cops didn't need to know that part of the transaction. He thought he was helping a pimply-faced seventeen-year-old kid purchase his first vehicle, that's all.

During the ongoing, hours-long questioning, things got heated a time or two, but VV held to his timeline of facts. The authorities, part of a joint task force that was investigating the Barrington Hills shootout, conferred with one another after all the questions were asked and came to the same conclusion—Vihaan Virk had done ab-solutely nothing wrong.

Back at his business, VV wearily picked up the newly arrived mail from his desk and noticed that one of the envelopes in the short stack had no postage or return address on it.

All that was written on the envelope was: "Owner."

VV ripped the envelope open with his grease-covered fingers and pulled out a typewritten note that read: "You have the use of a Dela-van, Wisconsin, lake house for the rest of this month. It's all paid for. The key for the place is at Enright Realty in the town of Dela-van. Tell them you have confirmation number 0703882. The fridge is stocked. Sorry for your troubles. Enjoy."

There was no signature on the note.

43

PIES AWOKE the next morning, took a long hot shower, and then borrowed another clean T-shirt from Jenny, before he headed out on foot to Milena's house.

The night before, he didn't have enough in his pocket for a cab ride, so he had walked, in the dark, the two-plus miles from the 16th district to the halfway house.

He still needed to retrieve his money, lock-bump, and smartphone from the basement stairwell at the Chlebeks' house. No one followed him this time as he made his way back to the heart of Edison Park, he was sure of it. Pies arrived at the rear porch at Milena's, to retrieve his property, by mid-morning.

Milena would still be attending to customers at her shop, although her morning rush would be dwindling by this hour.

Pies was still quite sore from where he had been shot by Panzera, and he could definitely use some more rest. But the apology was happening today. It would take place in the next few minutes.

After this final task was completed, Pies wasn't sure what he would do. The detective's business card was still in his front pants pocket, and he seriously considered going back to Von Bargen to give him all the details of how he'd been deeply involved in the Barrington Hills fiasco.

That was one option.

A second and third were still not coming to him.

He would more than deserve whatever came at him once he was "violated" back to Stateville and a trial was set for his long list of new crimes. The odds would be quite good that the Outfit would have him killed while he was in prison. Once the organization learned how he played factions of the Outfit against one another, until certain individuals were killed, he'd be set for execution himself. But he was now confidently banking on no one else in the Outfit knowing how much Milena Chlebek meant to him—the only ones who had known were in the ground now...moldering.

Milena was safe, he was sure of it.

Pies would violently go after anyone who tried to hurt him—he wasn't about to be murdered without a fight—and yet he only had so much strength and will of spirit left in him.

And the fact of the matter for Pies was he deserved the ultimate punishment for killing his love Vicki Chlebek. So, there was that....

As he crossed over the Metra train tracks in Edison Park he was, oddly, at peace with himself. Some of that serenity was courtesy of reliving the deep recessed and agonizing childhood memories of when his father was murdered. It was a painful realization, but the repressed memories benefited his psyche to know what really happened all those years ago. For all this time Pies had felt abandoned by his father, but his dad didn't want to leave him. His father loved him and would've always watched out for him...had he lived.

Pies continued walking toward his meeting with the mother of the woman he killed. Milena would be keenly aware of Pies's sincerity because his apologetic words would be nothing but genuine.

The Metra train's crossing lights signaled and chimed, and the gates began to lower—and an idea instantly came to mind. Pies looked up to see which of the three sets of tracks the incoming train was traveling on. He shuffled from the middle rail to the one on the right, where in the near distance he saw the huge and brightly illuminated headlight of the train closing in on him.

He slipped the smartphone from his pocket, bent to one knee, and pretended to tie his shoelace. As he did this, he placed the smartphone on the right rail of the incoming locomotive. He no longer needed Sam Panzera's burner phone.

The train sounded its ear-deafening horn, and Pies quickly righted himself and made it safely off the train tracks. He watched as the slow-rolling front car obliterated the smartphone and the train came to a halt at the Edison Park station.

Pies walked up to the alley opening behind the bakery and watched as Milena pushed through the shop's rear door with a bulging plastic garbage bag in hand. She went over to the dumpster, lifted the lid, and tossed the bag inside—and that's when she and Pies locked eyes.

Without hesitation, he headed down the short alleyway and faced Milena, who stood and anxiously awaited his arrival.

Pies and Milena were about three feet from one another and stood silently.

Pies felt the tears beginning to well in his eyes, and he started to tremble. Milena was having the same reaction to Pies's presence.

Before either one said a word, they fell into a tight embrace.

They stayed like that for a few moments—and then Milena gently pushed Pies back to an arm's length. She thoughtfully searched his eyes with her own.

"I'm so sorry," said Pies.

"I know, Jakub...I know," said Milena softly.

Pies wanted to say so much more. He just couldn't.

Milena considered him through smiling, tear-filled, eyes. She said, "You're such a man now, Jakub. Look at you. My Blaze would be proud of what you've become."

"Proud?" asked Pies in a confused and croaking voice.

"Oh, yes, Jakub. He loved you like a son. I love you like son... We knew you didn't do... We knew it was an accident, Jakub," she said through her tears. "We always knew. We forgave right away."

Pies grabbed her tightly again and hugged her.

"I was ashamed I never came to visit. You know, at the prison," she said. "After Blaze died, I got...lost. You know, lost?"

Pies gently pushed away. He understood perfectly.

"Oh, I have to show you now," said Milena.

"What?"

"We have to go now. You see, now... Now I am ready. I'm ready now, Jakub. Come. We'll take my car. I want to show you," said Milena.

"What do you mean?"

Milena smiled and said, "You just wait there, Jakub."

She disappeared into the bakery, was gone for about a minute, and returned with car keys dangling from her fingertips. She pointed to a tiny, blue two-door car.

"Please, come. It's not too far," said Milena excitedly.

*

THEY DROVE south on Milwaukee Avenue for some time—past the Chicago 16th police district building.

Milena cleared her throat and said, "Thank you for having the lady look out for me, Jakub. The one with the walking dog. I was okay, but I appreciate that you were looking out for me. It was sweet. I knew you did that. Those men in the parked van never bothered me."

Pies just grinned. Milena Chlebek was nothing if not the most observant person he knew.

"Is she your lady?" asked Milena.

"No. I mean, I...don't know....," said Pies. "I don't think so...anymore."

"I won't question no more, Jakub," said Milena through a knowing smile.

They kept traveling for another mile or so in silence.

Pies could see the Shurz High School grounds on his left, as Milena pulled the car into a parking space on the right. She turned the engine off and said, "Here, Jakub. You must know," said Milena. "You must see for yourself."

Pies cautiously got out of the car and looked around, but he wasn't really sure what he was looking for.

Milena went up and onto the sidewalk and walked toward the third storefront from the next street corner.

Pies, utterly confused, followed along.

"This is why I write letter to parole people for you, Jakub. This is why I tell them that I love you and that you didn't do the thing like the people think you did. You were trying to save my Vicki, not hurt. I know that. Blaze knows... My Blaze knew that, too, my Jakub. I asked them to let you go," said Milena.

Pies was completely stunned.

He'd thought this entire time that the Outfit, or at the least Sam Panzera, sprung him from Stateville. His mind quickly raced back to the few times Panzera, Silano, and Brosi told him they were desiring the use of his expertise *after* they heard of his pending release. They were just taking advantage of Milena's warm-hearted benevolence.

Pies recovered enough from the revelation, and he finally looked in Milena's direction. She was happily raising her hands toward the sign above the storefront located there on Milwaukee Avenue.

The sign read: Vicki's Art House.

Pies stepped forward and looked through the glass of the storefront art school. It was a good-sized space. There were many, many original paintings hanging from every available bit of wall space.

Some of the works of art were Vicki's original paintings.

Currently, there were fifteen young female students at work inside, a decent mix of preteens from all races. Every single one of the girls had an expensive-looking easel in front of her and a colorful paint palette in her non-brush hand. The instructor, a bespectacled African-American woman in her late twenties, offered expert advice as she made her rounds among the students. The female students were obviously not from upper-middle-class families, though. Their clothing was clearly worn and threadbare.

Milena gently took Pies by the hand and led him inside the school. As they crossed the threshold, everyone there turned in their direction. Milena playfully motioned for the instructor to keep teaching and to ignore them.

In a whisper Milena said, "This is what I did with the money you left in the backpack. She'd be so proud of the school, yes?"

"Yes," whispered the surprised Pies. "She would."

Pies looked about the room, and noticed a few of the girls' mothers, and one father, sitting on the floor near the front windows.

One mother in particular, a delicate-looking Latina woman in her
thirties, wearing a simple white top and blue jeans with a hole in the
left knee, had her fidgety two-year-old son with her. As she looked
his way, he could see that she exhibited a fresh black eye and that
her arms were lightly bruised, too.

"We help people who need the help, yes? We pay for everything.
The supplies and teachers. All of it. But...this is not about art and
painting pretty pictures," said Milena.

Pies looked questioningly at Milena.

"This is confidence builder for the young ladies," whispered Milena. "Some of the girls need help finding their heart, Jakub. Their
strength."

His eyes, again, wandered about the space.

"I know you, Jakub. I know you since you were little boy. And I
know that you think you deserve punishment," she continued softly,
"for Vicki."

Pies took in a sharp breath.

"You need to stay out of the prison, Jakub. There are people... The
people come here, some of the mothers and some fathers. People
who could use your kind of help. I know the things you do. The
crime things. I understand now, after what happened with the Zielinskis, that your crime things come from the heart, not a bad place,"
said Milena. "You could use your *umiejetnosc*...what do you call? Skill.
You know, your skill, to help people. Jakub, there are so many people who need help. So, so many..."

Pies's eyes darted about the space. The brightly colored paintings
hanging on the walls comforted him and allowed his emotions to
even out and his breathing to settle. He considered all of the fore-
thought and the work and the creativity that had been poured into
the paintings. Some of the young ladies attending classes at the art
school were probably living in some rather precarious situations,
and yet their paintings were so bright and hopeful.

There was a green-colored painting in the far corner that captured and held Pies's full attention. It was rudimentary piece that depicted a tan-colored and scruffy-looking dog sitting on a vast green lawn. There was a small blue and white striped ball sitting next to the dog's front left paw.

Pies studied the painting for a few seconds, and then an image flashed into his mind—that of the little boy with the British accent near Bertena's Place. He wore a golf shirt the same shade of green as the lawn in the painting. The jet airplane logo on the little boy's shirt was the same blue hue as the striped ball.

In that instant, Pies knew that he had to go and find the boy and help him. Pies would also want to retain the job at Bertena's Place if he was going to remain free on parole. This time he and Bertena would make his employment circumstances legal and aboveboard.

When he peeled his eyes away from the painting, Pies noticed the Latina woman staring at him intently. He considered her a bit more carefully, taking special notice of her black eye. He offered her a grin and a quick nod.

The Latina woman tried to return the gesture. Her attempt didn't quite work, though. Through trembling lips, she mouthed the words, "Thank you."

ACKNOWLEDGMENTS

JAY AMBERG, Sarah Koz, and John Manos—the cumulative and finely tuned gray matter that composes Amika Press—I thank you for your creative encouragement and for kicking me in the back pants pockets when it was required. While I'm in an appreciative mood, there's this. You never forget the first times you were treated as an adult by an adult. For me, that was in seventh grade at Lincoln Junior High School in Park Ridge, Illinois. Helen Prey, an English teacher, and Quentin Uptegrove, our history teacher—two no-nonsense leaders who did not suffer the pre-hormonally induced whims of whiny twelve-year-olds—were the first people outside of family to instill a sense of confidence in me. What may have seemed like harsh treatment to some of the other students was really a building of adult-type self-assurance, a professional-level skin-thickening exercise that has lasted and served me well all these years. Here's to all of the great teachers who've found their way into our lives. Thank you.

MATT HADER'S circuitous route to becoming a professional writer followed an unlikely path through post-collegiate classes at The Second City, on-air shifts in Chicago-area radio station studios, and work as a 9-1-1 communications officer. He's had numerous screenplay options and production deals over the years, and in 2011 his first novel, *Bad Reputation,* was published, followed by six more stories that expanded the *Bad Reputation* universe. Matt served for a time on the board of directors of the nonprofit American Screenwriters Association, and he's a current member of the International Association of Crime Writers (North American branch). He and his wife make their home in Barrington, Illinois.

* 9 781937 484590 *